"Althea, watching, saw Marjorie at this point gaze at Mrs. Henshaw in an oddly yearning fashion, saw her gaze for a long moment and then drop her eyes while an expression of resigned sadness came over her face."

Another adventure from the pen of Sarah Aldridge, whose legion of fans now have seven novels to read and reread. In this we follow the fortunes of Althea from her boring though modestly comfortable life in Baltimore when she goes to live with her aunt Marjorie at age fourteen and finds a world with far wider horizons.

When her studies take her abroad to the University of London she is drawn into the world of 1930's intrigue that lead to World War II and into the arms of . . .

MISFORTUNE'S FRIEND

SARAH ALDRIDGE

MISFORTUNE'S FRIEND

SARAH ALDRIDGE

THE NAIAD PRESS INC.

1985

Printed in the United States of America
First edition

Typesetting by Sandi Stancil

Library of Congress Cataloging in Publication Data

Aldridge, Sarah.
    Misfortune's friend.

    I. Title.
PS3551.L345M5 1985   813'.54   84-29610
ISBN 0-930044-67-3

Photo by MIC

Photo by MIC

WORKS BY SARAH ALDRIDGE

TO

TW

MISFORTUNE'S FRIEND

SARAH ALDRIDGE

I

Althea could not remember herself before the iron brace. She had read in autobiographies and memoirs that other people could often remember scenes and places and even people they had encountered when they were very young, bits and pieces of their very early lives, of themselves as very young, certainly before they were six. Some of them talked about remembering looking up at people from their cradles, of being conscious of their surroundings before they could talk, of being conscious of their own very essence as infants and very young children.

But she knew nothing of herself before she wore the iron brace on the leg that had been withered by infantile paralysis when she was six. She had never talked about this with anyone. She supposed it was logical to assume that the illness, which had not quite taken her life, never-theless had taken away all memory of what went before. The epidemic of the disease that summer of 1913 in Balti-more had killed her mother, and her other relatives did not talk about it, especially after her father, unable to face the problems thus created in his life, had walked away, leaving her to her mother's parents. She remembered only her life since, held captive by the iron brace, never able to run and play freely with her cousins, always tethered to an adult, aware that her crippling was something to which her relatives tried to be resigned, though they tried, often without success, to hide their impatience. None of her married aunts wanted to have her around them for long at a time. They were all middle-aged women — her own mother had been the youngest child of her grandparents. She knew that they were alert among themselves to see that each did not have more than her share of this burden. So she was left chiefly in her grandmother's house. Her grandmother, a stately woman, provided conscientious nursemaids but gave her little personal attention.

She was fourteen, in 1921, when she left her grand-mother's house to go and stay with her Aunt Marjorie in Washington. She knew that her grandmother never entirely approved of this daughter — of the fact that she had never married — every woman, her grandmother implied, had an opportunity to marry, if only she did not turn it down. All her other daughters had families, who gathered around on the appropriate holidays and birthday and wedding celebrations. All except Marjorie, who lived alone in her own house, without husband or children.

Instead of marrying Marjorie had gone traipsing off to the ends of the earth, under dangerous and sometimes not entirely respectable circumstances. During the Great War she had been in France and then in the Balkans with the Red Cross and afterwards she went to Russia and the

Near East with the rescue missions and sent home to her
mother and sisters graphic accounts of the starving children
and homeless people she was surrounded by in the regions
where war and revolution had laid waste the land. Her
mother had been forced to admit that Marjorie's doings
were valuable — feeding the hungry and succoring the af-
flicted — to admit that Marjorie's efforts were motivated
by humanitarian ideals, especially when foreign governments bestowed medals on her for valor and devotion in
the wrack of war and famine. But there were always reserva-
tions in this grudging acknowledgement — particularly
when Marjorie's photograph appeared in the newspaper,
in uniform, standing at attention while some high-ranking
official pinned a ribbon on her chest.

And after the fanfare had passed Marjorie did not
show any indication of settling down to a domestic routine,
to a normal life as a spinster. She had settled down in Washington and became one of the administrators of the national
headquarters of the Red Cross. This seemed to provide
her with opportunities for sudden and extensive travelling,
to the sites of disasters, to international conferences.

In fact, Althea realized, the only reason her grandmother
decided to send her to stay with Marjorie was because of
her grandfather's illness. He was ill for a long time before
he died and someone, perhaps Marjorie herself, suggested
that the perpetual gloom of the house was not good for
a fourteen-year-old girl who did not have the normal physical
outlets of a healthy adolescent. She could not get away
from the house and join in the sports and games of her
unhandicapped friends. Althea did not think her grandmother was much swayed by this argument but she probably
seized the chance to be free, for the time being, of the
problem of looking after her as well as the old man. In
any case, Althea went to Washington to stay with Marjorie.

She was wary on first arriving at Marjorie's house on

the edge of Georgetown because, of all her aunts, she knew Marjorie the least. Marjorie had come to Baltimore to fetch her and had talked almost continually all the way on the train and from the station to the house. She had a loud, resonant voice that penetrated every corner of a room and for quite a distance in the open air. This was an important reason for her success as a public speaker. She was often on platforms, advocating some sort of social reform or drumming up financial support for charitable causes. She was a tall woman with a craggy face that in a man would have been considered handsome. In fact, she would have made an attractive, bluff, hearty man, thought Althea. Luckily, what she had to say required no responses from Althea, who was used to being the passive audience with adults. What her aunt was chiefly concerned with was the fact that she had enrolled her in Miss Armstrong's school for girls. Obviously, Althea was to spend the winter in Marjorie's house.

It took her a little while to get used to the tall, narrow, red brick house fitted into a street of similar houses. Inside, it tended to be dark, since the daylight came in only from the front and back, and it had long flights of stairs which would take her some effort to climb. But Marjorie gave her a big room on the first flight up, at the back overlooking the narrow strip of garden running down to the high wooden fence that shut out the alley. The first trip up the stairs Marjorie exclaimed in consternation the whole way up, as she helped her with a hand under her elbow. It was obvious that until that moment no one, not her grandmother, not Marjorie herself, had given a thought to the problem of stairs for a lame girl. But whereas her grandmother would have ignored the matter, assigning a servant perhaps to help her, Marjorie's dismay was openly and volubly expressed.

"Do you think you can learn to manage, Althea dear?

Are the steps too dangerous for you? Martha will always be ready to help you." She watched as Althea turned herself so as to grasp the bannister with both hands to steady herself. "You're really very clever about it, aren't you? But you must say if you need help."

Ordinarily Althea resented too much attention paid to her disability. Even well-meant concern was irksome and often she wished fervently that people would not cover their own embarrassment, their pity, with a flood of fluttering questions and comments. But Marjorie's awkward attempts to ease the effort of climbing for her had a quality of genuineness that overcame the resentment she at first automatically felt. For Marjorie, once satisfied that she would not harm herself, went on talking about other matters. It was Martha, Marjorie's black cook and housekeeper, soft-spoken, unobtrusive, who came unbidden to help her unpack, arrange her things, at night to go to bed and in the morning to get up.

Althea discovered, on her way to and from her own, a small room at the head of the stairs, right over the front door. What it had been originally used for Althea could not guess but Marjorie had filled it with mementoes of her own life. Althea, spending idle hours there when she was alone in the house — Martha out at the grocery store and Marjorie not yet home from her Red Cross office downtown — had found there mounted photographs of her grandmother and grandfather, family gatherings, wedding pictures, including that of her own parents, her mother's young face framed in the heavy lace of her bridal veil, her father's smooth and bland. These were all clustered on one side of the room, standing on table tops or hanging on the walls — people and events preserved forever in the motionless air of this never-used place.

On the other side of the room Marjorie had gathered pictures of her own past — herself one of many in class photographs, wearing a sailor blouse and dark skirt, holding a hockey stick, surrounded by the rest of the team. Again, Marjorie in a cabinet frame, stiff and strained at her graduation from college. But there was also a crowd of small pictures, many of them taken with a brownie kodak, some dim and badly focussed but all carefully mounted, of scenes of foreign places — camps in open fields, army tents, lines of drably dressed people waiting with bowls in hand for soup being ladled out by stout bustling women in uniforms and white overalls. These, Althea supposed, must be pictures of Marjorie's two years with the Red Cross in the Balkans at the end of the Great War. Finally there was a photograph of Marjorie herself, in uniform — a skirt down to a few inches of her ankles, and a military coat reaching halfway down her thighs, with big pockets and a broad belt, a white shirt with a man's collar and tie, heavy laced high shoes and a brimmed hat with the insignia on a band in the front. Althea studied the figure and the face whenever she saw this photograph. Ramrod straight, Marjorie stood at attention, her head turned to one side as if before a reviewing stand, in front of a line of other women similarly clad. They stood in a city street, a large American flag hanging from a massive building in the background. Obviously this was a moment of rest in a parade, a ceremony held to mark the return to New York of the group with which Marjorie had served abroad. Althea searched her aunt's features, stern, proud, even haughty, and yet saw in them the sympathy which had become familiar to her in the last few days, softening Marjorie's most positive declarations. Glancing back at the faces of her other relatives, Althea saw that, yes, Marjorie was different. You would expect her to be more receptive, more yielding than her grandmother, for instance, less blandly self-centered than her other aunts.

These pictures were supplemented by a glass case,

standing in the middle of the room. In the bottom of it were school trophies — for Marjorie herself as a champion archer, for the hockey team which she had captained in games against other girls' schools. On the upper shelf of the case were medals and ribbons, awards for bravery, for valiant service under fire, for competence as a nurse and administrator in war-desolated, famine-stricken areas — certificates on parchment with highly embossed lettering, letters, some of them in French, some in foreign languages Althea could not read, signed apparently by heads of state or other exalted personages.

Althea did not have much trouble getting used to the new school. She already knew how people reacted to her, to her thin, bony body — scrawny, was Martha's word — her iron brace. At first the other girls were embarrassed and made uneasy by the sight of it. Then they adjusted quickly to the idea that she would not be taking part in games and outdoor play — that she was somehow, automatically and subtly outside the full scope of their lives. The fact that she was bookish — that she was far ahead of them in reading, English, French, arithmetic — was taken to be a natural result of her handicap. Even her teachers seemed to assume that since she could not run and play games like the others, she would be studious and a good scholar. She was used to this juxtaposing of her physical with her mental state, of regarding the one as a necessary corollary of the other. Nowadays, as she grew more truly thoughtful, she wondered sometimes what would have happened if she had not liked to read, had not been content to find sedentary pleasures to take the place of what was natural at her age.

Marjorie, for the first week or so, paid her an exaggerated attention, nervous at the responsibility she had undertaken. Althea supposed that Marjorie at her age had been quite different — a hearty, robust girl who played a large part in helping her school team to win hockey matches and liked a rough-and-tumble sort of social life with her schoolmates. She must have been then an adolescent version of the tall, vigorous woman with ginger-colored hair she had grown into, with the same florid complexion and loud, authoritative voice. So probably she felt at a loss about dealing with a pale crippled child who had had, even at this age, more than an average share of misfortune — a physical handicap, a frail body, neither father nor mother and no brothers or sisters.

Althea knew that Marjorie did not approve of her father and his escape from responsibility. Perhaps also Marjorie felt a niggle of self-reproach. For hitherto she had made no real effort to become acquainted with her niece. She had the excuse, of course, of the fact that for so many years of Althea's life she had been caught up in the great events of the war and postwar years, rarely spending as much as a month at home.

Now she hovered over Althea, taking her to school in her own car — she had a Packard motorcar and was one of the first women to drive herself about Washington — and arranging for one of the teachers to bring her home in the afternoon. She asked frequently whether Althea felt all right — was she happy — was she treated fairly at school?

"You must let me know at once, Althea, if anything is the matter. Don't suffer in silence. That would be foolish. I know I am often very busy and sometimes preoccupied. So speak up if you need anything or if anyone is being unkind. There is nothing that can't be set right, but I must be told about it."

Her anxious gaze as she said this told Althea of her real dismay in not knowing how to deal with something subtle, not out in the open, her inner uncertainty about facing situations that could not be named and defined in plain terms. Realizing this, Althea felt uncomfortable in her turn and a little guilty that she was annoyed by these anxious attentions, instead of grateful for Marjorie's kindness of heart. Marjorie was a vigorous woman, now with gray in her hair but with a fresh, youthful complexion. She usually wore well-cut suits of broadcloth or tweed and walked with a purposeful stride, as if never in doubt about where she was going. To most people she must have seemed a woman who was entirely certain of what she was doing, who was to be relied upon to have the right answer for any practical problem, however undecided everyone else might be. Now she seemed at a loss as to how to carry through this situation which in her exuberance she had created.

Althea said as reassuringly as she could that everything was all right. Oh, yes, she would say if anything went wrong.

After the first few weeks Marjorie's concern lessened as she got more used to having Althea and her requirements in her life. Marjorie's afternoons and evenings were often filled with social and public affairs. Martha was always there, always there when Althea came home from school, so there was no worry about her arriving at an empty house. Often Althea ate dinner alone with Martha in the big airy kitchen. She enjoyed these evenings with Martha as a receptive audience for the stories she liked to tell, sometimes embellished, of the girls and teachers and incidents of the school day. Martha, a tall dark woman with a long face and deepset noticing eyes, gave no sign that she was surprised or puzzled by anything she said.

When Marjorie was home to dinner she often talked about public events that involved her interest or her work. Althea was fascinated by this untrammeled flow of talk about politics, world happenings, people in public life. At home in Baltimore dinner had been a silent meal, since her grandparents had very little to say to her or to each other. Or if one or two of her aunts were present the talk was endlessly about family squabbles, new dresses or gossip about their friends. Nobody paid any attention to her, as an uncomprehending child. Marjorie seemed unaware of such an attitude. Perhaps it was partly nervousness, an eagerness to make Althea feel at home and at the same time a feeling that she did not know what to talk about to a fourteen-year-old girl. So she talked at length about the League of Nations, about the Nineteenth Amendment which gave the vote to women — "Such a bizarre idea," she said, "that a woman shouldn't have the right to vote just as a man, and it has been so long in coming about." She pulled herself up short and looked directly at Althea. "Of course, your grandmother has very different ideas about this, I realize that." She waited as if to give Althea a chance to say something but Althea said nothing.

As September came Marjorie began to talk excitedly about the Disarmament Conference. It was talked about, she said, to take place at the beginning of the year. "It is for the limitations of armaments, Althea. Nothing could be more important than to prevent future wars. Wars are such destructive things. There is no excuse for them. No one ever gains from them and so much is lost. The great nations must disarm. Otherwise they will be at each others' throats again."

She was an ardent supporter of President Wilson because of his efforts for a lasting peace. She forgave him, she said, his halfhearted support for the campaign for women's suffrage, especially now that it had been successful. She was indignant because the United States Senate had failed to ratify the League of Nations Treaty. Eventually, she said, the United States must join with other countries to bring about security for all peace-loving people and an end to armies and the manufacture of munitions.

At first Althea was at sea in listening to her, not understanding the bases of her arguments, not knowing the current

controversies that underlay what she said, not remembering
events that obviously were still vivid in Marjorie's memory.
But gradually she began to identify some threads of thought
that came through Marjorie's repeated and vehement statements. At school Althea's civics teacher sometimes held
discussions about current events. Most of the girls who
attended them were older, but it was tacitly accepted that
Althea was the star. She boned up on history and political
events, translating Marjorie's protests against the blindness
of American foreign policy and especially politicians, into
judicious and calmly stated propositions. She was pleased
and amused to notice that even the teacher was impressed.

Occasionally Marjorie pulled herself up short and said
something like, "I'm sorry, Althea. Of course you can't
realize the importance of what I am talking about. But I
get so upset by people's shortsightedness when it comes
to the big forces that are shaping our world." But then
she plunged again into a discussion of the current phase
of political events that aroused her.

Althea would have liked to have told her that she knew
about the Bolsheviks, that she had read about the Russian
Revolution, that she found all this very interesting. But
the habit of not talking about her own thoughts and opinions
when surrounded by her relatives was too strong. She read
the newspaper each day that Marjorie discarded in the
wastebasket after breakfast. She read about Sacco and
Vanzetti, two Italian immigrants being tried in Massachusetts
for murder but the fact that they were anarchists seemed
to be more important than what they had done. So she
asked Marjorie what anarchists were. Her question caused
Marjorie to stare at her for a moment and instead of answering she said, "Why do you want to know?" Wary,
Althea did not say, "because I want to know why it is so
important that these men are anarchists." Instead, she
said she had been reading something in the newspaper,

which said that anarchists were dangerous because they threw bombs to assassinate people. Marjorie said, Yes, they did sometimes. Anarchism was a political philosophy that held that it was best to do without government, because all governments were oppressive. "But of course that is impossible, as any reasonable person would understand. Some people are fanatics and you can't deal with them."

Sometimes Marjorie, spurred on by some incident in her day's activities, told anecdotes of her experiences in Russia and the Balkans at the end of the Great War — how she with her unit of Red Cross workers had travelled on crawling, crowed trains across miles of devastated countryside, to bring what succor they could to starving and homeless people. With fervent memory that shone in her eyes she talked about the masses of famished beings who pressed around them when the train entered a station, the beseeching hands raised to each window, the orphaned and abandoned children trailing her in the streets and clustering around her when she sat down to eat in some dirty, unkempt place that still had a little food to sell at high prices to the fortunate. These stories held Althea spellbound. As she listened to them she understood the nostalgia that underlay Marjorie's voice. In spite of the tragedy and the heartbreak, Marjorie recalled those days with a kind of regret. There was something more than the miseries of the time involved. Althea felt Marjorie's sense of the value to herself of the unstinted effort, of the immediacy of life's demands that she had experienced and that now came back to her in the midst of her safe, untroubled present.

One morning when Althea came down to breakfast she found Marjorie giving instructions to Martha. "She will arrive," she was saying, "sometime today. I'm sorry I can't be more exact, because Mrs. Henshaw failed to state in her letter which train she expected to take. So

I'm afraid I must ask you to keep to the house until she arrives."

Marjorie went into detail about the arrangements she had decided upon — which bedroom Mrs. Henshaw would use, what her requirements might be. "She likes tea first thing in the morning." Althea, standing by her chair waiting for Marjorie to sit down, watched Martha. Martha's deliberate movements disguised the competent swiftness with which she carried out her work. Now she stood in front of Marjorie, her hands clasped on her white apron, listening attentively. Mratha never wrote anything down, even complicated recipes. Probably, Althea surmised, she could not read or write. She never forgot to deliver a telephone message nor its precise wording. When, as now, she waited to hear Marjorie's instructions to the end, there seemed to be a trace of skepticism in her manner. Seemed to be, Althea thought, because she was not sure what the expression in Martha's eyes was. Perhaps it was that Martha had learned to discount as temporary some of the enthusiasm which so often took possession of Marjorie. And Marjorie seemed pleasurably excited at the prospect of this visitor's arrival.

That afternoon, just as Althea got home from school a cab stopped in front of Marjorie's house. Althea was still in the hall, taking off her coat, for it was a chilly day. As she stood watching through the window panel at the side of the front door, Martha came from under the stairs from the kitchen and stood beside her, silently.

They saw the cabman open the cab door and a woman still seated inside, one foot on the running board, her hands busy with a large handbag in her lap, obviously searching for money. Presently she handed money to the driver, who then gave her his hand to get down. While she walked to the door, he drew from inside the cab a large suitcase and several cardboard boxes, which he brought to the doorstep. The bell rang as the man tipped his cap and returned to the cab.

When Martha opened the door Althea, standing back in the shadows of the vestibule, stared at the woman who stood on the doorstep. She was a little taller than average, slender to the point of thinness, dressed in a nondescript coat and skirt and a white blouse and shabby walking shoes. Under her black-brimmed hat her hair, a mixture of blond and white, straggled in wisps. Her face was pale with a lined, delicate skin, with no trace of cosmetics. Her pale blue eyes looked out sharply through steel-rimmed glasses.

"How do you do?" she said to Martha. "This is Miss Seymour's house, is it not?"

An Englishwoman, thought Althea, but then Marjorie had told her that Mrs. Henshaw was coming from London. Martha said, "Yes, ma'am. Miss Seymour is not home but she's expecting you."

She took hold of the handle of the suitcase and brought it inside and then reached methodically for each of the other pieces of luggage. Mrs. Henshaw stepped into the vestibule. Without the least glance at her surroundings she looked at Althea and said, "You are Marjorie's niece, I expect."

Althea, startled out of her absorption by being addressed directly, stammered Yes and then tried to pull herself out of her spectator's trance. "I'm Althea, Mrs. Henshaw."

"Well, Althea," said Mrs. Henshaw, "perhaps we should help this good woman carry these upstairs." She took hold of one of the roped boxes and started towards the stairs.

Althea heard Martha's annoyed "tcha!" But then Mrs. Henshaw's sharp eyes caught sight of the brace on Althea's leg. She exclaimed, "Oh, my dear! I did not realize!"

She said nothing more and went up the stairs carrying a box and another piece of luggage, followed by Martha with the suitcase and another box. Althea waited until she heard the door of the guest bedroom close and then laboriously climbed the stairs and hid herself in her own room.

In the evening when she came downstairs she hesitated at the threshold of the sittingroom door, hearing the sound of Marjorie's voice punctuated by Mrs. Henshaw's higher-pitched, quick responses. She did not want to go in but she knew that Marjorie would send for her if she did not, so she slid into the room as quietly as she could.

Marjorie was saying, in a voice charged with indignation, "But don't they see that barbarism will only lead to more barbarism? Now —"

She stopped abruptly, aware that Althea had come into the room because Mrs. Henshaw had turned to look at her. Marjorie exclaimed with her usual extravagance, "Oh, Althea, you must come and meet Mrs. Henshaw. She has come from London to attend the Disarmament Conference! You know, I have been telling you about it, how important it is to the future of our country and in fact, to the future of the whole world." She laid her hand on Althea's shoulder and drew her close to her. Instinctively Althea resisted at first and then submitted, a two-step response she recognized in herself. In her grandmother's family kissing and hugging was briefly and hastily done when on occasion it seemed to be required. Marjorie had the same skittish way of touching anyone. This gesture was the most spontaneous she had ever shown to Althea. Althea did not look at Mrs. Henshaw but she was aware that the sharp, bespectacled eyes were searchingly upon her.

Marjorie went on, eager to fill up the gap in conversation, "Althea is very interested in world events. She is a good student — in fact, her teachers say brilliant." There was an odd note of pride in Marjorie's voice that surprised

Althea. At home with her grandmother no one paid any attention to her school work. It seemed to be taken for granted that, with nothing else to do, she must be a good student. No one expressed surprise or pleasure when she did something better than expected or when one of her teachers praised her. But Marjorie was always asking her about what she was studying and whether she liked her teachers. She did not think that Marjorie always listened closely to her replies. But now it seemed that she paid a surprising amount of attention.

Mrs. Henshaw sat smiling at her while Marjorie talked about her. There was a knowing but sympathetic twinkle in her eyes, as if to say that they both understood Marjorie. Then she turned back to Marjorie and the conversation between the two women flowed on again. Althea, sitting near them, learned that Mrs. Henshaw was a translator and interpreter for the British delegation to the Conference, that she was greatly relieved to get the post because she had been without regular employment for some time and her funds had run low. When Marjorie exclaimed in dismay at this — "Oh, Janet, you should have let me know!" — she made little of it — "Of course, Dawkins, I could not place my burdens on you" — and went on to talk briskly of other things.

They began to talk about their wartime experiences. Mrs. Henshaw had been in Serbia, serving as an interpreter at the American unit of the Scottish Women's Hospitals at the Salonica front in 1917. She reminded Marjorie of the chaos they had both encountered there, how brave the Serbians were in fighting the Austrians, the Hungarians, the Turks, with few guns and little ammunition. Marjorie seemed absorbed in all the events she recalled and understood the political implications of them. Althea, who had read in her history books that it was a Serbian who had precipitated the Great War by shooting an Austrian grand-duke, was only half-comprehending. The women, no longer aware of her presence, talked on through dinner and she left them afterwards still lost in reminiscence in the sitting-room when she went up to her own room to do her homework.

But the next day she was alone with Marjorie and asked for explanations. Marjorie said vaguely, "I'm afraid it is too complicated. You'll have to learn about it in school. It was all a tragic mistake and once the great powers got into the war, nothing could stop it. Janet and I were only there afterwards, to pick up the pieces."

"You've known her a long time, haven't you?"

"Oh, yes. We were schoolmates in Scotland when I was in my teens — your age, Althea. You know, my parents — your grandparents — sent me to this school in Scotland because it was recommended by one of the Scotsmen my father knew in his business. Your grandfather did a lot of business as an importer of Scottish things. Well, I met Janet there in Edinburgh the first day, when I arrived. We've been fast friends ever since." She paused for a moment, looking down, as if assailed by poignant memories. Then she went on. "Janet's name, at that time, was Welby. She comes of a very good Yorkshire family, though they disinherited her."

Althea looked at her in astonishment. She had read in novels about people being disinherited but she had never expected to meet one in real life. "Why?" she demanded.

Marjorie hesitated, as if she found she had plunged ahead too thoughtlessly. After all — Althea could see what was passing through her mind — the child is only fourteen, though she seems such a little old woman. But she replied, "Her parents did not approve of the man she — wanted to marry. He was brilliant but penniless, not of their class of society, and he held political opinions they did not like."

"Was she happy?"

Marjorie was startled. "Oh, you mean, after she left her family? Well, I suppose she must have thought she loved him a great deal to defy her parents like that. But she has not had a very happy life."

"Why?"

But now Marjorie was irritated, probably because she thought the conversation unsuitable to have with an adolescent girl, and she said shortly, "I really can't go into all that, Althea. I don't think I should discuss Janet's troubles with you — or anyone. She has never really confided in me about that part of her life. I have only bits and pieces of information, some of it from other people."

Nevertheless, Marjorie did provide other items about Mrs. Henshaw's past. Henshaw was not the name of the man whom her family disliked. He was Jewish and they had separated. He had returned to Germany, where he was from. After a while she had become reconciled enough with her parents so that they provided the means for her to go to Sommerville — one of the women's colleges at Oxford, you know. It was at Oxford that she met Roger Henshaw and married him. He became a very famous archeologist. Marjorie did not mention divorce. That was not a word she would speak to Althea. The fact that Mrs. Henshaw had married a Jew was passed over, yet Althea did not have the impression that he had died.

It was late October when Mrs. Henshaw arrived, two weeks before the Disarmament Conference was due to open, on November 12. She was rarely in the house during the day and very often in the evenings she and Marjorie went out together to meet people in hotels. Mrs. Henshaw knew a great many people, it seemed, and whenever she noticed in the newspapers the mention of any new arrivals for the Conference she at once went to seek them out. It was obvious that her presence caused a disturbance in Marjorie's normal routine. Marjorie seemed preoccupied with her even when she was not present. It was not usual for Marjorie to come home early in the afternoon but now she did frequently, as if the possibility of Mrs. Henshaw's being in the house brought her home. Althea came in from school one day to find her sitting alone in the sittingroom. She saw the back of her head above the sofa back, wreathed in cigarette smoke — that was another thing, Althea had learned, that Marjorie smoked cigarettes, though never when she visited her mother in Baltimore. Marjorie was not doing anything. There was not even an open book on the seat beside her. She was hospitable if absentminded when she asked Althea if she would like a glass of milk with her piece of cake. The tea tray sat on the side table. She must be expecting Mrs. Henshaw.

After a silence while she ate Althea asked, "Were you at Oxford with Mrs. Henshaw?"

Marjorie, surprised, said, "Oh, no. I was not at Somerville. No, I did not see Janet for a number of years after we both left Mrs. Dalshiel's school in Edinburgh. We wrote, of course, and that is how I knew what was happening to her. She often wrote me, wherever she was, so that I knew where to reach her. I think she needed me at times, since her family, even after they were reconciled, kept her at arm's length. She knew I would understand how things were between herself and her parents. I met them when I was in school with her, because I had nowhere to go on school holidays and the trip across the Atlantic to Baltimore took too long. They were terribly reserved. I remember how cold and formal I thought their lives were, even compared to what I was used to. They lived in a large brick house surrounded by gardens, close to York. They made a great question of privacy. The doors to all the rooms were always closed and you had to knock before you went in." Marjorie gave a short laugh. "Of course, it was deathly cold in the house, except where there were fireplaces, so naturally they kept the doors closed to keep out draughts. But you know, I really think some of the reserve of such people comes from not being freely in touch with their kind. It was just the opposite with Janet and me. Of course we were at the giggly girl stage and we had such fun together, but whenever we were required to join her parents it was as if a blight came down on us and we were as stiff and silent as they were. My mother told me later that they very much approved of me as a companion for Janet because I was so well-behaved, which surprised her very much, because she always considered me not as ladylike as she would like. They had no idea how Janet and I acted when we were upstairs in the old nursery."

Althea, listening enthralled at these revelations, thought "She's forgotten I'm Althea, and held her breath.

"So when Janet wrote and told me her difficulties with them about the man she was in love with, I could fully understand. I remembered that cold house and those stiff people so tightly bound up in their reserve that they could scarcely speak of anything but the most commonplace things, in uttlerly conventional phrases. I could imagine Janet, who could be so fiery when her feelings were aroused — she can even now — trying to reach them with her plea for sympathy and their repulsing her. They would never accept such a man. And of course, when she saw that she became even more vehement in clinging to him. You can imagine how it was when she told them that in fact they need not worry about having him for a son-in-law because he did not believe in marriage — he thought people should live freely together without such bonds."

Marjorie stopped abruptly, suddenly overcome with a realization of what she had just said. She kept her gaze away from Althea, who sat quietly waiting, noticing the flush of embarrassment that rose in her face. After a few moments Marjorie added, as if speaking to herself, "Of course, they were right. It was a very unsuitable relationship. It could not have succeeded. Janet's outlook and the young man's were so different, though she did not realize that at the time. And I suppose Janet's feeling for him was really infatuation, not the great love she supposed it was. She had nothing really to sustain her when he became sarcastic and showed her how contemptuous he was of her feelings, her opinions, her family. I expect that was his revenge for the humiliation he thought she had brought on him. She wrote and told me all this. I could see her gradual disillusionment in her letters. I was so distressed about it all. She was so far away. I am afraid that Janet has a way of seeing people only through her own feelings about them. She does not see them as they are."

Marjorie stopped talking and suddenly laughed awkwardly and said, "I'm sure you can have no idea what I am talking about. All I meant was that Janet and I have been very close friends, really, for a long time."

Disappointed, Althea tried to think of a way in which to lead Marjorie to continue the story. Had Mrs. Henshaw lived with the young man without marrying him? There was a real titillation in hearing about such a forbidden subject. Nobody but Marjorie would ever have spoken of it in her hearing. She made a valiant effort.

"But what did she do when her parents disowned her?"

"Oh, she went to live in London for a while. He was a member of a political group which advocated radical political changes. He was a clever speaker. He often appeared in rallies for men standing for Parliament who favored Socialism and the shift of power, to the working class. In the end he went back to Germany. Janet went with him, though I don't think he wanted her to. But Janet never does anything by halves and she had tried to accept his ideas. The plight of the downtrodden has great appeal

for her. However, I don't think she understood his view
of the matter. He wanted revolution, no matter how
violent — the wiping out of the injustice of the past by
whatever means and the triumph of the workingman. Janet
could never countenance such ruthlessness. She saw it only
as substituting one set of victims for another. He thought
her a sentimental fool. I was in London for a visit before
they went to Germany and I met him and realized how
mistaken Janet was in her estimate of him. I could not
enlighten her, of course, even though by then she was quite
disillusioned. She did not want to admit how wrong she
was. And I thought he was such an ugly fellow! There was
nothing to redeem the situation in his physical appearance —
dark, with a bad skin and a perpetual sneer on his face —
he did everything to make himself as unattractive as possible,
as if he despised smartness and neatness as part of the world
he was rejecting. If she had a taste for brilliant analytical
thought and dialectical debate, I suppose she could have
admired him for that. But I never thought that Janet had
an appreciation for that sort of thing — for abstractions
generally. I think his appeal for her at the beginning was
that he was alone and friendless, struggling against what
he considered injustice."

When Marjorie stopped talking this time she did not
begin again but only said brusquely that she had not meant
to go so deeply into relating Mrs. Henshaw's history. Althea
sat mute, held captive by the sense that here she had been
given a real glimpse into the world of adult people, of men
and women's relationships, that older people deliberately
kept so mysterious for her, of which she only occasionally
caught a snatch in the conversations of her grandmother
and her other aunts. She hugged herself together as Marjorie turned away to light another cigarette.

Each day when it came time to go home Althea felt
a quickening of her pulse at the thought of catching Marjorie

again alone and in a reminiscent mood while she waited for Mrs. Henshaw to come and join her for afternoon tea. Mrs. Henshaw had ceased to be a rather tedious, middle-aged woman with absentminded ways. There was, in Althea's mind's eye, an aura of something tantalizing, of tragedy not quite consummated, of a mysterious drama not finished and not quite understood. Each afternoon she found Marjorie by herself she tried to prod her into further stories of Mrs. Henshaw. Who was the man Mrs. Henshaw married?

"Oh, he was Roger Henshaw. You will probably find his name mentioned in your history books about the discoveries he made of ancient cities in Greece."

"Did she make up with her family?"

"Well, not altogether. He originally met Janet at Oxford — her truce with her family had included an agreement on their part to pay her way through Oxford — they were people who felt strongly about higher education for women and perhaps they were somewhat softened by thankfulness that she had come back from Germany a free woman. Everyone who knew him was surprised that Roger could take his mind off ancient Greece long enough to fall in love and marry. When he finally got to Greece he was disgusted with the gap between the noble antiquity of his dreams and the barbarous present. Janet was a greater realist there."

"Why is she so poor now?"

Marjorie seemed a little surprised at the question. "Well, Roger never had any money. Everything he received went into digging up the past. Janet could never feel the same about her parents. She is just like them, in fact — unyielding, unforgiving. She felt that what they had done was inexcusable, since they did not retract their opinion of the first man nor apologize for their actions towards her. She refused to accept any inheritance from them — though I believe they lost much of their affluence as a consequence of the Great War."

"Is that why she was in Greece?"

"She has been in Greece several times. She was there when I first went to the Balkans. But, yes, I suppose the first time was with Roger. He was very hampered by the political situation. This was before the War, of course, when there was so much underground unrest. And I'm afraid that Janet did not help. She became involved in saving the life of a man who was condemned to be executed as a rebel — his wife was a woman who wanted to revive ancient Greek customs and dances and festivals and that sort of thing. Janet helped in arranging for his pardon and exile. As it turned out, he wasn't very grateful. He seemed to feel it was a reflection on his manhood that he owed his life to a woman. Men are such silly fools."

She said this with such vehemence that Althea stared at her.

Mrs. Henshaw did not always return in time for tea but was delayed until dinnertime and sometimes later. One evening, after the Conference had begun, she came home bringing with her a dark-haired unhappy-looking young woman who did not look English but spoke with an English accent. It was rather late and Marjorie and Althea had already finished dinner. It had been arranged with Martha that they were not to wait for her on such evenings, since she never knew when the demands of her work would be sure to keep her till all hours. But there would be something of a meal ready for whenever she did come. Mrs. Henshaw, Althea had noticed, paid little attention to food.

The young woman with her was not talkative. She had a sallow skin and a half-angry expression on her face. This was Elsie, said Mrs. Henshaw matter-of-factly, as if this was sufficient explanation. Marjorie said, How do you do, Elsie. But to Althea she was the most un-Elsie-ish girl she had ever met. She ate methodically, apparently enjoying

Martha's chicken, intent on her dinner, as they all sat around
the dinnertable, bare except for the two places hurriedly
set for them, while Marjorie and Althea sat opposite them
to keep them company.
Mrs. Henshaw's soft, melodious voice carried them
through the evening. It became apparent that Elsie was to
spend the night. She had no lodging, Mrs. Henshaw explained, because no arrangement had been made in advance
for her, by some oversight when she was recruited to work
at the Conference, and of course Washington was bursting
with visitors. Althea noticed that Marjorie was somewhat
taken aback when Mrs. Henshaw said this, with only the
merest gesture towards the possibility that Marjorie would
object. Her "of course if it is too inconvenient" was left
in the air to be overwhelmed by Marjorie's eager invitation.
Marjorie stuttered a bit as she said something about telling
Martha. Althea heard her say under her breath that she
hoped Martha would not be upset.
Mrs. Henshaw dropped the subject at once, as if once
stated it was settled, and went on to discuss the day's events
at the Conference. Elsie said nothing.
Elsie stayed for a few days. Althea saw very little of
her, partly because, like Mrs. Henshaw, she worked increasingly long hours as the Conference's activities grew
more complicated, and partly, Althea guessed, because
Elsie did not like visiting Marjorie's house. Once — the day
after she had first come — they accidentally spent half an
afternoon together. Elsie was in the small front parlor when
Althea arrived home from school. Standing in the dimlit
vestibule taking off her coat and galoshes — there was a
drizzling November rain — she was aware of some slight
sound coming from the open parlor door. Since there was
usually complete silence in the house at this time of day —
the kitchen and Martha's quarters were closed off behind
the door under the stairs — she was transfixed for a few

moments, sitting on the big wooden chest Marjorie had brought from Italy, holding suspended the overshoe she had just taken off. She was early home from school today — Thursdays were always half periods for her since she did not take part in school sports. When she had put her things away in the small closet she limped as quietly as she could to the door and looked in.

The parlor was not much lighter than the vestibule, the windows dull grey with the wet November afternoon. There were glassfronted bookcases against the far wall and she saw that one of these was open, the pale light glinting on the pane. She had been thinking about Elsie on the way home and was a little disconcerted by finding her here before her. Elsie looked up as she heard the thump of Althea's foot in its iron brace.

"Hello," she said. Her eyeglasses winked in the dull light from the windows.

Why doesn't she turn the light on? Althea thought. "Hello," she replied politely.

For a few moments neither of them said anything, Althea because she rarely felt the urge to speak to break a silence. Perhaps Elsie also was shy. But Elsie did not give the impression of being shy. Instead you felt that she was contemptuous of the need to maintain politeness. She looked at the book in her hand and then hastily put it back on the shelf, as if the brief interest it had aroused had evaporated.

"Your aunt's books are pretty old, aren't they?" she said. "She must have finished with them long ago. I wonder why people keep that sort of old lumber around them?"

She came away from the bookcase toward the window and stood gazing out at the greyness. Althea, tired of standing, sat down on the settee. Elsie fascinated her, for no reason that she clearly understood, unless it was her essential foreignness. There were a few foreign girls at her school and they none of them, even the Japanese girl, seemed as alien as Elsie. Elsie's strangeness was from more than nationality. After all, she was apparently a British subject, from what Mrs. Henshaw said, with an English education. There was an air of the unknown, the mysterious about Elsie, not clearly defined as in the case of the Japanese girl, with her slant eyes and Japanese manners. Elsie gave the impression of having lived in a very different world and yet one related to Althea's, had lived through strange circumstances and bizarre events. But what could these have been, Althea wondered, to produce this so different outlook that appeared in the expression on her face. For one thing, she could not imagine Elsie in her grandparents' house in Baltimore. Even the Japanese girl would not have been so out of place there.

Elsie turned away from the window. She paused when Althea said, "Most people keep books they are fond of."

She saw the amusement in Elsie's dark eyes and realized that there had been a trace of resentment in her own voice, in an obscure defense of Marjorie. Elsie came back quickly with, "That is, if they live in one house all their lives. I've not had that experience. But not that I think I'd care for it. Why crystallize the past around oneself? I can't see treasuring the poetry of Owen Meredith, in any case."

Althea, who had read through all of Marjorie's books, remembered the copy of *Lucille* in its soft, luxurious, dark-brown leather binding decorated with gold leaf, with an inscription on the flyleaf from some friend of Marjorie's. She herself had thought at the time that this collection of books must date from some long ago romantic period of Marjorie's girlhood and had been vaguely uncomfortable at the idea that Marjorie, now so self-assured and positive in manner, had once felt the nebulous uncertainties of adolescence. But Elsie ought not to joke at Marjorie's expense. Besides, she ought to tell her that Marjorie had not lived in this house all her life. But she saw at once that this was not the point.

"I guess Aunt Marjorie doesn't remember what is in there," she said defensively.

But Elsie shot back, "That is what I said. Why do people cling to that old debris of their lives, when it has become without meaning to them?"

Talking to her further, Althea discovered that Elsie was always that way in any discussion — instantly on the attack, sharply critical, impatient, her quick mind running rapidly ahead, her contempt barely disguised for anything she perceived as slowness and sentimentality. The conversation at the dinnertable became argumentative, contentious, finally acerbic, as Marjorie responded to her barbs. There was no more of the duel that had gone on before, between Marjorie's voluble monologues and Mrs. Henshaw's tenacious interruptions. Occasionally Mrs. Henshaw struck into the talk to say, perhaps, that Elsie felt strongly about whatever she was saying and was too vehement accordingly. It was only with Mrs. Henshaw that Elsie's manner softened, and she would break off what she was saying with a short laugh, as if to say, well, that was good while it lasted.

Althea was aware that even Martha became silently involved, standing at the sideboard waiting to hand the plates, her head turned to one side so that she could catch a glimpse of Elsie's face, her own face registering briefly indignation, angry amusement, unbelieving outrage. Althea understood Martha's feelings. Martha was more aware of Marjorie's weak points than anyone else. She was often impatient and annoyed with Marjorie's tendency to be carried away by some new enthusiasm and her way of inviting newly met acquaintances into the bosom of her home as if they were already lifelong friends. But now she plainly resented the skill with which Elsie goaded Marjorie into extreme statements, her amusement at the red-faced vehemence with which Marjorie refuted something she said expressly for the purpose of creating this reaction.

In the kitchen in the morning, while she packed Althea's lunch, Martha muttered angrily, "That girl don't have no manners at all. She'd be in the street with no roof over her head if it weren't for Miss Marjorie."

Fortunately Elsie did not stay long. After a few nights, she announced that she had found somewhere else to live and without any ceremony removed her belongings from the bedroom and was gone. Althea heard Martha mutter, "Good riddance."

At first they saw nothing at all of Elsie, only heard of her in incidental glimpses in Mrs. Henshaw's accounts of what went on at the Conference. She did not come to visit them once she had left the house, as if, they having served her purpose, she had dismissed them from her life. Althea was aware that Marjorie's feelings — so much more sensitive than you might imagine in such a downright person — were hurt, and Martha made no bones about what her own opinion was of such lack of courtesy. Mrs. Henshaw was also aware of this, because once or twice she murmured excuses for Elsie — she was so very busy, she was overwhelmed by the great responsibility thrust upon her because she was such a clever, reliable girl. Marjorie made no responses, as if she did not want to acknowledge the state of her feelings.

Christmas drew near and Marjorie talked of Althea going back to Baltimore to spend her school holiday with her grandmother. Althea wished passionately that this did not come about. A great gulf, created by the short three months she had been with Marjorie, seemed to stretch between her present self and the child who had come to stay. Waking in the morning she thought at once of being required to return to her grandmother's house, void of this beneath-the-surface excitement of new knowledge, new people, this prospect of some new view of what the world was really like. She had learned to be more independent in dressing herself, in fastening the brace on her leg, though Martha was always ready to come and help. In Marjorie's house she felt like an independent person, almost an adult, since Marjorie had no experience in dealing with children and therefore did not treat her as one.

But in the end, to her great relief, her grandmother decided that she was unable to cope with Althea over the Christmas holidays. Marjorie was very apologetic, dreading to inflict pain, assuming that Althea would take this decision of her grandmother's to be a rejection of herself, that she would mourn over this exclusion from the family gatherings.

"Of course, Althea dear," she assured her anxiously, "we'll go over to Baltimore for Christmas Day, that is, if your grandfather is not worse."

But Althea, remembering the boredom and constraint of these family affairs, how hollow she felt this enforced conviviality to be, felt nothing but elation at the idea that she would stay with Marjorie and go only as a visitor when Marjorie took the train to Baltimore.

What interested her more were the small parties that Marjorie gave in the late afternoons, before dinner. All sorts of people came, people known to Marjorie and also to Mrs. Henshaw. A good many were foreigners, some of them wearing strange costumes — the women in filmy lengths of colored cloth wrapped around their bodies, or full trousers and sleeveless jackets over embroidered blouses, or full-skirted colorful dresses with masses of embroidery over the shoulders. The men were sometimes in turbans or fezes and were highly scented like the women. Martha was obviously often disapproving but she seemed not entirely at a loss, as if she had encountered some of this before. Althea supposed that she herself was not really invited to these affairs, but Marjorie said nothing about her presence, apparently not noticing that she followed Martha around with the plates of canapes or trays of punch and sometimes rather absentmindedly introduced her as her niece. She was aware that Elsie never appeared. Martha did not refer to this but Althea thought that some remarks in her absence passed between Marjorie and Mrs. Henshaw — in fact, that Mrs. Henshaw had invited Elsie more than once and was disappointed that she did not appear. Then at last Christmas came and a Christmas tree, laden with glittering varicolored balls and ropes of tinsel filled one end of the parlor. Dinner that evening was a hasty pickup meal and the doorbell rang intermittently through the next few hours as people came and went. At last, as it got near midnight, they were alone, Althea and Marjorie and Mrs. Henshaw. Martha had departed sometime before, to go to whatever family she had of her own — a sister, Marjorie said, and some children who lived on the other side of town. Mrs. Henshaw, in a rare moment of quiet, sat on a hassock close to the tree. Marjorie was circling the room, emptying ashtrays and straightening the cushions.

Presently Mrs. Henshaw said, "Dawkins" — Althea had learned that this was the nickname Mrs. Henshaw had for Marjorie — something to do with the nursery rhyme about Margery Daw — "do you remember Welby?"

Marjorie stopped what she was doing, her hands suspended in the air, and looked over her shoulder at Mrs. Henshaw. Finally she said, a little breathless, "Of course, Jan. Is it really the first Christmas we've spent together since then?"

There was a melting softness in her voice that astonished Althea. As the two women went on talking, she heard of the Christmas Marjorie had spent in Yorkshire with Janet's family — of the snowy town, the waits coming into the kitchen for a nip to keep out the cold, the leaping glow of the blazing logs in the fireplace — but no Christmas tree, a foreign custom to Janet's people, imported from Germany into England in Queen Victoria's reign by the Prince Consort. There was a mellow reflection in their voices of the childhood excitement of that far off time, cut off now not only by the passage of years but by the destruction of the Great War. Althea held her breath with suspense as Marjorie moved over to where Mrs. Henshaw sat. She stood beside her for a moment and then Mrs. Henshaw put her arm around her and she leaned down and they kissed. Althea knew she was witnessing the surfacing of an old emotion, that the women before her were suddenly swept up in the remnants of the feelings that had overflowed in their adolescence.

With Christmas and New Year out of the way the work of the Conference seemed to settle down to a steady gruelling pace and Mrs. Henshaw's time was wholly occupied. She arrived just before dinner, breathless with apologies, her soft fine hair straggling about her head, her eyeglasses twinkling as she moved her head nervously from side to side. She had not time now to come home for a cup of tea with Marjorie before returning for a few more hours work.

But then one afternoon when Althea got home from school she found both Marjorie and Mrs. Henshaw in the parlor, having tea and the small sandwiches Martha placed on the side table by the window. Marjorie called out to her as she stood in the hall, undecided whether to go in, and invited her to join them. Mrs. Henshaw sat in the middle of the settee, bent over a piece of needlework — she always seemed to have such a thing in the capacious canvas carry-all she carried with her everywhere, ready at hand to fill any idle moment. Probably she grew nervous if her hands — fine-boned, delicate-fingered, thin-skinned hands — they fascinated Althea — were not engaged in something. Half-absently Marjorie offered Athea a cup of tea and handed her the plate of sandwiches. Though the sounds of Althea's arrival had caught her ear and she had responded in this way, her attention was still firmly fixed on Mrs. Henshaw. Mrs. Henshaw was saying, "He is a very distinguished man — a man of considerable accomplishments. He was one of the most brilliant of the men at Oxford when I was there. You always found him speaking at the student rallies. He was always so forceful, so assured in the midst of the most chaotic political campaign. He was thought even in those days to have a brilliant political future. His rooms were the meeting place for all the liveliest people. They were quite different from anybody else's rooms — full of a jumble of real objects d'art and the freak of the moment.

"He's a wealthy man?"

"Well, no, not wealthy. His people were never more than well-off. But since the War — you know how much more stable our lives were before the War. The financial part was never much to the fore in our thinking. At least for people like us. Now, of course, we cannot take such ease so much for granted."

"And does he really show great interest in Elsie?"

"He's a widower — his wife died quite young. And everyone of course is always on the lookout for a suitable match for him. So one must discount gossip." Mrs. Henshaw stopped and took off her glasses and rubbed the lenses vigorously with her thumb. It was a gesture she made frequently and seemed to mean that she sought clarification of something in her own mind. But surely, thought Althea, those lenses must eventually become opaque.

"I think his interest is growing. At first I thought he was annoyed by her. Elsie is a very able young woman, but she can be quite aggressive when she feels she is in the right. Then she has been invaluable on more than one occasion when in the middle of a heated debate he needed information not readily obtained. He has learned to depend on her. She makes herself available at all times. She lives and breathes for the opportunity to be of service to him. She will work all night, if necessary, to be prepared for the next morning's session, even when the debate has gone on into the night. He is under a great deal of pressure — all the delegates are who take their responsibilities seriously — and she is there whenever he needs someone — before the sessions, perhaps, when he needs to sound out some new defense or argument that has come to his mind."

"I see," said Marjorie. "That is very lucky. She is an excellent handmaid. But how does he see her as a woman? It is obvious that she is infatuated with him."

Mrs. Henshaw was thoughtful. "He is now, perhaps, more concerned with her than he is aware."

"Would he consider marrying her?" Marjorie looked keenly at Mrs. Henshaw. "Is that what she wants?"

Mrs. Henshaw sighed. "Elsie is not concerned with marriage. She rather scorns the need for such a commitment —"

"Dear God!" Marjorie exclaimed. "Don't tell me she can be so foolish!" She would have said something further but Mrs. Hensahw had suddenly glanced in Althea's direction and she stopped abruptly.

Now it was Elsie's affairs that dominated the mood of anticipation in which Althea came home from school each afternoon. After that first afternoon, whenever she found Marjorie and Mrs. Henshaw together in the parlor, they obviously ceased whatever they had been talking about and Marjorie began at once to inquire about Althea's school day. It was Elsie they had been talking about, she was sure. Sometimes at odd moments through the evening, after they had gone upstairs to their rooms and then come down again to assemble for dinner, she overheard some scrap of further discussion between them but the moment they heard the thump of her iron brace they fell silent.

But Mrs. Henshaw did talk at length, in her soft
high-pitched English voice, of the day's events in the Conference and Elsie often figured in these accounts. Althea,
avid for details, caught the glances that the two women
exchanged that told plainly of some deeper meaning to
the phrases they used. Vaguely, with a maddening lack
of definition, she gathered that Elsie's affairs — or was it
an affair? — with the Englishman, had continued. At least,
she heard Mrs. Henshaw murmur "head over heels" and
that could only mean "head over heels in love." And he
either dallied with Elsie in secret and ignored her in public
or in fact ignored her altogether, while Elsie read into his
words and actions an invitation to intimacy. Althea thought
over the many novels she had read that hinted at such situations. What were the details of such intimacy — what bodily
contact did it consist of? Among the girls at school, because
of her imaginative use of the fiction she read, she had ac-
quired a reputation for sophisticated knowledge, an expert
acquaintance with the ins and outs of men's and women's
relationships. It was a reputation as fictitious as the sources
from which she got it. She had achieved it by means of a
lot of knowing comments, half-phrases, a telling silence
at crucial points of talk when the girls were pooling their
stock of information. The girls had come to look upon her
with a mixture of astonishment and respect. They did not
know that her sources of information were all literary,
helped out by her quickness at picking up the disguised
meanings of what adults said, the talk of servants among
themselves. But she was surprised that the girls accepted
her remarks as wisdom and therefore had adopted the habit
of checking their own conjectures with her. She knew that
some of the reason for this — and this was a facet of her
life that always brought pain, no matter how familiar it
was — was that her lameness took her out of the group of

her peers — her lameness put her outside of the common experience, set her aside psychically — the genesis of being a witch, she thought wryly.

But though surprised and a little apprehensive, she was careful to cultivate this reputation. It offset to some extent the other reputation she had of being so phenomenally brainy that no one in the school, not even the bigger girls in the classes ahead of her, could compete with her.

Now the history of Elsie offered the first opportunity for observation at close hand of a real life drama. Or at least she could watch its progress through its effects on others closely involved. Elsie obviously occupied Mrs. Henshaw's thoughts in most of her free time and when she and Marjorie were together this overriding preoccupation excluded any other topic of conversation. Mrs. Henshaw in her concentration on the subject often forgot that Althea was there, and Marjorie, her attention likewise caught, forgot to remind her. As the days went on Althea was aware of a heightening tension. It was something that Mrs. Henshaw seemed to bring into the house with her, so that even Martha began grumbling to herself in the kitchen, muttering half-phrases that Althea could not entirely piece together — "why'nt she keep it to herself — ain't no call to get everybody upset — what's it to do with Miss Marjorie?"

Then one evening, a little before dinnertime, there was a commotion in the hall downstairs. Althea, peering down over the bannister, saw that Elsie had arrived and that she was being interrogated by Mrs. Henshaw and Marjorie. What was the matter? What had happened? But Elsie said loudly, "I won't do it any longer! I won't dangle like this! He's got to make up his mind. Why should he expect me to wait on him, do all the details for him and not give me any thanks, not even when we're alone?"

Althea saw Marjorie pluck anxiously at Elsie's sleeve.

"Come into the parlor," she said. "We can talk better there."

And the three women went into the parlor and the door was closed and their voices reduced to a murmur. It was considerably later when they all actually ate dinner. Althea, driven by hunger, limped downstairs to join Martha in the brightly lit kitchen. The moment she stopped on the threshold she knew that Martha, whose back was turned to her, was angry. Martha was an excellent cook and her dinners were delicious, prepared with an exactness of timing to arrive on the table at the point of perfection. So no wonder Martha was upset. But there was also, Althea knew, the underlying vexation she felt about the intrusion into the household of Elsie and Elsie's troubles.

Martha glanced over her shoulder. "Looks like we're going to be held up for quite a while," she said. "You can have one of those biscuits to keep you going."

Althea picked up a hot biscuit and bit into it. "What's the matter with Elsie?"

"Don't know and it's none of my business, I guess. Except she's ruining the dinner for everybody else."

But it was in fact not too long before Marjorie came hurrying into the kitchen and said, "Oh, Martha! I'm sorry. You can serve now. Come on into the diningroom, Althea."

She was obviously trying to speak calmly but there was a breathlessness about her that betrayed her agitation and Althea heard Martha's "Tcha!" as she watched for a moment Marjorie's retreating back.

At the table they all sat at first eating the soup in silence. Silence was rare when Marjorie and Mrs. Henshaw were present. It seemed now to be imposed by the heavy gloom that had settled over Elsie. Althea watched her covertly. Elsie's sallow face was a study in suppressed emotion. Much of that emotion was anger, indeed fury. But there was also scorn, a desire for revenge, and — Althea gave her another secret glance from under her eyebrows — yes, anguish. Althea had never before been near anyone who was so obviously consumed by hostile passions, whose body seemed to seethe with feelings like a pot of boiling water about to overflow. The silence was finally broken by Mrs. Henshaw's voice, beginning to speak of some happening in the Conference which would be reported in tomorrow's papers. Loyally Marjorie responded, disjointedly, as if her own composure was disrupted by Elsie's troubled presence. Elsie continued to stab at the food on her plate, as if to some extent she was venting her feelings on the fried chicken and sweet potatoes. Mrs. Henshaw gazed at her but made no effort to draw her into talk. When the meal was over Elsie unceremoniously left the diningroom and went upstairs to Mrs. Henshaw's room. Althea saw no sign of her when a little later she herself went up to her own room to do her homework. She was aware that Marjorie and Mrs. Henshaw spent a long time together and were still downstairs when she went to bed and turned out her light.

The next day she discovered that it had been decided that Elsie should move back to stay with them. Elsie, Marjorie explained, was going through a difficult time, "and Janet is such a binder-up of wounds. She has always been that way."

Elsie moved into the room she had occupied before. And having moved in, she stayed in the room, not leaving the house even to go to the Conference. In the evening Althea heard Mrs. Henshaw, standing at the door, pleading through the door panel with her to come down and have dinner. She was unsuccessful and came down the stairs after a while with a worried frown on her face. This time it was Marjorie who talked almost without interruption through the meal, anxiously seeking to dispel the gloom that had settled over the meal.

For the next several days there was a hushed air in

the house, as if no one wanted to raise her voice to a normal pitch. Martha muttered to herself and Althea heard her say, "You'd think there's going to be a funeral." Elsie did not come down to breakfast, but then she always had said that she did not eat breakfast. About midday, said Martha, she left the house, presumably going to work. She came back promptly at six o'clock, in time to get ready for dinner. At dinner she sat like a thundercloud, eating if she liked the dish set before her, pushing it away if she did not. Althea was aware of Martha's unvoiced outrage and also of Marjorie's distress at Martha's injured feelings. But Mrs. Henshaw's attention was fixed on Elsie. When Elsie got up from the table and headed for the stairs, Mrs. Henshaw watched her go with anxious eyes and at the first possible moment followed her, for what was apparently a long session of commiseration, in Elsie's room.

After that, quite often in the afternoons when Althea arrived home from school, Marjorie and Mrs. Henshaw sat together in the parlor, having tea and little sweet biscuits. The pace of the work at the Conference had slackened. There were snags, it seemed, in the negotiations which required long meetings among various groups of the delegates before they all could come again to convene in public sessions. Temporarily Mrs. Henshaw was not as much in demand as she had been. But Elsie seemed busier than ever. She was the mainstay, said Mrs. Henshaw, of the section of the British delegation to which she was attached.

At first when Althea came in the two women would interrupt what they were saying and for a while there would be a forced conversation on subjects that they assumed were of interest to her. But Althea learned that if she took a book from the glass-fronted cabinet and began to look at it, they accepted the idea that her attention was straying and returned to a soft-voiced continuation of their own talk.

"Of course, you see," said Mrs. Henshaw, "I'm afraid

that Elsie has been too forward. As you know, she is a girl with a great deal of ambition. She is always striving for success in anything she does. And now she is infatuated with this man and she does not realize that her manner and her actions are embarrassing him and are disagreeable to those who work with him. He also is ambitious — a handsome, attractive man who has drawn to himself many admirers and supporters. He is a highly effective public speaker who is able to persuade even his enemies to accept his political views even against their inclinations. But in his private aspect he is quite different. I know him well, from the past, as I have told you. He is a reserved man. He lost his young wife and newborn child. I suppose you can say that he has devoted much of his emotional energy to his public career. As far as women are concerned, he is easily attracted by a pretty woman and not too wise in dealing with women who imagine themselves in love with him."

"Do you think that perhaps Elsie has mistaken his attitude to her?" asked Marjorie.

"Well, perhaps yes. Though I think it would be hard to reject Elsie when she turns the full power of her feelings on one. She is a much more powerful character — in herself, I mean — than the other women with whom he deals. She is also more intelligent than any —" Mrs. Henshaw seemed to hesitate — "perhaps with one exception."

She was thoughtful when she said this. Marjorie sat waiting for her to continue and then said, "Is there, then, someone else in whom Sanford is interested, someone he might think more suitable, from his point of view?"

"Certainly more suitable, from the point of view of his background and his ambitions. She is, in fact, the daughter of a peer and therefore a woman who would be of considerable value to him in his political career."

"Oh, dear! Poor Elsie, then."

But the expression on Mrs. Henshaw's face was one of shrewd calculation. "Perhaps not. I do not think we can assume that Elsie is seriously outclassed. This other woman does not know of Sanford's relationship with Elsie — if one can call it that. It is within Elsie's power to let her know of it."

"Blackmail? But if she is so infatuated with him, would she want to do such a thing — undermine his public character?"

"Elsie is capable of ruthless action when she is enraged — or feels slighted. That is part of her nature."

Suddenly Marjorie glanced across the room at Althea and the conversation ended.

Disappointed, nevertheless Althea hugged to herself the richness of these revelations. Each day as she hurried home from school — she had money for a cab whenever one of the teachers could not bring her — she eagerly joined the two women in the parlor, gratified to see that as they got more and more used to her presence the freer they were in continuing their private talk. At first, and in spite of the information she gleaned from the reading of novels, there was a good deal which puzzled her in what Mrs. Henshaw had to say about the motives that underlay Elsie's behavior and that of the man Sanford. But she was quick at picking up explanations and the drama grew in intensity. Sanford was a complex person, said Mrs. Henshaw. He came from a strict family background with narrow religious views and though he had a name for radical political opinions, he was not prepared to see his personal life exposed to public criticism. He was very conservative when it came to the duties and proprieties of a woman. No matter how brainy a woman might be, she could not in the nature of things successfully compete with a man in any professional or intellectual capacity. Certainly there were intelligent women — without them the race would return to savagery. But her intelligence was to be used in her role as helpmeet to a man worthy of her respect. If she was well-educated, so much the better, he approved of higher education for women. But that did not change the basic pattern of her position as a woman.

Marjorie did not listen to this outline of the ordained sphere of women without a good deal of indignant protest. Althea enjoyed it when the two women left the subject of Elsie to discuss how women should behave. It was Mrs. Henshaw who temporized. "My dear Dawkins, there you go. Not everyone has your particular gifts. A great many women — the majority, shall we say — do very much better for themselves by humoring men. Why not let men think they have the last word, when it certainly is not the case? Life is a good deal easier if you don't argue with them. And you get a good deal further in what you want to achieve." But Marjorie would not agree. "Jan, you know how I feel about that — women getting what they want by cozening up to men's weaknesses. I think that is despicable — beneath a woman's pride. And you know that you never do that on your own behalf, only for the benefit of someone you think needs your help." Obviously the two women had carried on this argument for the length of their friendship and they did not mince their words. Marjorie, said Mrs. Henshaw, was a visionary. It was not really important for a woman to appear to be a man's equal in every respect. What was more important was that she use the power she had to achieve her own purposes. No, no, no! Marjorie exclaimed.

Finally Marjorie burst out, "What a terrible hypocrite you are, Janet! Even now I cannot believe it!"

Mrs. Henshaw was not disturbed. "One must always use the weapons one has at hand, Dawkins. One must be practical and achieve results here and now and not in some chimerical future."

Then they came back to Elsie. "But, Janet," Marjorie objected, "I do not see how you can expect Elsie to succeed by adopting such methods. If Sanford cannot accept the idea of a wife whose opinions would differ from his own, he surely would not contemplate marriage with Elsie. She is the opposite of the woman you are portraying. She is the epitome of the forceful woman who will have her own way. She would never for a moment knuckle under. In fact, it seems to me that this other woman in whom Sanford is interested is more the type you believe would be successful in catching him. Really, what a disgusting way for a woman to act! How destructive to one's self-respect! I am sorry for Elsie's unhappiness and I do not find her a sympathetic character, but I should hate to see her try to buy happiness by denying her true nature." She paused for a moment to look directly at Mrs. Henshaw, who did not reply. "And you, Janet, you know very well you've never acted by those principles in your life."

Mrs. Henshaw smiled and said nothing.

One afternoon when Althea arrived home and stood in the vestibule taking off her coat, she noticed a quietness in the house, no muffled sound of voices in the parlor. Marjorie must be alone. Perhaps Mrs. Henshaw had not yet come. She opened the door carefully and was surprised to see Elsie sitting by the window smoking a cigarette.

Elsie turned toward her. "Oh, it's you," she said.

Althea, disconcerted, said nothing. She went over to sit on the settee. For a while Elsie ignored her, continuing to gaze out of the window at the wintry bareness of the trees. Then suddenly she turned around and said, "You expected to find your aunt here, didn't you?"

"She usually is."

"Well, she and Mrs. Henshaw went to a special session of the panel on prisoners of war. Even if you have disarmament, you still have prisoners of war. Your aunt was in the Balkans at the end of the War, wasn't she?"

Althea nodded. Elsie was silent and abstracted again for a while and then she seemed to rouse to the idea that they should carry on a conversation.

"What do they teach you in your school — anything of importance?"

Althea stared at her. Nobody had ever asked her such a question before. "Well, we have English literature and history and algebra and French."

Elsie's upper lip curled a little. "The same old pap. How do they expect anybody to leave school ready to deal with the modern world if they just teach you about poetry and how to do sums?"

"Sometimes we have discussions about current affairs," Althea offered timidly.

"What do you call current affairs?"

"Well, just now we're reading about the Disarmament Conference and studying nineteenth century European history as a background." She spoke gravely, anxious that Elsie should approve.

But Elsie laughed derisively. "I can imagine what you're told. What you should really know is that it's all miming — shadow boxing — the big countries trying to bluff one another. Nobody is sincere. If they really want to bring about lasting peace, they'll have to face the fact that the economic structure of the world is all wrong. If you don't change that, fiddling around with political structes won't mean anything. But of course you can't expect people — men — who have a stake in the present status of things to welcome revolution. Look at the Russians. They started out bravely enough. But I'm afraid the rot is setting in there too. Everybody is too busy protecting his own interests."

She went on at some length. Althea listened to her, fascinated. Elsie's voice rang with an enormous bitterness.

Althea had often been aware of a sense of passion seething just under the surface when she was near Elsie, even a silent, sullen Elsie. She also dimly understood that what Elsie was voicing now was a personal, emotional indignation, that she was venting a deeply felt resentment of personal injury that had little to do with the defects in the political basis of the Disarmament Conference. She felt coming from Elsie the pain of a raw, bruised bleeding heart, the heat of a passionate despair that burned like a fire in Elsie. She could find nothing to say in the face of this, did not think that her voice could be heard in the midst of Elsie's turmoil.

Elsie went on lecturing. "What they really ought to teach you about is the change that should be made in society — what the Russians have been trying to do — about Karl Marx, about —" She stopped, as if discouraged by her own words and Althea broke in eagerly, "Aunt Marjorie was in Russia."

Elsie looked at her as if her train of thought had been interrupted. Althea hurried on, "Right after the revolution. She has told me all about the starving people."

Elsie turned away impatiently. "That is all they talk about — the starving people. They don't think about all the people who starved before because of an unjust social structure. They don't understand what it means to try to redesign a society, a society that was still in the feudal age, with an illiterate, ignorant people. Nothing like that is ever done without hardship for some — for a lot of people, in fact. How could it be otherwise? Don't you realize that in order to create a new society in a backward country like Russia you have to destroy the old and build everything up from the ground? I'm so tired of hearing people talk about the Bolsheviks as if they were devils. What do they know about them? They don't understand that there are a lot of people all over the world sunk in just that sort of benightedness —"

Althea listened bewildered and at the same time enthralled. She had never heard anyone talk this way and she realized that even Marjorie probably would be horrified at what Elsie was saying. Althea had heard people talk about the Bolsheviks as a terrible threat to the world, to world peace, world stability, even civilization. In the current affairs class there had been references to Bolsheviks and anarchists, glancing references, for the teacher was discreet, and she had read in the newspaper about Emma Goldman and Alexander Berkman, anarchists and sympathizers with the new Russian regime, who had been imprisoned and then deported for their political views. She stared at Elsie, fascinated. Was Elsie a sympathizer with these opinions? It had not occurred to her that she herself might actually meet someone with such violent views. There was this quality of barely suppressed passion in Elsie, something she had recognized the very first time she had encountered Elsie.

But nevertheless, at this moment, she knew that Elsie's fervor in talking about world revolution was not fueled by an abstract, impersonal passion for the reform of society. The core of Elsie's passion was the torment in her own heart over unrequited love for a man. That was the source of the heat, the almost smell of physical desire that radiated from Elsie. Althea was struck by a sort of awe.

Elsie stopped what she was saying, aware at last of Althea's fascinated stare. She seemed to relax for a moment and said, in a contemptuous tone, "I'm quite sure your teachers wouldn't approve of all this. You'd better not mention me to them."

Althea was captivated by her sudden descent to the personal, the intimate — like a goddess stepping down from Olympus to speak to a mortal. Elsie seemed all at once much nearer to her in age and feeling. It was the first time that Althea had ever felt this about a woman so much older than herself — as much as ten years, perhaps. She said impetuously, breathless with the hint of confidentiality, "Oh, I never tell anybody about what happens at home."

Elsie looked at her searchingly for a moment and then an odd smile appeared on her face. "I believe you are a little mole, aren't you?"

Althea, disappointed and yet puzzled, dropped her eyes.

After that afternoon Althea sought moments to be alone with Elsie or at least without the oppressive weight of Marjorie's and Mrs. Henshaw's active participation in their tete-a-tetes. It was seldom that she could be with Elsie entirely alone, but she made efforts for them to be together at one end of the room while the two older women talked at the other. Elsie's physical presence drew her like a magnet. Standing near her she felt an almost irresistible impulse to reach out and touch her. At the dinnertable the talk between Marjorie and Mrs. Henshaw, which up to now had so enthralled her with its glimpses of odd people and strange events, went by her now without arousing her interest. Elsie, sitting there chiefly silent and morosely abstracted, her intense inner preoccupation making it seem that a dark cloud hung over her, claimed all her attention. Covertly she examined Elsie. Elsie, she had to admit, was not a pretty woman. Her skin was sallow and at the time of her monthly period, pimply. Her hair was black and straight and hard to manage so that it could look neat and lustrous. Her present emotional state did not enhance her looks. Her large nose tended to be red and shiny and the sullen set of her mouth disfigured her face, erasing the glowing attraction of her large dark eyes. Yet after all she was wrapped in the mantle of a great romantic tragedy. Unrequited love — producing despair, unbearable sorrow. But in Elsie it seemed to produce anger, a towering rage that flowed out of her to anyone nearby. It was that, perhaps, that created this magnetism that drew Althea to her, helpless to resist this pull.

When she was alone with Elsie for any length of time, which was seldom, after a while Elsie came out of her preoccupation with herself enough to notice the effect she was having on Althea. Then there was a mixture of indulgence and disdain in her smile, as if she understood very well, better than Althea herself, what Althea was feeling and found a certain absurdity — and even a sort of pleasure — in it. Seeing this, Althea was for the moment devastated but at the same time overjoyed by the idea that a secret terrain had been created between them. She had never had this sort of relationship with anyone — an intimacy of spirit that by shutting out other people magnified her feeling of herself as herself, not as the schoolgirl Althea, not as Marjorie's niece, even as the person she thought of herself as being. She was both herself and a character in a drama, a drama of the most exquisitely intimate and enchanting kind.

These tete-a-tetes became more frequent. Perhaps this was because Elsie no longer seemed to feel compelled to give as wholeheartedly of herself, of her time, to the work of the Conference. February was approaching and with it the end of the Conference. Althea came to know an Elsie she had never suspected — still a self-absorbed Elsie, but a vulnerable Elsie, an Elsie who was wide open to the stings and arrows of outrageous fortune — they were doing Hamlet as the school play this year and Althea savored the language of the soliloquies. Elsie, she decided, was a queen of tragedy. The intensity of her feelings, the concentration of her scorn and vengefulness on the man she nevertheless adored, made her more than a figure for sympathy. Elsie never made even the most distant allusion to him but Althea, clued in by Mrs. Henshaw's explanations to Marjorie, saw at once and without doubt who it was that was the cause and the object of Elsie's frantic grief. It was obvious to her that Elsie realized that she knew of and understood the situation — or else did not care whether she did or not — nor did she care if she exposed herself to Althea's observation.

Finally there came the evening when Althea came upon Marjorie and Mrs. Henshaw deep in conversation, so absorbed in what they were talking about that they scarcely noticed her presence.

"Yes," Mrs. Henshaw was saying, "it has been officially announced. There are statements in the London papers that confirm this. Oh, yes, Elsie has seen them. She knows the matter is settled and done. No, she was not prepared for it. It came as a surprise — though it should not have. But he had not ceased to act towards her as if the situation is what it always was. He gave her no inkling that he was seriously considering marriage with someone else. But the announcement says that he will marry the Honorable Miss Parker next month, when he returns to England."

"And how is she taking it?" Marjorie's voice was avid with curiosity.

"I'm afraid not very well. I suppose she has refused to see that there was any coolness in his manner. She broke down, with me, this afternoon, and I have persuaded her to take a sedative and try to sleep."

"You mean she is here, in the house?"

"Oh, yes. In her room. I have thought of a solution for the moment — something to tide her over till she can regain her equilibrium. She will need some sort of work after the Conference closes. She must earn her living and I know that she has given no thought to it. I have put the wheels in motion to obtain her a post in the Secretariat of the League of Nations at Geneva. She will be invaluable there. In fact, I have approached Sanford himself to use his influence." Mrs. Henshaw's eyes flashed as she looked over at Marjorie. "He understood perfectly that I consider it the least he can do and I'm sure he will act. Though, of course, Elsie must know nothing about this." Mrs. Henshaw paused for a moment. "A most unfortunate business. But she has such a passionate nature. Reason cannot prevail at such a time."

But Althea noticed that she did not speak as if this was something that could be avoided. There was nothing in her tone that indicated that she thought Elsie might have done otherwise than follow the demands of her emotional self, that she might have had better sense than to have become infatuated with an unsuitable man. Althea, observing this, wondered. Mrs. Henshaw obviously felt only sympathy for Elsie's despair and heartsickness but she treated it in much the same way she did Althea's withered leg — a sad but inescapable misfortune. Althea thought of what Marjorie had said about Mrs. Henshaw's own unhappy romance. Perhaps that was the reason for her acceptance of Elsie's hopeless love as something that could not be escaped but only endured.

Apparently Elsie made no problem about falling in with Mrs. Henshaw's scheme for her to go to Geneva. At least, Althea heard no protests, no fierce rejection, coming from her room when Mrs. Henshaw went in there to talk about it, to help her plan for her departure. Mrs. Henshaw did announce to Marjorie that Elsie was leaving at once. The Conference was winding up and Elsie had been granted an early release from her post. She would go at once to Geneva, on a ship that was sailing from New York to Southampton within a week. She was leaving most of her belongings behind. Mrs. Henshaw would gather them up in due course and take them along with her own when she herself left Washington.

"But what will you be doing, Janet?" Marjorie inquired. "Do you have a place to go to? Some secure work?"

"Well, no. Nothing I am going to do immediately. You know, of course, I have a small income — from Roger, you know — not enough to keep me and I am afraid it is shrinking. But I can always find work as a language tutor. And you have been so kind that I have had no expense here and therefore have quite a little fund to fall back on."

"Oh, Janet! You know you can always count on me if you need anything!" Althea noticed tears in Marjorie's eyes. "You need never want for anything, you know! You really need only let me know!"

Mrs. Henshaw patted her arm and said soothingly, "Of course, Dawkins. I've always remembered that but I'm doing very well. I have never really been on my uppers. I shall go to Geneva with Elsie's things. I feel rather a responsibility for her, even now —" here Mrs. Henshaw paused and exchanged a long look with Marjorie — was there something there, Althea wondered, that was understood between them? — "and I shall be able to see how she is getting along. I'm sure I shall find something to do in the meantime. I'm afraid this has been an embittering experience for her — it could not be otherwise."

Elsie herself was more withdrawn than she had been at any time during her stay in Marjorie's house. She did not make the sort of sallies she had when she first arrived — seeking opportunities in the conversation to expose Marjorie's goodwill as basic stupidity or Mrs. Henshaw's inveterate sympathy with the miserable as missing the point of an unjust society. But she also seemed to have achieved an appearance of self-possession so that at the dinnertable, although not talkative she spoke enough to dispel the weight of gloom that she had so often brought with her. Althea saw that Martha observed this difference also and was relieved but not mollified. Probably she did not depend on the continuance of this new social grace. Althea noticed that she would every now and then cast a suspicious glance at Elsie's face as she handed the plates around the table.

In the afternoon, when Althea got home from school, Elsie was almost always alone in the parlor, since for this school session Althea's schoolday was shorter than it had been and it was too early for either Marjorie or Mrs. Henshaw. She was surprised to find Elsie almost amiable, asking a question or two about her schoolwork and listening to her answers without caustic comments. But most of the time she was silent and abstracted. Her taciturnity made Althea relapse into silence. In those long moments of quiet, Althea began to feel the sense of mute communion, as if her sympathy flowing wordlessly to Elsie was accepted gratefully by Elsie. This gave her a soft, trembling inward lovingness, a yearning fondness in which Elsie was embedded, as if cradled in her arms. She had never felt this before towards anyone. Elsie became in her dreaming thoughts both the heroine of a romantic tragedy and the pathetic victim of cruel injustice — the ravishing heroine of a terrible story, whose pure and unstinted love was rejected by a cold and self-seeking man. She was not aware that for long moments she sat gazing at Elsie, who seemed unconscious of her adoration. When she was alone thus with Elsie a tremendous need filled her to reach out and touch her — the need for a physical fulfillment of some sort, which she could not identify, was almost beyond bearing. Once she did put a hand on Elsie's arm, unable to prevent herself. Elsie had been startled but did not fling her off. Instead she had looked at her as if wondering what she wanted and had then smiled in an indulgently contemptuous way.

At night, in bed, Althea was overcome with the sense of Elsie's presence even in her absence. She had never been an easy sleeper and now she lay awake, in a waking dream centered on Elsie. She imagined all sorts of situations — impossible, she knew, in the cold light of day — when Elsie was kind, happy to be with her, weeping in her arms to calm her own sorrow, confiding her inmost agonies of love. So powerful were these waking nightdreams that in the morning she was slow to get up, dawdled in dressing, until she was roused by Martha coming to see what she needed.

The time before Elsie was to leave was short and these few afternoons passed like the wind. The day came which was to be her last. She was leaving the next morning, early. Althea was so mesmerized by her own absorption in fantasy that she scarcely realized this fact. She was in a fever of impatience the whole morning at school, wondering if Elsie would not be in the parlor when she got back shortly after lunch, skipping her last class period. But Elsie was there. But there was a difference. Elsie was not slumped in an armchair in her usual apathy, scarcely responding to Althea's greeting. Today she was pacing up and down the room. She turned sharply at the sound of the door.

"Oh, it's you," she said, in a tone of disappointment.

"I got off early," said Althea, breathlessly. "I said you were going away and Aunt Marjorie wanted me to come home early."

Elsie paused in her pacing. "Why did you do that?" But she did not really seem interested in Althea's answer and turned away to her own thoughts.

With dismay Althea recognized the return of the savage anger of the days after the announcement of Sanford's marriage. "I'm so sorry you are leaving, Elsie."

She herself was aware that her voice faltered and was in fact almost a whisper from the emotion that overwhelmed her. Elsie after another glance at her, turned away and stood staring out of the window. Desperately Althea went on talking, "I shall miss you so much, Elsie. You're not like anybody I've ever known. You don't talk like the girls and the teachers at school. Oh, Elsie, aren't you a little sorry you're going away —?"

Elsie gave an angry laugh. "Of course I don't talk like the girls and teachers at your silly school! Good God! What do you take me for? No, I'm not sorry I'm leaving. I'm delighted I'm leaving. I could not have stood another day in this place."

"But, Elsie, doesn't it make you a little sorry that I'm so unhappy about your going away?" Althea was near to tears.

Elsie whirled around and Althea saw that her eyes were blazing. "Don't go sniveling like that! I never could stand all this schoolgirl slop! It's sickening — and all this mooning around over me. It's just your age. I don't know why girls have to get so drivelling just because they're going through puberty. I never did. And thank God I don't have to be a teacher in a girls' school. No, I'm not the least bit sorry I'm leaving. I just want to go away from this place. I never want to see it or you or your aunt or this house again. I want to forget I was ever here. I want to put all this behind me and forget it ever happened."

Althea, the tears running down her face, hobbled over to her to catch hold of her arm. She hung on, looking up into Elsie's angry face, hung on so tenaciously that Elsie could not shake her off. "Elsie, I know he was dreadful to you. If only I could do something to make you feel happier. Elsie, I really love you."

"God!" Elsie exclaimed, glaring down at her. "You silly little fool! Take your hand away. This is ridiculous!"

Althea, trying to stifle her sobs, clung to her arm, lowering her head to bury her face in the cloth of Elsie's dress. Before Elsie could fling her off, Althea implored, "Elsie, don't you like me at all? I do love you —"

Elsie, enraged, gave her a violent push which sent her sprawling on the floor. Suddenly calmed by the consequences of her action, she exclaimed, "You miserable little cripple! See what you've made me do." She leaned down hastily to help Althea up. "Did you hurt yourself?" But Althea was beyond her now. She could not prevent Elsie from pulling her to her feet and drawing her onto the settee. But once there she put up her hand and pushed Elsie away.

Elsie, still angry but chagrined by her own harshness, went on. "I just can't stand all this sentimentality. It hasn't got anything to do with your lameness. I'm sorry I said that. But it's true, what I said. You're just going through a phase of growth. You'll forget all about this in a little while. When you're grown you'll have more sense. You haven't any idea what you're talking about now. Love!" Elsie's laugh was harsh. "That's a lot of nonsense — just a game to get you into hell —"

She raved on for a few more minutes, but Althea had ceased to hear anything more than the sound of her voice. Presently the room was quiet and she realized after some moments that Elsie had gone away and that she was left alone. After a while, when Marjorie came, she sat silent and unresponsive. Mrs. Henshaw's arrival soon after diverted Marjorie's attention.

Because Mrs. Henshaw was so concerned with Elsie's departure and Marjorie was flustered by the commotion this seemed to cause, neither of them noticed the stricken whiteness of Althea's face nor her complete silence. At dinner Martha looked at her several times anxiously and tried unobtrusively to coax her to eat her dinner. The next morning Althea stayed in bed, telling Martha she did not feel well. Martha, thinking she was having a bad time with her period, brought her hot cereal for her breakfast and said nothing to Marjorie, who went off with Mrs. Henshaw to see Elsie off on the train.

As she lay in bed Althea felt at first only a great numbing bereavement. She stayed in bed for several days, rousing herself only to say No, no, when Marjorie, alarmed at this first time that Althea had shown any sign of illness beyond an ordinary cold, insisted that she should call the doctor.

"But Althea dear," Marjorie remonstrated, "if you feel too ill to get up we must have the doctor. I cannot allow any neglect. You don't have a fever, I know, but perhaps there is something else —"

In the end it was Martha who dissuaded her. Martha, whose instinct seemed to tell her that something was here that ordinary medicine could not reach, shook her head silently and Marjorie, seriously reluctant, left off and said they would wait a day or so. Perhaps, she thought, she's just a little girl and all that schoolwork is too much for her.

Althea, the moment she was left alone again, sank back into the morass of her own despair. She had no will to make the effort to get up from her bed and dress and drag that ueless leg through the routine of a normal day. Between waking and drowsing she dwelt on the image of Elsie, the remembrance of Elsie, the memory of Elsie's way of looking and speaking. In a sort of effort at self-protection she tried to absolve Elsie of blame. After all, Elsie had been in the agonies of rejected love. She could not have been feeling and thinking as she normally would. But again and again she came back to it: "You miserable little cripple." Shrinking within herself at the pain of the remembrance, she found she could not forgive that. Elsie had said she was sorry — Elsie who never accepted blame, who denied that anyone could ever make her feel guilt for anything — Elsie had said she was sorry. And perhaps she was, the essential Elsie, who must be good, must be loving. But she could not convince herself. And each time, as the remembrance of the phrase came back, she felt a little harder, a little less soft towards the memory of Elsie.

In a calmer mood she began to think of Elsie as Elsie, not the woman who had called forth such a passion of adoration from her. She writhed a little inwardly, at this stage of her recapitulation, at her own childishness, at the unthinking eagerness with which she had sought to be something to Elsie of what Elsie had become to her. Of course Elsie was contemptuous, Elsie was full of scorn for such mawkish, unfledged physical feeling. But need she have been so contemptuous? Of course Elsie was very different from anyone she had ever known. Elsie was brilliant — Mrs. Henshaw never ceased to talk about Elsie's brilliance. The very quality of her mental endowment made her impatient and scornful of lesser souls. But should this call for contempt? Elsie was like steel, a glittering swordlike metal immune to the dreamy softness of her own child's nature. Elsie's emotional nature was like a fiery furnace, ready to consume and at the same time ready to do battle with a contending fire. But how many fires could contend successfully with Elsie's? Slowly, Althea buried the memory of Elsie, the demand for Elsie's love that still cried in her body, the consciousness of Elsie as a doorway once opened into a mysterious great world beyond childhood and then slammed shut. All that lingered finally in her consciousness, to rise again and again at unexpected moments, was the phrase: "You miserable little cripple."

With Elsie gone, Marjorie's household settled down to a different routine. Althea, when she came downstairs the first day — it was a Friday and they said she was not to go back to school till Monday — was aware of the quieter atmosphere in the house. Martha settled her in the sunny window of the kitchen and brought her breakfast there. She felt a certain contentment, as if she had truly been ill, and at ease with Martha, as if Martha, who could not know the real nature of her malaise, nevertheless understood that she was soul-weary and in need of a special sympathy. She stayed there through the morning, content to sit and read George Eliot's *Middlemarch*, which had been assigned

her for her next term paper. Martha had fetched the book
from the glass-fronted cabinet in the parlor and Althea
could not refrain from remembering Elsie's caustic comments about what people harbored in their mental attics.
When Marjorie came home in the afternoon she went into
the parlor and they waited for Mrs. Henshaw's arrival to
have tea.

"Do you feel better, Althea?" Marjorie asked anxiously,
the whole aspect of her manner betraying the combination
of concern and puzzlement that had been hers all the while
Althea had been upstairs in bed. Usually Althea rejected
any attempt to help, but this time she accepted the support
of Marjorie's arm, comforted in spite of herself by the worried solicitude in Marjorie's craggy face as she bent over
her. Marjorie herself seemed aware of this uncharacteristic
willingness to be helped and was made uneasy by it.

Mrs. Henshaw came in shortly after they were settled
in the parlor, arriving in a flow of talk about the day's
events, until she saw Althea and broke off to inquire how
she was. "I'm so glad, dear child, that you are feeling so
much better and so pleased to see you down here."

Althea gave her a searching look, wondering if Mrs.
Henshaw's greater sophistication had enabled her to guess
what lay behind Althea's illness. She returned Althea's
gaze and then, nodding briskly, went on with her talk. But
even though her inquiries were brief and sandwiched in
between remarks dealing with other matters, she did not
give the impression of being perfunctory in her interest.
It was something to do with her eyes, Althea decided,
when she inquired about you her eyes gazed directly into
yours, as if other concerns were for the moment, however
brief, forgotten.

She spoke often and at length about Elsie, while Althea
screwed up her courage to listen without flinching. Such
an unfortunate business, Mrs. Henshaw said, the whole idea

so unsuitable in every way. She could not imagine why a man like Sanford should allow himself to become involved with a girl he must know was completely outside his own sphere. But unfortunate chiefly for Elsie, whose capacity for feeling was so extraordinarily intense. It was foolish of her to allow herself to become embroiled in an affair with someone like Sanford, who most certainly could not reciprocate fully — whose public life precluded the possibility of any such connection. But after all, Elsie could not help herself. She had fallen in love.

Althea, watching, saw Marjorie at this point gaze at Mrs. Henshaw in an oddly yearning fashion, saw her gaze for a long moment and then drop her eyes while an expression of resigned sadness came over her face. Marjorie murmured something meant to be in agreement with what Mrs. Henshaw was saying but offered no comment of her own about Elsie. Was she remembering — were they both remembering — Althea wondered, Mrs. Henshaw's own unhappy love story?

Mrs. Henshaw reported after some days that Elsie was well established in Geneva, had found a convenient place to live — and she and Marjorie discussed for some minutes just where Elsie's *pension* must be located, recalling to each other the details of Geneva's landscape. During their time at the Scottish school they had been sent together, it seemed, to Geneva for a summer holiday to improve their French and their health, and they remembered it now with a gleefulness that brought to Althea the savor of their youthful selves.

"I shall be going over there in a couple of weeks or so, Dawkins, to join her," Mrs. Henshaw said. "She seems to expect me to stay with her for a while and of course she wants her things."

"But what will you live on, Janet?" Marjorie objected.

"Oh, I shall find something to carry me for a while. I

can always give English lessons, you know. And besides I have my little nest-egg that I have gathered up while staying here with you." She smiled, the sweet, charming smile that sometimes came into her face when she was talking to Marjorie, and put her hand out to pat Marjorie's arm. Althea saw Marjorie blush. "I cannot offer you anything for my keep, I know —"

"Certainly not!" Marjorie's eyes blazed.

"So I shall give Martha a small present. She has been most attentive."

"That is not at all necessary," Marjorie mumbled, "though I'm sure Martha will appreciate some token from you."

They went on talking about what had to be done before Mrs. Henshaw left.

Going to school again Althea found that her acute sense of loss, of the worthlessness of all effort, abated a little. But the excitement, the eager hopefulness with which she used to look forward to each day had gone. The habit of diligence in studying helped her. She did not want to be idle, because then she lapsed into brooding. Conjugating French verbs and writing essays on the English romantic poets filled the time, but the bright glass that had overlaid everything, giving such a feeling of the new, the marvelous, to her lessons, to her discussions with her teachers, had gone. She no longer enjoyed astonishing and entertaining her classmates with her fancies and worldliwise statements. She knew that her teachers noticed this change in her, that they missed the eagerness with which she had jumped into the talk in the classroom. One or two of them tried to spur her into action but stopped when she stiffly rejected them. They supposed, no doubt, she thought, that her brief illness had sapped her small amount of physical strength and they left her alone.

The day came when Mrs. Henshaw's trunks — she had a flat metal-bound one and one that could stand on its end and open like a wardrobe, and another, newer, more elegant one that belonged to Elsie — were fetched away by Martha's brother, who came with his horse and cart to take them to the railway station to be sent ahead of her to New York and put aboard the steamer. Althea, coming out of the fog that usually enveloped her now when she was alone for any length of time, noticed that Marjorie was not only almost silent throughout the afternoon and dinnertime but that her eyes looked red, as if she had been crying. Her responses to Mrs. Henshaw's remarks were murmured, incomplete sentences without a clear meaning. But Mrs. Henshaw did not seem to notice.

The next day Marjorie did not go to her office but instead waited about the house while Mrs. Henshaw made her last preparations. Althea said she did not want to go to school and Marjorie's attention was so completely distracted that she merely nodded agreement, making no effort to find out what was the matter. Somehow Althea felt she could not miss Mrs. Henshaw's departure — she could not go away from the house with her still present in it, to return to a house half-empty — that seemed to her how it would seem. She had a powerful sense of the impending change that would be brought about by Mrs. Henshaw's leaving — a withdrawal of the warmth and cheerfulness that seemed to fill it when she and Marjorie were together — in spite of Elsie, in spite of Elsie's gloom and tragic presence. Even Martha was disturbed and as usual she showed her uneasiness in a certain shortness of temper as she helped sort things out and found containers for the always overflowing odds and ends that Mrs. Henshaw found she had to take with her.

They all three finally accompanied Mrs. Henshaw to

Union Station, in two cabs, Marjorie and Mrs. Henshaw in one with several parcels and Althea and Martha and the rest of the luggage in another.

"How is she going to carry all this mess of things?" Martha demanded, staring at the several cases piled on the floor of the cab crowding their feet. On her lap she held an old-fashioned hatbox tied with a cord.

Althea sought to soothe her. "There'll be porters at the station."

"But they cost money. She ain't got no money. Miss Marjorie'll take care of this end but what about when she gets to New York? All them crowds of people in the station there. She'll be robbed. She cain't hold onto all those things by herself."

Althea looked at her, surprised by the degree of worry showing on Martha's brown, usually impassive face. Why, she thought, Martha was almost as upset by Mrs. Henshaw's going as was Marjorie and yet all the time Mrs. Henshaw had been staying with them it had been Martha who had borne the burden of extra work, of looking after her comfort. It was amazing — Martha, so often sardonic, who gave people such short shrift, had been captured in the net of Mrs. Henshaw's sympathy like everyone else, was as ready to come to her aid as anyone else, was as alarmed as anyone else at the uncertain future that seemed to loom out there ahead of her.

Mrs. Henshaw herself seemed unconcerned. When they were gathered together in the station, standing on the open platform under the long narrow shelter beside the empty train track, she continued to talk, in her light, high-pitched gentle voice, to Marjorie as if they were sitting by the tea-table in the parlor discussing the day's events. Martha and Althea stood a little to one side. Martha's eyes were fixed watchfully on the parcels and bags heaped around them. At last at the end of the track the train appeared, tiny in the far distance, looming larger as it came slowly down the track, and they all watched it as it came puffing to a stop beside them.

As it came to an abrupt halt, Martha reached for several of the pieces of luggage and Marjorie, her attention caught, sprang into action to collect a few more. The porter who had brought the things from the cabs on a handcart, appeared to help. Mrs. Henshaw with greater deliberation, picked up a case and a bundle tied with string. Just how it was done Althea did not know, but at last all the boxes and bundles were finally hoisted on the back platform of the coach into which Mrs. Henshaw had climbed. The trainman, after standing nonplussed for a moment surveying the mass of baggage, had joined in the operation of getting it aboard, Mrs. Henshaw talking to him in the meantime, saying that she hoped that the train would not be crowded and that no problem would thus arise. The trainman seemed too bemused to contradict her.

Althea, unable to climb the steps without help, could only imagine how everything was disposed of. They must surely have filled the seat which Mrs. Henshaw had chosen and also the rack above. Several pieces were left piled on the train platform. Mrs. Henshaw was not perturbed. Martha returned to Althea, muttering under her breath, and presently Marjorie and Mrs. Henshaw appeared once more at the train door and stepped down onto the platform to wait until the conductor signaled for departure.

Althea heard Marjorie protesting, "But, Janet, I would willingly have got you a firstclass ticket! You don't have to travel in the coach!"

"I would not think of it, Dawkins. Remember, I have an allowance for return travel to England. I wish to stay within that. I am grateful for all you have done — that goes without saying. The coach is quite comfortable. It is only for five hours. I'll be aboard ship by five o'clock this evening. I'll drop you a line before we sail."

Althea watched as the two women stood together, suddenly quiet, — tall ungainly Marjorie bending slightly over the shorter, frailer Englishwoman. They were not looking at each other nor were they touching, but there seemed to be a communication between them that was wordless and motionless. It was a moment fixed in time. Then the trainman called out, "All aboard!" and Mrs. Henshaw reached up to give Marjorie a swift kiss on the lips before turning quickly to mount the train steps. The three of them stood together as a little knot watching the train disappear down the track in billows of white steam.

They turned away to walk back down the platform to the gates and the station waiting room. Althea, walking beside Marjorie and Martha trailing a little behind them. None of them spoke. Then Althea, anxious, glanced up into Marjorie's face and was shocked to see that tears were running down her cheeks. She looked away, embarrassed and speechless as Marjorie tried to staunch them with her handkerchief. She had never imagined that Marjorie would ever give way so in public to womanly weeping. She glanced over her shoulder at Martha seeking help but Martha merely shook her head and made some exclamation she could not understand, striding past them to lead the way to the ranks of cabs waiting at the far end of the station. Marjorie continued to weep throughout the trip home and once there, without a word, climbed the stairs hastily to her own room and closed the door. When Althea saw her next her eyes were still red but her face was set in a determined composure. Martha was grim and uncommunicative throughout the rest of the day.

Every so often through the months that followed Marjorie had a letter from Mrs. Henshaw from which, at dinnertime, she read excerpts to Althea, about Geneva, about the workings of the League of Nations, occasionally about Elsie. Whenever Elsie's name was mentioned Althea was aware of a suppressed grunt of disapproval from Martha. Elsie, it seemed, was forging ahead, making a place for herself in the field of international affairs. She was, said Mrs. Henshaw, so amazingly competent in handling discussions of economic and social problems that came with the postwar period. There was never, at least in the passages Marjorie read aloud, any hint of Elsie's private life — whether she still pined for Sanford, whether her ardent feelings were becoming fixed on someone else.

To Althea the whole story of Elsie's sojourn in Marjorie's house had retreated into a land of mythologic haze. The Elsie who had aroused such violent emotions in her somehow vanished, was not the Elsie Mrs. Henshaw wrote about. Perhaps, she told herself, this was because she knew nothing about Geneva. She could not visualize Elsie in her new surroundings. But she knew within herself that this was not the real reason. The Elsie she had adored had vanished because she had never existed. Reluctantly she admitted this to herself. Yet when the memory came back to her of Elsie, the real, live Elsie, standing by the bookcase in the parlor talking about the books, of Elsie's passionate outbursts disrupting the placid air of Marjorie's house, then Althea felt with double intensity the Elsie who had swept her up into a strange place where emotions crowded out thought, where nothing went according to the rules she had been taught to live by. When she was alone she sank back into the misery of her loss, drowning again in the feeling of being forsaken. But then, she reminded herself, Elsie had never shown the remotest love-interest in herself, so how could she be forsaken if she had never been claimed? And then her deepest memory called back the little moments when Elsie, racked by her own despair, had softened momentarily and listened to her eager stories of school and teachers, as if grateful for this disguised love-offering.

The spring came, flowering gaily, brilliantly through April. The school year was coming to an end. The lilac bushes massed in the corners of the playing grounds filled the air with their enticing perfume. The mornings broke with a bright sun in a pale blue sky. The cool embrace of April turned into the warmth of May. Althea knew that the question would soon arise about her going back to her grandmother in Baltimore. Marjorie said nothing about it but for some time now Marjorie had been much more silent than usual when they ate together at dinner. Sometimes she roused to a wild sort of talkativeness, hopping about from subject to subject without much connection between them. Every so often she seemed to remember that Althea still went to school and that she should inquire about how things went there and Althea could see that she strove to pay attention to her answers. There was a great chasm, Althea realized, between the time before and after Mrs. Henshaw's visit.

The last days of school came and still Marjorie said nothing about her going back to Baltimore. She knew the reason was that her grandfather still lingered. At last in June he died and at last the sense of suspended animation among the family broke into a frenzy of activity. Each day Marjorie, voluble once more at breakfast, bustled off to take the train to Baltimore. Althea regretted the sudden change. For three weeks now, since school was out, she had luxuriated in a dreamy inertia, a form of mourning for what had gone before. Marjorie had made sporadic efforts to rouse her, as if now and then she awakened to her responsibility as Althea's guardian, questioning her — Did she want to do this? Didn't she want to do that? Wasn't there something she would like to do? But Martha left her undisturbed, merely prodding her to eat her breakfast, her lunch, seeming to recognize that this was a necessary passage of adolescence that would in time pass. Althea spent most of her time in the parlor with a book in her hand. This was a consecrated place now, in her mind — consecrated to the shade of Elsie, to the memory of the afternoon tea ritual that had provided Marjorie and Mrs. Henshaw with an intimate moment nearly every day. Marjorie had abruptly left off the habit of having tea in the afternoon when Mrs. Henshaw had departed.

But now everything was focussed on her grandfather's funeral. Althea could not summon up any real feeling of grief for him. She had known him only as an elderly man who was sometimes jovial but more often irascible and whose interest apparently lay outside the house in Eutaw Place. He had a lot of grandchildren older than Althea, and she, with the acute sensibility of the crippled, believed that he avoided her because of her withered leg. Her grandmother, though undemonstrative, had been much more someone on whom she relied. But now she was aware that she had grown out of being a child in that household. She had grown into being almost an adult in the smaller, more cheerful, easier world of Marjorie's house, secure in the friendship of Marjorie and Martha. She found she dreaded going back to Baltimore, something she had up till now taken for granted as bound to happen — that at the end of the school year she would go back to Baltimore.

The day of her grandfather's funeral arrived. For the first time she was to go with Marjorie to Baltimore. Martha fussed about her appearance, about the way she was dressed, about her hair, brushing its glossy length again and again, as if anxious that she should be a credit to herself, to Marjorie, under her grandmother's scrutiny. It was a long day, climaxed by the big funeral at the church of St. Michael's and All Angels, and the long procession to the cemetery, with the anti-climax at her grandmother's house filled to overflowing with aunts and uncles and cousins. Althea waited with apprehension to see what would happen. Marjorie had said nothing about whether they — or she — would stay in Baltimore, though Althea was cheered by the fact that they had brought no night things with them. Marjorie herself was in a frenzy of nervous activity, restlessly moving from one room to another, talking incessantly, irritating her mother with unasked advice, commenting not always favorably on the arrangements her brothers-in-law had made.

But at seven o'clock in the evening she had come to fetch Althea from the group of cousins with whom she was and announced that they must hurry to catch the last evening express train to Washington.

The next day, at breakfast, Marjorie said, "Althea, you have liked being at Miss Armstrong's school, haven't you? You seemed to do pretty well there."

Althea said, Oh, yes, and waited.

For a while Marjorie sat gazing down at her half-finished breakfast. There was a frown on her strong-featured face. She had the vulnerable skin of those with ginger-colored hair. Her hands as well as her face were covered with freckles. She flushed readily at any stress, as Althea had early learned and learned also that this was one of the things her grandmother disapproved of in Marjorie. Now Althea could see her natural high color heightened as she struggled with her thoughts.

Finally Marjorie inquired, "Would you like to stay here with me and go back to Miss Armstrong's in the fall?"

Althea felt a great leap of joy in her heart. "Oh, yes, Aunt Marjorie!"

Marjorie, gazing somewhat perplexed at her suddenly glowing face, protested. "But it must be rather dull for you here. There are no other people — you never see your cousins — there is nothing —" She stopped, as if belatedly realizing that there was not much difference in Althea's mode of life in Baltimore from that here with her. There was always the barrier of her crippled leg between her and other children her age. She said then, with a hesitant note of apology, "You see, it's your grandmother. She is very upset by your grandfather's death and she feels she needs a while for her nerves to calm down after this long strain. Oh, Althea, dear, I don't mean really that she doesn't want you with her! It's just that she doesn't feel that she can look after you the way she should. But if you really want to go back to Baltimore you could go to the Girls' Grammar School as a boarder and just be home for weekends —"

Althea interrupted, eager to bring an end to these hesitating suggestions. "Oh, no, I'd much rather stay here with you. I like Miss Armstrong's school. If I went away, I'd miss you and Martha. I'd like to spend the summer here and go back to Miss Armstrong's in the fall."

She could see the relief on Marjorie's face, relief mingled with some lingering misgivings, as if Marjorie felt this was too easy a solution to a difficult problem, too easy and therefore somehow not altogether honorable. Several times in the next few days Marjorie raised the subject again, as if worrying at a nagging doubt, but Althea realized that for the time being at least all the responsible members of her family welcomed the idea of her staying on with Marjorie, of having her thus off their hands.

It was a placid year that followed, quite unlike the foregoing winter. By the end of the second school year everybody had seemed to have forgotten that there was any other way in which the problem of what to do with Althea was to be solved. It was entirely natural that she should live with Marjorie. In the spring there must have been some consultation among her relatives that Althea knew nothing about, for presently Marjorie announced that she was to be formally appointed Althea's personal guardian in place of her grandmother. Althea had been told that her father had died somewhere abroad in somewhat mysterious circumstances or at least circumstances that were not completely explained to her. His contact with her family had been sporadic for a long time. When she was older she came to realize that his years of alcoholism had finally caught up with him while he lived among disreputable companions in some distant place.

Marjorie was saying to her now, "Of course, Althea, since you are more than fifteen now, you don't have to accept me as your guardian. You can tell the judge that you want someone else."

Marjorie was looking at her with an anxious frown when she said this, but Althea said quickly, "Oh, no, no. I'd much rather have you."

"Well, then," said Marjorie, "that is settled. Of course, the property you have inherited from your grandfather is administered by trustees. I have very little to do with them. When you get older you can learn more about it."

The years slipped by and Marjorie's house was her home, the base from which she went to visit her grandmother, her aunts, and to which she returned, the place she thought of as being where she belonged, with Marjorie, with Martha. A good part of the time the three of them lived their separate lives. She was aware that there was a great deal of Marjorie's life, of Martha's life, that she knew nothing of — though sometimes she caught glimpses. And on the other hand they neither of them intruded into her private life, her thoughts, what she did that was out of their ken. Sometimes Marjorie, evidently prompted by a feeling that she was shirking her responsibility, would ask her questions — how did she like her new teachers, were the other girls friendly, did she want to invite some of them to visit, was there anything she would like to do outside of school? Althea answered these interrogations with carefully elaborate, essentially uninformative replies. She knew that one of the lasting effects of Elsie had been a change in her own attitude to the people around her. Her innermost thoughts and feelings were to be sheltered behind a strict reserve. She found that if she was agreeable and apparently interested in what someone else had to say about herself, she seldom noticed that Althea had little to say about herself. Marjorie might sometimes be uncertain about her answers, her doubt showing in her face, but she did not press the matter. Martha would occasionally give her a speculative, sidelong glance but she said nothing.

She was still a schoolgirl when she became aware of Marjorie's women friends. They came, singly, to spend a few days with her, a few weeks, sometimes a month or so. Usually they were women Marjorie had known in college — women with the same background as herself, Easterners, from well-to-do families, unmarried or at least if once married not now attached. Sometimes they were women Marjorie had met abroad, in that all-important period of her life when she had been in the Near East, in Russia, in her early work with the Red Cross. Sometimes they were women she encountered in the many trips she made around the United States for the Red Cross.

At first Althea, when she was introduced to them, saw them only as friends of Marjorie's, without any second thoughts about who or what they might be. But in one instance, when the woman who came to stay for several weeks was from abroad, — a vivacious, demonstrative woman who threw her arms around Marjorie frequently and talked in innuendoes, which she did not explain but emphasized by glancing at Althea — the thought of Mrs. Henshaw came unbidden but strongly into her mind. This conjunction of ideas set her musing on Mrs. Henshaw and Marjorie. Mrs. Henshaw went back a good deal further in Marjorie's life

than any of these other women. She wondered how it was
that Marjorie spent such a long time — from her thirteenth
to her seventeenth year — abroad in the Scottish school.
When she asked a question about this once Marjorie had
seemed half-surprised, and then a little vague in her reply,
saying that it had just happened, perhaps her father, Althea's
grandfather, whose business interests linked him with mer-
chants in Scotland, had been persuaded by his friends that
a good school in Edinburgh was just the place for a teenage
daughter. And her mother, Althea's grandmother, had liked
the idea because — "Well, you know, Althea," Marjorie
had explained, with one of her self-deprecating little laughs,
"I was a terrible hobbledehoy — not at all like you." There
was, Althea realized, when she thought about it, a great
gulf between the intensity of Marjorie's feeling for Mrs.
Henshaw and her attitude towards these other friends. The
difference came out in the way Marjorie acted towards these
other friends. She never used any formality in dealing with
them. Even with those whom she had known only a short
time she very quickly fell into a cosy comraderie, traded
all sorts of jokes Althea did not understand, giggled like
a schoolgirl, especially after she had had a cocktail or two
before dinner or several glasses of wine with it.

The first time Althea noticed this was in the Christmas
holiday of her third year at Miss Armstrong's school. The
guest this time was an old college mate of Marjorie's, a
woman who like Marjorie had never married. The visitor
was already in the house when she arrived back from a
visit to her grandmother. She had been nonplussed at the
strangeness of Marjorie's behavior, the way she laughed
loudly without cause, clasped her friend on the shoulder
to emphasize whatever story she was telling, seemed oblivious both of Althea's presence and Martha's disapproving
frown. Then late at night, when Althea had long since gone
to her room and was reading in bed, she heard hurried

whispers and suppressed giggles on the landing outside her door, as if either the guest was being invited by Marjorie into her room or Marjorie was joining the guest in hers. She was struck by the resemblance in their behavior to that of girls in the school when they sought to defy rules. But these were grown women and Marjorie was in her own house. Thereafter Althea became acutely aware of the archness of manner of the two women at unexpected moments and was embarrassed on their behalf. She had looked at Martha the next morning, wondering what effect this would have on her whose puritanical instincts were easily reflected in her face. Martha had a very strong sense of her own dignity and did not sympathize with those who lost theirs. But now Martha paid no heed to any of this and went about what she was doing, cleaning the house, cooking the dinner, serving it, with her usual bland indifference. It was with relief that Althea finally realized that she would not have to listen to a lecture from Martha about people who did not know how to behave, a lecture in which the meaning would be closely veiled in heavily emphasized obscurity.

Then she realized the truth — that Martha knew Marjorie a good deal better than she did, that Martha had learned all there was to be known about Marjorie over a good many years and that she had a deep affection for her that made allowance for her weaknesses, indeed excused them, as a sort of loyalty to Marjorie as sometimes the victim of her parents and sisters.

One evening in the kitchen, Althea, sitting on a stool by one of the shining white tile counters where Martha prepared the food for their dinner, made an exploratory comment about Marjorie's current guest. Martha gave her a brief glance over the carrots she was scraping and then said firmly, answering the intent of her remark rather than her words, "Miss Marjorie has her own friends. They aren't the same as your grandmother's. Some of them are right nice. But she's too generous. She gives too much away and sometimes she's sorry afterwards. But that's her way. You can't change that."

Althea listened avidly, waiting for something further, which did not come. This was the only time Martha had ever made a direct comment to her about anyone, much less Marjorie. Even Elsie, who had roused such indignation in Martha, had not prompted her to say to Althea what she felt. Watching her now she saw that Martha's face was closed as usual. She knew that Martha had been with Marjorie as long as Marjorie had lived in this house. For two weeks out of the year she went away, where to, Althea did not know. Marjorie said that she had a sister with a brood of children who were always in need of Martha's help. She had a brother — he was the man who had come to fetch Mrs. Henshaw's trunks to take to the station — an industrious soft-spoken man very like her in appearance who owned a horse and cart and was often hired by people like Marjorie to move furniture and who came several times a year to wash all the windows in Marjorie's house and carry away things she discarded.

Marjorie also, Althea learned, knew a great deal about Martha, because occasionally she let drop some detail of Martha's history.

For one thing, she learned that it was some years before the Great War that Marjorie had moved to Washington from Baltimore and bought her house. It was plain from the way she spoke that she had done so because she was deeply and publicly involved in the women's suffrage movement — Althea remembered that among the souvenirs in the little room over the stairs there was a picture of her marching as a suffragette — and that conflict with her mother over the subject had become too great. Martha had come to her at that time. In fact, it was Martha who stayed in the house and guarded it while Marjorie was abroad at the end of the War.

Marjorie said, "She's never left me in all that time except once, when she was mesmerized by a spellbinding black preacher who gathered around himself a big congregation. He was very good at exhorting people to repent their sins and give up all their worldly goods. A lot of his converts became ecstatic, hysterical. I never did understand why Martha got involved. I'm sure she never committed any big sins and heavens knows she hasn't much in the way of worldly goods. But she went off after him, with a whole crowd of others."

Marjorie had, after Martha was gone for several months, given her up, but one day she had appeared in the kitchen, looking thin and hollow-eyed, so worn and shabby that Marjorie had exclaimed when she saw her.

"She didn't say anything to me," Marjorie recalled, forgetting Althea saw, that she was talking to her and only remembering the event. "I was so sorry to see her like that. She is a proud woman. She didn't say anything to me — she was fixing dinner. I hadn't hired anybody else as a regular servant while she was gone. I was always hoping that she'd be back. I just couldn't talk to her — it was something about the way she looked at me, rather fierce, as if daring me. But next day she was the old Martha and we've never talked about it since."

Her mother, said Marjorie, had not approved of her taking Martha back. "But I was very happy to. I think it must have been that she had reached a point where she needed to explode some suppressed emotions. There are moments like that in anybody's life."

Althea, eyeing Martha covertly after hearing this, pondered what lay behind that intense reserve, except the kindness and warmth of heart she had learned was there from the first day she had come to Marjorie's house. Althea did not continue through these years at Miss Armstrong's school to be the steady, brilliant student she had begun as. She was glad that Marjorie's attention was often distracted from her by the visitors, because she sometimes felt guilty and yet at the same time she knew she was not going to make the necessary effort to improve. She knew it was perverse of her not to keep her mind fixed on the subjects she had to study. She learned easily and well anything she set herself to study. Yet there were days and even weeks when some demon of disorder took possession of her and she stubbornly turned away, to daydream, to idle away hours in inconsequent thoughts. She knew that she baffled her teachers, who could not understand why she so willfully refused to make good use of her time, who met in her a wall of indifference and sometimes flamboyant cynicism. They appealed to Marjorie for enlightenment. Althea knew this because Marjorie made stumbling efforts to inquire why she was not doing better in school, why she seemed to have lost her zest for mental exercise.

"I can't understand it, Althea dear," she said, gazing at her in puzzled dismay. "I never was a great one for books. When I was your age it was Janet — Mrs. Henshaw — who had to help me get through my school tests. She always explained everything to me and told me what was in the books we were assigned to read. I never have been a great reader. But you're so different. You're so clever. You seem to enjoy studying, books and things like that."

"Because after all, what else is there for me to do," said Althea, savagely completing her thought, goaded by some irresistible impulse to hurt Marjorie. She was ashamed when she saw the stricken look on Marjorie's face.

At the worst moments of this period of rebellion her teachers' protests — perhaps through Miss Armstrong herself — reached her grandmother, and Marjorie, alarmed and defensive, had begged and pleaded with her for an explanation, for a return to the happy studiousness of her first year. But she knew she could face down Marjorie and callously did so, recognizing in Marjorie a basic grieving pity for her lameness, the dreadful and insurmountable barrier that stood between her and the history of tomboyish, joyful adolescence Marjorie looked back upon as a golden age. And Marjorie stood between her and the censure of the teachers, Grandmother and her other aunts, not so much as complaining to her of her intransigence and the tax it placed upon Marjorie herself, so consistently at a disadvantage with her own family.

So her progress through Miss Armstrong's school was ragged, delayed by having to take over again subjects she neglected, by stretches when she refused to go to school but sat at home reading. After a while the spirit of revolt in her seemed to abate. In her inner consciousness she accepted as inexorable the fact that her crippling would dominate the whole of her life, would set the measure of the accomplishments she might aspire to, would always be the string that held her back from a free and untrammeled choice of activity.

The one lasting result of this arduous change in her inner life was the abrupt change in course that her intellectual and aesthetic interests took. She looked back now on herself in her first year at Miss Armstrong's school with a sort of wonder combined with compassion — an eager little girl, immersed in the English classics, feeding her own inner hunger with the poetry of the Romantics, dreaming of unformed yet luxurious longings with literary idealism. It was a perfectly acceptable thing to everyone, her teachers, her family, since after all she was never destined to be able to fulfill any of the normal social and sexual needs of her kind of young lady. But — and here her mind tried to switch away from the thought — Elsie had changed all that. After

Elsie, she could never convince herself, even in half-dreaming, that there was in the end a happiness in life, a fulfillment that would be open to her. She had even at that stage thought about suicide — after all, what was it all about — this striving, merely to win approval from those around her? But there was a natural toughness in her that not so much rejected the idea as simply turned away from it.

So she arrived at the time to go to college — later than had been expected of her — everyone had supposed that she would have breezed through preparatory school at double speed, to leave well ahead of her contemporaries in age. When she was criticized for this, Marjorie defended her. Why should she be expected to outdo all the other girls? Of course, the answer was implicit: because her physical life was so blighted that she would naturally excel in mental pursuits. Althea absorbed these conversations between Marjorie and her teachers — her grandmother and her other aunts treated the matter with indifference, since braininess was not a family concern. Their concern was rather with what to do with her when she could no longer continue in school. Althea seethed at all this, which she had gathered from conversations spoken out of her hearing but which reached her in reflected comments. What business did any of them have thus weighing up the elements of her life? At moments when they were together but silent, as at dinner when no one else was present — none of Marjorie's intimate strangers being present — Althea was aware of Marjorie's eye upon her, sympathetic, pitying, worried.

What she did not realize at first but gradually came to understand was that Marjorie had another, more formidable battle to do on her behalf. She herself, in spite of the carelessness of her scholastic work at Miss Armstrong's, nevertheless had always assumed that she would eventually go to college, so she was surprised when one day Marjorie asked her if she wanted to go on with her education. She did not tell her that her grandmother was raising objections to her going to college. It was risky — and unnecessary for her to go away from home. She did not need to get training to earn her living. She would always be provided for. It was a needless risk for her to go where she must live among strangers, rely upon strangers to look after her because of her lameness and frail health. Althea learned of this conflict between her grandmother and Marjorie from fragmentary remarks that Martha made. When the basis of the argument became clear to Althea she flared up at Martha — "What do you mean, my grandmother says I can't go to college?"

Martha looked into her angry eyes and turned away to beat a bowl of eggs. "Your grandma — she don't understand how you feel. Miss Marjorie knows you need a little air. She knows you could have an accident, fall down and hurt yourself bad, and sometimes you need some help, don't you? But she thinks you ought to have a chance at doing for yourself."

So she was already angry and belligerent when Marjorie suddenly asked if she would like to go to Goucher. It was right there in the middle of Baltimore and she could live with her grandmother. Marjorie was astonished at the violence of her refusal. No, she would not go to Goucher. She wanted to go somewhere else, anywhere else.

"But, Althea dear," Marjorie pleaded, "why not? It would be so much easier and it is a good college. I went there, you know, and you'd have certain advantages as being my niece."

Yes, thought Althea hotly, and look how long it took you to get away from home. She knew Marjorie was studying her face intently but she kept her lips stubbornly closed. Then Marjorie sighed and said no more at that time. The next day, having evidently thought further about it — and talked to Martha? Althea wondered — she remarked, "If you don't want to live in Baltimore, where would you like to go? She did not mention Goucher again. She was aware now that her refusal was making it more difficult for Marjorie but she could not give way. It seemed to her she had always known that to her grandmother she was not a complete person — as if the shrunken state of her leg necessarily affected her whole being, physical, mental and spiritual — but chiefly social. That was it. Her lameness, her puny body made it impossible for her to fit into the scheme of life her grandmother accepted as proper for a girl like herself. It was in fact a life-sentence to immaturity, helplessness, dependency.

But Marjorie prevailed and she went to another college, not too far away to be back at Marjorie's house for frequent visits. As unobtrusively as possible Marjorie provided for her to be looked after and in the shock of reality when she first found herself among strangers unused to her disability she was grateful for this thoughtfulness, though she never mentioned it.

But though she could come home frequently she deliberately stayed away until the Christmas holidays. It was then that she saw with a greater clarity the question of Marjorie's visitors. She came back with greater sophistication. She had begun to learn to deal with the physical demands of daily life, about stairs, about managing her clothes. She had also begun to learn about the unconscious callousness of many able-bodied people. The other girls never made any attempt to include her in the clandestine parties they organized out of sight of the college authorities. They assumed that she would have no interest in boys — or more realistically, that boys would have no interest in her. Or, in the case of some of them, an interest in other girls — she had learned to recognize among them the sort of erotic attraction that Marjorie and her friends displayed. The brutality of this attitude towards herself infuriated her but she realized that in her innermost being she was glad to be so excluded, because in fact she wanted to deal neither with boys nor girls on a physical basis. They all seemed to her childish. She turned from the thought of physical intimacy of any sort — the dark spot in her memory, of Elsie thrusting her away in repugnance loomed always in the back of her mind.

Now she saw Marjorie much more as a contemporary of her own. Of course, Marjorie was closer to her than her other aunts. Marjorie was middle-aged — her own mother had been the youngest of her grandmother's daughters and there was a spread of some years in age between her and Marjorie, but there was a subtle difference between Marjorie and the other middle-aged women she knew. Perhaps it was because she was independent, free of the limitations imposed by husbands and children. Marjorie's intimate life was bound up with her women friends. Althea was still ambivalent about these intruders into Marjorie's household, but she did not resent them as she had when she was younger. She had come to realize that Marjorie was in fact seeking something she never found. And some of these women were amiable, some of them intelligent and very well educated. She even came to like some of them, those who were entertaining company at the dinner table and those who had some interesting special knowledge to talk about.

It was one of these, a professor in a western university, who during her first year in college changed the course of her intellectual life. She had drifted into college with the same sense of aimlessness that had hampered her last year or so at Miss Armstrong's school. The poetry and literary appreciation that had so governed her romantic yearnings when she was fourteen had lost their power to enthrall her after Elsie, but in her stubborn inertia she had done nothing to put something else in their place. But now, listening to this woman she suddenly saw the appeal in studying about the economic structure of society, the hard, unsentimental facts of economic history. This was something real, with the bite of reality, of the rawness of the basic facts of human existence.

As usual it was Martha who first received evidence of this new enthusiasm. Through the years Martha had listened patiently when Althea sat in the kitchen and talked about the importance of literature as an art and recited poetry. Martha had served as her sounding board when she rehearsed Shelley and Keats and Edna Millay, whose poetry had seemed to her at the time the true voice of herself, as the absorber of the emotions that swelled within her so violently they threatened to burst her body. She did not stop to consider what Martha's view of all this was. And Martha never seemed to fail in the role of appreciative audience and comforting presence.

So she was brought up short by the change in Martha's manner when the scope of her own interest shifted, when she laid aside romanticism in literature as a sentimental sham and turned to what she took to be the stern realism of economic theory as forming the essence of human society. At first, when she began to talk about economic theory, about the dialectic of social progress based on economic realities, Martha had shown surprise and then suspicion. She began to argue back, indignant and sometimes angry at the new gospel that Althea preached. When Althea outlined the theories of Adam Smith, described his idea that every man naturally wished to better his own lot in life and that in doing so he contributed to the good of society, Martha, trying to follow the argument, nodded in uncertain agreement. It sounded very like the outlook of the world in which she had always lived. But when Althea started on Karl Marx and his prediction that through revolution the world would eventually become a classless society in which working people would finally get their just deserts, Martha was outraged.

"Miss Althea, does Miss Marjorie know they teach you all that stuff in school? I don't think she'd like it.''

Althea, smiling at the idea of Marjorie paying any attention to such things and moved by a spirit of mischief, said, "But, Martha, what's wrong about people getting their fair share of the world's goods? Most people like you, work for their living. Why shouldn't you get a share of the profits?"

"What are you talking about? I don't have no complaint about Miss Marjorie. She pays me good wages. If you ask me, Miss Althea, you're mixing with a lot of people who are out looking for trouble. And I'll tell you one thing, don't you let your grandmother know you're studying all that stuff. She sure wouldn't let you stay in college." Martha went off about her work muttering under her breath. Althea, thoughtful, gently closed the book she had been reading.

But it was a warning. It had not occurred to her that her grandmother had the slightest interest in what she studied at college. It was just the general idea of higher education for women that she mistrusted. She had objected, unsuccessfully, to Marjorie's going to college. Much of what Marjorie had done thereafter she attributed to the poison of a college education.

From Martha she learned that what-to-do-about-Althea was a continuing burden in the minds of her grandmother and her other aunts. Since no one expected her to marry, what and how was she to be settled for the rest of her life? Althea recognized the fear that lay behind this — someone must always be on hand to provide her with a home and suitable care, and no one wanted to be faced with this responsibility. She watched Marjorie to see whether she showed any concern about this. Marjorie herself, it would seem, gave no particular attention to the future when Althea would be of age and able to control her own money. But now and again she saw an annoyed, half-angry, half-baffled expression on Marjorie's face that evidently meant that the rising chorus of family debate was beginning to wear on her nerves.

One evening, when she was sitting in the kitchen, Martha said, "Your grandma do keep on at Miss Marjorie about what to do with you."

"Is that what's the matter with her? Ever since I got home she's been grouchy and nervy."

Martha nodded. "They're all wondering what to do with you when you get out of college."

Althea, angry, demanded, "Why do they have to think about that? Aunt Marjorie isn't going to turn me out of the house just because I've finished college." She paused and looked at Martha inquiringly. "Is she?"

Martha patted her arm. "Miss Marjorie always has been right glad to have you here with her. It's her sisters. They've got guilty feelings. They've let Miss Marjorie look after you ever since you came here as a little girl when your grandfather died. So they have to make a big noise to cover up their feelings."

Althea looked silently at the floor for a moment and then raised her eyes to look at Martha. "You've never minded having to look after me, have you, Martha?"

A rare smile appeared on Martha's face and there was a twinkle in her eye. "What would you do about it if I did?" She turned back to what she was doing as if to dismiss such foolishness.

This conversation gave Althea considerable food for thought. First she seethed with indignation at the picture her relatives seemed to have of her — a burden, someone without mind or feelings, since having a withered leg seemed to exclude a person from the normality of the human race — but gradually her spirits grew calmer and her mind cleared. It was up to her to find a solution to her own problem — what to do with her life — and at least she could count on the moral support of Marjorie. In college, as in Miss Armstrong's school, she was always a little distant from the people around her. It was assumed she was not interested in boys and in fact she wasn't. Her mingling with other people was purely on an intellectual basis. On any other basis she felt detached and outside the world she lived in. She could get passionate debating social values. She was respected for the energy and articulateness of her opinions on all sorts of things. People liked to argue with her, enjoyed the warmth she showed only in these sessions of intelligent talk. She enjoyed what she was studying now. She was tantalized by newspaper items about anarchists and other such groups. Was what they were seeking really only utopic and impossible to achieve? She had read a lot about the several religious and social communities attempted in the 19th century in America — the Shakers, Fourierists at Brook Farm, the Amana villages in Iowa. Could human beings be supposed capable of putting into practice a system of society that would negate violence, the exploitation of the weak by the strong, the aggrandizement of the few at the expense of the many? And if such an effort could be made, how could it be achieved by bomb-throwing and the killing of selected personages? She found that she could weigh all this dispassionately. The pursuit of the answers intrigued her.

The summer passed and October, 1929 came and the stock market crashed. To Althea it was an exciting and fascinating event, a landmark in economic history. Its causes, its immediate effects, the repercussions it had on society — she read avidly and with concentration on everything about it that she could find, debated endlessly with those within her world who realized its implications. She did not relate it to herself until as Christmas came she went home to spend the holidays with Marjorie. Then she discovered that Marjorie had spent anxious weeks assessing

the damage to her own investments and income. The afternoon of Christmas Eve they spent in the parlor, gazing out
on a scattering of snow whitening the small front garden.
Marjorie is getting quite grey, thought Althea, turning to
look at her and noticing the fading of the once brilliant
red hair.

Marjorie said, with anxious care, "There really isn't
anything for you to worry about, Althea. I've talked to
your trustees and the lawyers and they say that all the
companies your capital is invested in are quite sound.
Your investments are all quite conservative. You're not
likely to suffer any great loss — none of us will. Of course,
the way things are going, we'll all have to expect a drop
in income. There'll be less money coming in. It's the
people who are losing their jobs that are in a bad way."

Marjorie gazed at her with kind anxiety. Althea was
nonplussed. It had not occurred to her to relate these recent
public disasters — the bankruptcies, the paying off of large
numbers of people in factories — to a possible threat to
her own source of income. In fact, she never thought of
the money that came to her so automatically. Until she
was twenty-one, Marjorie had paid her bills, had supplied
her with pocket money. She knew that the money came
from a trust fund her grandfather created. Now that she was
of age, her trustees paid her expenses and sent her a monthly
check. The main sense she had of this was that she was independent, that she could choose to do what she chose, to
live where she wanted, though it would never have occurred
to her to make a change of any sort. Otherwise she was
vaguely aware that she was well enough off but not rich.
All through college there had been girls who cultivated
her because she came from a well-to-do family. She had
come to recognize the kind of attentiveness that some young
men paid her, uninvited. But she had not seen herself as
a potential victim of an economic collapse. There were

girls with her in college who, as the months went by, suddenly became silent and anxious, girls who announced that they would not be coming back next semester, some girls who admitted unhappily that their families were in financial trouble. She was also aware that there were more idle people on the streets, seedy looking people with an increasing hopelessness in their faces. She read the unemployment statistics in the papers, felt the breath of economic disaster — but at secondhand. It had not occurred to her to think of herself in such danger.

Marjorie had gone on talking. "I really don't know how things will go. I hope you will leave things in the hands of your trustees for the time being. As you know, you will soon have full control of your money. But until you are older, especially the way things are in business, I think it would be better to rely on the judgment of —"

Althea interrupted her. "I'm not going to do anything silly. Until I've made up my mind about a lot of things I'm going to leave everything as it is. Let's not talk about it any more. And please don't worry about me."

Marjorie gazed at her doubtfully. But all she said was, "Well, of course, Althea, you must do what you think you would like to do."

Her grandmother died during her senior year at college. Althea, home for the funeral, noticed at once that Marjorie was not affected by it in the same way as by her grandfather's death. When her grandfather died, Marjorie was stirred up into a burst of frenetic energy, talkative, in constant motion, ready to take on any task whether invited to or not, eager with advice and criticism. This time she was completely subdued, as if her normal ebullience was deflated. Her emotional turmoil now was displayed not in energetic response to stimulus but in an uneasy acceptance of defeat, as if her mother's death aroused feelings of guilt, of self-reproach for unspecified sins of omission, for which she could no longer atone. Uncharacteristically she answered Althea's remarks about the details of her grandmother's funeral, about her grandmother's last wishes, with hesitating vagueness. She seemed timid in dealing with her sisters and brothers-in-law, unwilling to challenge anything they said, any decisions they made. It was obvious that when she was alone she cried a good deal, for her eyes and face showed signs of this. Althea observed that Martha looked at her often with perplexed concern.

In the kitchen, watching Martha prepare dinner, Althea said, "She's terribly upset. She wasn't like this when my grandfather died. But she never did get along with my grandmother, did she? She was always complaining about how grandmother did not approve of this or that."

Martha gave her a long look, as if what she said sparked a new thought. "I guess maybe that's why. She thinks she wasn't a good daughter."

"Oh, Martha, how could she think that?"

Martha mulled over the problem. "Your grandma didn't like the way Miss Marjorie lived. She thought it wasn't ladylike. She should've got married and had a husband and done all the things married ladies do. Your grandma didn't approve of Miss Marjorie living like a bachelor girl and going off to foreign countries by herself like that."

"But Aunt Marjorie is a heroine, Martha! She did a lot to help people who were starving and in danger of their lives." Althea's eyes shone at the remembrance of Marjorie's tales of adventure in the Balkans — the arduous travel in Red Cross vehicles on bombed-out roads surrounded by refugees fleeing before encroaching armies, desperate flights in army planes to succor the wounded and dying — Marjorie had said that after the war, when she was one of the first to fly from Paris to London she felt no novelty, only the gaiety of a holiday spree.

Martha's response was laconic. "I guess that's so. But

your grandma just didn't think she should be there doing all that."

When the funeral was over and they came back to the house Marjorie seemed to revive somewhat. She roused herself to pay attention to Althea. The first question she asked was, What did Althea want to do when she graduated at the end of the college year?

"I haven't thought it out," Althea answered cautiously. "I'll probably go to graduate school."

"But where, Althea dear?"

"Oh, I don't know. I said I haven't thought it out."

The spring of 1931 came and Althea came home to stay, with no plans fixed in her mind about her own future. She became aware, before many hours had passed, that Marjorie was uneasy, as if anxious to speak of something and yet unwilling to broach the subject. She seemed absentminded while they ate dinner. Afterwards, when they sat together, she asked some desultory questions about what Althea had been doing during the day, obviously not attending to her answers. After a few minutes' silence, she asked, hesitating, "What do you want to do this summer, dear? Have you made any plans?"

Wary, Althea hedged. "Oh, I don't know. Why? Is there something you want for us to do?"

"Oh, no! I just wondered if you expected to be here in Washington or had thought of going to summer school elsewhere, perhaps."

She faltered and Althea saw her blush lightly. It was the first time it had ever occurred to her that Marjorie might not want her there. Ever since she had come, as an uneasy schoolgirl, Marjorie had always seemed to have unquestioningly accepted her as a permanent adjunct to her own life. So now Marjorie's confusion, Marjorie's embarrassment, surprised and dismayed her. She said stiffly, "Well, I certainly don't have to be here, if it's inconvenient —"

"Oh, Althea dear, I don't mean that at all! This is your home, of course, and you must never leave it unless you want to go somewhere else, and then you must come back here whenever you want to. No, no, dear, I do not mean anything like that. But you've sometimes spoken of going on to graduate school and I thought perhaps you had plans —"

Althea's first resentment melted at the eager contrition in Marjorie's voice. But her curiosity was now aroused. What was prompting Marjorie? Marjorie, so transparent — so uncalculating —. She said cautiously, "I've been thinking of going to summer school somewhere." Seeing the anxious frown on Marjorie's face, she asked, probing in a carefully casual voice, "What are you going to do this summer?"

Marjorie's explanation rushed forth, eager and somewhat confused. "Well, you know, I have only a month's vacation — if we don't have any national calamities — though I must say the economic condition of the country is such that we're getting all sorts of requests for help in feeding people — desperate people. So I hadn't planned to go away. I said I would consider myself on call. Miss Goodacre hasn't had a real holiday for years. She is so self-sacrificing. If I stay here, I can be on call to fill her place in case of emergency." She hesitated but the strength of her pent-up yearning impelled her forward. "I've invited a friend to spend the summer here with me. That is, I have suggested it and she seems eager to come. She is someone I've met in Chicago when I was out there last October. She has never been East before and I thought she would enjoy it. But then it occurred to me that you would not find it very cheerful being here with two middle-aged women, so I decided to tell you about it ahead of time in case you wanted to make other plans —"

Marjorie's apologetics flowed on. But why, Althea wondered, doesn't she want me here? She never bothered about me when she's had these friends here before. Is it because I'm not a child any more and she doesn't want to have me here criticizing her? Does she think I haven't understood the hidden meaning behind these friendships before this? Althea took a sudden decision and found herself voicing as certain a vague idea that had been hanging in the back of her mind for several months. She had wondered about going farther away from home for her graduate work, spurred by a strong inner feeling that she wanted to go beyond the shelter of even Marjorie's soft restraint. Every time the idea had come to the surface in her mind she toyed with it, imagining going further away on the East Coast, to the West and even — here her blood quickened each time she had thought of a real plunge into the unknown abroad. Yet each time she had thought about this she had drawn back and tucked it carefully away. She could not hurt Marjorie, she could not show ingratitude, and yet she asked herself whether this was to disguise from herself a deep fear, a basic mistrust of her own capacity to look after herself. But she had to test herself.

She blurted out, "Well, to tell you the truth, I have some plans I wanted to talk to you about." She plunged into explanations, abandoning the careful preliminaries she had sometimes composed, yet astonished at the confidence with which she spoke about these half-formed ideas as if they were already viable plans. "I want to go abroad. I want to study abroad. I feel cooped up in what I'm doing. I think it would be a good idea if I went abroad and learned to deal with different kinds of people, to expose myself to other ideas. I'd like to go abroad for a year or so."

Marjorie gazed at her speechless, then said, "But, Althea dear, that is rather a tall order. You've never been anywhere except right here close to home. I thought some time or other you and I might travel a bit. But the time never seemed to be right for that. I don't know how you would manage by yourself, without someone to help you when you needed help. Of course, perhaps we could find someone who could go with you —"

Althea interrupted with sudden anger, "I don't need to be looked after! I manage very well on my own — a lot better than you realize. I'm not a child any more. Oh, I know, whenever I've gone anywhere you've always made arrangements so I'll be protected. I don't want that any more. You're always kind, Aunt Marjorie, and I don't want to be churlish, but I don't need all this cosseting. I really don't. If I didn't have any money and had to earn a living, I'd have to look out for myself and I could do it."

"Oh, yes, yes, darling." Marjorie's voice had the soothing tone she always used when she realized that she had stepped on Althea's toes. "Yes, I'm sure you could always manage. But there isn't any reason, really, to be heroic, is there? If things can be made easier, there's no reason not to."

"Well, I want to go abroad and I want to go alone. I want to go to London. I've written and they say I can take courses at the University of London. And I want to try the new London School of Economics — you know, the school Beatrice Webb and her husband have founded. I'm sure there are all sorts of new ideas I can pick up there. I've talked to people — professors at college and they all know people abroad, especially in London."

Marjorie looked at her with half a smile. "You have been busy, haven't you, dear, and you've kept all this to yourself." There was a rueful note in her voice.

Smitten with remorse, Althea said quickly, "Oh, I've just been projecking around." Purpose she used the phrase her grandfather used to excuse some scheme he had had in mind without his family's knowledge. She thought to mollify Marjorie with it.

Marjorie nodded, thoughtful. "Well, I'm glad you've

picked London. I shall write to Janet. I am not sure where she is just now but I'll get in touch with her."

Althea gave her a sharp look. "You mean Mrs. Henshaw? But I don't want her running my affairs."

Marjorie's tone was aunt-like. "Now, Althea, she won't do anything of the sort. But you've got to have somewhere to live. You can't stay in a hotel all the time. That's not a nice way to live. Dear, you must let me help you arrange things and Janet is just the person. I shall be very much worried if I wasn't sure that you would be all right."

Althea, stubbornly frowning, shrugged. She could not stop Marjorie from writing to Mrs. Henshaw. She supposed this was a natural thing for Marjorie to do and, glancing at the worried look on her face, decided not to protest further.

Marjorie went on speaking, half to herself. "Janet will know just what to do, the best sort of arrangements for you. I'm sure she knows people at the University, too. It can make all the difference, Althea, to your enjoyment of your stay if you have the right sort of place to stay and know a few congenial people." She lapsed into silence for a while. Then presently she said, "When were you thinking of going? Of course the term at the University does not begin till the autumn."

Althea was aware that some other thought had arisen in Marjorie's mind, probably about the friend she proposed to invite for the summer. She said as casually as possible, "Oh, I thought I'd go soon, to spend the summer in England before I have to settle down to study. I can get passage on a United States Line freighter — I've been reading about them. They take just a hundred passengers and they go straight to London, right up the Thames. I think that would be fun."

"Oh, dear! That's very short notice. And I wonder if you wouldn't be more comfortable in one of the Cunard ships."

"They're a lot more expensive. I'd enjoy the other more. And why not go now? I don't feel like settling down to anything else."

"Well, then, we must start getting you ready at once. I'll go and write to Janet at the last address she sent me."

Althea wandered out into the kitchen to tell Martha. So all this vague, romantic dreaming that had preoccupied her for the last year had suddenly been brought down to reality. She felt a twinge of dismay and then a tremendous exhilaration, as if the whole tone of life had changed from a prosaic monotony to a promised pageant of electrifying events. She sat down on the stool by the counter and said, "I'm going to England, Martha. I'm going to spend a year studying at the University of London."

Martha's hands paused and she glanced up, giving Althea a look from her dark, sharp eyes. "That's a long way from home. What do you want to do that for?"

"Oh, it's not all that far away." Althea was airy, thrilled by her own intrepidity. "I think it's about time I got out on my own. Don't you think so?"

Martha cast her another, more dubious glance. "You'd better be mighty careful."

There was something deflating in Martha's tone, but Althea noticed that she said nothing really discouraging or indicating a lack of confidence in Althea herself. After a moment she added, "Probably is a good thing for you to try things out."

They were both silent for a moment and then Althea said, "Anyway, Aunt Marjorie will be glad I won't be underfoot. She says she is going to have a visitor here this summer."

"She told you?" There was another quick glance of Martha's eyes.

"Yes. Do you know who she is, Martha?"

Martha did not answer. Althea persisted. "But you know her?"

"No'm."

So. Martha does not like this. There was some difference here from the visitors Marjorie had had before. "She's coming in July. I'll be gone by then."

"Me too." After a pause Martha added, "Don't know why she invited her while I'm gone."

Of course, Althea remembered, Martha was always gone in July. It was an immutable fact of life that Martha took her holiday in July. She wondered about Martha's grumpiness. Was Martha jealous, jealous of the idea that someone would be here installed in the house in her absence, using her kitchen, absorbing Marjorie's attention?

"Perhaps it's just by chance. Maybe Aunt Marjorie forgot about you not being here in July."

Martha gave a snort of scorn. "No, ma'am. She wouldn't forget I always takes July."

"Well, then, why is she doing this?"

Martha did not answer. She shrugged and then said, with a trace of indignation, "She say that she didn't want to give me no extra trouble." Obviously Martha did not accept this explanation. "If you ask me, this is somebody she thinks a whole lot of — somebody she thinks is different from the other friends she invites here. And I don't even know her."

"She says she met her in October when she was in Chicago."

"Don't take long sometimes for Miss Marjorie to get taken like that by somebody." Martha's tone was as cryptic as her words.

"You'll find out all about her when you get back — if she is still here."

"I reckon she will be. I reckon she's going to live here."

"You mean permanently?" Althea was astonished. The chief characteristic of Marjorie's enthusiasms was that they were brief — at least, the first intenstiy of emotion was brief, though often her friendships endured for years in a comradely way beyond that. Marjorie was never quarrelsome.

Martha shook her head uncertainly. "Whoever she is, she's sure impressed Miss Marjorie."

"And you won't get to see her and find out what she is like till she's been here for a while."

Martha seemed to flinch. It was exactly the central spot of her uneasiness. Defensively she said, "I don't expect her to be any great wonder. What impresses Miss Marjorie don't necessarily impress me."

The puzzle faded somewhat in Althea's mind as the days went by, filled with details of getting ready for her trip and with the inner excitement that welled in her at the thought of this new and unprecedented step into independence. Occasionally, talking to Marjorie and noticing the vagueness in Marjorie's eyes — which must come, she thought, from Marjorie's concentration on her own anticipations — her curiosity awoke. But Marjorie, though obviously suppressing a great deal of feeling, managed to quell her own impetuosity and answered her questions with mild evasions. She always turned the conversation back onto the details of Althea's preparations for going abroad.

Marjorie announced one afternoon, when she arrived home from her office and had time to look at the letters that had come in the mail, "Oh, Althea, I think we have the answer to where you should stay in London, at least at first. I've heard from Janet, from Mrs. Henshaw. My letter finally reached her. She does not expect to be in England when you get there but she has given me the name of a woman who keeps a boarding house in Bayswater. She caters to Americans especially, though English people who live abroad also stay with her when they're in England. She says you will be comfortable there and certainly quite safe. Shall we write to her? She is Miss Maple."

She waited, half-expecting, Althea could see, to receive a sulky No. But Althea agreed promptly. Of course Marjorie was right. She had to have a secure place to stay, somewhere where her special needs would be recognized and accommodated. And besides, she was riding the crest of the wave of exhilaration that had gradually been building in her. It was a brilliant afternoon. The sun shone with a blinding whiteness on the little garden outside the parlor window and the street beyond, where the overarching elms cast black cool shadows. The curtains at the open windows blew inward with the brisk breeze. The blue sky shone above, limitless, intense in color. She had been soaring there with a feeling of freedom about to be claimed, of the adventure about to be hers, unhampered by any consideration of the time and means and bodily impediments. Why should she throw the dampening cloud of her own moodiness over Marjorie's eager helpfulness?

Marjorie had gone on talking. "I think there is no question that we can rely on any recommendation of Janet's. I do wish she herself was going to be there. She could make things so much easier for you and I would feel that, since I cannot be there myself, she would be an utterly reliable deputy."

Althea wanted to shout at her, "I don't want her to be there! I don't want anybody to be there, anybody I've known before. I want to be free! I want to invite the moment — any moment, every moment! She shifted in her seat by the window and felt the weight of the brace on her leg. She sighed and answered Marjorie. "Yes. That would be nice. But I don't think I need anybody."

"Miss Maple is very central. It won't be difficult for

you to get about. You'll have to rely on cabs, of course, and that is a consideration when choosing a place to stay. I think Janet took that into account." That was as near as Marjorie would come to saying that Althea could not hop on and off the big red buses in Oxford Street and run down the stairs of the Underground. In her abstracted face Althea could see the shadow of some youthful passage in her own life that had left a lingering remnant of happiness in her memory. "You've heard from the people at the University? They agreed to what you want to do? You'll be in touch with them as soon as you get to London, won't you?" Marjorie's questions interrupted the daydreams to which she had returned, threatening to bring to earth the airy structure of her imaginings.

"Yes, of course. That part has all been taken care of. The Dean has written. She knows people there."

"You must make arrangements with the bank so that monthly checks can be transferred regularly. Barclay's is the bank I always dealt with in London."

"I've done that."

Marjorie smiled at her. "You're very efficient, my dear. You must keep in close touch with me, Althea. I shall worry very much if you don't."

"Oh, yes, of course, Aunt Marjorie."

Marjorie insisted on going to New York with her, seeing her through the hazards of train travel, waving her off from the dockside as the ship moved into the Hudson River. The vessel was dwarfed by the giants in the berths around it — the Leviathan, the Ile de France, the Mauretania. The ten days aboard passed for her in a welter of new experiences. Fortunately the passage was calm and she soon learned how to use her cane to steady herself when the gentle motion shifted her from side to side. She smiled to herself, thinking of Long John Silver and his pegleg. At journey's end she was up on deck in time to see the ship enter the Thames, move slowly past Gravesend — Pocahontas was buried there, she remembered — slipping by the outskirts of the half-seen great city on either side wrapped in the foggy greyness of early morning. Her first days in London were passed in a haze of wonderment — seeing the things she had only read about before, taking the dimensions of this ancient city. She was intoxicated from the first moment she was driven through it from the dockside to Miss Maple's. She was here alone, with an unprefigured future ahead of her. She drank in a deep draught of the wine of independence.

There was a letter from Marjorie awaiting her at Miss Maple's. She had learned the name of the newcomer in Marjorie's life a few days before she left Washington — Gwen. Gwen, it seemed, was not due at Marjorie's for another week. Marjorie said they both missed her — she and Martha — very much and she must remember her promise to write often. Althea, putting the letter down, wondered fleetingly if Gwen's arrival would cause a lessening in Marjorie's attention. But without Martha as the ready recipient of her enthusiasms she needed Marjorie. Only to Marjorie could she unburden herself of the tremendous joyfulness, of the half-fearful hopefulness with which she was bursting. Only Marjorie could understand even a fraction of the wonder that possessed her.

The second evening she sat in her room writing to Marjorie. She had written a long letter in installments on shipboard — the freighter had taken ten days to cross the Atlantic. She had posted it — or at least placed it on the hall table at Miss Maple's to be taken to the post office — when she first arrived. She began with an account of Miss Maple's establishment. It was a tall house just off the Bayswater Road close to Hyde Park, which once had housed the numerous family of an eminent Victorian scholar. Like a great many such dwellings it had been given up by the last of that family, left alone and impoverished as the consequence of the Great War. Miss Maple, a genteel spinster, the practical daughter of a scholarly clergyman now dead, had sunk her small inheritance into the property and had for ten years made a bare living from catering to overseas visitors, giving them the semblance of the comfort the house had once provided its owners. It had become sought after by staid Americans and by English people on furlough from the outposts of empire. At the moment, Althea wrote, there were only two other guests besides herself — an elderly American woman who had lively tales to tell of her many trips to continental Europe before the Great War and an Englishwoman of about the same age who had apparently recently retired as a missionary in the Far East. Althea had encountered them both for the first time at dinner on the day she arrived.

Tired and somewhat daunted by the strangeness of things, she had supposed the almost unbroken silence in which the meal proceeded was the usual custom. She had come to the table late, barely awake from the nap she had taken, and Miss Maple had murmured her name to the two women. Halfway through the soup the elderly American, a pretty woman with softly dressed white hair and alert dark eyes, had said, "You must be the young woman from Washington. I should like to welcome you. We're compatriots. I'm Judith Atwood, from Philadelphia."

Althea murmured, "How do you do? My name is Althea Richards." She noticed the Englishwoman, a short stout woman with iron-grey hair plainly dressed, had raised vigilant eyes to stare at her.

The silence recommenced. Occasionally Miss Atwood made a brief comment, but Althea could think of nothing to say to carry the conversation along. The other woman remained completely and conspicuously silent. When the meal was over, oppressed by the weight of disapproval in the air as well as her own tiredness, Althea went to her room.

"I'm writing to you now," she said to Marjorie in her letter, "just before dinner and I wonder if the same thing will happen again."

The morning after that first meal, coming slowly out of a heavy sleep, she lay for a moment orienting herself. Obviously at Mrs. Henshaw's behest, Miss Maple had provided her with a large room on the ground floor, with windows giving onto a silent, dead-end street, all stone and paving and iron railings guarding other tall, quiet houses. Getting out of her warm bed into the chill air — London mornings, she found, could be chill even in summer — she pulled on her dressing gown and dragged her way across to the nearest tall window to see again the scene that had struck such a cord of the sense of history the afternoon before. When she had looked out after her trunk had been placed in the room and Miss Maple had left, she had at once felt the silent but powerful impact of the deserted grey-stone landscape. As she watched now, a man in shirtsleeves and a servant's waistcoat had come up from the basement quarters of the house across the way and stood for a while leaning on the railing as if seeking a change of air. When he retreated once more down the steps the street was again without a human presence. It fascinated Althea — this scene that suggested a great world moving invisibly and unalterably behind this empty, still facade that gave no evidence of its existence except for the impervious, unchanging blocks of stone raised up sometime in the last century to house — what? — the world of an empire now badly shaken and perhaps beginning to crumble. Looking out at the window again this morning she felt the melancholy of the grey, quiet day, a misty dampness hanging in the air. But it was a melancholy full of past grandeur, of the ghosts of the magnificent past that still lived in the poetry and novels she had absorbed through her growing years. It was a suitable backdrop, she decided, for her coming explorations of London. The next few weeks she lived a self-absorbed life. Some of the people to whom she had introductions were in town and she dutifully got in touch with them. And then there was the ever-fascinating problem of learning to find her way around, to test the scope of her ability to move about the great city on her own. The time she spent at Miss Maple's was limited chiefly to breakfast and dinner and sleeping. Various other people transiently in London appeared and disappeared, none of them talkative but their presence broke up the impasse that seemed to exist between Miss Atwood and Miss Barrett — that, said Miss Maple, was the name of the unsociable Englishwoman. Miss Atwood often met her in the hallways — she had the impression, when she thought of it, that Miss Atwood sought to waylay her. A natural thing, she supposed, for an expatriate American to do.

She very often spent part of the day at the British Museum. She realized that this was one place she would frequently be. The splendors within made her forget the fatigue she often felt and the bad weather that invaded even the summer in London. Late one afternoon she came back to Miss Maple's. There was a small room that lay between her own and the diningroom. It was furnished with a settee and a few nondescript chairs and was referred to as the lounge, where tea was served at five o'clock and where the guests might linger awaiting their evening meal. When she limped into the room she saw that Miss Barrett was seated there reading a newspaper. Instantly the memory of the tension that had surrounded the two women — Miss Atwood and Miss Barrett — at her first few evenings came back to her. Perhaps, she thought, glancing covertly at Miss Barrett, it was only that the two women were incompatible and they were bored by their enforced companionship. But Miss Maple had seemed especially nervous — she was a nervous woman anyway — as if she was waiting for disaster to strike.

There was nothing about Miss Barrett to give hope for geniality. Her severely oldfashioned clothes fitted her stout body as if sewn into place. Her hair, now grey, was dressed with a smoothness that allowed no strand to escape. Her eyes behind the rimless glasses glittered with the intensity of her stare. She put down the paper as Althea came in and stared for a moment at the brace on her leg. Althea, always conscious of the thump it made no matter how she tried to minimize its awkwardness, sat down in the first chair she reached.

Miss Barrett said, in a voice of displeasure, "I'm afraid we're rather cramped here. This is rather a bad change from the past. Miss Maple has always had an excellent reputation among those stationed in the outposts of empire as providing a most comfortable house, where on modest means one could depend upon an unchanging standard of consideration. It is too bad to discover that even she is affected by the same sort of selfish interest that is contributing nowadays to the decay of quality everywhere."

Althea listened to her in bewilderment. Miss Barrett had never done more than acknowledge her presence in an abrupt manner. Now she ran on in the same vein. Gradually Althea understood that Miss Barrett was complaining of the fact that the big comfortable room that had previously served as the guests' lounge had now been converted to the more profitable use of a bedroom. It had been large enough to allow several groups to gather undisturbed by each other and there was even room for a piano.

Althea said timidly, "Perhaps Miss Maple can't afford to keep it that way."

Miss Barrett smiled unpleasantly. "Exactly, Miss Richards. She has become more concerned with money than the welfare of her guests."

"But perhaps she doesn't have any choice. It must be difficult to make enough money just now, with inflation and all that."

"So she maintains. And of course it is you Americans who have the money now." There was deep resentment in Miss Barrett's voice. "It is you who can afford the luxuries." She spoke as if there had been some malign conspiracy in heaven to bring about this state of affairs.

"Well, we have a depression in the States now, too, a very bad economic depression. There are a lot of people out of work and without money." Althea's anger began to rise, more at her tone than at her words.

"So we see. There are so many of you over here now." The sarcasm in her voice was heavy. When Althea did not answer, she went on, "Of course, I am not placing the blame on you. And I understand, of course, since you are lame and cannot climb stairs, that you require a room on the ground floor. But Miss Maple should not have accepted you as a guest. It is regrettable that everyone's comfort should be disregarded for the convenience of one person. It is to her financial advantage, of course."

Anger swelled in Althea. "I think you are very unfair, Miss Barrett. You should not be complaining to me."

Miss Barrett smiled smugly. "I think you should know how things stand." She picked up her newspaper and held it in front of her face.

Althea sat and seethed. She wanted to go at once to Miss Maple to demand an explanation but glancing at the clock on the mantel she saw that it was almost time for dinner to be announced. Presently Miss Atwood came into the room, glanced briefly at Miss Barrett's turned-away face and moved over to Althea, making a face and smiling.

"Ah," she said, "I see you are home early today. Did you have a good day?" She seemed not to notice the short answers that Althea gave her.

The next morning Althea awoke with one thought in mind, to protest to Miss Maple, and she went in search of her before she set out for the day's activities. She came upon her in the cubby by the front door which Miss Maple used for an office. Miss Maple was a spare, nervous woman in her fifties, with a soft voice never raised to express the anger and frustration she must often have felt towards servants and guests. She glanced up as the soft thudding of Althea's approach stopped at her open door.

"Oh, my dear Miss Richards!" she exclaimed, at the sight of Althea's angry face. "Is there something the matter?"

"Miss Barrett —" Althea said and noticed that at once Miss Maple's face first flushed and then turned white — "is disturbed because she says my room used to be the guests' lounge and she resents the fact that you have rented it to me for a bedroom."

She thought for a moment that Miss Maple was going to cry. But she seemed to pull herself together. "Dear Miss Richards, I'm so sorry that Miss Barrett has upset you. Please don't pay attention to her complaints. She is an old patron and I must give her consideration. But I am afraid that she is too outspoken. She does not realize that she offends people."

"Yes, but it is true that you sacrificed your lounge for me and that this will prevent some of your former guests from coming back?"

"Oh, dear me no! Why, dear Miss Richards, I will be quite candid with you. You know that times are very hard indeed. I used to have many people come to stay with me — a waiting list, in fact. People from abroad liked to come and stay with me. But you know there are not so many travellers now. I have been having a difficult time making ends meet. What you are paying me quite compensates me for any loss. And I do appreciate having you here. There are not so many who will miss the old lounge. Do believe me. I am truly sorry that Miss Barrett spoke to you as she did. She is elderly, you know, and used to expressing her opinions without regard to the feelings of others. So overlook what she said, please." She stopped, out of breath, her plea continuing in her eyes.

"She doesn't like Americans, does she?"

There was suddenly a look of dignified reproach on Miss Maple's face. "I imagine that she told you that I am favoring Americans over other guests. That is quite untrue. I have made the arrangement for you because Mrs. Henshaw asked me to. Any request of Mrs. Henshaw's will always receive my first consideration, twenty Miss Barretts notwithstanding. Like so many, I owe much to her."

Althea's anger ebbed. She allowed Miss Maple to cajole her into a better humor. But that evening at dinner she found it hard to eat. She kept her eyes on her plate but she was aware of the triumphant glances Miss Barrett sent her way and also to Miss Atwood. Obviously Miss Atwood was at once aware of a new ingredient in the tension between herself and Miss Barrett. Althea saw the inquisitive glances she sent to her and to the other two women. Miss Maple, pale and tight-lipped, looked at no one.

When the meal was over, Althea, the last to leave the table, was surprised to find Miss Atwood lingering in the hall, anxious to speak to her. "I thought," she said cheerfully, "we could have some coffee together and talk a bit. We can use the lounge. This is the evening Miss Barrett always goes out to some church gathering."

She smiled brightly as she said this, as if placing the two of them on a conspiratorial footing. Reluctantly Althea agreed.

"After all," Miss Atwood went on, walking slowly

beside her, "we're fellow Americans and we ought to hold up each other's hind leg."

Althea said nothing and they entered the lounge and sat down together on the settee. Miss Atwood turned a little sideways towards her.

"Miss Barrett complained to you that you have deprived us of our old lounge, didn't she?"

Althea shot her an angry glance. "Did Miss Maple tell you?"

Miss Atwood laughed her high, tinkly laugh. "Oh, dear no! Miss Maple is the soul of discretion. Oh, no. I know Miss Barrett very well. I expected that she would find some way to upset you."

Althea said, bewildered, "But why should she?"

Miss Atwood put her hand on her arm. "Oh, really, it has nothing to do with you — except that you are an American. I am an American. She dislikes me — why is too long a story. So she now dislikes Americans. So of course she upset you to show how much she objects to Americans."

Althea shook her head. "I still don't understand it."

"Of course you don't — because you don't know what went before. Miss Maple did not tell you that. I suppose I should tell you all about it after all. You see, when I first came here Miss Barrett and I used to have very lively conversations about all sorts of subjects. She is, as you've noticed, very opinionated. I have often felt sorry for the poor wretches who were at her mercies in whatever organization it was she managed until she retired. She must have bullied them terribly — for the good of their souls, I suppose. I also discovered that she is a very ignorant woman — knows only so much history as is consonant with her idea of the grandeur of England. Unfortunately one evening I mentioned a book that had just been published, about the private life of Queen Elizabeth, about the impropriety of the behavior of her uncle Lord Howard when she was his ward in her teens, etc. No doubt you have heard all this discussed. It raised the question of Queen Elizabeth's physical nature — whether, in fact, she never married because she was not fully a woman. As any intelligent person would, I found it a matter of great interest — the effect this lack, if it did exist, on the course of history and so forth. But Miss Barrett took violent exception. In fact, she acted as if I had written the book. She took it as an insult to herself as an Englishwoman. She would not listen to any reasonable argument or even to my disclaimers of being a supporter of the theory. Such opinionated people never do listen to anyone else. She is nothing if not consistent. Not that that worries me at all. But I'm afraid it has made things rather awkward for Miss Maple — only two guests here most of the time and those two won't speak to one another. I'm so glad you've come. Miss Maple doesn't have the flow of visitors she used to have, though we've had several recently, as you know. I don't know how long she is going to be able to keep this going."

Althea made no response when Miss Atwood paused. She was all at once aware that Miss Atwood had moved much closer to her on the settee. Presently she began to stroke the glossy dark brown hair that framed Althea's face. She said in a coaxing voice, "You're such a dear little thing. And such pretty hair."

Althea shrank from her touch. She was deeply disturbed. She was suddenly reminded of some of Marjorie's friends. One or two of them had tried to pet her, cooing at her as if she were indeed a little girl. She had only vaguely understood the subtle overtures at the time. Now they seemed crystal clear to her. They were what she had vainly and un-understandingly sought from Elsie, these soft strokings and coaxing sounds. They roused something in her — a physical yearning that once had perplexed her and that now she shrank from as dangerous — dangerous because they would undermine her resistance to intimate contact, a resistance she felt she must make. In moments when she sought to reason out her feelings she wondered why she must resist and yet when the opportunity was there a real revulsion came up in her. She did not face the fact squarely but she knew underneath all her rationalizations that she could not respond unless there was between her and the other a basis of loving kindness. She did not doubt that Miss Atwood felt kindly towards her, but she also knew in her bones that her attraction for Miss Atwood was simply that there was no other choice for her, no one else at hand to satisfy a purely physical need.

At length, with a little half-hidden gesture of disgust, Miss Atwood moved away, taking up again the flow of chat with which she had begun. Althea listened with half an ear. When she wrote to Marjorie the next day she did not report candidly all that had happened, certainly not her own feelings. Marjorie would have been indignant, both about Miss Barrett and Miss Atwood, and besides there was that deep-seated shyness of hers at giving any unguarded hint of hurt or sadness. Instead, in writing, she strove to present the happenings at Miss Maple's as a comedy, an opportunity to enjoy human frailty in bright, satirical colors.

When she had been in London a month she received from Marjorie the first letter in which there was a mention of Gwen. Marjorie said: "your letters have been marvelous — downright brilliant, Gwen says. Your account of Miss Maple's is like a play — wonderful, so vivid, so entertaining. Gwen says to tell you that we can hardly wait from one episode to the next."

Althea, reading Marjorie's letter in the quiet gloom of a London Sunday afternoon, sat thoughtfully afterward. "Gwen says," "we can hardly wait." So now there was Gwen.

II

It was the third day of stormy weather and the Marine Parade at Brighton was half-lost in rain sweeping in from the Channel. August was not yet quite at an end but summer had already gone. Even with the fire lit, Althea's hotel room felt musty and close and by ten o'clock she was out on the Parade, struggling with the rain and wind. At the first shelter she sat down to watch the rolling sea and tried not to notice the dank, penetrating smell that hung about such places whenever the sun had fled. At first she saw no one. She seemed to be quite alone. But Mrs. Henshaw had likewise felt the restlessness induced by bad weather. She saw her presently, walking out of a wisp of heavier sea-fog that had encroached onto the Parade from the drenched beach. Wrapped in a mackintosh she was a dot of a different grey from that of the somber horizontal layers of sea, pavement, housefronts and sky. She came towards her with a quick nervous step and, reaching the shelter, sat down beside her, a little breathless from the wind whipping along the Front.

"I hardly expected to find you out, my dear," she said, taking off her glasses and wiping the streaming lenses with the corner of her cardigan which she had pulled out from under her mackintosh. "There is such a strong wind. In fact, I thought of inviting you to join me in a walk, for the benefit of the fresh air, but decided it would not do for you."

Althea did not respond. As usual she resented the careful consideration that kindly people showed her, even when it was as delicately put as Mrs. Henshaw's statement. She did not want to be taken care of. She knew she often hurt Marjorie's feelings when even with her she had rejected a minimum of cossetting. It was only with Martha that she had accepted thankfully a helping hand — probably, she thought, because Martha's kindness was laden with a certain sardonic humor. As a matter of fact, she had been very glad that Mrs. Henshaw had appeared at Miss Maple's just when she was recovering from a touch of the flu that the doctor said threatened to become pneumonia. In some fashion — because she made a point of not complaining in so many words — Mrs. Henshaw had divined that she was unhappy at Miss Maple's and without more ado had suggested that they go together to Brighton for a little relief from the staleness of the end of summer in London.

She looked now at Mrs. Henshaw, covertly, comparing her present appearance with what she remembered of her ten years ago. She saw a spare, fine-boned woman who had lived through many hardships. Her way of peering through her glasses, which she had now put back on, with nervous quick glances, made her sometimes seem sharp and inquisitive, until her eyes rested on you — friendly, keen blue eyes, sometimes with a touch of vagueness.

She turned them on Althea now. "Such a pity to have so much rain and fog for a holiday. But one can never depend upon our English weather. Perhaps this afternoon it will be clearer and we can enjoy a stroll."

She spoke with a matter-of-fact sympathy. There was a touch of impersonality in Mrs. Henshaw's kindness. In some unobtrusive way she prevented you from feeling that you were singled out from among humanity as disabled or incompetent, that your shortcomings were not of your own creation. She made you feel that she was an exception to the rest of the human race and that sympathy and charity were a special province of hers and not to be received from her in the same way as that dispensed by anyone else. Althea's deep-seated resentment, which had built to a climax during her solitary stay in London, began to fade. This was part of the magic of Mrs. Henshaw's presence, something she remembered from the past. For a while Althea had been carried along by the strangeness, the novelty of aloneness, of idleness, with the new duties of the autumn safely in the future. But then, in spite of herself, she had become prey to a feeling of forlornness. The silent quarrel between her two fellow guests had added anger to her melancholy. She could feel nothing but indignant anger towards Miss Barrett. Yet she did not want to be Miss Atwood's little friend. It was almost a relief when she came down with a feverish cold and then the flu and could stay in her room. But the stillness of the room, unbroken except when Miss Maple and the servant brought her trays of food, proved too seductive. She knew she was over the flu. She should get up, bestir herself, try to revive in herself the avid interest of her first weeks in London. Nevertheless, she pushed away the impulse and turned over in bed toward the wall with its paper of streamers of faded roses. Tomorrow she would make the effort. Tomorrow she might have a letter from Marjorie. Marjorie's weekly letter had failed to arrive for the first time. Was it because of irregularity in postal service across the ocean or had Gwen caused Marjorie to forget to write?

She was astonished when there was a knock at her door in the middle of the morning and when she answered, not Miss Maple but Mrs. Henshaw walked into the room and came to stand by her bed. She recognized her at once, as if it had not been ten years since the day they — she and Marjorie and Martha — had seen her off at Union Station.

Mrs. Henshaw had said calmly, "My dear Althea, I'm so sorry to find you ill. Miss Maple says you have been here in bed for a week or more. What does the doctor say?"

Althea sat up. "There's nothing really the matter."

"Then, my dear, you should be up." Mrs. Henshaw went over to sit down in the armchair near the window. "It is very lowering to stay abed when one is over these things."

"But why are you here? Aunt Marjorie said you would not be in London till winter."

"I did not expect to be, but unforeseen circumstances now require me to be. I have had a very tiresome time during the last few months. Now that I have settled myself here in London I should like a few days' holiday. Will you come with me to Brighton? It is the nearest and most convenient place for a rest. I'm sure it will cheer you up."

She spoke as if the fact that Althea needed cheering up was self-evident. And so they had come for a week's stay. It had started to rain immediately but Mrs. Henshaw insisted on going out at every break in the weather. She herself did not mind the wind and rain. It brought a delicate youthful pink into her otherwise usually pale face.

She said, "It's very homelike. I've been in Greece and the Balkans and it never rains like this there — this quiet, gentle, persistent drizzle. I've often thought about the effect of climate on the national character. Here in England we do not have the extremes of temperature and dry and wet that prevail in other parts of the world. It was King Charles I, I believe, who remarked that there was nowhere else where one can be outdoors more days of the year. He was not speaking, surely, of those who have no choice but to endure what God sends.''

Althea, listening to her gentle, soft persistent voice, felt the gloom that had fastened on her slowly lift. Sometimes Mrs. Henshaw lapsed into silence, busy with the knitting she often carried about with her in a stout canvas bag. At least, her fingers were busy in that way. What, Althea wondered, occupied her equally busy mind? The days of ten years ago in Marjorie's house came back to Althea — the remembrance of herself as an adolescent learning her place in the new school and in a new world, of Marjorie and Mrs. Henshaw as two old friends recalling their own girlhood, of Elsie — but here her reminiscence came to a full stop as it always did when her thoughts reached back to Elsie.

Mrs. Henshaw was saying, "I know that the weather is something we all like to discuss. It is, in fact, a very useful topic of conversation when nothing else seems suitable. But though we — I mean, English people — complain a good deal of our own — and indeed foreigners even more so — we are spared most of the great natural catastrophes that are visited upon those who dwell elsewhere. For example, earthquakes. Oh, I suppose there have been earthquakes recorded in the British Isles but nothing producing the death and destruction I have just witnessed in Croatia. Whole villages destroyed and sometimes whole families wiped out. And in primitive places, like those desolate mountains, the initial damage is inevitably followed by famine and disease. Why was I there? Oh, I was in Trieste.

I had gone there in response to the appeal of an old friend. She had taken refuge in Trieste from the political enemies who had ambushed her son in Dalmatia. We felt some of the earthquake shocks in Trieste but no real damage was done. I volunteered my services to the Serbian government. They needed everyone who could care for the injured. It was the same region, you know, where your aunt Marjorie had gone with the Red Cross after the Great War. Long ago, when I married Roger Henshaw, I decided I should be prepared for the emergencies that would surely arise in the remote regions of the world where he carried on his archeological work. Then twenty years ago I ran an improvised hospital in Smyrna during an outbreak of plague. So the authorities were grateful for my offer of assistance. Oh, yes, they thanked me very touchingly — with a medal and plaques — the sort of things Marjorie has in her house there in Washington as mementos of her wartime service. But unlike Marjorie, I do not have a place to put such things. I never know what to do with them. I gave them away to a home for orphaned children in Tirana. They seemed to want them, as mementos of me, they said, poor dears. But, as I was saying, we are indeed blessed here in England to live in a temperate climate, without the upheavals that nature can bring."

Althea watched her as she fell silent for a few minutes, counting stitches under her breath. It was obvious that Mrs. Henshaw did not think of anything as such universal inconvenience as the weather as having any bearing on her own activities. If it rained, she went out nevertheless, though with umbrella and mackintosh. It never seemed to occur to her to complain of the weather or to stay indoors on account of it.

When she had finished counting her stitches she said, "Then there is no one here — no one in London — whom you know well, no one who is a particular friend of your aunt. You are very much on your own. I wonder that Marjorie allowed you to come under the circumstances."

"She couldn't stop me." Althea was belligerent. "I'm of age. I have my own income. She would not try. She understands why I wanted to come — away from everybody, everything, to be on my own."

She was aware of Mrs. Henshaw's eyes fixed on her for a moment, sharp, probing. Then she looked back at her knitting. "One treasures one's independence, of course. And of course it will be better when you begin your studies — you'll be meeting people. But you have no friends here, no one to appeal to in case of emergency."

"I don't expect emergencies. I think I can avoid them."

"Really, my dear?" Again she was aware of Mrs. Henshaw's sharp eyes. "Well, we shall see. Of course, now that I am here, you will have me in case you need me."

A doubt crept into Althea's mind. Was Mrs. Henshaw back in England because Marjorie had let her know about Althea — or had Miss Maple?

Mrs. Henshaw went on, "It is brave of you, Althea, and really quite understandable. One must try one's wings. So you have undertaken to carve out a place for yourself in the world."

"Yes. I don't fit in with the girls I went to school with. They're getting married and having children. And my cousins all ask me to be godmother to theirs. But I don't intend to spend my life as the quintessential maiden aunt."

Mrs. Henshaw laughed, the gay, uninhibited laugh that Althea remembered from the past. "Oh, dear, no! How tiresome that would be!"

The rain began to sweep in greater gusts from the sea and they left the shelter, Mrs. Henshaw bundling up her knitting and thrusting it into her canvas bag in order to have a hand free to steady Althea against the wind as they crossed the wide Front to the hotel. There was a firmness to Mrs. Henshaw's grasp on her arm that she could not have shaken off and she found in fact that she did not want to be free of it. Again she noticed this quality in Mrs. Henshaw's forthright kindness, that placed her outside Althea's usual defensive response to proffered help.

It rained nearly every day they were at Brighton and in the afternoon they sat in the hotel's lounge looking out at the squalls sweeping across the dark Channel waters. Althea, wrapped up in the books she had brought along to read, knew nothing of the few other guests, but Mrs. Henshaw was soon informed of all their hopes, hardships and misadventures, even down to the servants. She had an almost unconscious ability to provoke the confidences of others, an ability she exercised with an absentminded skill developed through long practice. The only really sunny afternoon she insisted on hiring a Bath chair for Althea, for a stroll along the Front, while she walked beside it. Althea, amazed at herself for agreeing to this, listened to her soft continuous voice. She could never really be boring, she decided. She had the quick, various intonations of a university-bred woman, a familiarity with the formal discussion of political and economic subjects — she had very soon learned that Althea now focussed her interest on economics as the basis of society and she had much to add to Althea's knowledge. What constantly astonished Althea was the extraordinary hodge-podge of opinions she expressed, about the political scene of England, in the Balkans, from the most radical to the most hidebound conservatism, with no apparent awareness of the strangeness of the mixture. She never spoke of religion except to dismiss theology as a matter for serious consideration. The need for the socialization of every sort of charity seemed to her beyond question. Yet the preservation of middle-class society, with the individual's right to privacy of every sort and free choice of opinions, she said, was the true bulwark against savagery. It was the real difference between civilized and primitive peoples, she said. She doesn't really, thought Althea, deal in abstract ideas. To her, every situation, every fact, was so important at the moment that it crowded out all other situations similar or antagonistic, past or future. She had picked up phrases and ideas from the vast number of people and groups of people with whom she had mingled over the years, using them and seeing them always in the context of the persons and circumstances of the moment. She never spared the time to reconcile the discrepancies between them. She seemed to spurn the need to rationalize them, to sort them out into a whole. Perhaps it was that she did not see a coherent pattern in human affairs. Even the ideal of a society she seemed to assume was just that — an ideal. It had no useful function in the practicalities of life.

Surprisingly — to Althea — a good deal of their time together was spent in silence. For though Mrs. Henshaw talked, in her quick, light voice, cheerfully and at length whenever she seemed to sense that Althea needed rousing from melancholy, she nevertheless often sat quiet. Perhaps she was preoccupied with some private problem. Perhaps her presence here now was an interruption of some other situation and her thoughts reverted to the unfinished business she had left behind. Often when they sat together, on the Front or in the practically empty lounge of the hotel, she would be knitting with concentrated speed, her thoughts far away from the needles and wool in her lap. She usually sat hunched forward, peering absently at her needles through glasses that slid nown on her nose. Her hands, the skin of which had the same wrinkled delicacy as that of her face, worked with nervous quickness. She was almost entirely colorless, for her faded hair, done up as if hurriedly and without attention, and the pallor of her skin were of almost the same tinge of greyish yellow —

she must once have been very fair. The fierce sun of the climates in which she had spent so much time had drained her fine skin of its natural rosy color. She could never have been really pretty, for her nose was slightly crooked, her mouth too large. But there must have been something extremely engaging in her appearance as a young woman. Now she was weatherbeaten and her clothes lacked any vestige of fashion. They were beautifully sewn, for she made her own clothes, but they were shapeless and hung on her dispiritedly. All her energy was in her actions and these were sometimes erratic from the vigor with which she moved. Althea, watching her, knew she was seeing her in a new light. Ten years before, in Marjorie's house, she had seen her simply as an adult, as someone inexpressibly removed from herself by so many more years of life. Now she was tantalized by the thought of Mrs. Henshaw as a young girl, as the girl with whom Marjorie was first a new friend, then the closest of companions. How to imagine the freshness of thirteen, fourteen years of age in the woman she saw before her? How to imagine the bond that had grown between her and the brash, undisciplined Marjorie, by turns aggressive and overcome by shyness?

Mrs. Henshaw seemed unaware of Althea's close scrutiny. Sensitive as she was to the psychic state of someone in need of some sort of help, spiritual or material, she was nevertheless blind to the image she presented of herself. Althea needed comfort, reassurance, the sense of a friend at hand. This she was instinctively supplying. After a few days Althea was chagrined to realize she had, without consideration and at the time unconscious of the fact, laid bare to Mrs. Henshaw the unhappiness she had felt through her teens, the psychic reasons for her turning away from literature to economics as a field of study. Some inner warning signal made her leave out all mention of Elsie — yet she wondered if Mrs. Henshaw did not remember her fit of despair when Elsie had left for Geneva, whether she did not have her own surmises about the effect of Elsie's departure, for occasionally, while Althea was talking, she would raise her eyes in one brief instant from her knitting. Nor did Althea say anything about the presence of Gwen in Marjorie's house. She wondered if Mrs. Henshaw knew about this, whether Marjorie had written to tell her of this new visitor. Mrs. Henshaw said nothing about it, though she often spoke of Marjorie and of receiving letters from her.

The last afternoon they spent at the seashore, while they stood at the head of the Pier, leaning on the railing and gazing out at the misty Channel, Althea felt that Mrs. Henshaw was somehow suddenly cut off from her and the familiar atmosphere of the seaside resort, wrapped up in some other world utterly strange and unrelated to anything she knew about. She seemed to herself all at once only an interruption in Mrs. Henshaw's life, as if Mrs. Henshaw had laid aside her more pressing concerns to enter for the moment into Althea's affairs and now she was about to, had already, withdrawn. To bring her back, Althea murmured urgently, "Can't we stay a few more days?" But Mrs. Henshaw patted her arm and said, "No, I must go back. I must go back."

Althea burst out, "But I don't want to go back to Miss Maple's."

At the tone of desperation in her voice Mrs. Henshaw's full attention instantly returned. "But, my dear, then you must find somewhere else. I can see that perhaps it is not the happiest solution for you."

On the second level of her mind Althea realized that she had seen into the problem at Miss Maple's. But the urgency of a need for change overrode this recognition. "I'd like to have my own place — especially for the winter — somewhere where I would have some things of my own."

Mrs. Henshaw was thoughtful. "I must give it some thought. I am sure I can find the sort of thing you want." Steeling herself Althea insisted. "But I want to make my own choice."

Again Mrs. Henshaw patted her arm. "Of course, my dear, of course. But you must let me guide you. Marjorie would be very upset if I left you entirely to your own devices."

By instinct, thought Althea, she knows she can always invoke Marjorie to persuade me. Mrs. Henshaw had gone on speaking. "I am certain I can find the right place for you — somewhere where you can have your meals prepared and served and someone to look after your needs otherwise. You can go back to Miss Maple's for a few days until I can make some inquiries."

Thereafter, with every moment that passed until their departure for London, Mrs. Henshaw seemed to recede into her own preoccupations, as if she had settled for the moment what must be done with Althea and therefore was free to consider other problems. With every moment Althea felt that she was further and further from the center of Mrs. Henshaw's attention. As they stood in the train station, gazing at the magazine stall, carefully and unseeingly reading over the covers on the rack, Althea asked if she could come to see her in London. "I do not have your address."

Mrs. Henshaw was suddenly entirely with her. "Oh, of course! I intend that you should. I shall not leave you to your own devices, my dear, no matter how independent you wish to be. I believe I can find you suitable rooms in a convenient neighborhood, somewhere near to the places you intend to go often. There is nothing at all wrong with Miss Maple's, but I see that it is not right for you."

They settled into their seats in the train compartment, silent and once more remote from each other. Althea glanced from time to time at Mrs. Henshaw and saw that her eyes were straining toward London.

The train came into Victoria Station and Althea followed Mrs. Henshaw onto the platform. It was plain to her that Mrs. Henshaw's mind was now entirely absorbed by a contemplation of whatever it was that lay ahead of her. In spite of herself Althea was prompted to make one last effort to recapture the place in her attention that she had held these last days. Like a child afraid of abandonment she put her hand out to grasp Mrs. Henshaw's arm.

When Mrs. Henshaw turned to look at her there was impatience and annoyance in her glance but instantly, calling herself back from the future to the present, these feelings were banished in a look of affection. "My dear," she said hastily, "I shall be in touch with you in a day or so. I still have not given you my address, have I? Oh, I must have something to write on in here!" She began frantically searching through the large shabby black handbag that hung on her arm. Althea hunted through her own pockets and thrust a small memorandum pad and pencil into her hands. Accepting them, Mrs. Henshaw scribbled hastily and gave the pad and pencil back to her. As she reached down to grasp the handle of the canvas bag that was her chief piece of luggage Althea said, "Let me take you home in my cab."

But Mrs. Henshaw said with uncompromising firmness, "Oh, certainly not! All that distance and out of your way! The Tube will take me there very quickly."

"But you have so many things," Althea protested, eyeing the stray books Mrs. Henshaw clutched under one arm, the sack of nameless objects that hung from one hand, the mackintosh draped over her other arm.

"Indeed no. I can manage very well. Do help me put this coat on. That will be one less thing to carry."

Obediently Althea held the coat for her as she disengaged one arm and then the other to put it on, saying as she did so, "Come to my house whenever you feel like it. I am most anxious to see more of you."

Althea watched her walk quickly away across the vast, untidy, grimy space lit by streaks of sun filtering through the glass roof of the station. A vivid memory returned to her of Union Station and the concerted efforts of Marjorie and Martha and the trainman to get her and her belongings onto the train. But then she had had some of Elsie's things to take with her. The smile faded from her face as she turned away to call a porter to carry her own small case and hobble toward the sidewalk where the cabs drew up.

As she approached Miss Maple's she felt a twinge of remorse. Her heart sank a little at the thought of Miss Maple, of Miss Maple's desperate struggle to keep her establishment going. But Mrs. Henshaw had seemed untroubled at the thought of any disappointment Miss Maple might feel at the loss of a long-term, well-paying guest. She found she had returned to Miss Maple's in a new mood. It was true that her life was empty of that urgent love of the future and what it might bring that filled the hearts of others. What was it, for instance, that so absorbed Mrs. Henshaw's energies, urged her forward to every new episode without a backward glance, her eyes already focussing on some future drama? It was true that there was a promise in the bustle of many people's lives, no matter how hectic or how commonplace they might seem to be, a promise that all this, whatever it was, would lead to something brilliant or satisfying or rewarding, and if not any of that, justifying, justifying their existence. Perhaps this was all an illusion, but it was an illusion that held most people fast to whatever it was they strove for. She brushed aside these musings as the cab reached Miss Maple's.

The next day she set to work to find herself another place to live. She scanned the advertisements in the *Times* and wondered how one chose from them the places one would bother to look at. She hesitated to begin and she tried not to admit to herself that it was her lameness that created this hesitation — not only her lameness in itself but the effect it invariably had on those she dealt with. She sat in the small lounge to read the newspaper, far less intimidated now, in her new mood, by Miss Barrett or anyone else. Miss Atwood came in to find her there and after greeting her said, "Miss Maple says you will be leaving us."

Althea looked up in surprise into her bright, inquisitive eyes. Since the episode on the settee Miss Atwood had treated her with a slightly contemptuous offhandedness. She had not expected that Miss Maple would confide in Miss Atwood.

Miss Atwood, seeing her surprise, smiled in obviously triumphant amusement. "Miss Maple says you have decided you must have more ample accommodations since you will be in London throughout the winter." She leaned closer to Althea and dropped her voice, in a show of conspiratorial confidence, as if they were in a crowded room. "You can imagine how agitated Miss Barrett is. She cannot wait to see whether we shall get our old lounge back. She will claim credit for that if we do."

Althea's anger returned in full force. "I've no interest in Miss Barrett," she said and made a show of going back to read the newspaper.

The next morning there was a note from Mrs. Henshaw on her breakfast tray — she had not gone back to eating her breakfast in the diningroom with the two old women. The note contained a list of addresses. Mrs. Henshaw had lost no time in making her inquiries. In her narrow spidery handwriting she said, "My dear Althea, I have heard that there is a house near Paddington which is shortly to be ready for occupancy by students or other such visitors to London. I have made inquiries about the woman who is undertaking it — a Mrs. Tyndal — and find that she is in every way recommendable. I am so sorry that I am unable to go and see it with you, but I have stopped by and spoken to Mrs. Tyndal. It is the first address on this list. Do let me know whether you like her rooms."

Althea studied the address. It was not too far from Paddington Station and was convenient to everywhere she wanted to go or to the means of getting there. She toyed with the idea of trying to go there on the bus or in the Tube but she had never attempted to board one of the big red buses and she had been told that there were a great many stairs in the Tube, that one could not always expect to find a lift. Everyone she spoke to seemed to assume that she could not manage them. Yet she thought of it, with a quickening of her pulse, tantalized and yet fearful of trying it for herself. She ended by taking a cab.

The house was a tall one in a terrace of similar houses, with a flight of six steps up to the glass-paneled front door. When she had paid the cabman and was left alone on the pavement she looked up at the windows. Counting the floors — she caught herself, remembering the English custom of counting the first floor up as the first story and not the second — she saw that it had three floors by the English way of reckoning, four flights of steps to her. A flight of steps led down at the side into an areaway onto which the windows of the basement looked out. There was an air of spruceness about the place that set it off even from the fairly wellkept houses on either side, and there were pots of geraniums and ivy set about inside the areaway. Her ring was answered by a small smiling woman clad in a gingham dress. Her hair was drawn back from her face and coiled in a neat bun on the nape of her neck. Her complexion still showed a country rosiness, not yet bleached to a city pallor.

"Oh, yes, Miss Richards!" she exclaimed in a lilting voice that at once caught Althea's ear. "Mrs. Henshaw told me to look out for you. How do you do? May I take your wrap? I am Mrs. Tyndal."

Mrs. Tyndal was newly arrived from Wales, Althea shortly learned, with an unempoyed husband — "the times are very hard, miss, as I am sure you know" — and two half-grown children to support, in the hope that London could provide a greater opportunity for earning their living. The times in Wales, she said, were much worse than even in England. She had only just advertised for lodgers — it had taken a while to make the house clean and ready for them — and Mrs. Henshaw had been one of the first to answer. "She said she was looking for rooms for a young American friend."

Mrs. Tyndal paused briefly to give Althea another bright smile. She would be delighted to have Althea. Mrs. Henshaw had explained all her requirements — meals to be prepared and served, regular service for her rooms. This was something she did not expect to provide for all her prospective lodgers but it was understood to be part of her arrangement with Althea.

"There is only one obstacle —" Standing together in the hall she paused to look up at the stairs. She had tried to explain to Mrs. Henshaw, but Mrs. Henshaw had been in a great hurry. She paused again and Althea saw the instant glance of her eyes downward, the merest wink of her eyelashes, towards Althea's lame leg. She understood that Althea would prefer the rooms on the first floor — there were no rooms to let on the ground floor — for then there would be only one flight of stairs. But she was so sorry, the first floor was already bespoken, by the family of a young woman from India, who had come to London to study at the London School of Music. Here Mrs. Tyndal stopped and waited anxiously for Althea to speak.

Althea gazed past her to the flight of stairs. Twenty steps. She had a habit of counting steps. That meant, if there were two flights, forty steps each time she went up or down.

Mrs. Tyndal was speaking eagerly again. "Oh, the next flight is not so long! This is the worst."

Althea considered. She knew she was growing bolder. Marjorie's house had had a flight of fifteen steps to the landing on which her room was. She was coming out of her cocoon. You didn't get out of a cocoon without some travail. Damn the steps. She would learn to endure them. She had a feeling of sympathy toward Mrs. Tyndal. Perhaps it was not entirely reckless to make this experiment.

"I want to try the stairs," she said finally and new hope revived in Mrs. Tyndal's face.

But Mrs. Tyndal hesitated. "I'm so sorry. Of course, if you find it won't do —"

They climbed slowly together up the flight of steps, Mrs. Tyndal eager to help her but Althea determined to manage alone. At the landing they stopped while she caught her breath and weighed the problem of the next flight. As Mrs. Tyndal had said, they were not so many. When they had climbed these Mrs. Tyndal flung open the door on the landing. She could have a large sittingroom, a small bedroom and her own bathroom facilities. From the windows she looked out onto the garden within the railing in the middle of the square. It was one of the few such gardens in London, said Mrs. Tyndal, that had been opened to the public. The gates were open during daylight hours.

"I'll try it," said Althea. "But you must agree to release me from the arrangement if I find I cannot manage." Listening to her own voice, Althea was surprised at the firmness and sagacity with which she spoke.

"Oh, look you to goodness, Miss Richards!" The Welsh exclamation rang with the mixture of hope and contrition in her voice. "I would never try to hold you to it if you could not manage!"

Mrs. Tyndal led the way down the stairs. As they reached the first landing, she paused, as if something still troubled her. She looked toward the door on the landing. "These are the rooms of the young lady from India. You will not mind sharing my house with her?"

"Mind?" Althea was puzzled.

"She is quite a dark young lady — from Madras, I think they said."

"But why should I mind?"

"Well, I have been uneasy about letting to her, but her family is paying very well. They want her to be in a quiet, safe place. I could not bear to lose the money. But sometimes I wonder whether it is too big a risk — friends have mentioned this to me. They have said that perhaps I might not find other lodgers because of her."

"But why?" Althea said, still mystified but beginning to understand.

"She is *very* dark, you see. Of course, she dresses in their style of clothes and obviously has very nice manners and speaks English well —"

Althea cut her short. "I don't see at all what this has to do with me. She sounds like the sort of person you should have here."

Mrs. Tyndal's voice rose in pitch with her sense of relief. "I thought that, perhaps, since you are an American —" She did not finish the sentence but talked cheerfully as they went down the final flight of stairs. This venture, this house, said Mrs. Tyndal, was very much a gamble and she was not a gambler by nature. Only the dire need of finding some respectable means of livelihood had brought her to this great teeming wilderness of London, and she was fearful of anything that she might do in her innocence and lack of knowledge that might scuttle her frail craft in such dangerous waters. The young Indian lady was the daughter of a well-to-do businessman in Bombay, who had paid the rent for a year in advance. His agent had been his brother, the young woman's uncle, a serious, bespectacled middle-aged Indian who gave her unimpeachable references but who also questioned her at great length, because, he said, his family must be absolutely assured of the respectability and safety of the nest in which his niece was to be placed. She was to study music.

"He said," Mrs. Tyndal finished, "that he took it for granted that my other tenant would be a woman, someone of quiet habits. He will be pleased to hear of you."

Althea, suddenly struck by the humor of these intricate negotiations, laughed. "Perhaps he'll suspect *me*, when he hears that I'm an American."

Mrs. Tyndal joined in the laugh. They were standing now in the entrance hall. She glanced at Althea in puzzlement. "Isn't it odd that a foreigner like that, someone from such a strange place, should come here to study music? They don't have the same kind of music as we do, do they?"

At first Althea was surprised by her knowledgeability and then remembered that the Welsh were a musical people. "They don't use the same scale, I believe, as our music. It is a pentatonic scale, isn't it, like the Scottish and perhaps your own Welsh?"

Mrs. Tyndal looked dubious but did not question what she said.

On her way back to Miss Maple's Althea thought over her decision. She would have to learn to ration her goings in and out, so as to limit the number of times she climbed the stairs. But this was something of an old habit already. And Mrs. Tyndal offered her advantages. She herself would provide Althea's meals; modestly she said she was accounted a good cook. Althea would never have to go out in bad weather or if she felt unequal to the stairs. If ever she had a guest, all she need do was to let Mrs. Tyndal know and that could be arranged for. Arriving in her room at Miss Maple's Althea sat down and wrote a letter to Marjorie.

She felt a great relief when she finally moved in with her belongings. For the first time she felt she had achieved a home of her own, temporary though it might be. Mrs. Tyndal was as good as her word. She showed herself a kind-hearted, sympathetic woman, never seeming to forget Althea's special problem yet never obtruding unwanted pity. Nor did she, as Althea once or twice feared, make a nuisance of herself in gossiping at length when events brought them together. She did occasionally, when Althea noticed a careworn look on her face and offered sympathy, confide her worries, as if relieved to have a receptive ear to which to unburden herself.

One day, coming to Althea's room to bring fresh linen, she had talked of her daughter, a girl of seventeen, who had had the good fortune to find a place as a nursery governess in the family of a businessman who could still afford such things. She hastened to add, before Althea could speak, "Oh, she does not live with them! She just goes there early in the morning and comes home in the evening. I think she is too young for me to allow her away from home overnight."

Althea, sensing that there was some unspoken reservation in Mrs. Tyndal's statement, waited.

"Indeed, I wonder if I should allow her to work in such a family at all. But we do need her wages, especially now."

"But what is the matter? Is she unhappy there?"

"Oh, no. Quite the contrary. She likes them very much and the children seem very fond of her. And the mother is a kind woman."

"Well, then, what is the matter, if she is treated

132

properly?" Althea began to think of tales she had read
about girls being victimized by their employers, sexually
pursued by the men in the family.

"Oh, yes! She likes them very much, as I said. She is
always telling me stories about her mistress — how nicely
she is dressed and how well-mannered the children are.
She says they are all musical. One of the bigger girls plays
the piano very well, and they appreciate her own love of
music — we're Welsh, of course. And the house is beautifully furnished. She can't say enough about how kind and
cultivated they are."

"Then why are you worried? Does the man, perhaps —?"

But Mrs. Tyndal stopped her. "Oh, no, no! She says
she almost never sees him, he is such a busy man. And the
relatives who come there are polite to her but not familiar."

At first she thought Mrs. Tyndal was going to leave it
at that but then she rushed on. "It is my conscience. You
see, the family is Jewish."

She gazed apprehensively at Althea, who looked back
at her in surprise. "But why should you be upset about
that?"

Mrs. Tyndal hesitated. "Well, but you see, if we feel
that Jews are not our sort, we should not profit from dealing with them, should we?"

"I still don't understand," said Althea stubbornly.

Mrs. Tyndal flushed. "But, look you to goodness, Miss
Richards, you don't think it isn't proper?"

"Do you really feel that way yourself, or has somebody
else said that to you?"

Mrs. Tyndal did not answer but looked down so as not
to meet her eye and Althea went on, "We don't have to
perpetuate all these old prejudices, do we? If these are good
people and your daughter likes them and they treat her
well, what else is there to it?" As she spoke Althea felt the
weight of the history of religious persecution through the

ages. And Mrs. Tyndal came from some remote corner of Wales, where the past still probably bore down on its inhabitants, even if, like her, they had left behind the rigid grip of a narrow religious background.

Mrs. Tyndal looked up at her again with a hopeful gleam in her eye. "Well, if you don't see anything to object to —"

Althea said firmly, "Nothing at all."

Mrs. Tyndal never referred to the subject again and Althea supposed that she had taken her own reassurances as deciding her doubts. Occasionally she met Mrs. Tyndal's daughter, known simply as Glad, on the stairs or when she sometimes brought up the tray with her meals. Glad was a pretty blonde bright-eyed girl who did not give the impression that she worried much about such abstractions as her employer's religious belief. She was bubbling with a scarcely concealed cheerful excitement at being in London, with an acute sense of the dignity that was hers because she was earning her own living and contributing to her mother's income. Glad had left behind the ancestral shadows that still troubled her mother.

Sometimes also Mrs. Tyndal talked to Althea about the anxieties that beset her in meeting the expenses of running her house. There was a third story to the house and several young men lodged there, students from abroad. They never lingered on the stairs or in the entry, but ran up and down from their own quarters early in the morning or late at night as if the main events of their lives took place elsewhere and they came there only to sleep or change their clothes. Mrs. Tyndal had covered the stairs with sturdy carpet to minimize the sound of their passage. Besides, she told Althea, she had made sure they were sober and diligent young men before she had taken them in. At least, thought Althea, they are when they're here.

It was obvious that the rent of her own rooms and those

of the Indian girl below her were Mrs. Tyndal's main support. Sometimes she encountered the Indian girl, who was as dark as Mrs. Tyndal had described her, with white, white teeth. She wore a jewel in her nostril and colorful garments of a sheer material wrapped about her in layers. In bad weather she wore stout English boots and a heavy tweed coat, an incongruous combination of the airy and the practical that captivated Althea. Otherwise she was aware of her only in the sound of her piano as she struggled with Beethoven and Debussy. Althea, alone in her room reading, would find herself wondering, as Mrs. Tyndal had, why such a girl from so distant and strange a culture should spend her time and energies on music that was so alien to her. But though she wondered she came to no conclusion, no more than she did in her musings over the odd glimpses she had of Mrs. Tyndal's view of the world.

She was a kind little woman whose care for Althea's comfort was shown in unobtrusive ways. She was also a good cook — not as good as Martha, Althea thought loyally, but then there were different dishes and different ways of cooking. Once she began to overcome the nervousness of her first days as a landlady she seemed also to lay aside her anxieties and chatted cheerfully, even merrily sometimes, about the oddly dressed foreigners who crowded the London streets, about the teeming life of the city so different from the stagnant gloom of her Welsh valley. Althea also discovered that she came from a convinced Socialist family — her father had been a fiery speaker at the coal miners' rallies. She was in doubt about the new National Government and its economic theories, which she confessed she did not understand, and she was shocked by the street fights reported in the newspapers between Oswald Moseley's black shirts and those who did not accept his admiration of the Italian fascists. "We don't want Mussolini here," she said, and spoke of her fear that her own son might be involved in the street fighting. The London police put all the fighters in jail impartially and she did not want her son to have a jail record. It interested Althea that Mrs. Tyndal's staunch socialism made her doubtful even of the example of Ramsay McDonald's Labour Party.

"Why, look you to goodness, Miss Richards!" she exclaimed, "How can you expect them to understand what a workingman's life is like?"

Coming into her rooms late one afternoon Althea sat down in the big armchair to rest for a few minutes. The stairs were a test of her strength sometimes more than at others. The day was waning fast, as it did in London in September. Looking out of her window she saw the railed garden that filled the center of the square. Even in the short time since she had come here from Miss Maple's the grass had become covered with fallen leaves from the surrounding plane trees. They had been raked up once and the piles were still in the corners. The gates of the garden were still open. Most of the houses around the square were no longer private residences but had become lodging houses like Mrs. Tyndal's, so that the public could now between certain hours of the day walk and sit in the garden. She went often to sit there on a bench and enjoy the quiet spot within the city's hubbub. Like all London gardens, it was perpetually damp, with moss growing in the more sunless spots. In the center, under a patch of open sky the big straggly rose bushes were still in bloom in spite of the chilly, shortening days. The melancholy the season, of the grey skies, added to her own sense of aloneness. Both Marjorie and Martha seemed far away — further than the geographical distance between London and Washington, because, she supposed, her world now would be so alien to both of them. There was only Mrs. Henshaw. Since she had moved into Mrs. Tyndal's house she had heard nothing from her. Was she out of London? Dwelling on her recollection of the seaside visit she wondered if Mrs. Henshaw really did bear her in mind. She assured herself that she must undoubtedly be only a minor character in Mrs. Henshaw's varied affairs. For a short while she wallowed in this sense of relegation to an isolated corner of the world but then she remembered how, though Mrs. Henshaw was so often abstracted, when she looked you in the eye she obviously listened to you with the closest attention, she seemed as absorbed in your state of mind as if there was nothing else to claim her interest. In a fit of self-discipline Althea told herself that she would in no circumstances go to find Mrs. Henshaw. But she remembered that she had Mrs. Henshaw's address, that it would only be sensible to seek her out and let her know how she did at Mrs. Tyndal's. She argued the matter back and forth in her own mind for several days, aware that she was surely drifting to a decision to go and find Mrs. Henshaw's house. At the end of the week, in the midst of a fine sunny afternoon, she went out into the square and hailed a cab and gave the driver the address in St. John's Wood that Mrs. Henshaw had given her.

It turned out to be a house in a street where the trees were still leafy. It was a smaller house than Mrs. Tyndal's, with only three storys — American style — and a garden at the back. She could see trees and shrubs over the fence that closed in the narrow passage between it and its neighbor. There was a small patch of grass behind an iron railing in the front, divided by the walk that led to the front door, up three stone steps. When she rang the bell she waited for several minutes before there was any response. Then the door was opened by a tall, bulky man with bushy blond hair. For a moment she was afraid that he would sweep her off her unsteady balance by the rush of his movement, since it was obvious that he was not answering her ring but had been already on his way out of the house. He checked himself in time and stared down at her in surprise.

"Oh, I say!" he exclaimed and stopped nonplussed before adding, "I expect you want Mrs. Henshaw." He stepped back and craned his head around to look back into the hallway. Althea thought he was about to shout and braced herself for his bellow but he did not. Instead he made a gesture to her for her to come in and at the same time sidled by her, saying, "There's somebody about, I'm sure. Sorry, I can't stop now." He leapt down the steps and strode off down the street.

Althea stood still in the vestibule, the street door still open. It had not occurred to her how she would find Mrs. Henshaw — whether she was lodging in a house with other people, whether the house was her own and that others lodged with her. The house was quite still around her. The soft breeze of the fine afternoon wafted into the door. She could hear the stir of the leaves of a small tree that framed the window of the drawingroom into which she could see. At least she supposed it was a drawingroom since it was furnished with chairs and a sofa, a long narrow room that must extend the depth of the house. In the far end of it there was a large square desk in front of a bow window that looked out onto the garden beyond. It was heaped untidily with piles of papers. On the chair behind it she recognized the large shabby canvas bag that held Mrs. Henshaw's knitting and other nameless belongings. The sight of it reassured her. This must indeed be the house Mrs. Henshaw lived in.

She heard someone coming down the stairs. A very fair young woman dressed in a grey flannel coat and skirt and wearing a small hat perched on one side of her head stopped as she reached her and stood looking at her uncertainly. Althea asked, "Is Mrs. Henshaw in?"

The young woman glanced into the sittingroom and

said, "I really don't know. She is not there, is she?"

An American, thought Althea. "How can I find out?" The young woman hesitated. "I don't know." She looked up the stairs as if seeking inspiration. Perhaps if you go in and sit down — she is not usually away for very long — unless she has gone to the Foreign Office —"

She left the sentence unfinished and continued to stand in front of Althea helplessly.

"I'll do that," Althea decided, glad of a chance to sit down in a comfortable chair.

As if relieved, the young woman went out of the door, murmuring something Althea could not hear. Althea chose an upholstered chair near the doorway from which she could see and be seen from the hall. The stillness of the house was once more unbroken, except for the rustle of the leaves of the maytree casting its shade over the outside steps. She was nervous and tired from the effort to get here but the tranquil quiet of the afternoon — London sometimes enjoyed these moments of general mildness even this late in the year, and the turmoil of the city seemed far away in this spot, perhaps a reminder of the countryside so long ago built over by these suburbs — soothed her and she waited patiently.

She was actually startled by hearing Mrs. Henshaw exclaim, "Pshaw! Wide open again," as she came up the outer steps and walked in the door. But her annoyance was swallowed up by the delighted smile that appeared on her face when she caught sight of Althea. "Why, my dear! How glad I am to see you! You've been very much on my mind. Have you been waiting long?"

She did not wait for Althea to reply, walking quickly the length of the room to the big desk and depositing on it the voluminous black handbag she was carrying. I've never seen her without some sort of bag like that, thought Althea.

"It's so tiresome, waiting in the offices of these people. They pretend half the time, I believe, that they are too busy to see me. They try to discourage me in that way. They hope that I shall get tired and lose interest. They are much mistaken. They should know that by now. They simply make me more determined."

"There is something important you want them to do?"

"I intend that they shall allow Victor to enter the country. It is such a foolish business. He has no political ambitions. He could not plot a coup if he wanted to. He is harmless and yet they treat him as if he were the most dangerous creature ever to attempt to enter England."

Not enlightened, Althea asked, "But who is he? Where is he coming from?"

"From America, my dear child. That is part of the trouble. The American authorities have said that he is dangerous and that they will not let him return to their country next year. You surely are aware of the fuss the American officials are making about people holding radical political views. And poor Victor. He has a concert tour all arranged beginning next year early. It is outrageous, really."

"You are trying to arrange for him to come to London?"

"Yes. His friends have been able to arrange a concert season for him here, to tide him over."

"Where will he go if he can't come here?"

"Why, Paris, of course. The French are not so silly about these things. Or if they make a fuss, he can go to Switzerland. But how is he to live?"

"He is a musician?"

Mrs. Henshaw sent her a surprised glance. "Why, yes. He is Victor Karandy, the cellist. He is young but already very well known. I believe your aunt was one of his patrons when he gave a concert at the Walters Gallery in Baltimore several months ago."

Still bemused by what she said, Althea was about to ask more questions but a glance at her face told her that Mrs. Henshaw's thoughts were too far away to be reached for a further explanation. Mrs. Henshaw sat down at the desk and, taking newspapers from her carry-all, sorted them quickly in front of her. Presently she sighed and said, "I shall simply have to go and see Willie Rowan. Fortunately he is close to the Home Secretary and the superior of these men I have been dealing with. He will remember Roger. They were at Oxford together."

This decision seemed to settle her mind for the time being and she shuffled the papers together and put them back in the carry-all. Then she looked up at Althea as if fully aware of her presence for the first time. "My dear, how are you? Do you find your rooms satisfactory?"

Althea nodded.

"I saw Mrs. Tyndal only briefly one day when I was on my way home. She seems a competent little woman who keeps her house very clean. She told me that she scrubs the front step every morning, a habit she was trained to at home."

A fleeting memory of Baltimore's white stone front steps passed through Althea's mind. "Yes, it is very clean and she is a good cook and I'm very comfortable."

"And the stairs?" Mrs. Henshaw's eyes were sharp. "But then there is only one flight."

"Oh, no, two."

"Two! But she assured me —"

"No. She told me that she tried to tell you that the first floor was already taken by an Indian girl, but you were in too great a hurry."

Mrs. Henshaw looked chagrined. "That is most unfortunate."

"Oh, I manage very well," said Althea, with more

unconcern than was the fact. "It is a matter of getting used to it."

Mrs. Henshaw was silent for a moment as if mulling this over and then decided not to pursue the subject. "Have you written to your aunt about it?"

"Oh, yes. And I've a letter from her directed to Mrs. Tyndal's house. She does not write as often as she used."

"Oh? Well, I expect she thinks you are settled now. And of course she knows that I am here."

Althea studied her face, now again somewhat abstracted. "Also she has a friend staying with her. So I suppose she doesn't have so much time for writing letters."

Mrs. Henshaw's abstraction vanished. "A friend? Who can that be?"

"All I know is that her name is Gwen."

"Gwen? How strange. I know no one of that name. And she has not mentioned her in her letters to me." There was an undertone of resentment in Mrs. Henshaw's voice.

Slyly Althea added, "She is a new friend, someone she has met recently. I have not met her. She came after I left."

"Odd," said Mrs. Henshaw, more to herself than to Althea.

A sound in the hall called her attention. A girl put her head in at the door.

"You're here, Mrs. Henshaw? How did the interview go? Are they going to let Victor in?"

As she spoke the girl came into the room. Althea saw that she was a tall, slim girl with a fresh complexion and bright brown hair cut short and fitting her small head closely. She wore a tweed skirt and jacket and heavy-soled walking shoes.

Before answering her Mrs. Henshaw said, "Althea, this is Fern Merrill, who is studying at the Royal Academy of Drama. No, Fern, I am afraid nothing is yet resolved."

As she was speaking a telephone rang and she got up quickly and went into the hall to answer it, saying over her shoulder, "Don't leave, Althea, I have much to talk about."

The girl called Fern made a comic face at Althea and said, "I wonder when she will be back."

"You mean, she will go out again?"

"Who knows? If it's something to do with Victor, she will forget you're here. Nothing ever stands in her way when she is on a crusade."

"A crusade?"

The girl smiled a bright attractive smile. "She is always on a crusade. Haven't you noticed? When someone is to be rescued, she will leave no stone unturned." Fern, still smiling at her, leaned back against the desk and folded her arms. "Perhaps I'm assuming too much. Do you know Mrs. Henshaw well?"

Althea hesitated. Did she know Mrs. Henshaw well? How did one know someone like her? She said, "I've known her since I was a child. She is a friend of my aunt's."

"Oh, well, then, I don't have to explain her to you."

"But I've never seen her in — in this sort of way. I don't understand what she is doing. She is not like anyone else I've ever known."

"She's quite an unusual person, I'd say." Fern contemplated her for a moment, her clear blue-grey eyes fixed on hers. "You think about people, don't you? And, of course, knowing somebody when you are a child isn't the same as seeing them as a grown-up. It's a different perspective, isn't it? Still, if you have known her as long as that you must know that she is always ready to save somebody from disaster, present or impending. She has a sharp eye for a lame dog. She can spot one trying to get over a fence a mile away. Did you know that it was Charles Kingsley who said that — 'helping, when we meet them, lame dogs over stiles?' He said that is what honest Englishmen do. In this case it is an Englishwoman and she doesn't wait to meet them. She goes looking for them.''

She has a lovely voice, thought Althea, and she talks like an American — or does she? "Are you going to be an actress?"

Fern laughed. "Mrs. Henshaw made it sound a lot more certain than it is. You're wondering why I'm here in her house, aren't you? Well, I'm one of her lame dogs. My parents don't like what I'm doing. They didn't want me to come to London by myself. She persuaded my mother that I'm perfectly safe here with her. Of course, really, I can do what I like. I'm of age, twenty-two, to be exact. But I don't want to give them a bad time, poor things. But I don't want to stay in Berlin with them.''

Fern stopped speaking and they listened for a while to the sound of Mrs. Henshaw's voice in the hall. There was indignation in it, reasonable argument, cajolery but no compromise.

Althea said, "Where are you from?''

"That's a big question. No, I'm not English but my mother is. You guessed that. You're wondering about how I talk. I'm American but I haven't lived in the States. My father is in the army. He's been military attache at the embassy in Berlin for the last five years. I went to school in Switzerland. You're from the States, aren't you?''

Mrs. Henshaw came back into the room, saying, "I really did think that he would have second thoughts after I spoke to Willie Rowan.''

Fern grinned at Althea. "Sir William Morehouse Gordon Rowan, KCB.''

An expression of slight surprise crossed Mrs. Henshaw's face as she glanced at Fern. "Yes, of course.'' Silly girl, her manner seemed to say, too quick by half. "He was a great friend of Roger's — my husband. He was able to obtain permission for us to go to Greece in 1910 when everyone else said it was impossible. He has always kept in touch with me and I know he will see that Victor is allowed to enter the country. Such a foolish business. He realizes how foolish it is. As if Victor could be a danger to anyone."

"Not Victor himself, perhaps," said Fern, "but maybe some of his friends."

"Friends! Those dreadful men! They are no friends of his. He is in as much danger from them as anyone."

"Oh, yes, just so," said Fern, glancing at Althea knowingly.

Althea could see that she would have none of Mrs. Henshaw's attention, so she did not linger after Fern went out of the room and up the stairs. For several days, back in her own rooms, she pondered her visit. Mrs. Henshaw had invited her to come any afternoon. There was always tea to be had whether she herself was there or not. She had looked keenly at Althea for one brief moment of close scrutiny. "Althea, you must not be too much alone, especially until your courses at the university begin. It is not good for you. Do come. The people in the house like to gather at that time. You will find things of interest to talk about."

She said this firmly, in the tone of voice she used to people she had judged to be, at least for the time being, unable to reach their own decisions. The first afternoon after that when Althea went to the house she found the door open. A babble of voices greeted her when she went in but no one in the group of people scattered about the drawingroom gave her more than a glance and a nod. Fern was not present nor Mrs. Henshaw. Althea sat down in the chair she had used before. A cup of tea would have been welcome but she hung back from pushing her way through the throng to the table where the cups and teapot stood, knowing that it took careful balance for her to manage a cup and saucer and her cane. She was absorbed in watching an argument about English politics between two young girls and a man when she was startled by a man's voice at her elbow.

"Shall I get you a cup of tea?"

She looked up into his face and recognized the man who had run out of the house the first time she had visited. He was smiling down at her with confident ease. He was ruddy and vigorous, with twinkling blue eyes — the epitome, she thought, of Kingsley's honest Englishman, ready to help lame dogs over stiles. Her immediate impulse was to say No, I'm not your lame dog, but she checked herself and said Yes.

He brought her the cup and a tea biscuit. "We've already met, I believe."

She took the cup with thanks and again said Yes.

He continued to look at her quizzically. "You're from the States, aren't you?"

"Yes."

"On a visit to see the sights of London?"

"No. I'm going to study at London University and the School of Economics."

He opened his eyes wide in admiration. "You're interested in economics?"

She nodded.

"We need some new ideas on that subject. What do you think of our friend Mussolini's corporate state? You Americans seem to admire him no end."

"Not all of us."

"Ah, well no. But your bankers and business people. J. P. Morgan is helping to finance him, isn't he, and your Lincoln Steffens says he is the leader of the future."

"He also has a lot of admirers here."

"Yes, it is true. He has bemused some of us also. Bernard Shaw calls him Superman and Austen Chamberlain and Ramsay McDonald vie to outdo each other in praising him. And of course we have our lunatics. Oswald Moseley and his brave little men in black shirts who go out to brawl in the streets. Imitation is the sincerest flattery, they say."

Althea looked up at him again and saw that his eyes were still fixed on her as if he was curious to see what her reactions were to his remarks. Why? she wondered. Did he just like to bait people and she seemed a likely target? She said nothing and almost at once he relaxed his intentness and said goodhumoredly, "Well, I'm sure our national troubles will provide you with considerable interest. Our first Labour prime minister has succeeded in getting himself repudiated by his own party because he consorts with our national enemies, the Tories. These are stirring times."

She thought he was mocking not only the British political situation but also herself. Vaguely she recognized his manner as being deliberately aggressive, a particular sort of gambit to arouse her attention while at the same time overcoming any defense she might put up to his inquisitiveness. But, again, why? His behavior smacked too much of bringing up a cannon to kill a fly. Perhaps it was only because she was an American and that intrigued him. She began to revise her first opinion of him.

He became more personal. "I see that you did find Mrs. Henshaw. She is sometimes elusive, hard to pin down. Especially when she is in pursuit of a quarry. Have you known her long?"

"Since I was a child."

This seemed genuinely to surprise him.

"Really? Most of us are more recently made friends. Has she been in the States, then?"

"Yes," said Althea shortly and did not provide any further explanation. He talked on for a while and then seemed to lose interest or perhaps remembered something else he wanted to do and she was left to sit quietly once more, watching the dwindling group of people.

Among those who were left she recognized the vague, fair girl she had encountered on her first visit. Althea realized now that she was older than she had seemed then, that she was in fact a woman in her thirties. They stared at each other across the room, Althea waiting for a sign of recognition, the other woman returning her a puzzled gaze, as if wondering where she had seen her before. The woman spoke only briefly to those near her and before long she went out of the room, disappearing unobtrusively.

Towards the end of the afternoon Mrs. Henshaw arrived, as dusk was closing in. Althea was now alone. There was an unaccustomed weariness in her step, as she crossed over to the depleted table and poured herself a cup of lukewarm tea and ate the remaining scone. She came to sit near Althea.

"Did you meet any of the people who were here?" she inquired in her usual kindly and absentminded manner.

"Yes," said Althea. "Who is the fair woman who looks so distraught?"

Mrs. Henshaw raised her eyebrows, nonplussed. Then she said, "Oh, yes. Mary Hilary. She is also an American."

"I haven't talked to her. She stayed on the other side of the room. But she was here the first time I came to find you. What is she doing in London?"

Mrs. Henshaw's eyeglasses glinted in the light of the lamp that had been lit. "Unfortunately she married Victor."

"Why unfortunately?"

Mrs. Henshaw seemed to consider for a moment, as if seeking a beginning for her explanation. "It is an unsuitable marriage for her — for both of them. Her family does not approve. And Victor does not really know what to do with a wife. I am afraid that he feels that marriage hampers him — and so it does."

Mrs. Henshaw got up and began to tidy the room, picking

up newspapers that had been flung down here and there and dumping ashtrays into a bag. It was obvious to Althea that she moved about doing this automatically, preoccupied with something else and at the same time a small murmur of disgust came from her, as if she disapproved of the need to do this. Althea knew that there was a servant who came in to help sometimes but otherwise those who dwelt there looked after themselves. Finally, when she said she was going, Mrs. Henshaw paused long enough to ask her whether she was comfortable at Mrs. Tyndal's, not listening to her answer.

In the lamplit street Althea stood for a while considering whether she would walk to the corner where she was likely to find a cab. Then she noticed a bus in the distance and hobbled quickly to the stop. This time she would try it, since the bus had only a few passengers going towards the center of town. Her heart beating fast from the decision, she managed to board and find a seat near the door. Getting down near Mrs. Tyndal's house, she stumped along the pavement, exhausted by the physical and nervous effort and also excited by a sense of triumph. It was still just dusk and the street lamps came on as she passed, irradiating the soft, misty evening air till all was luminous. She would always remember this time of evening, at the end of a day like this, as a special event in what she thought of already as her London.

When she reached Mrs. Tyndal's house and entered the vestibule she found a group of people standing in the subdued light — a very dark Indian in a business suit and two women shapeless in the swathing folds of filmy, light-colored cloth that covered them from head to toe. The trio shrank back, murmuring something she could not understand, the man gesturing politely for her to pass. She did so, saying Thank you to one side and the other, and began to climb the stairs. She recognized in their gentle politeness a certain shrinking from her as a cripple. At moments like this she remembered the first days at Miss Armstrong's school, when the girls, embarrassed by her iron brace, had behaved with an exaggerated formality until they had time to go away and whisper together. She knew also that some more unsophisticated people feared her appearance in their midst — rather as if she possessed the evil eye — and that Martha had had scathing comments to make about them.

When she reached the first landing, the trio of Indians began to come up the stairs, the man leading the two women. At her own door, a flight higher, she paused to look over the bannister and saw them gathered in a knot in front of the door of the Indian girl's rooms. The subdued light on the landing caught the whiteness of the man's collar above his dark coat as he stood softly clapping his hands before the closed door. She turned away as the door began to open.

The fine weather held. The next afternoon, in the hazy October sunshine, Althea took the bus that traveled the length of Sloane Street and the King's Road, on its way to Chelsea. It was nearly empty and she sat by the window watching the small shops and the people who went in and out of them, enjoying vicariously the bustle of the pavements, the colorful flowers on barrows, the fabrics, chinaware and house decorations in the windows. She was absorbed in this reverie when a touch on her shoulder startled her and she looked up into the face of the tall slim girl with the small head and closely trimmed hair.

"Fancy seeing you here," said Fern, sitting down beside her. She was dressed in the same tweed suit and she was hatless.

Althea managed to say, "It's such a nice day —"

"And riding the bus is a fine way to see London. It's a pity you can't go up on top."

Her frankness caused Althea's shyness to recede. "I

thought I'd go and see Chelsea before I got too busy with my schedule."

"Oh, yes. Americans always go to see Carlyle's house and George Eliot's and the Rossettis'. We're great shrine-visitors, aren't we? Perhaps because we don't have so many at home. Or so I suppose. I know almost nothing about the States firsthand. I feel like a fraud when I'm talking about being an American."

"You do?"

"I've never lived there. I was born in China, when my father was stationed there. I was in the Philippines when I was a small child. And I spent the War in England. My mother did not want to go to the States while my father was in France. After that I went to school in Switzerland. Oh, look, this is where we get off."

Fern stood up and waited in the aisle for Althea to clamber to her feet. Althea, contrary to her usual response to such solicitude, grasped her outstretched hand to steady herself. When they stood on the sidewalk together she asked, "But did you intend to get off here?"

"Oh, I wasn't going anywhere special. I'd like to come along with you and see the sights. Here, take my arm. Let's cross over here to the Embankment. You can start off by seeing Whistler's river."

Obediently Althea took her arm and they crossed to the riverside and stood watching the river traffic — the slow, unswervable barges, the faster launches, the little craft dashing in and out. The damp mild air hung over the silver water filtering the sunlight into an enveloping pearl grey haze, softening the unromantic bulk of the structures on the other bank.

Fern said, "You see why Whistler liked to paint here."

"He lived near here?"

"Oh, yes." Fern turned around to lean her back against the parapet and gaze at the houses visible among the trees across the roadway. "Sometimes, you know, I think I'd like to be an artist. London always has that effect on me."

"Instead of being an actress?"

Fern made a face. "It's just a game, you know." She glanced at Althea's puzzled face. "I mean, coming here to study dramatics. I had to have a reason for leaving my parents. I had to think of something to do that my father would agree to support me for. He doesn't like the idea of my being an actress but on the other hand he's crazy about the stage. I don't mean that he'd ever want to be an actor — at least, I don't think so. He's always been a military man from West Point on. But he loves going to the theater. If I make a big success he'd be tickled to death. Though I don't think there's much chance of that."

"Why not?"

Again Fern glanced at her. "To tell you the truth, I don't think I have that sort of gift. Oh, I've some talent. I can make a good show of it. But I don't feel, inside, that I have the stuff that great actresses are made of — and if you can't be the prima ballerina, why be in the corps de ballet? I think if you really have a gift for something, nothing can stand in your way. You'll go ahead and do whatever it is you are impelled to do, regardless of the circumstances, regardless of how it affects other people."

Fern stopped, and Althea who was gazing at her all the time she was speaking, saw the brooding look come into her face. It was a very mobile face, narrow, large-eyed, with a small mouth that was now firmly closed. An actress's face — expressive of whatever passing emotion was called for by the script.

Fern said, "Sometimes I think I'll give it up and go to the Slade school with the painters instead. I like to draw. I like messing with paints. But then I don't think I'd rival Whistler, either."

"Would your father object to that?"

"Oh, Dad — well, I don't think he'd like it but I don't think he'd cut me off with a shilling. What he'd object to most was that I couldn't stick to one thing, that I don't have any perseverance. What he doesn't understand and never will is that this is a kind of restlessness that makes me feel this way. He'd say I needed to get married and settle down to having children. Ugh!"

"Have you been in any plays?"

"Oh, you know, the usual thing you always start out with — Shakespeare. 'Speak the piece, I pray you, as I promised it to you, trippingly on the tongue: but if you mouth it, as many of you players do, I had as lief the town crier spoke my line. Nor do not saw the air too much with your hand, thus, but use all gently: for in the very torrent, transport, and, as I may say, in the whirlwind of passion, you must acquire and beget a temperance that may give it smoothness. O, it offends me to the soul to hear a rambunctious periwig pated fellow tear a passion to tatters, to very rags, to split the ears of the groundlings, who for the most part are capable of nothing but inexplicable dumbshows and noise: I would have such a fellow whipped for o'erdoing Termagant; it out—Herods Herod: pray you, avoid it.' "

Althea, recognizing Hamlet, laughed. Across the roadway a solitary passerby stood still for a moment in amazement, watching Fern's gestures, and then continued on his way.

"You do it very well."

"I suppose the theory is that if you can do Shakespeare, you can do anything. But you know, you have to have practice — in a theater, going on stage before the crowd, and parts are hard to come by. Everybody's looking for work right now. It is pretty discouraging competing against people with established reputations, people who already have an in with managers and producers." Fern paused and gloomed for a bit, gazing across the road. Suddenly she asked, "It's lunchtime. Do you have the price of two meals?"

"Oh, yes, of course."

Fern looked at her with a quizzical smile and mocked, "Why, 'yes, of course.' Would you like to go over there to that pub? A lot of so-called bohemians turn up there — the well-heeled variety."

They crossed the roadway and entered the old building which had a large sign over the door. They sat in a quiet corner, with a mullioned window behind them throwing odd color patterns on the highly varnished small table, eating their steak-and-kidney pie and mashed potatoes with a glass of ale. For a while they were silent and then Althea asked, "Are you an only child?"

Fern nodded, "More's the pity."

"You'd like to have brothers and sisters?"

"Well, I don't know about that. But if there was more than one of me, my parents wouldn't concentrate on me so much."

"How does your mother feel about what you are doing?"

"She doesn't worry about me the way my father does. Mummy is more easy-going, I guess you'd call it. She thinks I'll survive, whatever I do. The only thing she worries about is my getting into trouble and that means having an affair and getting pregnant. She's not like Dad, thank goodness. Dad's all for discipline. I'm glad I'm not a boy. He really would ride me then. When I was little he was always threatening to take a strap to me. He never did. I don't know really whether it was an idle threat but I don't think Mummy would have let him. She draws a line about some things and when she does she is not easy to override. But if I'd been a boy — Well, I expect I would have run away from home before now. How about your parents?"

"They're both dead."

"Oh. Then you're an heiress."

Althea stared at her, suddenly angry. "Does that necessarily follow?"

Then she saw that Fern was laughing. "Well, no. But
you seem to have means, money you don't have to earn.
So you don't have to be rescued by Mrs. Henshaw from
destitution — or from going on the streets to a fate worse
than death. How disappointing for her."

Althea, still unsettled, said grudgingly, "I'm sure I have
other deficiencies that arouse her sympathy."

Hearing the bitter edge to her voice, Fern said hurriedly,
"Oh, now. You said you were old friends with her."

"Yes. That is, she is a very old friend of my aunt's —
the one I live with. Yes, I know. I'm lame, and that makes
her want to take care of me. But there are other things. I'm
uncomfortable with strangers. I don't make friends easily."

Althea thought, Why am I telling her all this?

Fern, spearing a piece of meat, chewed for a moment.
"All because you are lame. Well, you can get over that.
That's why she has invited you to come to her house, isn't
it? — succoring the lonely. I think perhaps she likes that
better than feeding the hungry." Then suddenly impatient,
she burst out, "If she spent half the energy she does helping
all sorts of people out of difficulties that are usually of
their own contriving, she would be famous or wealthy, or
both. She is a brilliant woman. But there's no discipline,
as my Dad would say. As it is, she scratches a living teaching
foreigners English and being a translator at international
conferences. It is a great waste."

"There must be a lot of people who are thankful for
her kindness."

"Or should be. Oh, yes, I suppose there are some who
appreciate her. But it isn't sensible, really, is it?" Fern
turned her bright gaze on Althea again. "It is not as if she
expected a reward of any kind — in heaven, if not on earth.

She isn't a religious woman. She doesn't go to church, like you. She is a rationalist and a firm agnostic. I've heard her talk about that — about the fallacy of looking for divine punishment or reward for something done during one's life here on earth. Yet she seems to be driven by something, by an impulse to take in the whole of life and the world and something beyond, which she otherwise denies exists — the something beyond, I mean." Fern suddenly laughed. "Wouldn't she be surprised to hear me!"

"You're quite eloquent."

"It's my stage manner. What do you think of her?"

"I?" Althea was nonplussed. I never thought about her in that way. I think it is that she hates cruelty. She cannot endure the thought of cruelty — whether it is people being cruel or — or —"

"Life generally. Don Quixote and the windmills. But she is so much more practical in the way she goes about it. Yes, I believe you are right. She doesn't think that any religion, any philosophy, any political goal can excuse or soften the fact of cruelty. That's why you can't pin her down to anything. She won't be committed to any one side of anything. If you're a victim, you're a victim and it doesn't matter why."

They ate in silence for a while. Then Althea said, "Who is the tall man?"

Mistaken for a moment, Fern glanced around the room. Then she realized that Althea could not be speaking of the other people in the pub. "Oh, I see. You mean Adam Milner — at Mrs. Henshaw's. Why? Did he move in on you?"

"He was the only one who paid any attention to me when I went there yesterday."

Fern made a face. "That sounds like him. You're new, so he comes nosing around to find out who you are and why you're there."

"Well, at first I though he was just being amiable."

"Welcoming the stranger in our midst. Pushy, isn't he? As the English say. Well, the trouble is that I don't think he is an Englishman."

"He's not an Englishman? He certainly looks like one, talks like one —"

"Too much like one. He's probably a very good actor. Oh, it's too complicated for me to explain."

"Why is he staying at Mrs. Henshaw's?"

"He doesn't look as if he needed rescuing from anything, does he? At first he was not living in the house. He came there at teatime. Somebody brought him there one day and he kept coming back until, when there was a room vacant, he rented it. There are a lot of people who come to tea there just for the company, you know. Mrs. Henshaw always has very interesting people gathered around her and others like to come and talk and listen. Anyone is welcome, as far as she is concerned. She has one prohibition. No beer or spirits. If you want that, you have to go elsewhere. But otherwise you can come and preach anarchism, or bolshevism, or any brand of religion or anything else. Half of the people you saw there don't live in the house. They come for the fun — and free tea and scones. That must cost her a bit."

"He doesn't look as if he is short of money."

"Oh, I'm quite sure he is not. But you never know what sort of people are attracted to her. With some it's just loneliness. Some of them are very peculiar — fanatics of one kind or another. And then sometimes you meet somebody influential and important in a social or political way, in the government or business. They've come into her life sometime or other and they remain her friend forever."

"Why are you staying there?"

"Why do you suppose? My mother knows Mrs. Henshaw. She has worked with her at some sort of charity benefit and she's convinced that she is a saint. So if I stay there, my mother doesn't worry about me. And then I'm always short of funds — my mother knows that is bound to happen and she feels I'm safe with Mrs. Henshaw — I won't starve or go on the streets."

"But doesn't your father send you an allowance?"

"The bare minimum. He says if I insist on taking up a precarious career, I'd better get used to adversity. It's his way of trying to break me. He doesn't think I've got the guts to stick it out. I'll get tired of doing without all the luxuries I'm used to and come trailing home with my tail between my legs. That's why I had to ask you for the price of a meal. I always run short a week before remittance day."

When they left the pub the fine day greeted them with a mellowed afternoon warmth of blue sky, golden sunlight. The trees, still leafy, cast foreshortened shadows on the paving. Carlyle's house was around the corner, said Fern. George Eliot's was a block away. We can see them from the outside, said Althea, unwilling to spare any time from this soft, easy companionship, her desire for sightseeing ebbing. When they boarded the bus it was almost empty and the quiet privacy of their good fellowship continued. But by the time they reached Piccadilly Circus and Trafalgar Square the crowds pressed around them and Althea grew apprehensive. Fern, as if sensing her nervousness, said, "Don't worry. I'll go with you to Paddington. Yes, it is out of my way, but that doesn't matter. Anyway, I'd like to know where you live."

Fern helped her off the bus and onto another. Why, Althea wondered, don't I resent all this care? She knew she so often bewildered and offended those who tried to give her help in such situations. But now with Fern there was none of this habitual resentment. With Fern she was docile, accepting the help of her arm, the shelter of Fern's body in the pressing throng. They got down from the bus and walked along the quiet, leaf-littered street.

"You have your own rooms?"

"Yes — a flat, really."

"That's what I should like to have. This is it?"

They climbed the steps to Mrs. Tyndal's door and Althea opened it.

"Ground floor?"

"No. Two flights up."

"Two!" Fern looked down at her, her eyes going to the iron brace.

"Oh, I can manage all right. An Indian girl has the first floor."

They began the slow climb, Fern keeping step with her, silently. They arrived at Althea's door and walked into her spacious sittingroom. "You see," she said proudly, "it is very nice when you get here — not at all poky."

Fern was at the window, gazing down into the square. The sun lit up the yellows and browns of the autumn leaves. "Yes, it's nice. But that's a terrible job for you, climbing all those stairs. Couldn't you find anything else?"

"Not so pleasant. Mrs. Henshaw found this for me — only she thought I would have the ground floor. But the Indian girl had spoken first. I like Mrs. Tyndal — she is my landlady. She would be hard to match."

"She takes care of you?"

"Oh, yes, very well."

They left the subject and began to talk about London. Or at least, Althea listened, for the London Fern talked about she had not encountered, the London of behind the scenes at the theater. The times were terrible, Fern said, but there was no decline in the kind of plays and actors available. There was a lull at the moment in the theater season, but within a few weeks Noel Coward's *Private Lives* would be opening again and some other new plays.

Althea's visits to St. John's Wood were frequent after that. What she thought of as the bohemianism of the style of life at Mrs. Henshaw's house fascinated her. On her next visit after her lunch with Fern in Chelsea, she found Fern in the hallway and was invited up to Fern's room, a small room at the back of the house but with two windows. The bed was tumbled, the chairs draped with clothes, the floor strewn with play scripts. She gazed about in surprise.

Fern, noticing her expression, said humorously, "Looks a mess, doesn't it? I forgot to clean it up before I went out. Here, let me clear this stuff away and you can sit down."

Sitting down in the chair Fern cleared for her she tried to take her eyes away from the confusion. She had never before been in a house where the beds were unmade at three o'clock in the afternoon. Or at least if they were not, a guest was not invited to see them.

Fern said with a trace of defensiveness. "I don't have Mrs. Tyndal to tidy up for me. Mrs. Henshaw can't afford a maid to do the rooms. That's part of our understanding with her — we look out for ourselves."

Althea asked, to change the subject, who was the young man with the sleek fair hair she had passed in the street, coming from Mrs. Henshaw's door. She did not say that he had run down the steps, meeting her face to face and when he noticed her crippled leg, had backed away with a look of horrified dismay.

Fern said, "That must have been Victor. Did he act funny when he saw you? He's as superstitious as an — actor."

"Victor — you mean —?"

"Victor Karandy, you know, the cellist. He's the genius of the age on the cello, they say. He's been in the States.

He is the one Mrs. Henshaw has succeeded in getting the authorities to allow into England."

"Yes, I know about that. But what is all the fuss about — if he is a musician?"

"Well, the theory is that he is a dangerous subversive — at least that is what the American immigration people say. He has been expelled from the States and won't be allowed back in."

"Why? Has he been mixing with anarchists or the like?"

"I don't think so. No, I don't think he has any political opinions, much less designs on overturning the government. Victor just had the wrong father."

"What do you mean?"

Fern hesitated for a moment. "Do you know anything about the Balkans?"

"Not very much. My aunt Marjorie was there at the end of the Great War. She did Red Cross work. She talks about it a lot. She was in Serbia and she tells stories about how brave the Serbians were in fighting the Austrians and Hungarians without modern weapons. She admires that sort of gallantry."

Fern nodded as if recognizing the nature of Marjorie's enthusiasm.

Althea went on, "It was the great romance of her life. She felt she was witnessing an epic unfold — you know, the revolt of the Slavs against the tyranny of the Austro-Hungarian empire. Of course, she admits there were terrible battle wounds and typhus and filth and afterwards famine for the civilians." For the first time Althea was conscious of having to defend Marjorie's great adventure — for the first time to see it as less than heroic, as instead a great waste of human resources.

Fern had been picking up the sheets of play script lying on the floor. She muttered something and Althea demanded what she had said.

"All this militaristic glory! Didn't it ever occur to you that it was nothing more than a bloody game for professional soldiers so that they can show off their superiority over anybody else? The Romans parading their captives to the populace, the Indians carrying off scalps, the Prussians goose-stepping in front of the Kaiser?" Fern angrily cast down the papers in her hand.

Althea said coolly, "Our military heroes are nothing but cat's-paws for those who seek economic power. The Romans conquered for the sake of wealth as well as glory. That's what the Kaiser had in mind, too."

Fern looked up at her from under her eyebrows. "And there are those in Germany who are talking the same way now — 'we lost the war because we were cheated and betrayed.' So you're not taken in by all that? If you're a politician and you want to fight a war, you first get everybody stirred up about national destiny and the sublime nature of personal sacrifice. I suppose I don't have to point out to you that it's a man's game. Women are simply for consolation and binding up wounds — and cleaning up the dirty mess when the fighting is over. It's the warriors who go to Valhalla. The Valkyries only do the transporting. Look at your aunt Marjorie. She went to pick up the pieces, didn't she?"

"I'm quite sure she would never have enjoyed the fighting — killing people."

"I'm sorry. I get carried away when you talk about military glory. Arma virumque cano! Of arms and the man I sing — how accurate old Virgil was. It all seems such a fraud."

Althea looked at her shrewdly. "You don't agree with your father about that either, do you?"

Fern sat down on the edge of the bed and looked down at the floor. "No. That's really what is at the bottom of it. I don't accept his view of society. When I was younger I used to flare up and argue with him about history or about what was going on in Europe or the States. I don't think it is right to put people in jail simply for their opinions or bar them from the country when they have no record of violent actions, just because they are anarchists and pacifists and so on. My father says I'm all wet, that I don't know anything about it. These people are potentially dangerous, he says — they are likely to go around throwing bombs and disrupting the public order. He says I'm just ignorant and that I've been influenced by the wrong people. He threatened to send me to a boarding school, a Catholic school, where the nuns would teach me discipline and how to obey and not let me read newspapers. He said it was a mistake to send me to that school in Switzerland where they believed in modern education and student meetings and that sort of thing."

"Why did he send you there?"

"Oh, that was my mother. She wanted me somewhere close at hand so I could come home for holidays. She didn't really care about the school as long as it was respectable and taught me the usual things. Dad didn't really think about it because, after all, I'm just a girl. If I'd been my brother, the son he always expected to have but never did, I'd have been sent to the States to one of those fortresses they lock boys up in — military schools, you know."

"Has he changed his mind about you?"

"I don't know. I think it is just that he realizes that now I'm an adult and he can't dismiss my opinions out-of-hand. He's bull-headed and narrow-minded. Well, he's a professional military man and he can't afford to see any side of a problem except the one he's been taught in the Army. I think he'd be scared to admit any contradictory ideas. He just takes the surface of a situation and a handful of cliche'd thoughts — prejudices, I suppose you'd call them — and acts on them. To probe beneath is unsettling, unhealthy, he'd say. He can't see what's happening in Germany right now. He dismisses Hitler as a street rowdy and he is half-inclined to believe there is something to these stories about Jews being the real instigators of the War for their own profit."

"There are other people who believe that."

"That doesn't make it true. Perhaps it is true that the postwar settlements — the reparations and all that — have made a lot of Germans resentful and ready to fight again and show the world they are not really losers. And Jews have always been made the scapegoats in such situations. Of course there are warmongers and munitions makers and I suppose some of them could be Jews, but to say that they are all underminers of the Fatherland and villains and in league with the Russians — that sort of thing is vicious."

"I've read Keynes' *Economic Consequences of the Peace*. A few people have foreseen all this for some time."

"But they've always been discounted as radicals and pacifists and therefore not to be listened to. It's terrible to see what is going on now in Germany — all this street-fighting and Jew-baiting. Really that is one of the reasons I wanted to get away. I was getting sick at my stomach at what I heard in the news and even saw in the streets. I decided I couldn't stand it and then listen to Dad defending the Reichswehr — the German army — one professional soldier to another, you know. I don't think he ever thinks about where all this will lead. Suppose this little rat Hitler and his brownshirts get into power — Dad says that isn't possible. The Prussian military tradition wouldn't allow it. But I think it will happen if people are not aware enough of what is going on."

"Well, perhaps, the decent people in Germany won't put up with it. They must have had enough of war just like everybody else."

"I wouldn't count on that," said Fern gloomily.

They sat in silence for a while. Then Althea said, "But what is this about Victor? What did you mean when you said he had the wrong father? Was his father an anarchist or bolshevik or something?"

"Victor's father? Oh, no. Victor's father was a Serbian patriot. That is something else. Don't ask me to explain Balkan politics because I can't. Victor's father fought against the Austrians in the Great War and afterwards he led one group of people who were trying to form a government in his native region — you know, there are so many factions in that part of the world. The Hapsburgs always did their best to keep local animosities alive for their own benefit. Victor's father was finally murdered by some of his political enemies and his closest friends had to flee. Some of them came here to London and others went to the States and they all got into trouble with the police because of their intrigues and fanaticism. The trouble with Victor is that he hasn't the least idea of politics and racial partisanship. But to his father's friends he is the son of a revered patriot and martyr. They expect him to live up to that role. There is a colony of his father's people here in London now, plotting away to free their homeland — that's what they call it. They're enemies of the government that is now running their country and they want him to be their rallying point. They embroiled him in their affairs while he was in the States — there is a contingent of them there too — and that is why the United States Government told him to leave and not come back — in spite of the fact that he has commitments for a concert tour next year. They all seem to forget that he is a musician, first and last. You see what a boy he is. To his countrymen he is the focus of a sacred cause, to which, they say, he is pledged out of filial piety if for no other reason — the blood of martyrs, you know, and all that stuff. But he can't abandon them — they won't let him go, for one thing. Poor Victor. He is really bewildered by it all. He's the most naive person in the world. It is piti-ful."

"How did Mrs. Henshaw get involved?"

Fern sent her a satirical glance. "Well, he's a prime case of someone who needs rescuing, isn't he? She met him somewhere — must have been in Paris. Oh, I remember now. It was because of Charles." Fern paused and turned her head, listening to sounds from downstairs. "It sounds as if Mrs. Henshaw has come in. Let's go down and have some tea. I'll have to tell you about Charles some other time. It would take too long now."

She came over and resting her hands on the arms of Althea's chair, looked down into her eyes. "I don't know why I'm talking to you like this — about my father and why I wanted to get out of Berlin. I'm not inclined to talk like this to anybody else. It seems too personal — how I feel about my old man and his way of seeing things and my own feelings. I wish sometimes I could be like all the other girls I know. They just don't think about what's happening in the world. They're interested only in their own lives. They don't realize how these things could affect them. They accept whatever's easiest. Or else they are in the arts or music and they say it isn't any of their business. Artists and actors and musicians are not political people. It doesn't matter to them what kind of a government they live under. They don't even think it is important when I point out what is happening to some of their own kind in Germany right now. They say that's just because they are Jewish. They don't see how that sort of thing works. How it could be anything — because you're black or have red hair or they don't like your style of living. See what has happened to Victor, through no fault of his own." Fern straightened up, abruptly silent.

She is suddenly doubting me, thought Althea, and put up her hand to reach Fern's arm. "I don't know anything about what you're talking about except what I've read. I don't have parents and Marjorie has never made me do anything I didn't want to do. I don't know if that is a good thing."

Fern cast her a startled glance. "I don't know. It probably saves you a lot of guilty feelings. Well, let's go downstairs."

Impulsively she reached down to grasp Althea's arms and raise her from her chair. For all her slenderness there was a remarkable strength in her hands. Why do I let her do this? Althea demanded of herself.

They stood for a moment close together, waiting for Althea to get her balance. Then swiftly Fern put her arms around her, hugging her fiercely and kissing her on the lips. Althea, helpless in her embrace, clinging to her for support, stared into her eyes. She did not try to draw away but stood leaning against Fern, her hand on her shoulder, conscious of a feeling of pervading comfort, wanting to prolong the moment. Neither of them said anything as they released each other and turned away to start downstairs.

Mrs. Henshaw was sitting by the tea table. Standing over her was the tall man Fern had called Adam Milner. As they came into the room he took a cup of tea from Mrs. Henshaw and started to stir it. He took a careful sip of the hot liquid and then looked around. Spotting Fern he came over and began to talk. He ignored Althea and she limped across the room to Mrs. Henshaw.

"Do sit down, my dear," said Mrs. Henshaw, removing her canvas carryall from the chair beside her. "Have you heard lately from your aunt?"

"Oh, yes. I usually hear from her every week or so," Althea murmured promptly, but the question surprised her. Had Mrs. Henshaw also lately heard from Marjorie and about what?

"Her friend is still staying with her."

Althea, her attention fastened on Fern across the room, replied absently, "Yes, — Gwen." She saw Fern shrug her shoulders, half-angry at something Milner had said to her. Did Fern like him? Was there something between them? "Do you know anything about her?" The question reached the outer edge of her mind. "No. I have told you that she came after I left." Milner moved closer to Fern, talking into her ear, as if pressing her to answer him. Fern, her hands in the pockets of her tweed skirt, shook her head impatiently.

"... it seems so odd." She had lost the beginning of what Mrs. Henshaw was saying and made no effort to reply. Her eyes were riveted on Fern. Fern had a natural grace. She stood draped against the high back of a chair, her long legs crossed at the ankles, her hands clasped loosely in front of her. She knew nothing about Fern except what Fern had said about her parents and her disagreement with her father. A despairing unhappiness took hold of her as she watched Milner draw closer to Fern, as if he assumed some right to display intimacy in a crowd this way. Was there some tie between them? The other people in the room paid no attention, as if this pairing off of the two of them was a usual thing.

Mrs. Henshaw's voice grew a little louder, as she became aware that Althea was not listening. "It is unlike Marjorie to express such fulsome praise of anyone. I have wondered if perhaps she has fallen prey to someone with an axe to grind. Don't you have any inkling, Althea, who this woman might be and what is her interest in your aunt?"

Her attention caught for a vivid moment. Athea thought, This is fantastic. She must know that Marjorie has always had crushes on women. And to talk to me about it! She must be alarmed. She said, "Oh, no. I don't know anything about her. Marjorie almost never mentions her in her letters to me — just occasionally."

Before Mrs. Henshaw could pursue the subject, they were joined by the fair vague girl called Mary. "Oh, Mary, how are you? You are very relieved, I know, about Victor." Althea brought her gaze away from Fern to see the blonde, distracted woman she had met in the doorway on her first visit to the house. Mary glanced at her briefly and nodded.

"Oh, yes, of course! It has been magnificant of you, Mrs. Henshaw! No one else could have succeeded. I cannot tell you how grateful I am. What could we have done without you? I know it has been a terrible task to get Victor into England." The plaintive voice trailed off.

"Yes, yes, my dear. Now don't be unhappy. I know the future is not settled, but I am sure everything will work out." Mrs. Henshaw leaned over to pat Mary's hand.

But her sympathy seemed only to release the flood of helpless loneliness that was pent up in Mary's heart. Her tears overflowed. "I am so frightened. While I was here alone, waiting for Victor, I was so fearful of what might happen to him. Now Victor seems to be surrounded by danger — such threatening people, and the place where we are living is so sordid — so dirty and noisy. I never saw London like this. My parents always stayed in the West End. Victor doesn't seem to mind it. He says he is used to it. He says it doesn't matter. He is just afraid that his cello will be stolen. He takes it with him everywhere. It is dreadful to live like this."

Mrs. Henshaw, eyeing her carefully, asked, "Your parents won't send you any money?"

"How can I ask them? They are entirely unsympathetic with Victor. They say if he is an anarchist or communist, they won't have anything to do with him and the sooner I leave him the better. I don't know what to do. We won't have any money left at all in a little while."

"My dear! Well, drink this tea. It will make you feel better." Mrs. Henshaw thrust the steaming cup towards her and Mary took it mechanically. "Naturally Victor has no money coming in if he has no professional engagements. We can't expect him to give music lessons. Perhaps if I go to see McGregor — that is the name of his agent, isn't it? — I can persuade him to give Victor an advance against his performance at the Albert Hall next month. Now do pull yourself together, Mary. Victor has told me you are lonely. But since you have been in London before, you must have friends here. No? I suppose perhaps you are shy about getting in touch with them —" Mrs. Henshaw trailed off for a moment and Althea knew that she was thinking of Mary's parents — well-to-do, culture-seeking Americans whose visits abroad introduced them only to hotels and museums. "In any case, you can make new friends. Victor, I know, is entirely taken up with his music and his fellow musicians. You must not allow him to cut you off from other people. If you do not like the people who surround him you must seek others."

Mrs. Henshaw's positive tone seemed to strengthen Mary. She wiped away her tears, and sipping her tea, glanced around the room. She certainly is not as young as I thought she was, Althea thought, studying the long, pale, delicate-skinned face. She must be older than Victor.

Mary said, "I don't mind his fellow musicians, though some of them are rather odd. At home I was on the music committee for the orchestra supported by my city. That is how I met Victor, when he came to play as soloist one season."

"And you married him against your parents' wishes," Mrs. Henshaw concluded.

"Oh, not exactly! Victor is so — personable, you know, such a fastidious man. Of course you know that. My parents were uneasy about my marrying someone so foreign, but they did not dislkie him and they admire his musical gifts. It was only later that they disapproved, when they learned about his political associations — such strange people gathering around him."

Althea saw Mrs. Henshaw give a little nod, as if confirming some thought of her own.

Suddenly Mary burst out, "Those dreadful men! They never leave Victor alone. He has given them all our money in the hope they will leave him in peace. But they do not. He curses them and grows so angry that I am afraid he will do something desperate. But they pay no attention. They might as well be made of wood or stone. Victor gets upset. When I ask him why doesn't he simply order them to stay away from him, he says they are his people, he can't deny them. They do not like me. They think I have had a bad influence on Victor — turned him away from his father's memory."

"Do they threaten you?" Mrs. Henshaw demanded.

Mary shook her head. "I never speak to them. Can they speak English? It is Victor they come to see. Oh, Mrs. Henshaw, I am really frightened. My parents refuse to send me any more money because they know it all goes to Victor and he gives it to these vultures. My parents think that if they refuse to help me, I shall be forced to leave Victor and go back home to them."

"And would you go?" Mrs. Henshaw's question was as sharp as a sword thrust.

"Oh, I cannot desert him! And yet sometimes I feel it would not mean a great deal to him. I think he actually forgets about me very often." Mary's eyes had dropped and an expression of wistful sadness appeared in her face.

"Do these men demand money from you?"

Mary was slow to answer. "Not directly from me. They think I have money — that Victor married me because I have money. It is always Victor they come to see, and

they always speak in an incomprehensible language. If
Victor is not home, they simply go away. There are always
two or three of them together. I think they know that
they frighten me. They creep up the stairs at our lodgings
so that I do not hear them until they knock on the door.
If I am alone and get angry with them, they just stand
there and then leave. It is as if they had no nerves — no
feelings. Do you know who they are? Doesn't this seem
strange to you — this sort of thing happening in London?"
Mrs. Henshaw took a sip of tea. "Oh, no, not strange
at all. London is a magnet for people like this — people
who have left their own countries in protest against oppression of some sort or have been driven out and have come
here as refugees. I do not know these men you speak of
as individuals but I can tell you that they are Victor's
countrymen. His father was an important man to them —
a martyr to their cause. They cannot understand why Victor
stands aloof from them."
"What do they want him to do?" Mary asked despair-
ingly. "What can he do?"
Mrs. Henshaw did not answer at once. Althea thought
that she was silently reflecting on Mary's inability to
understand the situation in which she found herself. Then
Mrs. Henshaw put her teacup down as if she had come to
a decision. "I think you must face the fact, my dear, that
in marrying Victor you have entered a world in which neither
your past experience nor your expectations have any value.
It is a highly political world and its politics are quite different from what you are accustomed to. These men who
dog Victor's steps are members of one group among many
who carry on a bitter hidden warfare for the dominion of
their country. They are in exile. At home there is a price
on their heads, I am sure. They seek to undermine the
present government of their country in order that they
may return to form a new one. Victor's father was a famous

warrior in their cause. They expect Victor to take his place as a focus for their loyalties."

Mary burst out. "But how ridiculous! Victor has no interest in politics. He thinks only of music. Oh, he gets excited sometimes after he has had a visit from these people, and talks about how his country will become great again as it was in the past, if only it can get rid of the strangers that have come to dominate it. But then he begins thinking about his country's music — its great songs, its composers who have in the past sought recognition abroad. How can he give up music for violence, for fighting?"

"No, he is not bloodthirsty and yet the whole history of his people, even his father's life, was filled with dreadful, bloody deeds — people murdered and thrown out of windows, people tortured to death, savagery inspired by the thirst for revenge. You must realize this, Mary. Victor, I am afraid, emulates the ostrich and sticks his head in the sand. But he cannot escape these people by pretending they are not here. I do not know how to advise you, except to counsel patience. Perhaps in time these men will realize that Victor is of no use to them, that he is not made of the stuff of warriors, like his father. But you must remember that there have been artists — great artists — great musicians — who have in the past been able to lead their countries — Paderewski, for example. I am distressed that you are short of money, that you haven't a suitable place to live. This may improve when Victor gets more professional engagements. But don't upbraid Victor. He cannot stand any sort of reproach." As Mary drew back, plainly disappointed at not having received a more decided answer to her questions, Mrs. Henshaw added, "I shall come to see you, Mary. Perhaps we can find some better sort of lodging for you, somewhere not so convenient for these men to visit."

Resigned, Mary stood and pulling on her gloves, said

goodbye. Mrs. Henshaw took off her spectacles and wiped the lenses with her thumb. Althea, seeing this, was transported immediately back to Marjorie's house ten years before. She longed to take them from her and remove the film that must obscure them. Instead, Mrs. Henshaw put them back on and picked up her teacup.

But Althea heard no more of what she was saying. Glancing across the room she was in time to see Fern walk out of the door followed by Adam Milner. The sight brought her back to the feeling of anger that had seized her when she had first seen them together. Why did Fern go with him? She seemed to indicate that she did not like him, but perhaps was this some sort of disguise for her real feelings? Dimly Althea was aware that the emotion that surged through her was jealousy — a violent, unreasonable wish to exclude everyone else from Fern's life. But had she any real reason to feel this?

The feeling was a cloud that enveloped her as she journeyed back to her own rooms, blocking her more reasonable self. Fern had kissed her, Fern had held her in a sudden, close embrace. And she had responded, unguardedly, not only with her lips but with a warmth that came from the very depths of her body. She had felt no impulse to shrink from Fern but instead to seek a closer bond. And yet, only a little while later, Fern had shown every sign of intimacy with someone else — with a man.

In her room in Mrs. Tyndal's house she sat in the deepening gloom struggling with this intimate monster, striving against what seemed to her a self-betrayal, a shattering of the coolness of spirit that she had so carefully built up through the years to protect herself from disappointment and despair and which now she herself was destroying.

Gradually her perturbation began to subside. She remembered, with an astonishing clarity, a memory unearthed from the careful burial of years, how she had felt under the tropical warmth generated by Elsie's bodily presence — the blossoming of her being, her eagerness to reach out beyond herself (so strange a thing in her experience), the bright and cheerful colors in which the world suddenly was clothed, the bubbling joy that trembled in her so close to the surface, that had spilled over, in fact, once or twice, beyond her power to hold it back, when she was near Elsie.

Mrs. Tyndal, coming with her evening meal, exclaimed at her failure to light the lamp, rousing her enough to make the expected sounds of response. But she spent the rest of the evening sinking deeper into despair, until the depth of her misery drove her to get into bed. There, at least, in the warmth and dark, she could seek forgetfulness. She took her clothes off slowly, looking down at her naked self in a scrutiny that she usually avoided. Of course Fern could not love her. Who could find attractive this bony body with its undeveloped breasts and shrivelled leg? In tears she got into the bed and put out the light, realizing for the first time that it had been Elsie who had taught her to hate her body.

For several days this rancor simmered in her, interfering with her reading in the British Museum Reading Room, making her brusque with people she met at lectures, preventing her from seeking out Mrs. Henshaw or the few acquaintances she made in London, diminishing the pleasure she had felt in being at last in an intellectual world where people spoke endlessly, wittily, penetratingly of ideas, of concepts. Her unhappiness showed so strongly in her manner that Mrs. Tyndal, bringing her tea one afternoon, lingered in her room, ignoring the array of books and papers spread on the round table. Typically Mrs. Tyndal would have entered with quiet steps and a brief Good afternoon and would have left again at once, overawed by the evidence of scholarly study. But this time she set the big tray down and said, "Do you feel all right, Miss Richards? This is a bad time of year for the influenza and such. Aren't you studying too hard?"

Althea, surprised, looked up to see the kindly anxiety in her eyes. No, she said, she was all right. She was just preoccupied with something she was studying. Why did Mrs. Tyndal think something was wrong?

"Well, you haven't been out much. And that young lady who came with you one day — she hasn't been back. I know you have not gone out with your American friends who come to fetch you in the evenings."

So Mrs. Tyndal really kept an eye on her, thought Althea. "Don't worry about me, Mrs. Tyndal. I'll have this paper finished in a day or so and then I'll be as sociable as ever."

November with its fogs and cheerless days was waning. One morning, shortly after breakfast, there was a knock on her door and she said, "Come in," thinking it was someone come to fetch her breakfast tray. But it was Fern who opened the door and said, "Hallo!" She was gay and smiling. But halfway across the room she stopped, aware instantly of the cold lack of welcome. Had she, thought Althea in anguish, in a turmoil of mixed yearning and rejection, meant to kiss me?

Instead Fern walked over to the window and looked out at the throng of people moving across the square from the Tube station on their way to work. She said casually, "I haven't seen you at Mrs. Henshaw's."

"I haven't been there."

"Oh. Well, I haven't been to tea very often myself." Fern turned away from the window. "I have a chance at a small part in the new production of Shaw's *Major Barbara*. It's not much. I walk on and say two lines. But it means I can be there in the rehearsals and all that."

Her suppressed enthusiasm welled in her voice. But Althea only said, "That's nice."

Fern exploded, "Yes, you can say it is that! It's my

first real chance. Oh, Althy, aren't you happy for me?"
Althea was silent and Fern turned away again. Presently
Althea asked, "Does your friend — that man — like the
theater?"
Fern turned back to her, puzzled and then enlightened.
"Oh, you mean Adam Milner. No, he doesn't like the theater.
Oh, he goes for social reasons — if he is invited or it seems
the proper thing to do. He hasn't any use for actors and
actresses."
They were both silent for a moment and then Fern
asked, "Did you think I didn't come to see you because of
him?"
Althea said nothing. Fern came over and knelt down
by the side of her chair. "Althy, I'm sorry but it was because of the play. I forgot about everything else — no, I
didn't forget you — but I didn't seem to have time. The
company is going on tour after the new year and with luck
I can go with them."
The coaxing tone of her voice softened Althea in spite
of herself. There was always this fresh, springlike, youthful
disingenuousness about Fern. Lost in her old masochistic
gloom the remembrance of this had faded and now here
was Fern, as enchanting as when she had first met her.
Fern, looking up into her face, noticed the lightening
of her mood. She chattered on and presently they were
on their old footing. When she left she bent over Althea
to kiss her, hesitating for an instant to see if she would be
accepted, and Althea did not pull back. She breathed into
Althea's ear, "Althy, I love you." Althea, unnerved by this,
was passive in her arms as she gave her one last hug before
jumping up and going out of the room.
The November weather prevented her from moving as
freely about London as she would otherwise have done
and she stayed closely to her usual daily routine. December
came and one day Fern came running in to say that she

had to go to Germany. "I have to spend Christmas with my parents. I'm leaving tomorrow. I tried to get out of it but they're not having any of my nonsense — that's Dad. I'm to spend Christmas in Berlin and that's that."

Fern was looking at her closely, her sharp, informed eyes examining her face. Althea looked away and said primly, "I expect you'll enjoy it."

Fern laughed and suddenly reached over and hugged her. "Oh, Althy! But it won't be so long." She looked down into Althea's eyes as if searching for something, holding her all the while closely to her. When she finally relaxed her embrace she said gently, "I'll miss you, Althy." Althea put her head on her shoulder in acquiescence.

Mrs. Tyndal, bringing her tea in the afternoon, came in with a cheerful smile. "Oh, whatever, Miss Richards! Do you know, Christmas is almost upon us. Are you going away for the holidays?"

Althea looked at her blankly. She had been aware that Christmas was drawing near. The scent of Christmas greens filled the shops, which teemed with more people than usual, apparently many of them from the provinces, as Fern called the rest of England outside London. But this fact had not made much of an impression on her beyond the realization that Fern would be gone. So she could only reply to Mrs. Tyndal that she did not think so.

But the next day she had a letter from Baltimore. Another aunt, an elder sister of Marjorie, was coming to London with her husband. They would be at the Grosvenor Hotel and they expected her to join them for the Christmas festivities. The letter was dated much earlier, at the beginning of December. It had been longer than usual on the way. Her aunt spoke of being at the Grosvenor on December 15 or perhaps a little before. Now it was already the fourteenth. Althea picked up the newspaper to verify the date. She could expect a visit at any moment.

Her aunt arrived the next morning, coming to Mrs. Tyndal's by cab, chiefly annoyed by the lack of a telephone by which she could reach her. Mrs. Tyndal did have a phone in her own part of the house, said Althea, and in an emergency she would take a message and allowed Althea or the Indian girl to use it to reply.

Her aunt, a big, robust woman who was used to having her own way, brushed aside what she said. "Oh, I daresay it is all right. It was just a nuisance, when we arrived at the hotel, not to be able to get in touch with you at once. I felt rather frustrated. But it is not important, because we expect you will come and stay with us at the Grosvenor while we're here. There's no point to you being here by yourself. I told Marjorie that was what I would do."

Althea, angry but not wishing to show it, murmured, "I can't do that. I've got all my things here. And everybody knows how to find me here."

"Oh, you can leave your things here, of course. And what do you mean by everybody? They must be the people we shall be seeing while we are here."

Althea spoke through her teeth. "I'm sorry, Aunt Susan, I have made a lot of friends. I have my own routine. I don't want to disrupt it."

Her aunt looked at her as if startled by this rebellion. "Oh, well, Mrs. Tyndal — that's the name of your landlady? — can tell them where to find you."

"I expect some of them will be put off by that. They expect to find me here and they're not used to going to the Grosvenor."

Her aunt looked offended. Althea could guess what was going on in her mind: Marjorie never did use good sense in looking after her. She said, "Well, really, Althea. You've been over here for almost six months. I should think you'd be glad to see us."

"Oh, yes, yes!" Althea hastened to make amends. "Oh,

yes, I'm very glad you have come for Christmas, Aunt Susan. But I think I'd better stay here and just come over to see you during the day."

Grudgingly her aunt agreed to this. Althea would spend all her evenings with her aunt and uncle in the staid, red-carpeted splendor of the Grosvenor. This wouldn't make much difference, thought Althea. Most of her usual activities would be suspended for the holidays anyway, like everyone else's, and Fern would not be in London. The middle-aged and elderly family friends who had dutifully kept in touch with her through the months she had been in London would certainly also spend their evenings with her aunt and uncle. She was prepared for an uneventful, traditional, family-dominated Christmas such as she had endured many times in Baltimore.

But in the daytime she savored the quiet pleasure of her own freedom, heightened by this parried threat. The next afternoon she went out to St. John's Wood to find Mrs. Henshaw. When she arrived around tea time Mrs. Henshaw was not there. She waited, thankful that Adam Milner was not present, regretful that Fern had already left. She had seen very little of Milner during the few visits she had paid Mrs. Henshaw in November. When she questioned her, Fern had said that he was away. He had some mysterious business to attend to that took him out of London often.

She sat down in the armchair next to Mrs. Henshaw's desk, idly surveying the stacks of letters and papers that covered its top. All at once Mrs. Henshaw came bustling into the room and flung her canvas carryall on top of the clutter. Her delicate skin was flushed from the briskness with which she had walked in the cold damp air from the Tube station. She swept off her hat and her fine-spun pale hair spread out around her head. She wore a dark skirt and a long-sleeved white silk blouse under her coat and seemed to feel no need for anything warmer in the chilly room. Her desk was in the corner farthest from the fireplace, in the grate of which there was always a heap of smouldering ashes into which anyone at any time might dump fresh coals as long as there were any in the coal scuttle on the hearth.

She was in the midst of a sentence — "so fortunate that most of my private pupils are going out of town for the holidays — oh, how are you, Althea? Of course, the school is closing down for a fortnight. Otherwise I don't know what I should have done. Dealing with government officials takes so much time. You'd think they would realize that even refugee children must be fed and clothed while decisions are being made about their disposal."

She threw her coat over the back of her chair and sat down. As if suddenly reminded of something she looked directly at Althea. "I have meant to ask — what are you doing about Christmas? I must write and let Marjorie know that you are looked after."

Althea was glad to be able to say, "My aunt and uncle from Baltimore have arrived. They are staying at the Grosvenor. They've come to spend Christmas in England."

"Oh, then, they will look after you. I am much relieved. I did not like to leave you so much on your own."

"Oh, don't worry. I don't need looking after."

Mrs. Henshaw cast her a brief glance, recognizing the injured dignity in her voice. She said smoothly, "It is always nice to have congenial company at this time of year. Marjorie would have been upset if you were left here alone. But she must have known that her sister and brother-in-law were coming."

"Are you going away?"

"I am going to Paris." She stopped abruptly and looked at Althea again. "Do you remember Elsie? She was with me when I stayed with your aunt in Washington ten years ago."

"Yes."

"Such a clever girl. You remember that at that time she obtained a post as a translator at the League of Nations in Geneva. She at once set out to make herself an expert in economic matters and political theory. She was able to study for a while at the Sorbonne. She has become one of the most valued people in the International Labour Office. She is a respected authority on the relations between government and labor, on the impact of economic development on society — especially in backward countries — and political affairs. She is taking her Christmas holiday in Paris. She had wanted to go to New York — she loves New York — but she cannot take enough time. She never comes to London — she dislikes England. So if I am to see her I must go to Paris. I have the opportunity. Princess Czerny has invited me to come and stay with her, so I can see Elsie at the same time."

Elsie. While Mrs. Henshaw talked on, Althea tested the memory, still tender to touch, in spite of Fern. "She's not married?"

There was a slight hesitation in Mrs. Henshaw's manner. "No. She says she does not wish to marry — though she has had several opportunities — excellent ones. She is very independent by nature — and then she has embraced some rather advanced ideas about the institution of marriage. She believes that everyone must be perfectly free in their personal relationships. That is all very well, but one's own freedom must always be balanced by one's responsibilities to others. I cannot accept anarchy in one's private life, any more than in one's public. But Elsie is quite adamant. Marriage, she says, is so outmoded a concept and it is nothing but a trap for a woman. She does not lack male interest. Men seem to find her fascinating. Perhaps as time goes on she will change her mind. Young people often do when they experience more of life."

Althea said nothing. Once again, she thought, is there an echo here of the young Janet Welby, in rebellion against her parents?

The approach of Christmas became increasingly obvious. There was a lot of coming and going in Mrs. Tyndal's private quarters, young people mostly, and lively parties in the evenings, with Welsh voices raised in singing, the hall festooned with holly wreaths. Mrs. Tyndal apologized to her the mornings after for any disturbance, but she said, oh, no, sometimes half-wishing she could have joined in the jollity. She was alone on the upper floors. The Indian girl had gone somewhere for the holidays and the young men upstairs had vanished. Even Mrs. Henshaw's house, when she went there for one brief visit to see her before she left for Paris, was decorated in a haphazard way with several stray wisps of greenery, no doubt put up by one of the lodgers.

The two weeks of Christmas passed more quickly than Althea expected. After Mrs. Henshaw left for Paris she spent more of the daytime hours than she anticipated with her aunt. She had forgotten, she realized, the massive steam-roller effect of her relatives' personalities. Used as she was to Marjorie's loose-reined ways, she had encountered her other aunts' driving demands only on occasion. Now she found herself caught up in going to shops — for knitted things, toys, china, all sorts of things to eat and drink put up in bottles and tins — she knew her aunt intended to return to Baltimore well supplied with luxuries for her own household and gifts for her friends. They went to art galleries, museums — her aunt had seen them before but a quick return visit was obligatory — matinees at theaters and concerts at the Albert Hall. She did not think all this was done so much for present personal enjoyment as from a sense of duty to her friends to whom she must report when she was back home. The first time or so they went out together her aunt consciously reminded herself from time to time that Althea was crippled, that her lameness must be taken into account. But within a few minutes, she had forgotten and Althea only reminded her when some situation, involving a long flight of stairs, proved impossible. It was a true lesson in independence, thought Althea, striving to keep up with her through the throngs, often frightened by the danger of being thrown off her precarious balance. But she was also wryly pleased by this neglect, for it could only mean that her own self-assurance had grown to the point where someone else took her independence for granted.

In the evenings there was always a social gathering in the suite of rooms her aunt and uncle had taken in the Grosvenor. Sitting in a corner, unwilling as always to call attention to her iron brace, Althea, watching, thought, We might as well be back in Eutaw Place — staid, bored, expensively dressed people talkative only about happenings in Baltimore.

Christmas came and then New Year's. Her aunt and uncle prepared to leave. They would go briefly to Paris and then return to New York from Cherbourg. The day they left Althea came back to Mrs. Tyndal's house with a sense of relief. As she stepped into the house she was welcomed by a cascade of Chopin from the Indian girl's rooms. So she was back, too. Things were back to normal, she thought, climbing slowly up the stairs, inundated by the waves of piano music. Was Mrs. Henshaw back, she wondered? But what she really wanted was to have Fern back. Sometimes she was dismayed at the thought that perhaps Fern would not return, that her parents would insist that she stay with them.

So a day or so later, her heart took a great leap, as she sat in her rooms with a book open in front of her, at the unmistakable sound of Fern's step on the stairs. She had not locked her door and Fern came in, bringing the damp chill air of January with her. Even as she came over and swept Althea into her arms, Althea saw that she wore a new winter coat and gloves and a fur hat, which she tossed off at once, shaking her short curls loose.

"Whew! I'm glad to be back!" She pulled off her gloves and walked about the room. "But I was lucky. I didn't have to spend more than a couple of days in Berlin. My mother persuaded my father to spend most of the holidays in Paris. She loves Paris. Paris wakes her up, she says. She dragged me through every shop in Paris, I swear — did I like this? Did this look better on her? Was the color all right? God! Even the women waiting on us thought I was a nuisance. I heard one of them say under her breath, 'Quel bête!' because I hadn't paid any attention to what she and my mother had been discussing for half an hour. The shopwomen in Paris love my mother. She hits it off with them right away. Paris wakes my Dad up too but he hates it. He doesn't approve of the French, though they were our allies in the War. He says they are flighty, unreliable. They don't make as good soldiers as the Germans. They need Napoleon, he says. They're too volatile — not solid like the Germans. Well, I must say, I don't think you could get the average Frenchman as regimented as the Germans. They hate authority. They don't like being told what to do. I said that just shows that it isn't easy to get them to put their brains on the shelf. Oh, we had a few arguments — we always do. Oh, I was forgetting! Mrs. Henshaw was in Paris."

"She told me she was going there."

"Oh, she did? Well, she must have decided to go after I left London. You know, I've told you that my mother thinks she is the most wonderful woman in the world. One day when we came back to the hotel from shopping there was a message that Mrs. Henshaw had called and invited my mother to come and have tea with her. I don't know how she learned where we were. But Mrs. Henshaw at the Crillon! You know, that's only for people with a lot of money."

Althea nodded. "Did you go?"

"Oh, yes. My mother was terribly pleased. We went and there we were being ushered into a very expensive suite with deep-piled rugs on the floor and sparkling chandeliers and those great overstuffed French armchairs — it really all called for cloth-of-gold evening gowns and tiaras. Mrs. Henshaw came hurrying through one of those tall white and gold panelled doors to greet us. She was dressed as she usually is — a white blouse with a high neck and a dark skirt. I was really carried away by the contrast. But no matter how she is dressed, you could easily believe that she is the grand dutchess of somewhere."

"She was visiting a friend — a Princess something who invited her to come to Paris. I understood that she is the head of some charitable organization that rescues orphaned and abandoned children."

"Yes, she told us that."

"Was Elsie with her — did you meet Elsie?"

"Elsie — yes. Do you know her?"

"I did, once. She stayed at my aunt's house in Washington, years ago. She came with Mrs. Henshaw then. I've not seen her since."

Fern, catching a tone in her voice, looked at her curiously.

Althea asked, "What is she like now?"

"Well, you know, she is an official at the League of Nations now — quite a high-up one. I wouldn't say she is a good-looking woman but she is quite striking — and very forceful. She came in while we were chatting with Mrs. Henshaw. She had on a Russian fur hat and a fur coat, with a lot of bangles, earrings, that sort of thing, very soignee. I must admit I felt we were peasants in comparison, when she swept into the room and acknowledged Mrs. Henshaw's introductions with a kind of absentminded graciousness. What an entrance that would have made on the stage! But she gave Mrs. Henshaw herself a keen look, as if she really wanted to know how she was. In fact, I think perhaps she was disappointed to see that Mrs. Henshaw was not alone, so that she could tell her something of importance to herself."

"Did she stay and talk to you?"

The tightness in Althea's voice reached Fern's ear. "Not really. Oh, she stayed a few minutes and we all made polite conversation. But it was obvious that she had no interest in us. After a while she got up and went off into another room. I suppose she knows Mrs. Henshaw's hostess. My mother is very curious about her. When we were coming away she was speculating how even a high-up official of the League of Nations could afford to dress like that. She is apparently not married, so my mother wonders if she had a friend, a male friend, who keeps her in such luxuries." Fern glanced at Althea but Althea sat frowning at the floor, as if she might not have heard all she said.

Fern decided to go on talking. "If that is so, I wonder what he makes of Mrs. Henshaw? She is obviously a very important person to Elsie. It is amazing how people become attached to Mrs. Henshaw. There she sat, in the midst of all that ornate splendor of shining floor and magnificent furniture, such a quaint sort of figure, with that hideous old canvas carryall she always has with her, apparently only intent on the person she is concerned with. Her hands are always busy. Have you noticed her hands — such fine-boned, soft-skinned, agile fingers that seem to have a life of their own. My mother gets so upset when she sees her take off her spectacles and rub her thumb over the lenses — you've seen her do that. Well, anyway, she is remarkable. She reduces everyone, no matter who they are, rich or poor, gifted or stupid, weak or powerful, to their essential nature. We all have a common denominator to her."

Fern glanced again at Althea. Althea had raised her head and now answered her glance. Encouraged, Fern said, "You know, there is something else that my mother was speculating about. Mrs Henshaw is very fond of Elsie. In fact, she acts as if she was her daughter. She is the only person I have ever seen Mrs. Henshaw treat in a truly intimate way — just something in the air in those few minutes when Elsie was with us." Fern looked at Althea again. "She couldn't be her daughter, could she?"

"What!" In her own ears Althea's voice sounded like a shout.

Taken aback, Fern said, "No, I suppose that's fantastic. There is no physical resemblance between them. Elsie is dark with big features — not at all like her. Did Mrs. Henshaw ever have children?"

"No. I'm sure I would have heard about them from Marjorie. She has known Elsie all her life — Elsie's life — I think."

"Well, she was married before she married Roger Henshaw, wasn't she?"

"Not married. She was disinherited by her family because she had an affair with a man they didn't approve of."

Fern whooped. "An affair! Mrs Henshaw!"

"It was all very unhappy. Marjorie says it was tragic, really, because she was young and very much in love."

"And just as stubborn as she is now, I'll bet. Who was this man — someone from the lower orders?" Fern's voice was mocking.

"He was a Jew — a German Jew — a very brilliant man."

"Oh, that was it."

"Yes, and he was a socialist and believed in free love — no marrying. But he had been married before and I suppose divorced."

"Then is Elsie his daughter?"

Althea looked at her for a long time. "It has never
occurred to me that Elsie was anything but a protege of
hers. I wonder if Marjorie knows and has never said. She
is very loyal to Mrs Henshaw — Janet, that is, to her. She
would not say anything she did not think Mrs. Henshaw
would want talked about." She lapsed into silence, thinking of Marjorie's house and Elsie and herself.

After a while she became aware that Fern had not said
anything. She felt a soft touch on her cheek. Fern had
come to stand beside her chair and lean over her.

"What are you thinking about, Althy?"

"I loved Elsie when she was staying with us." It was
a simple statement but she astonished herself by making
it. Only to Fern could she have spoken the words.

Fern was looking down into her eyes, her own full of
sympathy. "But Elsie didn't love you. Was it very bad?"

When Althea did not respond, she turned away and
said as if to dispel the sadness, "I saw Mrs. Henshaw again
on the boat train. She had somebody with her — a poor-
looking little woman who had left all her relatives and
belongings behind in Germany. It is very sad to see somebody like that." Fern paused and then burst out. "It's
like coming out into fresh air to get away from there, Althy!
There's a sense of menace there, something oppressive, even
if you don't realize just what is going on. People are getting
so that they don't talk out loud, as if they are uneasy that
somebody might be listening. There are all these groups of
bullies marching about, in uniform — all this Prussian heel-
clicking and military shouting. I sat in the window of a
hotel — I went to visit a friend — all one afternoon and
there was this constant marching to military music. In
fact, I was scared to go out with some of my old pals at
night — this was in Munich. You hear about people just
disappearing — people trying to get visas and leave the

country or just dropping out of sight. But my father still won't believe that the Germans will fall for Hitler. Just the same, all you have to do is go and see one of these rallies — just thousands of people all yelling themselves hoarse in a kind of hysteria. As far as I am concerned the handwriting is on the wall but Dad can't read it. He says the Nazis are tolerated because they're a protection from the Communists. Good God! Do you have to embrace one devil to protect you from what you think is another?"

She talked on, brimming with the energy of her indignation. Althea, bemused now with the happiness of having her there once more, in the same room with her, let the talk flow by her with an uncharacteristic heedlessness. There might be grave portents of future disaster in what Fern was saying but for the moment her own inner joy bubbled up and overflowed.

She suddenly realized that Fern was talking about something else. "Do you remember that when I left there was a chance that I'd get to go as understudy in a company that was going on tour?"

Althea felt a quick check to her euphoria. "Are you going to get it? Are you going away?"

"Not yet. These are early days yet. But I'm to have a chance at it."

In the days that followed Fern alternated between effervescent good spirits sparked by the hopeful outlook for her stage career and the same taciturn moodiness that had so often quenched her natural cheerfulness before her visit to her parents. Althea wondered about this. She had not gone again to Mrs. Henshaw's house, waiting to hear definitely that she had come back from Paris, and therefore she had seen nothing of Adam Milner. Fern did not mention him. Where was he?

Then a few days passed and Fern did not come to see

her. When she did, at first she had little to say, but then she seemed to make an effort to rouse herself from the cloud of thought in which she was lost.

"I say, Althy, would you like to go and see the new show at the National Gallery?"

"What is it?"

"The drawings and prints of Kathe Kollwitz, the German artist. I think you would find it interesting. I've seen her work in Berlin."

They went in the bus, Fern lapsing into silence, Althea intrigued as always by the throngs in the street and the traffic milling about Trafalgar Square. They walked slowly through the exhibit, Althea caught up almost at once in the tragic, emotionladen portrayals in black and white of human suffering. She caught her breath at the impact made on her by these powerful depictions of the effects of war and poverty. Spontaneously she turned to Fern, forgetting Fern's brooding silence which had brought some constraint to their companionship.

Fern's preoccupation fled under her shining eyes. "Wonderful artist, isn't she? Do you see there — her working women — do you see how she makes you feel their despair, their anger, but also their determination to survive — these destitute women in their ragged clothes, with their half-starved children standing outside the closed factory gates."

Althea smiled at her, happy that Fern's withdrawn taciturnity had gone in this burst of enthusiasm.

Fern went on eagerly, "You realize, don't you, that Kathe Kollwitz has always shocked and upset conservative people. Why, back before the War, when she was to be awarded a gold medal for her Weavers' Cycle, which was about a sixteenth century working people's uprising, the Kaiser ordered that it not be given to her because he was afraid of the political statement it made." Fern broke off and then said with a laugh, "I wish I had been born with a real gift as an artist. Instead, all I have is the desire to be able to do something worthwhile. It doesn't matter what the medium would be — painting, music, even speechmaking, rabble-rousing — some vehicle to make a protest against all the hypocrisy we live with. You know, Kathe Kollwitz is one of the people who is getting into more and more trouble with those who are coming into power in Germany."

"What kind of trouble?"

"Political trouble. Anybody who is a real artist, a real creative person, is looked upon as an enemy of the state. These people are trying to make everybody conform to what they call being German. They've forgotten what Germany was in the past — the writers, the poets, the philosophers, the composers — people who could not live in an environment restricted to militarism and enforced conformity. You have to be an Aryan, whatever that's supposed to be, and that means anyone who doesn't believe in the master race or is a Jew or doesn't want to be a mindless follower of this miserable little idiot Hitler, is outside the law and fair game for the bullies. It's sickening, and my father is always making excuses for them. He says Germany has been badly treated by the French and English and that it is only natural that they'll follow a leader who will promise them a rebirth of pride in their country. I don't buy that. You can be proud of your country without trying to demolish somebody else. What kind of a country can it be that is based on the oppression of some of its citizens? What kind of a government is it that comes to power by organizing gangs of rowdies — that's all the Freicorps, as it's called, are — to attack people in the streets and murder them with the connivance of the police?"

Althea, noticing that Fern's fervent voice had called the attention of a guard peering through the gallery door, put her hand on her arm. Fern stopped and glanced around. They were almost alone. Then she shrugged. But Althea, uncomfortable, said, "Let's walk around a bit."

They went slowly through some of the surrounding galleries where the permanent collections were hung. At first Fern paid no attention to the paintings, her thoughts still centered on Kathe Kollwitz and her social protest. But all at once she seemed to become aware that they were surrounded by opulent canvases of elegantly dressed women and forceful, powerful men in impeccably tailored clothes against sumptuous backgrounds of expensive furniture and art objects.

She let out a low whistle. "Why, look where we are! No less than a gallery full of Charles Russet's portraits."

She stopped in front of a large canvas displaying a self-confident, reserved woman meticulously dressed in the style of 1910, her hair in a pompadour, seated in an armchair contemplating the viewer with a full stare that just missed being challenging. Althea, leaning on Fern's arm, bent forward to read the plaque under the picture. Fern said, "It's his wife, of course. You wouldn't get very far with that lady, would you?"

"She's pretty formidable."

"I was going to tell you about Charles, wasn't I?"

"But you never have."

"Let's sit down here," said Fern, leading her to the long bench in the middle of the gallery. "Well, he was a close friend of Roger Henshaw, the archeologist, Mrs. Henshaw's husband. They were all three at Oxford together. As a matter of fact I gather that people wondered why she chose Roger instead of Charles. He had that sort of charm for women. Let's say he had money, he had good looks and he was a brilliant painter, once he settled down to it. As you see." Fern glanced around at the paintings on the walls. "But later in life he got bored with painting — or dissatisfied with what he was doing and became embroiled in politics — the politics of the Left. He wouldn't be pinned down to a particular party but he believed in radical reform. This was before the War, of course, before the Russian Revolution. He became involved with the revolutionaries in the Balkans. He decided he had to help them throw off the yoke of the Austro-Hungarian empire. But he wanted to bring about social revolution as well as independence — for the Macedonians, the Albanians, all that lot. He was quite a wealthy man to begin with but he was careless of his wealth — ran through his own money, but his wife managed to safeguard the major portion of her own so that she still lives in comfort now down in Dorset.

"Mrs. Henshaw has a story about him in Greece. She was there with Roger, who was on an archeological expedition. Charles was detained by the authorities. He had gone on a walking tour that presumably was a cover for some other activities. His wife had stayed in the hotel at Athens. She did not like primitive living conditions and when she learned he was arrested she picked up in disgust and went back to London. But of course that's not what Mrs. Henshaw would do. She began working to get him released. Roger refused to have anything to do with the situation — he was afraid it would endanger his expedition. It took her hours of dealing with governmental officials but she finally managed it. When she got back to London after Roger's death — he died in Turkey of typhoid fever — she found Charles up to his ears in refugee intrigues. He had abandoned his painting — neglected the commissions he had for paintings — left his studio closed up. His wife had left him. She could put up with his philandering — I suppose she thought that was inevitable with such a man — but she could not stand the sort of men he was associating with and she was mortified at being identified as the wife of a man who was in trouble with the authorities. That's

when he began living openly with Mrs. Owens and there
was a big scandal."

"Mrs. Owens?"

"She was originally Nettie Henrietta Challoner from
Georgia — a very popular actress on the American stage.
She was married to an Englishman but apparently she forgot him when she met Charles. It was her money he was
living on then. She didn't mind all his revolutionary friends.
One of them was Victor's father. Charles became very close
friends with him and he was the one who persuaded the
father to give Victor a proper musical education and it was
Mrs. Owens who paid for it."

Fern looked around the gallery again. "There isn't a
portrait of her here, though he did several. He went back
to painting for a few years before he died. Victor was a
little boy then of course and probably pretty bewildered
by it all and Mrs. Henshaw would have noticed that, of
course. She has been his friend since."

"I see. Did you say his wife is still alive?"

"Yes. She lives in Dorset. She will have nothing to do
with anybody who knew Charles — except Mrs. Henshaw.
In fact, Mrs. Henshaw goes there to stay with her every
so often when even she admits she needs a rest. It's a
fine house set in an old garden at the foot of the Downs,
Mrs. Henshaw says, and when she wants a little solitude
a short walk takes her up within sight of the sea and out
onto the breezy peace of the cliffs." Fern looked at Althea
out of the corner of her eye and Althea laughed. Yes, there
was the echo of Mrs. Henshaw's voice. "And, you know,
all this is in spite of the fact that she has always stayed
friends with Mrs. Owens."

"And Mrs. Russet knows that?"

"I'm sure she does. Mrs. Henshaw never disguises anything. She found Mrs. Owens a few years ago — she had
lost track of her during the War — in Paris, destitute, living

in an attic room in an old building, in the middle of a winter so cold the water froze every morning in her washbowl."

"Where is she now?"

"I don't know. I don't think Mrs. Henshaw knows. Every now and then she mentions her and says she is worried about what has happened to her."

They wandered then in a desultory way through the other galleries on their way to the entrance. When they came out of the gallery a light drizzle had stopped and the sky had brightened as if with a promise of sun. They walked to the corner where a woman sat beside a barrow of roasting chestnuts. Althea bought a sack and they walked along peeling chestnuts and eating them.

In the midst of the silence Althea asked, "Did you have a quarrel with your father about coming back to London?"

Fern pulled the shell off a chestnut. "Not exactly. But there were just so many things I was quarreling with him about. And then I'm afraid he will find out about all the things I have been doing that he doesn't know anything about. My mother was getting worried and said I'd better come back here and stay with Mrs. Henshaw. Have I told you how she met her? It was in Paris a couple of years ago, when she was coming back from a visit to London and she lost her handbag in the Gare du Nord. It had her passport and some money in it. Mrs. Henshaw happened to be there too, meeting a train from Budapest with some refugees, and she rescued her, gave her money to get to the American Embassy. My mother stayed in Paris for a while and they became very good friends — you know how Mrs. Henshaw is. My mother helped her with her refugees — they were mostly women and children who were being brought from some famine-stricken place in the Balkans. My mother thinks Mrs. Henshaw is wonderful."

"Yes," said Althea. Walking along this way with Fern in the mild, quiet grey of the afternoon, in the midst of a teeming throng of people, she felt a deep contentment settle on her.

Now quite frequently Fern came to her rooms in the afternoon. It was a cold January, with a few fine, mild days sprinkled in it. Mrs. Tyndal provided them with a tea-tray, so that they spent the time quietly together instead of in the hubbub of Mrs. Henshaw's house. This meant that there was no opportunity for her to see Fern with Adam Milner and she wondered whether this was part of the reason why Fern came here instead. Fern slouched about her room, standing by the window gazing out at the leafless trees in the square below, occasionally mentioning the old lady leading her fat pug along its paths, or the postman dropping letters into the mail slots of the houses nearby. For the most part she was cheerful and there was only a trace of absentmindedness in her manner. Sometimes she came to sit on the arm of Althea's chair and looked down at her as they talked. Then Althea felt an undercurrent in her manner, as if she was waiting to see if Althea would make some intimate move, or would be receptive to one on her own part. As soon as she was aware of this, Althea involuntarily withdrew within herself, angry at herself for doing so, yet captured by a fearfulness she could not overcome. There seemed to be so much more in Fern's background, a much greater fund of sensual experience that froze any outreach of her own.

Very often Fern's mind seemed to dwell on Berlin and her father. It was as if, for all her independence, she could not sever the cord that linked her to her parents.

"The thing is," she said, "Dad doesn't know — he never did know — what I was doing most of the time. I went to classes at the University. Dad didn't understand why I wanted to do that. He thought I ought to find enough to do just doing what all the other American girls did — except that some of them were pretty wild. He wouldn't stand for me going out to parties and dances every night and coming home drunk. So I think he was relieved in a way that I wanted to go to school instead. But he still didn't understand it. Of course I speak German better than he does — I've spoken it half of my life and the people I mingled with didn't seem as foreign to me as they seemed to him. What he didn't know — and what I did everything to keep him from finding out — was that I joined a students' group that was really a political cell — radical, of course, most of them said they were Communists, but as a matter of fact very few of them were members of the Communist Party, but they all thought the Russian Revolution was the millenium. They were a lively bunch — full of ideas and wit."

"Did you agree with them?" Althea turned her head back to look up at her.

"I?" Fern mused for a moment. "Not really. Not all the way. That's my trouble, you know. I can't make up my mind — about anything, it seems." She jumped up from the chair arm. "I'm like Hamlet, you know. My resolution is always sicklied o'er with the pale cast of thought and my enterprises of great pith and moment turn their currents awry and lose the name of action. Me and Hamlet — great minds, you know." She grinned at Althea.

Althea said dryly, "You're play-acting — to yourself. Why, Fern? What are you afraid of?"

After a moment Fern said, twiddling the tassel on the cloth that covered the round table when it was not in use for eating, "I'm not really afraid. I just don't want trouble." She paused for a moment and then burst out, "I want to get out of the kind of life my parents live. I want to do something else — something that is more real, or more real to me. But I go a little way and then I get the wind up. I can't face conflict — real, honest-to-God conflict with my father — at least, I make him the obstacle. I suppose I'm not sure what the result will be — what I'll do, what I'll get into, if I break off from him. He's always been positive about the way he wants to live his life. You can't turn him away from the road he has chosen for himself. That simplifies things, doesn't it? He can't understand how anybody can be any other way — unless they're backboneless, worthless. If you have your eye fixed on a particular goal, you can take everything that happens along the way as necessary and not to be questioned. I don't have that kind of a mind. I keep wondering whether what I do have is worth the effort. As a matter of fact, I don't think my father would let me break away, at least not without a struggle. If I ran away, he would pursue me and fetch me back, even if I am of age. He'd say it is his duty as my father to save me from my own folly. I think he just has a need to bully me — bully somebody. My mother is no use that way. She just can't be bullied and she turns it all aside and leaves him clutching the air, so to speak."

Althea watched as she twisted the tassel around her finger, all the while looking down at the floor. But she did not say anything. This was strange territory to her, this surveillance of an active, demanding father. The nearest she could come to it was the recollection of the remote but threatening control that her grandmother had seemed to have over her, something lying inchoate behind the easygoing, affectionate concern of Marjorie.

"Of course, I could never argue with him very well," Fern was saying, "Because he always came down hard on my ignorance — that I didn't know what I was talking about and I knew I knew what I was talking about, because of the nights I spent in the students' hangout, listening. But I couldn't tell him that. Once or twice I just escaped being caught in one of the raids that the Freicorps made — that's what these Nazi bullies call themselves — on a place where I was. I could have been hurt in the melee — they're quite brutal — or carried off by the police when they finally arrived to break up the fight. And there'd have been hell to pay when Dad found out — not only because he'd forbidden me to get mixed up in these student protests but because he was in the U.S. military on diplomatic service and it would have caused terrible trouble for him."

"So that's why you came to London — to get away from all that."

"Fern hesitated for a moment. "I thought I had made a clean break. But I met up with somebody I knew in Berlin and he persuaded me to go to a gathering with him of several people who have left Germany — escaped, you might say, because they're afraid of what might happen to them if they stayed and the Nazis finally came into power — which seems to be happening. Many of them are clever, gifted people and Jews. I like being with them. They are so much more interesting than the kind of people I'd be mingling with otherwise. But —"

She did not finish what she was saying but stood silently playing with the tassel.

Finally Althea prompted, "But what?"

Fern raised her eyes to look at her. Althea saw in them the shadow she had so often noticed. Whatever it was that made Fern reticent behind her outward gaiety dwelt there now. Fern shifted her gaze elsewhere.

"You can't really escape anything by running away, can you? I suppose it wasn't only Dad that I left Berlin to get away from." She paused for a moment and stood still, dropping the tassel. Then she asked abruptly, "Do you have trouble discouraging men from trying to take you over, take over your life, pry into your affairs, No, I don't suppose you do."

The indirect allusion to her lameness angered Althea, yet in the next moment it cooled and in its dying flash she asked herself, But why does that make me mad? I don't want the trouble of discouraging a man's attentions. It's because it means a lack, of course. I'm limited and I hate the thought of my limitation. She glanced at Fern. Fern was unaware of the passage of fire through her being. She said shortly, "Is that your problem? Is there somebody in Berlin you ran away from?"

Fern looked at her but did not say anything. Althea saw her little shrug.

Fern stayed a while longer but for Althea a deadness had come over their being together. When Fern left she sat for a long time in a mood of deep unhappiness that was not dispelled even when Mrs. Tyndal came to get the tea-tray and gave her a letter from Marjorie that had arrived in the afternoon post. She read it through perfunctorily, only interested by the last sentences: Gwen complains that you've not sent any of those marvelous vignettes of an American in London lately. Are you all right, dear? Althea put the letter down with a feeling of distaste. Gwen.

She did not see Fern for several days and one afternoon, when the pale London sun gave the air a pleasant mildness, she went out to Mrs. Henshaw's house at tea time. The big room was full of people and sound. Some of the people she did not recognize. But Fern was not there, nor was Mrs. Henshaw. She talked for a while with Victor's wife Mary, until presently Victor himself came in, sauntering across the room, nodding to those who spoke to him, and coming to slouch nonchalantly against Mrs. Henshaw's desk, his hands in his pockets, a contented, amiable smile on his smooth sallow face. He kissed Mary, who hurried away to fetch him a cup of tea, and then looked down at Althea seated by the desk.

He had greeted her with a little half-bow and now he said, "I know your aunt, Miss Seymour. She was a patron of the society in Baltimore that invited me to play there for the first time. She was very kind, very enthusiastic about my playing. I remember her with gratitude."

His English was very good, without a marked accent, though there was a slight stumble over the "the" and "w" — enough, thought Althea, to add charm to his generally amiable manner. He went on, after she had murmured a response, "She had met my father when she was in Dalmatia, in the bad time there. She was very sympathetic to my people."

A recollection came to Althea of some of Marjorie's tales of heroic marches over stony mountains and rugged terrain by bands of people, women and children as well as the warriors, whole villages fleeing before an implacable, better-armed enemy. So Victor's father must have been one of the leaders of these refugees. In her letters home she had not mentioned Victor and his wife, hesitating to open up the abundant vein of Marjorie's reminiscence even by a casual reference to that part of the world. Now, perhaps, she should tell Marjorie of this encounter.

She said, "My aunt Marjorie was with the Red Cross in Serbia and southern Russia, in Albania and Greece — I don't remember where else. She has often told me about her experiences."

"I do not remember any of that. I was not there. I was here in London with my mother. I was only a young boy but I was already a musician. I began my professional career very young."

He can't be thirty, thought Althea, and remembered that Mrs. Henshaw had said that he had spent the war years in Paris and London, in exile with his mother, for the sake of avoiding an interruption in his musical training.

Before she could respond, Mary returned, a little breathless, as if the trip across the room from the urn had been fraught with some danger. Is she always like that? Althea wondered. But she was glad that Mary said Goodbye and hurried Victor away. She was about to get up and leave when Adam Milner appeared beside her chair. He smiled down at her with his usual direct, challenging gaze.

"You've not been to see us for a while," he said.

"I have been busy. I go to lectures every day and read in the British Museum Reading Room otherwise. That is what I came here to London to do."

"Ah, yes. I remember now. How is it going?"

His manner was entirely friendly and if she said she needed help, any sort of help, she knew he would instantly offer it. Yet she rejected the idea in advance. It's not because I'm jealous. The thought surprised her. There was another reason for her feeling of distrust. Fern had said that he was not an Englishman, in spite of the excellence of his imitation. If he is not what he holds himself out to be, what is he?

She said, "All right," not supposing that he had any real interest in what she said in reply to his inquiry.

He nodded and asked, "Do you see much of Mary and Victor? I understand they know some of your people in the States."

She thought, That's a curious question. "Why, no. I see them occasionally."

"Victor says he knows your aunt."

Growing more and more suspicious, Althea replied, "I believe he has met her. She is a patron of a musical society in Baltimore."

"But you did not meet him there?"

"No. I met him here for the first time."

He took another tack. "You and Fern are very good friends, aren't you?"

What business is that of yours? Althea thought angrily. She said, "You're full of questions, aren't you?"

He looked surprised and a little chagrined, as if he had not expected to be checked and also as if he had given himself away. He decided to laugh and make light of it. "Well, you're an American and Americans always arouse our curiosity." He glanced down at her crippled leg deliberately and said, "Of course, I see why you are one of Mrs. Henshaw's proteges."

Furious, Althea snapped, "You look able-bodied."

"So I am." He gazed at her as if weighing the effect of his remark. Then he said, "Mrs. Henshaw has need of some self-reliant friends."

Althea got up determinedly. He instantly came forward to help her up and in spite of her disgust with him she could not prevent him from lifting her onto her feet. He did it swiftly but carefully as if he was used to using his easy strength to help those more helpless. Or to destroy those too helpless to resist?

"Thank you very much," said Althea, stiffly, aware that she had become rigid at his touch. He knows I don't like him and guesses that I am jealous because of Fern.

When she got back to Mrs. Tyndal's the mild afternoon had turned into a mistily cool evening. The house was full of the sound of the Indian girl's piano — Chopin bringing an incongruous bittersweet romanticism into Mrs. Tyndal's staid, austere house. She remembered then with a sense of relief that this evening she was going to a dinner party at the Crandalls, Americans who entertained indefatiguably their compatriots visiting London. They would come to fetch her early. She often went out in the evening to such affairs. Marjorie had a large number of friends who were in the diplomatic service or who worked for American businesses abroad. She instructed all of them to look up her niece in London and dutifully most of them did. They took Althea to the theater, to concerts, to dinner parties — staid, predictable affairs at which there were few people as young as she. Mentally she compared them with the lively, happy hours she spent with Fern, alone or going to the sort of eating places and spontaneous parties where people from the theater predominated. She wondered what

Fern did on the evenings when they were not together. Sometimes Fern gave her an inkling by mentioning a nightclub, telling some anecdote involving the sort of people she never met, a mixture of bohemians and guards officers and society girls. Fern had a knack for recounting the gayer side of such affairs, dramatizing even commonplace happenings. But there was also a suspicion of darker, more threatening things and she remembered Fern's stories of Berlin.

One day Fern came and wanted her to abandon her usual routine and go with her to the movies. It was a German film, Fern said, with Marlene Deitrich, the new German star. It was a most remarkable film, called *The Blue Angel.*

"You know about Dietrich, don't you? She's a Prussian officer's daughter, with a 'von' to her name. But she is beautiful and ravishing and the greatest actress in motion pictures. Of course, they talk about decadence and corruption when they talk about her. In this film she is a prostitute, a courtesan, I suppose you'd call her, and she destroys the man who gets involved with her, a professor who loses his wits over her. I've seen her in nightclubs in Berlin. She is as marvelous in the flesh as she is in her films. That's one of the things I don't talk to Dad about. He admits she is an extraordinary actress and after all she is the daughter of a distinguished professional soldier — though perhaps that's more cause for shame. But he hates what she portrays. You know, he acts as if he was afraid of her."

"Afraid of her?"

"Afraid of what she represents. Lots of times men bluster and get angry about something because they feel it is somehow dangerous to them. Dad is that way. I used to wonder why he got into such a rage over some things, till my mother said something to me that gave me a clue. He's upset, she said, because he doesn't know how to deal with such a thing."

They went to a matinee showing of the film and Althea

knew that it pushed back the walls around her understanding of the world. It was not the sort of thing that it would ever have occurred to Marjorie, much less to her other relatives, to go and see. To be introduced, by the medium of the theater or the motion pictures, to the spectacle of a pathetic professional man unsuccessfully trying to disentangle himself from the toils of a vampire, to watch his humiliation at the hands of a classroom full of sadistic boys —!

The theater they went to was close to Mrs. Tyndal's house and they walked slowly home in the mild late afternoon.

Still under the thrall of the film Althea said, "That poor man. He acted like a bird hypnotized by a snake. And yet I didn't like him. I don't really sympathize with him, but I'm sorry for him, just the same. What a terrible woman — But why was she that way? She is fascinating — Dietrich, I mean. You say you have seen her? Is she really that beautiful?"

"Yes. She used to come to the most popular cabarets — places where you'd see all sorts of people — men dressed as women, a lot of actors and artists and journalists. This film made her. It is based on a novel by Heinrich Mann, you know. Originally it had a political basis. Lola-Lola was an agent for the Nazis and the professor became their tool because of his infatuation. But it is obvious that the producers of the film got afraid of Hitler and his supporters and they took that part out. I expect that Dietrich does not like what is happening in Germany these days and she's probably glad to go to America. The film is getting popular there too."

"I'm surprised at that."

"Are you? But it is such a powerful film."

"Yes, but Americans are more puritanical than Europeans, you know. Even Marjorie would probably not like it."

" 'Even Marjorie.' You always say that when you're talking about your aunt. She's not like the rest of the family, then?"

Althea smiled, more to herself than for Fern's benefit. "Well, yes, that is true. Marjorie is much more broadminded, though she doesn't call attention to that fact. There are her affairs, for instance."

Fern's eyes were bright with curiosity. "Her affairs? Do you really mean affairs?"

"Well, yes, I do. But not quite what you have in mind." How to say it? Althea wondered. My aunt Marjorie has affairs with women. I've never said it like that to myself. But whatever else could you call it? She sought around in her mind for words. "What I mean is that Marjorie gets suddenly very fond of someone — another woman — and for a while she'll be all wrapped up in her. Then it cools off. I don't know whether you'd call it an affair. Would you?"

"You mean, would I, myself, call it that? Or just 'you' generally?"

Why, thought Althea, looking at her in surprise, Fern is embarrassed. I never expected her to be embarrassed. She always seems to know everything already. Or is it because she thinks I'm such an innocent?

"I just meant, do you think something like that is the same as having an affair with a man? Going through all the motions. But if it is with another woman, nothing would come of it."

"You mean physically?" Now Fern was looking at her directly. "Why not?"

This time it was Althea who looked away.

They had reached the gate of the garden in the midst of the square. The weather, though still mild for January, was too damp and chilly for anyone to sit for long on the benches. At the moment they were the only ones walking along the curved paths between the grassy plots and groups of shrubs. But in the center of the garden was a statue, a bust on a granite shaft, of a Victorian statesman and philanthropist. Their attention was caught by the sight of a young man and woman running around its base. The girl, Althea saw, was someone she had seen at Mrs. Henshaw's, a student probably at one of the schools and colleges near Mrs. Tyndal's. As they watched, the young man snatched the young woman's purse from her hand, and climbing up the statue, hung it on a stone scroll on which the statesman's virtues were inscribed. He stayed, crouched against the head of the hero, looking down at the girl, who stood below him remonstrating in vexation. He took the purse off its hook and dangled it above her head, taunting her to come up and get it. At last, in exasperation, she turned on her heel and walked quickly away down the path to the nearest gate. Althea and Fern, coming along another path leading to the same gate, followed her out of the garden. But she was walking swiftly away, too far to be hailed. At the gate they stopped and looked back at the statue. The man still stood there, the purse in his hand. Suddenly he came running toward them and passed by, intent on following the girl.

For a moment they stood silent, aware of the rush of sensual feeling passing them. "The god Pan," said Fern, "in pursuit of a dryad."

"He's hardly Pan," said Althea sharply. "This isn't our gate, Fern."

They walked back toward the center of the garden. Then Fern stopped short and exclaimed, "Well, I'll be —"

Althea looked in the direction in which she was staring. Two women were sitting on a bench some distance away from them. If it had been warm weather and the shrubbery in leaf, they would have been in a secluded corner but now, with the winter bareness, they were plainly visible. Althea's first thought was that the chill of the afternoon was not the

most comfortable for sitting in the garden. Her second was
that there was something instantly familiar about the figure
of one of the women, the one who sat forward on the bench,
bending towards the woman beside her.

Fern breathed in her ear, "Mrs. Henshaw. What on earth
is she doing here?"

They stood together watching the two women on the
bench. Mrs. Henshaw, in her mackintosh and felt hat from
under which her fine hair escaped in wisps, appeared to be
talking with great earnestness to her companion, her hand
on the woman's arm. The woman sat at ease on the bench
as if it were a summer day, her head flung back so that
her face was plainly visible under the brim of her hat. Her
coat was flung open as if she felt warm. She seemed to be
paying little attention to what Mrs. Henshaw was saying,
though once she laughed loudly. As they watched, Mrs.
Henshaw stood up and with a little help the other woman
stood up too. Mrs. Henshaw glanced about as if she was
anxious not to be seen but her gaze did not reach them.
She steadied the woman's staggering steps down the path
to the nearest gate. It was evidently a hard task, for the
woman was bigger and heavier than she. But at last they
reached the street and as Althea and Fern watched, a cab
stopped at Mrs. Henshaw's upraised arm and they were
seated in it.

Fern said quietly, staring after the vanishing cab, "That
is incredible."

"I could see she was drunk. I suppose she's somebody
Mrs. Henshaw knows."

"Yes, but it's Mrs. Owens."

"Mrs. Owens?"

"The famous — the notorious Mrs. Owens, Charles
Russet's mistress."

"Are you sure? Have you ever seen her?"

"Yes. I met her once, when she came to the house one

afternoon and Mrs. Henshaw introduced me. I was surprised because she did not look much like the portraits Charles Russet painted of her. She has drunk too much booze since then, I suppose. She looks as if she is down and out."

"Does she live somewhere near here? I've seen her several times. I've noticed her because she's so down at the heel and always seems crazy — you know, walking along talking to herself, as if she's carrying on a conversation with someone else."

"I dare say. She is probably always under the influence, you know. Mrs. Henshaw hates drunkenness. She thinks it is the worst of all vices, since it leads to so many others. She has no patience with boozers. She thinks they've made their own bed and they must lie in it. She gave me a lecture on the subject once when I was late coming home and was a little the worse for wear."

"But she won't abandon her."

"No, of course not," said Fern and lapsed into a thoughtful silence till they reached Mrs. Tyndal's door.

A few days later Fern came to tell her that Mrs. Henshaw was indeed not abandoning Mrs. Owens.

"There's a lot of talk about her among the people in the house. Everybody knows how Mrs. Henshaw feels about drunks. But she seems determined to rescue her. It turns out that Mrs. Owens doesn't have anywhere to live. She was evicted from her last place for not paying her rent. So now she's coming to live in Mrs. Henshaw's house."

Mrs. Henshaw arrived with her one morning about eleven o'clock, said Fern, when the house was usually empty except for the servant. By eleven the slug-a-beds had usually turned out and gone off on their own business. Fern herself had loitered over breakfast — "I didn't get in till four o'clock and I couldn't sleep till daybreak, so I didn't get up till ten and then it took me a while to get dressed and fix an egg and some toast — I was just in the mood to dawdle — didn't like the idea of the rest of the day looming up ahead of me, I suppose. Anyway, I had just washed up my own mess — to save the servant a little work — when I heard a cab stop in front of the house and the cabman saying, Here you are ma'am. She's got a load aboard, ain't she? I looked out of the window and there was Mrs. Henshaw holding onto Mrs. Owens and trying to find the cabfare in that big bag she carries."

So Fern had gone out to help, motivated, she admitted, by curiosity as well as the spirit of friendship. Mrs. Owens stood swaying on the sidewalk, a vacuous smile on her face. Mrs. Henshaw paid the cabman in stern silence, plainly annoyed by his comment. Then she turned and without expressing surprise or relief, said to Fern, "Please take these parcels while I help her."

"You remember, Althy," said Fern, "how we watched her guide Mrs. Owens into the cab the other day when we saw them in the square. Well, it was really a comedy to see her getting Mrs. Owens up the steps. But she managed. It's fortunate that she did not have to get her up the stairs. You remember that Mrs. Henshaw uses that room behind the sittingroom for her own bedroom. It must have been a morning room, a breakfast room once, when the house was a gentleman's villa. Anyway, it is right there on the ground floor and she took Mrs. Owens to it right away."

Fern had followed them, carrying a large battered suitcase and a long cylinder — "like a carpet rolled up with the backing showing, about four feet long." When Mrs. Owens was safely deposited on the bed and beginning to snore, Mrs. Henshaw turned around and demanded peremptorily, "Where is it?"

"It was the cylinder she was anxious about," Fern explained. "She took it away from me and put it carefully into her cupboard, behind her dresses. What do you suppose it is — some fabulously rare oriental rug?"

Althea laughed, "Her only treasure left?"

"It must have some value, from the way Mrs. Henshaw handled it. But it wasn't heavy enough for a rug of that size."

Since then, Fern reported, Mrs. Owens was never sober, though nobody knew where she got the money to buy drink. At first she managed to borrow a few shillings from some of the people in the house. But that source dried up quickly. Adam Milner went so far as to speculate that she went on the street to get money. That made Mrs. Henshaw extremely angry. Mrs. Owens, she said, was respectable though unfortunate. She certainly was not going to turn her out of doors, no matter what was said. The weather had turned colder and wet and she would not be able to sleep at night if she thought that Mrs. Owens, houseless, would fall into a drunken sleep in some out of the way spot and freeze to death before she was found. There was nowhere for her to sleep except in Mrs. Henshaw's own room, on a couch made up as a bed. It was not a companionship that Mrs. Henshaw would have chosen, though Mrs. Owens, in the brief period of the day when she was sober, was an intelligent, perceptive woman whose eyes picked up more of her surroundings than others realized. She came sometimes to tea in the sittingroom in the midst of the others. She did not gossip but listened with a distant smile on her face. But sometimes also she made an unexpectedly shrewd remark about people and current events.

Mrs. Henshaw nevertheless seemed to enjoy this momentary companionship. Mrs. Owens, she said, brought back to her the remembrance of her younger, happier days, when Roger Henshaw and Charles Russet had dominated their respective private lives. Althea, observing these moments of Mrs. Owens' presence in the group, watched Mrs. Henshaw. Yes, it was true, said Mrs. Henshaw, that she sometimes missed Roger very much. In spite of his long absences from her — they were usually pursuing their own interests even when they were in the same country — she had always enjoyed his sharp mind, even his sharp criticism of much that she did, because he was always at the same time concerned about her safety and comfort. It must be, thought Althea, watching her and Mrs. Owens talking together, that Mrs. Owens' presence brought to Mrs. Henshaw the awareness that her own life had settled chiefly into one of surface relationships, with people she succored but were not her intimates. Mrs. Owens seemed to dredge beneath the surface without making any apparent effort to do so. Fern agreed. Yes, there was a subtle tie between them that held even while Mrs. Henshaw was guiding Mrs. Owens' stumbling steps down the hall to their now shared room.

Althea, meeting a half-tipsy Mrs. Owens at tea time, recognized this affinity. They were friends, she thought, though not as close as Mrs. Henshaw and Marjorie — that seemed a more fundamental bond. Thinking back to Marjorie's house ten years ago, she realized the difference.

She found Mrs. Owens' occasionally sharp comments intriguing. Once, looking across the room, she said, abruptly breaking a few moments' silence, "I don't like that man."

Following her gaze Althea saw Adam Milner lounging against the farther wall. "Why?"

Mrs. Owens' slightly unfocussed eyes suddenly focussed on her. "D'you have to have a reason for disliking somebody? I'd say he's playing a part, like an actor. That makes him dangerous."

"Why do you suppose he is here — with Mrs. Henshaw?"

Mrs. Owens gave a strange crow of laughter. "Why, I expect he pays his rent regularly. She has to have a few people who do that, to make up for the rest of us." There was a raffish gleam in her eyes. "We all batten on her, don't we? Oh, perhaps not you —" Her brief moment of clarity faded.

Another time she seemed to brood for a while, her eyes heavy-lidded, on Victor, who had come unexpectedly as usual into the room. Althea heard her mutter, "The faun — that's what I always call him. Charles used to laugh at that. But when he came into my drawingroom, when he was a child — he was only twelve years old, a child prodigy — he was frightened. He was in an utterly strange world — so much clever chattering. He was only reassured when Janet was there." She glanced sharply at Althea, "Mrs. Henshaw, you know. She did not seem so strange to him. It's a quality she has about her that dissipates one's fearfulness." Mrs. Owens' somewhat vague eyes focussed suddenly on Althea. "You've felt that, of course. She's always one's last resource. We can all depend upon her when all else fails."

Later Althea said to Fern, "You know, when she was young she must have been very attractive —"

"Mrs. Owens? Yes, I think she was a cheerful sort of person — nice to have around — so different from what I understand Mrs. Charles was." Fern's head was on one side as she looked at Althea. "But Mrs. Henshaw is friends with Mrs. Charles, too."

"That's what you've told me. She said something about Adam Milner."

Fern's head straightened up. "What?"

"I asked her why he of all people was living here. She said Mrs. Henshaw had to have a few paying guests to take care of the rest. But she said something else. She thinks he's an actor, but she didn't mean somebody on the stage."

"That he's playing a part," Fern amplified. But she did not say anything further.

But talking about him, thought Althea, doesn't dispel the barrier he seemed to create between them.

One evening she sat alone late in her room, reading until at last she grew sleepy and got ready for bed. There was no sound in the house, at least none that reached her.

The Indian girl was either still out or like herself quiet in her rooms. It was well beyond the hour when Mrs. Tyndal locked and bolted the front door. After this anyone wanting to enter had to ring the night bell that roused someone in the family quarters at the back of the house.

The sudden peeling of the doorbell roused Althea from her sleepy efforts to get into bed. Never before had there been such a loud clamor of the doorbell at so late an hour. Althea looked at the clock. It was far beyond midnight. Uneasy, Althea, halfway into bed, drew back and stood on her good leg, leaning against the beside. As the doorbell was rung another time, she moved across the bedroom to the sittingroom, supporting herself on the backs of chairs, the table and the doorjamb. As she reached the door of her sittingroom she heard the sound of Mrs. Tyndal coming from the back stairs to stand at the front door and demand who was there. Althea groped her way to her own door and out onto the landing so that she could peer down into the front hall. In the dim light of the ceiling lamp she saw that Mrs. Tyndal stood there in her dressinggown, her tall, gangling son standing behind her. Althea did not hear the voice of the person who answered but she heard Mrs. Tyndal's inquiry, "Are you alone?" and then the noise of the bolt being drawn and the door opened. Fern came through it. She wore a trench coat with the collar turned up and she was hatless.

She heard Mrs. Tyndal's high-pitched voice protest, "But she has gone to bed! She is never up so late!"

As if drawn by a sense of her presence, Fern looked up the stairwell. "But she's up! See!" She pointed up and called to Althea, "I can come up, can't I?"

"Yes, of course," Althea called down. "It's all right, Mrs. Tyndal."

Fern began to climb the stairs and Althea lost sight of her but heard her voice, more normal now, saying, "I am so sorry to have disturbed you, Mrs. Tyndal. Indeed I am."

A moment later she came into sight climbing the last flight of stairs. Reaching Althea she put her arm around her and helped her back into the room. Once there, with the door closed, she took off her coat and ran the fingers of both hands through the tousle of her hair.

Althea, aware that when their bodies touched she could feel the quiver in Fern's, demanded, "What is the matter? You're frightened."

She had sat down in the armchair and now looked up at Fern half-seen in the shaded radiance of the reading lamp.

Fern stood hugging her elbows. "I'm scared to death. I wish I had never set eyes on him."

"Who?"

"Adam."

"What has he done?"

"He started the fight. I'm sure he did it deliberately. He had his friends there. He didn't think the police would come so soon. He thinks he's in Berlin. He enjoys fighting — he enjoys hitting people — knocking people down, banging them against walls, making their blood run. He likes to batter people till he can see their eyes glaze and their tongues loll out of their mouths —"

Her nerves jumping, Althea said, "I've always known that he is a bully. It shows through his disguise. But what happened — where were you?"

"We were in a dive — I don't know just where. It was the third place we went to. I didn't get drunk, though he tried to get me to — I was too scared of what might happen. He was looking for somebody — I realize that now. We started out the evening with some other people — the kind that like to court danger — get a thrill out of mixing with shady characters. But at the second place we went to he suddenly dragged me out into the street. He must have found whoever he was looking for in this third place. There was a group of men around a table at the back of the room. It was not really a nightclub — just a small restaurant where regular customers come and sit through several hours, at all times of day — one of those places where the lights are dim and full of cigarette smoke and reeky. I noticed that after we had danced — there was a very small pad in the middle for dancing — and were sitting and having a drink, that he kept looking at the men in the back, so I looked at them too. They were foreigners of some sort — too swarthy and dark for Frenchmen or Germans, swarthy with black eyes and moustaches and their clothes looked cheap and didn't fit them very well. I thought at once that they must be refugees from eastern Europe — you can see them in Paris, gathered into clannish little groups. And they always seem to be plotting something. Sometimes you find artists and musicians among them, people who are escaping from some sort of danger. They always stick together — you know, 'I'm from the same village in Dalmatia,' that sort of thing. When the police come looking for spies and people with dangerous politics, they naturally drag in a lot of the others, who are harmless, really —"

"Like Victor. Was he there?"

"Victor? Oh, no. He has sense enough to stay away from that sort of thing."

"What happened then?"

"Before I was really aware of what he was doing, Adam got up and went over to the table where these men were sitting. He pushed himself into their circle — there were several men standing around behind those who were seated, as if they were watching a card game — and began saying something in German. I thought, that proves it. He is a German, Hitler's kind of German, a Nazi. You know, I've never told you. I knew him in Berlin. Sometimes he would come and join a group of students I was with — and thinking back on it, whenever he appeared, the evening ended in a raid or a fight. So I've suspected him ever since I met him here. Now there was no mistaking it. Whatever he was saying to them — I couldn't hear from where I was — it was insulting, because one of them suddenly stood up and tried to hit him. But he was expecting that and he dodged and hit the man in the stomach so that he doubled up. After that there was a general melee. You know how it is in a bar — no, I suppose you don't know — a lot of drunks or half-drunks just get into a fight for the sake of fighting. So there was this deadly business between Adam and the men he had attacked in the midst of a free-for-all. He is very powerful and swift and knows how to use his feet as well as his hands and he was able to avoid the knives they had. And all around there was this pointless brawl among the patrons who saw a fight and joined in it for the hell of it. I saw the bartender send a fellow scooting out to get the police, so I followed him as fast as I could."

Fern paused and wiped the palms of her hands on her dress. Her evening slippers were dirty and wet from her flight through the dark streets. "I was lucky. There's a fog but not thick enough so that I got lost and by some miracle I found a cab to bring me here. I thought I'd have to run the whole way — if a bobbie didn't pick me up."

Her fast breathing began to slow. "I can't afford being picked up. Can't you imagine how my father would react if he read in the London papers that I was arraigned in Bow Street on a charge of being involved in a brawl?"

Althea shook her head. "But why have you been going out with him, if you distrust him? You're afraid of him. Does that attract you to him in spite of everything?"

Fern gave her a despairing look. "No, no! I hate him!

I can't stand being near him, really. He makes my skin crawl. He's a spy, I know he's a spy. He's a police informer. And he's a sadist."

She faltered and Althea pressed her, taking revenge. "You go with him because he hypnotizes you, fascinates you with what you despise —"

"No, I swear that's not true! That's not the reason. Don't you see? He's been blackmailing me. He knows who my father is. He knew that in Berlin. He knows he can force me to go about with him because he can expose me to my father and then threaten my father with scandal. And I'm afraid that he won't stop with just making me go out with him. He'll try to make me go to bed with him —"

"Oh, no!" Althea's disgust showed in her voice, her face.

Fern dropped her eyes. "Oh, Althy, I'm not brave like you. I don't know why I'm such a coward." She suddenly dropped to her knees beside Althea's chair. "There's only one person who could make me go through fire. It's you, Althy. No, I'm not play-acting. It's true. I love you, Althy."

She put her arms around Althea's knees and buried her face in Althea's lap. Althea sat perfectly still, paralyzed by astonishment and a wish to believe. Fern, feeling her tenseness, sat back on her haunches, loosening her grip. "I've loved you ever since I first saw you — you remember? The day you came looking for Mrs. Henshaw and were having tea with her. You're not like anybody I ever knew before. For a while you seemed so bound up inside yourself that you would not let me in. But that's changed. Why do you suppose I came here? Oh, you can say that I came here because I needed to escape from Adam and the police and the Tube is no longer running and the cabfare to St. John's Wood is twice what it is here. But that's only part of it, Althy. I was terrified — terrified of everything, of my own life and I could only think of being here safe with you. Oh, Althy, nobody can protect me except you — protect me from all sorts of things."

She was quiet and leaned against Althea's chair. Althea did not stir but the tension in her body lessened. A strange feeling possessed her, one she had never been aware of before — of being in charge not only of herself but of someone else. A sense of strength bloomed in her. Whatever Fern needed she could provide. She put her hand on Fern's shoulder.

"Don't be so upset. He won't think of looking for you here — nobody will. Won't the police arrest him, along with the others, for breaching the peace?"

"I don't know. I told you I think he may be a police informer. That might get him off, if he's able to give them information about suspicious characters they're looking for."

"Even if he's a German — spying for somebody else?"

Again Fern sat back on her heels. "I don't know. I don't know whether they would know who he really is. You see, when I used to meet him in Berlin, he never paid much attention to me. It was only when he met me here that he became interested. As for the police here — whenever there is trouble — a stabbing, a shooting or a bombing or something of the kind, involving foreigners — naturally the police go looking for people who may be involved. Adam can tell them a lot, lead them to men who are hiding here in London. Some of them are deported to their homelands and I suppose are liquidated by their own enemies. I think he does some of this out of revenge, against people he does not like — or people he despises because they're not Aryans, members of the master race. He's a Nazi — a fascist — I've no doubt of that, at all."

"You say he's blackmailing you."

220

"He can tell my parents all kinds of lies — tell my father what I was up to in Berlin — say that I've gone to the dogs here in London —"

"But your parents won't believe that, will they?"

"You don't know my father. He'd be enraged when he found out that I had been deceiving him all the time in Berlin."

Althea did not answer. The room was very quiet. There was no sound in the house and beyond the closed windows the street was wrapped in a deadening fog. The little traveling clock that Marjorie had given her as a going-away present chimed a soft quarter hour. Four o'clock?

She felt Fern's hands urging her to get up. "Let's go to bed," Fern said, in a voice that seemed muted by the surrounding stillness. Althea did not resist the strong pull. Fern got her to her feet and steadied her till she got her balance. Aware that without her iron brace she could not walk without help, Fern stood close beside her with her arm around her. They walked together into the bedroom and across to the bed.

One of the features of Mrs. Tyndal's rooms that Althea had noticed when she first came to inspect them was the ample, comfortable bed. No doubt, she thought at the time, Mrs. Tyndal had envisioned her prospective tenants to be a couple, not an undersized crippled American girl. She remembered this now as Fern helped her into it and lifted her withered leg onto the bed with easy, matter-of-fact care.

The room was lighted only by the bedside lamp. The light was bright in a small patch. Otherwise there was a general luminousness. Fern stood near the bed, pulling off her own clothes. Althea watched as her naked body emerged — slim, long-legged, lithe, satin-skinned, rounded, flawless — a beautiful, healthy, unmarred body. As she tossed off her last garment, Fern glanced at her and then deliberately stood still to allow her full opportunity to stare and absorb the sight of her own nakedness. Then, just as deliberately she stepped over to the bed and got into it beside Althea, reaching for her as she did so. Competently, with unhurrying deftness she slid her arm under Althea as she stretched out so that their two bodies touched along their length, drawing the covers over both of them.

Enthralled, Althea lay perfectly still. This was finally it, the blissful moment of bodily communion, warmth, enveloping love, that she had dreamed about all her life, had mourned after as something that would never come about, had cursed her miserable, shrunken body as the barrier to. A sudden voluptuous release flooded her. At first, docilely, she accepted the command in Fern's touch. Amazed, she realized that she made no effort to withdraw, felt no impulse to shrink away as Fern's firm, deliberate hands passed over the boniness of her body, even when they reached and played along her shrunken leg, felt the outline of its wasted muscles. Instead, a thrill went through her that made her shudder deeply. Nobody had ever had this freedom with her body, nobody had ever been per-mitted to handle her with this assurance of welcome. Even when she had had to submit to help in washing and dress-ing, even with Martha, she had folded herself closely within herself. Fern had not hesitated, as if she was confident of welcome, as if she knew that Althea lay awaiting her touch. Now Althea felt herself burgeon, like a blossom soaking up the sun after a long spell of cloudy weather. She not only did not draw back from Fern's touch, she sought it — she pressed forward to feel Fern's fingers caressing her skin, gently rubbing the secret, responsive places of her body, her own welcome flowing strongly forth to en-courage, urge on this delectable exploration, this long-awaited awakening of the deepest well of feeling within her. She put her arms around Fern and held her against her in an unyielding grip.

After a while, as she slowly relaxed from this inescapable excitement, she moved herself over Fern, tracing with her fingers Fern's silken back, her slim, firmly muscled thighs, the taut wall of her stomach, the round handfuls of her hard-nippled breasts. Fern pressed against her and then drew away, to allow a little space for the play of Althea's hands, then came close again and writhed against her in ecstasy. They were murmuring to each other and yet neither knew what words were said. Slowly they sank together into the dark quiet warmth of the bed.

Althea awoke first, in the early light of day, a murky winter day that brought very little brightness into the room. She lay still, aware without surprise of the sweet weight of Fern's body lying against her. There seemed to be nothing strange or unnatural about this first waking in Fern's embrace. It had come almost as an inevitable event — unforeseen but at the same time, with hindsight, predictable. Certainly this could not be something ephemeral, something that would take place this once and never again. Fern hereafter was part of herself. The ambivalence of the last few months was gone.

A while later Fern stirred. She raised herself on her elbow to look down at Althea and then leaned over to kiss her. It was a matter-of-fact, unembarrassed kiss. You're mine, it said, or so it seemed to Althea. Fern sat up in the bed and stretched. Althea watched as she reached above her head, raising her small breasts into a long, graceful line from her narrow waist, shaking her head, set on her neck like a boy's. She put her feet out from under the cover and sprang lightly to the floor. Althea's eyes followed her long-legged figure go across the room to the gas-heater, set in the former fireplace.

"There are shillings on the mantel," said Althea, sitting up and pulling the bedclothes around herself.

Fern found the coins and fed several into the coin slot. She did not seem to mind the chill in the room but stepped to the window and pulled back the curtain to peer down into the street. Althea could see that fog lay beyond the window pane.

"You've a nice snug place here, Althy. And Mrs. Tyndal is a nice friendly woman. She didn't even get mad at me last night for routing her out of bed. I think if you ask her not to tell anybody that I came here last night, she wouldn't. And if she told you she wouldn't, she wouldn't, I'm sure."

"She's very honest."

"She brings you your breakfast, doesn't she?"

"Yes. What's the time? Seven o'clock? She brings it about eight o'clock. I have a kettle here to heat water on that ring. I can make us some tea."

"I'll do it. Do you have a robe I can put on?"

"Over there." Althea laughed in spite of herself when Fern put on the robe. It reached only to her knees.

"Oh, I don't think that's so funny. I can be Japanese, wearing one of those short coats they wear to work around in."

Fern filled the kettle at the wash basin and placed it on the ring. "Where's your tea and the teapot and cups?"

"There. Shall I go and find Mrs. Tyndal and ask her to bring two breakfasts?"

"What will you wager she will anyway? She must know I am still here. I couldn't have got out of the house without rousing her. It's locked up like a fortress."

She proved to be right. When Fern answered the knock at the door Mrs. Tyndal stood there holding a large tray with a double set of everything. Behind her stood her daughter Gladys with another tray holding the teapot and milk jug and toast rack. Gladys set her tray down and fled.

Mrs. Tyndal said, "Look you to goodness, Miss Richards! I hardly knew whether to bring your breakfast or not, thinking you might not be up so early. But I heard you stirring around."

For a wild moment Althea wondered whether there was some quality still in the air of the room that spoke of love satisfied. But she dismissed the thought as Fern said, "Thank you, Mrs. Tyndal. I'd have been in a bad way if you had not let me in last night."

"Two o'clock in the morning is no time for a girl like you to be out on the street alone." Mrs. Tyndal's voice was firm. Her tone made it plain that she expected some explanation.

"Yes. Well, sometimes you don't have a choice, do you?"

Mrs. Tyndal shook her head. "If I were you, I shouldn't go out with young men who do not have the proper respect."

Fern was supply compliant. "Of course, that is right, Mrs. Tyndal. I shan't go out with him again, I assure you." Fern paused and looked at Mrs. Tyndal, who waited expectantly. "I think I had better confide in you. I don't want anyone to know that I came here last night. Just because I took refuge here with Althea, I don't want to get her involved in anything."

Mrs. Tyndal eyed her appraisingly. Her eyes seemed to say, Young lady, you have got yourself into something you'd rather not. Aloud she said, "It would be a pity to get Miss Richards involved in anything that is not as it should be."

"Exactly. So, please, if anyone comes here asking for me, just say you don't know anything about me."

At first a slight frown appeared on Mrs. Tyndal's open face. Then she smiled brightly. "Well, that's true, isn't it? I don't know anything about you."

Fern laughed, relieved at her offered connivance. "And

I shan't tell you anything, so that you won't know. What Althea says doesn't count."

Still smiling, Mrs. Tyndal went out of the room.

"She has a soft spot for you," said Althea, and then asked, more seriously, "Are you afraid that Adam Milner will come looking for you here?"

They were dressed now and had moved to the table. Althea sat down and began to remove the covers from the breakfast dishes. Fern sat down near her and took the plate she offered. "I'm very uneasy. I don't see how he could find out that I came here — unless he guesses, knowing that I know you. But then I know some other people I could have gone to. And he doesn't know where you live."

"Why wouldn't he suppose that you just went home?"

"Perhaps he will — but he might learn from Mrs. Henshaw that I did not come home last night. But perhaps he did not get home himself — if the police detained him."

"Would Mrs. Henshaw know that you were not home?"

"I don't know. So if he asked her, she would be surprised and I expect alarmed, especially if he said he did not know where I was."

"She might read about the brawl in the paper."

"If it is reported."

They ate in silence for a while. Then Althea asked, "What will you live on, if your father learns about all this and cuts off your allowance?"

"On air — like a lot of theatrical people these days. Or do what Mrs. Owens does — sponge off Mrs. Henshaw. She won't throw me out for any reason. I'm a sacred trust from my mother. Or even without that. Instead, she would squeeze in another language lesson to support me and try to convince my parents that they shouldn't disown me."

"Don't joke," said Althea.

Fern put out her hand and touched Althea's. The

226

remembrance of the night before came flooding back to
them and for a few minutes they forgot about the problems
that came back with the day. Fern leaned close to Althea,
nibbling at her ear and making her laugh. Then Althea,
suddenly serious, said, as if her heart overflowed with the
love she felt, "Don't be afraid, darling. I shan't let anything happen to you."

A brief instant surprise showed in Fern's face. She
kissed Althea softly. "Of course you won't."

Fern left a little while after that, reluctant to go and
yet eager to find Mrs. Henshaw. Althea heard nothing from
her the rest of the day.

Next morning she was about to leave for the British
Museum when Fern ran up the stairs.

"Oh, Althy, you haven't gone yet!" She caught Althea
in her arms and held her close. Althea could feel the current of excitement in her.

"What is it?" she demanded, drawing away a little.
"What's the matter? Is it something to do with Adam
Milner? Have you heard what has happened to him?"

Fern released her, surprised by the question. It betrayed
where Althea's anxiety lay. "Oh, no, it's nothing to do with
him. He has disappeared. At least, he has not come back
to Mrs. Henshaw's house and she has said nothing about
him. He does disappear occasionally without explanation."

Fern wandered over to the window and stood looking
out at the misty rain. Althea waited. Presently Fern turned
back to her. "It's a funny thing, Althy, how you can want
something so much and then when it comes about, the
edge seems to have worn off of it."

"What are you leading up to?" There was a frown on
Althea's face.

Fern grinned at her. "Us. Me. You know how I've wanted
the chance at a real part in a good play. Well, I've got it.
You remember I was half promised it before I went away at

Christmas. But it means I go on tour. There was nothing I wanted more then. Now —" She stared at Althea, not finishing her sentence. Seeing the dismay in Althea's face, she realized more fully how her own joy in this prize so suddenly within her grasp was dashed by the knowledge that they would be separated. She would not have believed, at that time, that this could be so. The night they had spent together had changed it all. What she had thought would be unmitigated joy was suddenly a calamity.

"How long will you be gone?" Althea asked in a small, bleak voice.

"Three weeks. The regular understudy can't go. Oh, Althy, here it is, what I've so longed for and now I don't want to go!"

Althea, getting over her first dismay, said firmly, "Oh, yes, you do. Don't shilly-shally. You have to pay for some things, Fern."

Looking down into her resolute face, Fern nodded. After a moment Althea said, "You won't have to worry about Adam Milner for three weeks."

Fern, standing with her arms crossed, looked at her sidewise. "That's a mean one, Althy. I don't think about him. Let's not talk about him any more, shall we?"

During the days while Fern was gone Althea tried to stick closely to her own routine. But everything seemed to conspire to increase the great gap in her life made by Fern's absence. She lay in bed at night and wondered. How was it that in that first love-making they had both seemed to know what to do for the other's pleasure, had anticipated correctly the other's desire? For Fern, perhaps, this had not been the first time of loving a woman — she knew so little of what lay behind Fern. As for herself — she paused here in her thought. Was it imagination lit up by the deprivation of physical love that had always been her lot and which she had come to accept as inevitable and forever?

The time with Elsie — the longing for Elsie, for Elsie to respond lovingly, a longing so brutally denied — had taught her by its opposite what love-making could be, in her imagination. In the daytime, while she sat reading, even while she sat in the austere grandeur of the British Museum Reading Room, she was tormented by the desire that awoke between her legs as she thought of Fern. Reflecting on all this, she knew that the idea that this kind of love, which was never to be acknowledged aloud, could never for a moment seem unnatural or criminal. It had a quality of sweetness, of imperativeness, that gave it all the approval that the world withheld.

The world. The world could only condemn. Yet one couldn't live in a vacuum. Several years ago — was it nineteen twenty-eight? — Radclyffe Hall had published *The Well of Loneliness*, in the midst of great controversy and suits in the courts. Marjorie had somehow obtained a copy, which she did not place in the glass-fronted bookcases with her other books but kept in an inconspicuous place. She did not know that Althea had found it and read it: books were magnets for her — she could find them in the dark. She remembered that she had once heard some woman say, with genuine regret, that it was a pity that such a book had been published, for it had made life more difficult for many women who lived alone. Perhaps it was Miss Atwood who had said that. It was the sort of oblique remark she would make, though Althea did not remember discussing the book with her. She meant, I suppose, thought Althea, that it had caused many people to become more suspicious of single women than they would have formerly.

One night it snowed. Looking out of her window she saw the thick flakes coming down fast in the light of the street lamps. By midnight the sound of traffic and passers-by was muffled by the snow on the ground. In the morning, in the grey light of an overcast sky, she saw that the garden in the square was a pristine white expanse broken only by the dark shapes of the snow-laden shrubs. Mrs. Tyndal, bringing her breakfast, warned her against the idea of going out.

"You'll never keep your footing. It is slippery where people have trod."

Althea reluctantly agreed. Now if Fern had been here, she thought, she would have helped her. She could have ventured out with Fern's assistance. But as it was she was marooned for a couple of days, until a turn in the weather brought a thaw and water running freely in the gutters.

Then, as the weather cleared, restless, she went out one afternoon to Mrs. Henshaw's house. The dark, thick fogginess of February had lifted briefly and the momentary softness spoke of a possible spring. She was early and at first she did not think there was anyone else in the drawingroom. The gas fire had dispelled some of the chill and she moved closer to it. There were no lights on to dispel the gloom of the room.

A hoarse voice said out of dimness, "How d'you do? The tea things aren't here yet. It's always a toss-up whether the girl will bring them or somebody has to go and fetch them."

Althea turned around. Mrs. Owens sat in a chair close to the fire. She wore a heavy knitted jacket with big pockets bulging with a pack of cigarettes, handkerchiefs, bits of paper. Althea thought she recognized it as something Mrs. Henshaw's perpetually busy fingers had made. On her head was a turban of some sort. But though her voice was hoarse and her face blotchy, she did not appear to be at the moment drunk.

"Oh, I'm in no hurry," said Althea. "I've just come to see Mrs. Henshaw."

"You'll be lucky if you do. You haven't been here for a while, have you?"

"No. The weather has kept me in."

"Oh. Ah. Of course. We crocks can't get about like the others, can we?"

Althea glanced at her but she seemed unaware of any offense she might give by this statement.

Mrs. Owens went on. "She's not around as much as usual. Her political activities are taking up a good deal of her time."

"Political activities! Why, I didn't think she was interested in politics."

Mrs. Owens eyed her curiously. "Perhaps not in the sense you are thinking of. But she is always aware of what is going on in the political world — especially when someone she is concerned with is affected."

"Oh. I see what you mean. Victor, I suppose."

"Victor? Victor Karandy, the cellist. Yes. He is a case in point. But I don't think she is so much concerned with him just now. I think she has his affairs very well in hand. No. It's that pseudo-Englishman — what's his name?"

"Pseudo-Englishman?" Althea sat down opposite her and rested her cane against the chair arm.

"That tall conceited fellow, who always acts as if he has special privileges around here."

"Adam Milner. But why is she concerned about him?"

But instead of answering Mrs. Owens seemed to muse. "I wonder what it's like now." Then she was silent for a long time and Althea said politely, "You've lived in England, Europe for quite a while, haven't you?"

Mrs. Owens gave her a wry smile. "Yes. I'm an American and I still talk like one. I married an Englishman, you know. Poor fellow. He was a darling but he hadn't a chance when Charles came along."

"Charles Russet, the painter?"

"Of course. Who else? You've heard all the story from

Mrs. Henshaw, I expect." There was a trace of sly malice and pride in her tone.

Embarrassed, Althea temporized. "Well, she has mentioned —"

"Oh, she didn't approve, really. But she never lets a friend down. She's always been a very good friend to me. I think she accepts the idea that a grand passion cannot be confined within the ordinary bounds of a social convention like marriage. Charles, you know, was a great friend of Roger, her husband. I think she was once a little smitten by Charles herself. Roger recognized this fact but he never mentioned it." She paused but Althea said nothing. "Did she ever tell you about how she rescued Charles from the Greek authorities? Of course, that was before I met Charles. He was escaping from his wife. She detested those nihilists or Bolsheviks or whatever they were he was always giving money to — her money — he had run out of his own."

She seemed to muse again for a few moments. "You know, he brought Victor to see me. Victor was only twelve years old. This was before the War, of course, you understand, when Charles was trying to find a patron for Victor. He recognized Victor as a musical prodigy. You know about Victor's father, don't you? He was the nihilist or Balkan patriot or whatever you want to call him, whom Charles was subsidizing. Charles had a hard time convincing him that Victor should have special treatment as a musician, that money could be found to send him to a conservatory. So Charles brought him to one of my at-homes — I entertained a lot in those days. The boy was half-terrified by the life he had to lead with his father — the turmoil, the sudden flights from one country to another. He did not understand any of it. Victor has never had a political sense."

She suddenly stopped talking and listened. Her surprisingly sharp ears had caught the sound of the front door.

A whiff of the chilly air from outside drifted into the room. "Speak of angels and you hear the beat of their wings. Ah, Janet."

Mrs. Henshaw's high-pitched voice reached them. "Do pull yourself together, Mary. Victor is not in immediate danger."

She came into the room, bustling over to her desk to put down her canvas carryall. The Karandys followed her, Mary dabbing at her eyes, Victor slouching behind her as if reluctant to come in.

"Oh, Henrietta!" Mrs. Henshaw exclaimed, seeing Mrs. Owens, and then with an absent glance toward Althea, "How are you, my dear?" She turned then to Mary, who stood in the middle of the floor, still dabbing at her eyes. "Do have a cup of tea, Mary dear." She stepped to the table on which the tea things were usually spread and seeing it bare, gave an exclamation of impatience and hurried out of the room.

The four people she left behind stayed where they were — like figures in a tableau, thought Althea. Victor made no effort to comfort his wife but stood near her, nervously taking the handkerchief out of his breastpocket of his coat and putting it back. He had not worn a hat — I've never seen him wearing one, though Althea — and his sleek hair glistened from the fog-drops. When he saw and recognized Mrs. Owens, his face brightened and he stepped over close to her and began to speak in French — it seemed to be the language in which he felt most at home. A smile appeared on Mrs. Owens' face as she answered him. At last Mrs. Henshaw came back, carrying a tray of clinking teacups and followed by the maidservant carrying another with the teapot and the pitchers of hot water and milk and the sugar bowl.

"This will make you feel better," said Mrs. Henshaw

confidently, sitting down beside the tea table and pouring tea. Before she had finished the front door opened again and a couple of the other inhabitants of the house came in. Gradually the room filled as other people drifted in. But there was no sign of Adam Milner.

Althea, her attention on Mary Karandy, who had gravitated close to Mrs. Henshaw as if in a wordless seeking for reassurance, became aware that Mrs. Owens had got up from her chair and was drifting silently towards the doorway. For a moment it seemed that Mrs. Henshaw was unaware of her departure, but all at once Mrs. Henshaw looked in her direction.

"Henrietta —" she said.

Mrs. Owens stopped in the doorway and leaned against the doorjamb. Althea stared at her. In the half-gloom she seemed for a moment the beauty she had once been. Her skin shone pale and clear in the dim light and her dark eyes were brilliant. It was a momentary glimpse. She disappeared and Althea heard Mrs. Henshaw "Tcha!" She knows she is going to seek something stronger than tea, thought Althea.

The growing darkness from the fog thickening outside the windows warned Althea that she must go home. She was surprised that Mrs. Henshaw did not raise an alarm about this sooner — Mrs. Henshaw seemed never to overlook any real danger she might incur from her lameness. But she was now completely absorbed in some overriding preoccupation. Even her attention to the Karandys was perfunctory. As she was leaving she heard her say to Mary, "Fern is not here. You can use her room. I think it would be best if you did not go back to your flat just now."

Why? Althea wondered, buttoning up her coat to confront the fog outside. But in the hallway she found Mrs. Owens standing gazing out at the grey still afternoon. Surprised she waited while the older woman turned around to face her. I can't knock her down to get out of the door, she thought. She was more surprised to realize that Mrs. Owens was waiting for her.

"She won't let anybody go to the devil his own way, will she?" Mrs. Owens' voice was not as hoarse as it often was. There was an echo in it of a soft and seductive timbre. When Althea murmured a hesitating, "No, I expect not," she said, "Come into the bedroom. I want to show you something." She glanced down at Althea's iron brace. "There're no stairs to climb."

The room was brighter than the hall, lit by a window that faced the blank wall of the house next door from which the pale foggy sky light was reflected. In the far corner was a single bed, made and covered by a bedspread knitted from multicolored threads — another product, thought Althea, of Mrs. Henshaw's nervous, tireless fingers. Along the opposite wall was a couch with bedraggled bedclothes hanging half-off onto the floor. She can't keep her neat, obviously, thought Althea. There was a heavy scent of cigarette smoke laced with a trace of eau-de-cologne in the air. Mrs. Henshaw had a liking for that, Althea remembered. There was still another odor underneath — no doubt the gin that Mrs. Owens managed to acquire and drink.

Mrs. Owens wandered across the room to come to a stop near the door of the cupboard. For a moment, Althea, watching her gaze about aimlessly, wondered if she had forgotten what she had invited her in to see. But presently she went over to the closet and thrust her head and shoulders in amongst the clothes that hung there. She backed out, struggling with an unwieldy object. Althea suddenly remembered Fern's description of Mrs. Owens' arrival at Mrs. Henshaw's house and the long ruglike cylinder they had brought with them. Mrs. Owens brought it out now and dragged it to the center of the room. With an effort she lowered herself to the floor beside it and began to worry with unsteady fingers at the knots in the tapes that held the cylinder rolled.

Frustrated at first she stopped and looked up at Althea. "I haven't had it open since it was taken out of the frame." She gave a little laugh with such a genuinely happy sound that Althea answered her with a smile.

Mrs. Owens made a sweeping gesture. "Sit down there. When I get it undone I can hold it up for you to see."

Fascinated, Althea watched as she at last loosened the knots in the tape and undid them. One edge of the cylinder fell back and she could see that it was an oil painting. Mrs. Owens scrambled up onto her knees, and puffing, heaved herself onto her feet. After a moment of breathing hard, she reached down and seized the edge of the canvas and tugged at the cylinder. She unrolled it, pulling it up to her chin, peering over it at Althea.

In the grey light of the room the opulent colors of the painting glowed with the splendor of an Italian sun. It is hardly the way, thought Althea, to see a masterpiece, for the corners of the canvas fell forward, hiding part of the whole, and the clutching grip of Mrs. Owens' fingers drew it into billows and hollows that distorted the portrait. But Althea recognized it at once — Charles Russet's most famous painting, eclipsing the grand portraits that hung in the Metropolitan Museum, the National Gallery. It was a study of a woman dressed in a simple white frock and a wide-brimmed hat, her head thrown back in a confident way so that her eyes met the viewer's in a direct, challenging gaze. She sat in an ample wicker chair with a high, wide back, on a sunny loggia, with a frame of semitropical shrubs and vines that cast dappled shadows around her. Althea remembered that, when she was fifteen and still sunk in the morass of Elsie's rejection, she had come upon a photographic reproduction of it in color. It had captured her, for she had seen in it a revelation — a picture of enchantment, speaking of sunlit days and starlit nights, of the rapture of love-happiness, of abundant warmth and energy, of desire aroused, fed but not sated. She remembered the sullen, rejecting mood in which she had gone — an instinctive attempt, perhaps, to protect herself from the effect of that painting — with the other girls in her class — art appreciation was emphasized in Miss Armstrong's school — to a visiting exhibition of the works of European painters at the National Museum in Washington. But her picture had not been among them.

But here it was, all light and vibrant shadow and that seductive, confident woman in the midst of it.

Mrs. Owens' sudden, soft laugh interrupted her reverie. She turned to see Mrs. Owens' eyes upon her, gleaming with a trace of malicious pleasure. "Charles caught it, didn't he?" That lovely moment when we were at Rapallo — our first bit of heaven before the vultures and the harpies got their claws and teeth into us, to tear us to ribbons."

Suddenly shy, Althea stammered, "You've kept it safe all this time."

"Yes." Mrs. Owens' smile now was amused, well-meaning. "I thought you would appreciate it. You have sensitive feelings. You do know what love is. I can see that. I like you."

Althea blushed, ready to believe, for a wild moment, that Mrs. Owens had all-seeing eyes that could penetrate the outer skin to see what lay within. She watched, as Mrs. Owens, her mood suddenly changing to anger, snatched at the canvas, intending to roll it into a cylinder again. She will never succeed, Althea lamented, anxious now for the safety of the painting. Alarmed, she got up from her chair and hobbled over to try and hold one corner of it. Mrs. Owens, in an instinctive response, pulled it away from her. Her unfocussed eyes blazed.

"It is mine! He gave it to me. I've never left it out of my

keeping. They said it disappeared during the war. I hid it. I could not bear the thought that it would be destroyed." Her arms slowly relaxed and she let the canvas drop to the floor.

Althea, in despair, watched as she sat down again on the floor. Then, obeying an impulse, she limped as quickly as she could to the door and down the corridor to the drawingroom. Mrs. Henshaw still sat at the tea table, talking to Mary. As if warned by some sixth sense, she glanced toward the doorway and saw Althea. Without a word she got up and came over but without waiting for Althea to explain, she brushed past her and went quickly down the corridor to the open door of her own room. Althea, limping after her, arrived in time to see her step over to Mrs. Owens and hold out her hand.

"Get up, Henrietta." Her light, calm voice had a steely quality. Mrs. Owens looked up at her with a mixture of belligerance and slyness. Clumsily she got to her feet with Mrs. Henshaw's help. "Now help me roll this up." Between them they lifted the upper edge of the canvas and began rolling it back into a cylinder. "Henrietta, you should not have got it out this way."

Mrs. Owens flared up. "It's mine! I can do what I like with it!"

Mrs. Henshaw's reply was instant and firm. "That you certainly cannot. Of course, you own it but you have a responsibility to preserve it as an artistic treasure. You must not expose it to the risk of damage in this way. Come now, I'm going to put it back where I had it and you must leave it alone."

She lifted the heavy cylinder and carried it to the closet and pushed it back amongst the clothes hanging there. Mrs. Owens watched her do this and then turned her back as Mrs. Henshaw, motioning to Althea to go ahead of her, left the room.

In the corridor Mrs. Henshaw exclaimed, "How tiresome! She invited you in there?"

"Yes. I did not know that she wanted to show me the painting till she dragged it out."

"Had she talked to you about it beforehand?"

"No. I had no idea what she wanted."

Mrs. Henshaw signed, partly in relief. "I am concerned that she will talk about it to the others. It is invaluable and someone unscrupulous might try to steal it. You have never seen it? Of course not. How could you have? It is a marvelous painting, isn't it? It should be in the safekeeping of a museum. I shudder to think what might have happened to it during these past few years in Henrietta's hands. Oh, I know she guards it with her life. She would never sell it, even for drink. But there are so many moments when she has not been competent, when any stranger might have taken it from her, or any casual accident might have destroyed it. Now at least it is here. I must bend my efforts to see that it gets into safe hands permanently. Properly managed, its disposal could provide Henrietta with enough funds to live comfortably."

"But you say she won't sell it!"

Mrs. Henshaw gazed at her for a moment. "Yes. I fear that for me to persuade her to do so will be a fundamental task. How to persuade her? And then to find a purchaser in these difficult times? It must not go as a bargain." She was lost in musing for some moments and was preoccupied even when Althea said she must be leaving. "Oh, you must have a cab, then," Mrs. Henshaw declared and hurried away to see that one was fetched.

For several days after that the weather was too bad for her to go out again to St. John's Wood. The sleet that fell after the snow made the streets too dangerous for her. She missed Fern. Fern was not a letter writer but she did receive one or two brief notes, with fragmentary and disjointed accounts of what was happening in the touring company. Then there was a longer period with no word until one afternoon when the sky cleared and for an hour or so a soft silvery sunlight filled the square outside Mrs. Tyndal's house. She heard the doorbell ring and then Fern's voice exchanging greetings with Mrs. Tyndal and then Fern was in the room.

She came in and closed the door. Neither of them spoke. The great rush with which Fern had come in subsided into a quiet spell of loving outreach. Softly Fern came across the room to her and took her in her arms. They rocked together for an unregarded space of time. Then Althea sighed and Fern led her over to her armchair and sat down on a hassock beside it and leaned her head on her knee.

"When did you get back?"

"Last night — too late to rout you out. Mrs. Tyndal would not have liked that."

Althea traced the outline of her eyebrow and cheek with her finger. "I missed you."

Fern snatched her hand and kissed the palm. "I had a terrible time paying attention to anything. A couple of times I almost missed my cue. I was actually glad when the regular understudy decided to come after all. To tell you the truth, I think the director was glad too."

Fern's voice died away as she rose up on her knees to put her arms around Althea. Mumbling the skin of Althea's neck with her lips she quietly urged her out of the chair and half-carried her to the bed. They lay alongside each other as their hands pulled and tugged off their clothes. Feeling Althea's skin in the cool damp air of the room only partly warmed by the gas fire, Fern reached for an edge of the coverlet and rolled them both in it. They lay together, luxuriating in the warmth generated by their two bodies, seeking with their fingers the moist softness of their secret places — hers no longer, thought Althea with gratitude, secret from Fern's gentle, persistent touch. Her body rose to the insidiously demanding stroke, sinking back again after a moment into the delicious comfort of Fern's encompassing arms. Fern rolled over on her back, pulling her on top of her, inviting her to feel out the spring of her own rapture. For a while they were lost in the excluding sense of each other.

When they lay together again on their backs, gradually returning to the commonplace world, Althea said, "But did Mrs. Henshaw have a room for you?"

Fern, surprised, said, "Why shouldn't she have?" Then as another thought crossed over her mind, she added, "Did she give my room to Mrs. Owens while I was gone?"

"No. The last time I was out there the Karandys came in and Mrs. Henshaw told Mary that they could stay in your room for the time being. She said she did not think they should go back to their lodgings."

Fern frowned in perplexity. "My room was all right. There was nobody in it. In fact —"

Althea prompted her. "In fact what?"

"The Karandys are staying there but they have Adam's old room. And I don't think they are paying any rent. Mrs. Owens is still sleeping on the couch in Mrs. Henshaw's room."

When Althea did not respond, Fern said, "Adam has disappeared. Nobody seems to know what has happened to him."

"You haven't seen him?"

"I haven't seen him since the night I came here. I've been dreading the idea that he'll show up — that he'll make me go about with him as I did before. Oh, I know I said I wouldn't. But, Althy, I don't know if I can screw my courage up to sticking to that. Every time the door opens I'm sick with fear at the idea that he'll walk in."

"But why? You said you won't care if he tells your father."

Fern sat up in bed and put her head down on her knees. "No. It's not that. I think I can weather any kind of storm he stirs up with Dad. It's simply that I am afraid of him — afraid of him physically. He is a ruthless man. That is what frightened me so much that evening — why I ran away — not only because I didn't want to be arrested by the police, but because I was afraid of what he might do to me. He can't stand the idea that anyone will stand in his way — especially a woman."

"What would he do?"

"I don't want even to imagine it. He doesn't mind killing people. I don't know whether he would try to kill me, but he enjoys tormenting people — torturing them. He and his friends used to do that in Berlin."

"Yes, but he can't do that sort of thing here in London. He would get caught and punished. He must know that."

"He thinks he can do things that other people cannot. He thinks he is invulnerable and he has contempt for the English police. They're so soft, he says. They're always thinking of other people's rights. Oh, Althy, I wish I knew where he is!"

Althea pondered. "Have you asked Mrs. Henshaw?"

"She says simply that he has left — that he has vacated his room. She must know more about him. I have always thought she did."

Fern was not so certain. "She may have been deceived by him. He gives a very good imitation of the bluff Englishman. He'd be fine on the stage."

"That's what Mrs. Owens thinks."

"And Mrs. Henshaw does not probe very deeply into people's motives, you know, Althy. Her concern is with your present needs. If you are at a sorry pass, like Mrs.

Owens, she does not weigh up the good and bad of what brought you to it."

"Yes, but he is not at a sorry pass. It was not a question of having him in her house because he had nowhere else to go. Wouldn't even she wonder why he put himself there, amongst all those down and outs and political refugees and — aspiring actresses?"

Fern laughed and gave her a soft punch in the ribs. She sobered and said slowly, "I think she thought I was smitten with him and she knows that the surest way to fan the flame of an infatuation is to oppose it. She has had personal experience with that, you know."

"But if she had any inkling of what he was really like, wouldn't she hesitate?"

"I think she always thinks she can control things if they get out of hand. But she really must think she is omnipotent if she thinks she can cope with Adam and the sort of friends he had. She knows that things are getting bad in Germany. She has first hand evidence from some of the people she rescues. But I don't think she quite believes that people can be as bad as they seem."

They lay silent, each following her own thoughts. How wonderful this is, marveled Althea, revelling in the warmth of Fern's body beside her. I've imagined this — this human presence close to me, this woman's body responsive to mine — and I've thought for so long that it could never be — not for me, with my withered-up body and shrivelled leg — no, never —

Aloud she said suddenly, "There is one way you could solve the problem."

Fern shifted around to look at her.

"You could come and stay here with me. I can tell Mrs. Tyndal that you can't stay at Mrs. Henshaw's because you can't pay your rent."

"That would be lovely, Althy! But she would not believe

that. She would know that Mrs. Henshaw would never turn me out because I couldn't pay my rent. You know, she and Mrs. Henshaw have become good friends."

But Althea would not let the chance go. "I can say that you don't feel you can stay there if you can't pay — you don't feel you can be a burden on Mrs. Henshaw, take up a room she could rent to someone else, someone who could pay. And anything Mrs. Tyndal wants to charge extra I shall pay. I'm sure she won't object. She likes you."

As she stopped speaking Fern could feel her trembling with eagerness. Fern's practical objections faded. It was after all and above all a chance to be close to Althea all the time. And why not? Why not be here, the two of them together, while they could? Who knew what tomorrow might bring and why risk postponement of something as important as this to an uncertain future?

When she said, "All right. Let's try it," she was delighted by the great beam of happiness that lit Althea's face. What did anything matter against that?

Later, when she was going back to St. John's Wood, sober doubts arose, for shortly she would be confronted by the need to put in words what she would say to Mrs. Henshaw. She rehearsed one opening after another along the lines Althea had suggested. But none of them would do. If she told Mrs. Henshaw that she had no money, she would have to answer questions about her parents. Her father had not stopped sending her monthly bankers' drafts, though sometimes he ranted and raved in his letters about her coming home. If she said he had, Mrs. Henshaw was sure to write to her mother and then she would be known for a liar. No, she had to take another tack. Suddenly she thought of it. Of course. Since coming back from the theatrical tour she had a foot in the theatrical door. That was it. She needed to be closer in town, not so tied to the hours when the Tube and the buses provided transportation.

It was important for her to be on call just now, for the ever-possible chance of a role. Althea wanted to help with her career, wanted to provide the means for her to be instantly available if that crucial small part turned up which would launch her in the theater. Something like that, she thought, going up the steps of Mrs. Henshaw's house — if she could bring it off, avoid being undermined by those skeptical eyes, that tacit disbelief she had so often seen in Mrs. Henshaw's eyes.

But her carefully pumped-up courage, her diligently memorized spate of phrases, collapsed when she got into the house. Mrs. Henshaw was not there. No one knew when she would be expected to return. She had indicated that she would be away for a day or so, visiting in Dorset.

"Has she gone to see Mrs. Russet?" Fern asked Mrs. Owens, who burst into a loud laugh and asked, "Why ask me?"

Overnight Fern stayed in her room, caught in a net of anxiety. Each time she had heard voices in the hall she feared she would hear Adam Milner's deep tones. Then the house finally grew quiet and she fell into an anxious sleep. When she woke in the morning, to a pale sun lighting her room, she was suddenly resolved. She would simply leave, take her few belongings and go and join Althea in Mrs. Tyndal's house. Perhaps Mrs. Henshaw's new preoccupation would be great enough that she would not miss her for a while. And then Fern would just say that she had gone to stay for a while with Althea.

When she got back to Paddington, Mrs. Tyndal was at her door, just having washed off the steps to her house. This, she had early explained to Althea, was something that was taken for granted in the Welsh village she came from and she felt constrained to follow the custom even in this great dirty heedless London. Althea, reminded again of the rows of white doorsteps in Baltimore, thought, it gives her a sense of home. Fern, arriving with one suitcase, saw her standing in a shaft of smoky sunlight that reached the steps over the tops of the bare trees in the square, making them steam in the moist, mild air. It was still early in the morning and the streets were busy with people on their way to work. Mrs. Tyndal's slight, energetic figure was still as if she were enjoying this moment of idleness amongst other busy people. She has seen me, thought Fern. As Fern came within speaking distance, Mrs. Tyndal's eyes were fixed on the suitcase.

"Why, look you to goodness, Miss Merrill! 'Tis only eight o'clock."

Fern grinned at her. "And you never thought I could get up this early." Mrs. Tyndal had never seen her before afternoon.

"Well, being in the theater —" Mrs. Tyndal, Fern had learned, had a passion for the theater and a real devotion to actors and actresses.

Fern seized her cue. "That's it. I've come to stay for a few days with Althea. I'm too much out of things in St. John's Wood."

Mrs. Tyndal did not seem surprised, though she did not say that Althea had already told her. Fern found Althea eating breakfast from the tray Gladys had brought her, the morning's newspaper spread out on the table beside her. Fern was used to Althea's preoccupation with current events. She herself almost never read a newspaper.

"No," she said when Althea asked if she wanted some breakfast. "I don't want anything. Have you told Mrs. Tyndal?"

Althea nodded, her eyes still on the paper. Fern, put off by the cool reception, dropped her suitcase in a corner and said, half sulkily, "I can find somewhere else in a day or so."

Althea looked up in surprise and recognized in her face

the traces of a sleepless night. "Oh, did you have a hard time with Mrs. Henshaw?" She reached out her arms and Fern knelt beside her, to take refuge in them.

"No. She wasn't there. She has gone off somewhere. Nobody knows where she has gone. So I just walked out. I'll have to do my explaining later." She looked up into Althea's face, biting her lip.

Althea touched her cheek. "Don't worry, darling. It will be all right."

"Althy — I'm so — so out of sorts. Everything seems out of kilter. I don't really know where I stand with anything. I suppose it is because I'm such a weathervane."

"Never mind. You're safe here until things clear up."

Fern rubbed her face against her arm. "Althy, I do feel safer with you." Presently she rocked back on her heels and her eye lit on the newspaper. "What's so interesting?"

"Just something that made me wonder." Althea picked up the paper. It was turned to an inner page and she pointed to a short paragraph. "There is an item here about a statement made by the Home Office, in answer to an inquiry by a member of Parliament. The statement says that a number of aliens have been deported in the last week or so, most of them Germans, for stirring up civil disturbance. There is a reference to Oswald Mosley's fascists. Apparently they think these men were foreign agents who came here to teach Mosley's crowd how to terrorize the population — and I suppose to carry on some sort of undercover operations — undermine public opinion so that it will favor the Nazis. Mosley denies he had anything to do with them. But do you suppose Adam Milner was one of them?"

Fern gazed at her. "Perhaps he was. Perhaps that's why Mrs. Henshaw says nothing about him. She knows all sorts of people who could have told her."

Althea looked back at the paper. "It says here that these aliens have been in custody for several weeks and the inquiry by the member of Parliament — who is unnamed — was concerning whether they had been legally detained."

Fern gave a scornful laugh. "Do you suppose, if it were the other way round, that anybody in German would raise such a question? Not if Hitler had anything to do with it. His henchmen don't give a damn for anybody's rights."

"Including Adam Milner?"

"Especially Adam. I'm sure he is working his way up in the Nazi party. He ought to go far." Fern got up and walked to the window. Watching the parade of people passing through the square from the Tube station to their day's work — the men carrying attache cases, the women holding their coats close around their throats because of the cold, the twos and threes of schoolboys and girls chattering and dawdling, the occasional impatient pedestrian stepping rashly into the roadway to go faster than the throng — she wondered at the flow of orderly energy they represented, each individual intent upon his or her daily concerns, his or her future. How vulnerable they would be, she thought, to the wiles of some cynical manipulator ready to harness that energy for his own ends. Or would they? She turned back to say to Althea, "Althy, aren't you sometimes awed by what you see down there, all those people on their way to work, all of them accepting their lot in life as if there could not really be a change, for better or worse?"

Althea got up and hobbled over to stand beside her. "And if they did?" she asked, curious of Fern's thought.

"All that energy is power and yet they so seldom exercise it themselves. They so often hand it over to any bully ready to seize it." Fern broke off and then after a moment said, "Oh, Althy, if you had seen just one of those rallies the Nazis stage — the yelling mobs, that hysterical fool screaming about the master race, even decent, ordinary people caught up in that sort of bestial craving for somebody to take them over body and soul —"

Althea saw her shudder slightly. Anxiously she offered reassurance. "Don't be so upset. You've left that. If Milner has been deported, then you have nothing more to be afraid of."

"Ah, if I could be sure of that! If he is still in London, he can always come looking for me at the theaters. I cannot abandon my career. I must go in search of another chance." She broke off and was silent for a moment and then said, "Did you know that Mrs. Tyndal has a passion for the theater?"

"Does she? Well, she likes you to begin with and this should make her even more sympathetic."

In fact, during the next days that followed, Fern discovered that Mrs. Tyndal quickly developed a vicarious share in her half-successes, her occasional encouragements, her more frequent disappointments. Fern, she said, must not let discouragement take hold of her. There was always another day to go looking for a new start. To succeed she must keep cheerful, optimistic. That was the whole secret of success — to show someone else one's own enthusiasm. Althea was bemused by this unexpected loyal support. Part of it, of course, was the effect of Fern's own outgoing, mercurially cheerful nature, touching a spring in Mrs. Tyndal, calling forth a desire to see her succeed, to have a part in the fairyland quality of a stage triumph. Mrs. Tyndal seemed to give no thought at all to the fact that Fern had apparently settled into Althea's rooms to stay.

So they found themselves in a comfortable nest, undisturbed by any trace of a feeling of hostility in the air around them. It became a game, with Fern every morning setting out to try her luck in the theaters, ready to recount in every detail to Mrs. Tyndal how the day's effort went.

Althea, coming back in the late afternoon, found Fern in the midst of a half-acted out account of an interview with a play director or the result of a test for a walk-on role. The character of her life at Mrs. Tyndal's had changed completely. She was no longer the undisturbed bookworm. There was another dimension to her life now — alive, fluid, changeable, embodied in Fern — the accepting, unruffled, loving Fern, who took her flawed body in her warm and revivifying embrace every night.

Fern was startled the first time Althea came in on her little game with Mrs. Tyndal, but her surprise turned into an instant appreciation of a greater audience. She was delighted when she made Althea laugh.

Sometimes they went out in the evenings to a nearby little restaurant that Fern said served the sort of food one might find in a similar sort of place in Paris. It was rather dark, with checked table-cloths and candles in bottles and the patrons were nondescript. A sudden fearful thought crossing her mind, she asked Fern if they might not find Adam Milner in such a place, if he had not in fact been deported. But Fern said No. He would never come to such a prosaic place, catering to a very modest sort of foreigner, the kind that came to London to make a living, not to plot sedition against his own government. Look at the people, said Fern — staid working people with no great pretensions to education or intellectual interests. Why, the most there ever was in the way of entertainment was a musician or two playing the sort of semi-classical music that you expected to find in a tearoom frequented by solitary, middle-aged ladies in London on a shopping spree. The musicians were probably down-and-out friends of the proprietor eking out a living. They also went to an Indian restaurant recommended by the Indian girl, with whom Fern was almost immediately on friendly terms.

It occurred to Althea that sometimes perhaps Fern was

nostalgic for the more exciting, noisy, turbulent places she had been used to in other parts of London. Fern did not give the impression of being restless or dissatisfied but perhaps underneath that outward repose there was a current of discontent.

One morning as they sat eating breakfast she seemed pensive, unusually quiet. Althea waited, inwardly a little fearful of what this mood might mean. The day was mild and damp. Even in the heart of London there seemed to be indications that spring was on the way. Fern had reported seeing a crocus in the garden in the square.

Presently Fern said, "I'll just have to do it, so I might as well go this morning."

"Do what?"

"Go to St. John's Wood. I'd better go and see if Mrs. Henshaw is back. I don't want her coming here to find me."

"I'm quite sure that if she is back, you would already have heard from her."

"I don't think she'll like it that I've moved out."

Althea said, "I can go out there this afternoon, at tea time. If she is back, she will be there."

Althea could see in Fern's face that she was tempted by this offer, tempted by the opportunity to avoid doing something she did not want to do.

"What are you going to tell her — the reason for my staying with you?"

"Why don't I tell her the truth — that you're afraid of Adam Milner."

Fern smiled at her mischievously. "Is that the truth?"

Althea pretended to swat her. "It's what you said at the beginning."

They looked at each other for a long moment and then Fern nodded.

That afternoon a hazy sun lit the street as Althea reached

Mrs. Henshaw's house. The day was certainly a harbinger of spring, even though February had still a week to run. When she entered the sittingroom she saw Mrs. Henshaw sitting by the tea table knitting, as if she had never been away.

"Ah, my dear Althea. I'm so glad to see you." She reached out one hand to draw a chair closer to her and patted the seat to invite Althea to sit down.

Althea sat down. "I haven't been coming because I was told you were away. And the weather has not been very good."

"Yes. It would make extra difficulties for you. Well, I have only just returned. And of course there have been some changes here and there will be others. Our friends the Karandys are sailing for the United States within a very short time."

Althea said, surprised, "Why, I thought the United States Government wouldn't let him into the country again."

"Oh, that has been changed! The authorities have been prevailed upon to alter their view of Victor. Fortunately, he has some powerful friends who have been able to convince the necessary people that he is not a dangerous person. It is too tiresome! As if he knows enough about political matters to plot sedition!"

"But what about the people who gather round him — his countrymen?"

Mrs. Henshaw raised her head to give her a satirical glance. "And how is one to account for one's countrymen, and one's friends, and one's family, and one's acquaintances? Does one measure one's friendship, one's family ties by the yardstick of their political views? Do you investigate the soundness, from your own point of view, of the beliefs of the people you meet before you decide upon friendship with them? Well, perhaps there are those who do and then refuse to have anything to do with those who are of a different religion, or who hold a different concept of society or government from their own. Yes, indeed, there must be a great many people who do that, for witness the intolerance we see displayed everywhere." She paused and counted some stitches in her knitting. "Well, but that, after all, is something we can't change. It must be dealt with in a practical way. In any case, Victor's friends — chiefly music patrons who realize what an extraordinarily gifted musician he is — have succeeded in getting his status as an undesirable alien changed. He has a visa for an extended visit to the United States for a series of concerts. His patrons are guaranteeing his financial support, so he and Mary have no more money worries, at least for the time being. A most happy solution, don't you think? And, of course, you know your aunt has had a hand in this."

Because you put her up to it, thought Althea, watching her. She examined her face — the fine skin with its network of wrinkles around the eyes and mouth, the fair hair now almost white, the delicate narrow lips, the precisely cut eye-sockets — everything spoke of a softness, high breeding, cultivated sensitivity. But there was something more, an indefinable quality. There was something there that made you expect a sympathetic reception for your soreness of heart, your plaint of misfortune, unearned sorrow. There was a sort of sinking of self — that was it — in her manner. In dealing with you, she removed herself, her own feelings, her own beliefs, in order to minister to yours. Certainly she herself, Althea, had received that sympathy, that kindness, that careful attention to what she needed.

But it would be a mistake to suppose that under that soft exterior there was not an iron will, an unbudgeable belief in what she held to be the right thing.

Althea looked around the room and tried to see it as she had seen it the first day she had come there — the day she had met Fern. Now there were several people gathered into a knot at the far end, by the bow window that looked out on the winter bareness of leafless trees. Then, the view had had a mellow autumnal charm. In the group at the end of the room she recognized one or two of the girls to whom she nodded when they met on the stairs.

Aware that Mrs. Henshaw' eyes had stayed fixed on her while her own thoughts ranged, she said, "That means that Mary can see her people again. That should make her happy."

"Oh, yes, of course. They sail from Southampton on the Aquitania two weeks from now. We must arrange something of a farewell for them. As you know, Victor is a very affectionate young man. He will want to say goodbye to everyone who has been kind to him here in London and that is a tall order, as you can imagine." She laughed and Althea, surprised, felt a sudden rise in her own spirits.

But the next moment Mrs. Henshaw said, "But what about Fern? She is staying with you."

Althea nodded as casually as she could. "She came to stay with me because you were away and she was afraid of Adam Milner."

"Indeed!" Mrs. Henshaw's eyes bored into her. "He is indeed a dangerous man. So I have discovered. But thankfully he has been sent out of the country. She need have no further concern about him. Besides —" again she paused and then went on, "I had the impression that they were much attached to each other."

Althea's breath was suddenly stopped and then she exhaled. She thought, you never believed anything of the sort. She stared back at Mrs. Henshaw for a moment and than her certainty faltered. Perhaps in fact Mrs. Henshaw had thought Fern to be infatuated with him. She said lamely, "I hardly think so. He threatened her."

"With what?" Mrs. Henshaw's question was a pounce.

"With telling stories to her father about what she was doing."

Mrs. Henshaw looked puzzled. "What she was doing? Why, her mother was well-informed of her activities. I wrote to her often."

And that was so, thought Althea, aware of the midnight hours that Mrs. Henshaw spent bent over her enormous correspondence under a solitary lamp at her desk when everybody else was alseep or elsewhere.

"Well, she was afraid and so she came to stay with me." Mrs. Henshaw studied her for a moment. "Mrs. Tyndal has told me that Fern says she is staying with you because of the problem of getting to and from the theaters."

"Oh," said Althea eagerly, "that is true! Do you know, she has a chance now as understudy for a new production? And perhaps she will have a go at motion pictures. She is very excited."

Mrs. Henshaw gazed steadily at her. She said in a kindly tone. "I am very happy for her. But it is most unsuitable for her to be living with you, Althea."

"But why?"

Mrs. Henshaw's gaze was still kindly but there was a steely glint in her eyes. "Althea, I am not blind to the attraction between you and Fern. You are more than friends. You imagine yourselves in love — both of you. But you must stop it! It cannot go on! It is unhealthy!"

Her voice had suddenly risen so that Althea thought it must reach the people at the other end of the room. But their chatter seemed to cover it. Daunted by the sudden blaze in Mrs. Henshaw's eyes, she protested, faltering, "No. No. You are wrong."

Mrs. Henshaw's voice dropped, as if she was aware that she might be overheard. "I am not wrong! And soon others will see what you are — what you are doing. You will stifle each other. You will shatter your lives."

Althea was torn between anger and distress and did not answer. Mrs. Henshaw knitted with furious speed for several minutes. When she finally spoke again her voice was calm. "I must account to her mother. She came to London on a very definite understanding with her parents."

Althea burst out, "But, Mrs. Henshaw, Fern is twenty-two years old! She can take care of herself. Why, when she was staying here with you she came and went as she chose. You had no idea where she was or what she did. If you had, you would never have approved of her going out with Adam Milner."

"It is perfectly natural for a young woman to go out with a young man. She was infatuated with him. I did not know his true character at that time. It was not my business to interfere with that. Her mother would understand that. It is the sort of freedom Fern had at home, in Berlin."

Prodded beyond caution, Althea rejoined, "And do you know where she went in Berlin and the kind of people she went with?"

As if warned by Althea's manner, Mrs. Henshaw did not take up her challenge. She seemed to ponder for a moment. Then she said, "I do not really know what Fern has been doing. After all, she is young and eager for life. But I must set limits to what I can allow her to do with my approval. You must tell Fern that I expect her back here at once. Perhaps she has not realized that I am back in London. Mrs. Owens tells me that she came to find me while I was gone."

Althea, angry, did not reply. They both got up spontaneously.

Mrs. Henshaw's voice was sharp in response to her silence. "You must understand that I cannot allow her to stay with you."

Althea lashed out, "She's very upset. If she wants to stay with me, she can."

The tone of her outburst put Mrs. Henshaw back in command. She said only, in a dismissive voice, "Fern is sometimes too dramatic. She brings her theatrical sense into everyday life. You must not allow her to upset you — to override your better judgment." Softening, she put her hand on Althea's arm. "Do take care, Althea dear. You must remember that you are not strong. After all, I must act for you in place of your aunt Marjorie. She would be distressed if anything untoward happened to you."

In spite of herself, Althea's anger ebbed. They began to walk together into the hall to the front door. A sense of dismay took possession of her as she traveled back to Paddington. She felt unarmored for a struggle with Mrs. Henshaw. But she was in no doubt about the reason for Mrs. Henshaw's demand. Behind her vehemence was the fact of Marjorie — of what Marjorie meant to her.

Fern, reading a play script, looked up when she came into her sittingroom. She broke off, exclaiming, "What's up, Althy? Is something wrong?" She jumped up to help Althea take off her coat.

Althea stood looking at her with a troubled frown on her face. "She is home. And she says that Adam Milner has been deported. Therefore, there is no reason why you shouldn't go back to live with her. In fact, she does not believe that it was ever necessary for you to leave. She thought you were infatuated with him and she wasn't going to interfere."

"Oh, Althy! Didn't you tell her about it being easier for me to get to the theaters and all that?"

"She had already heard that story from Mrs. Tyndal. She says you must go back there." Althea sat down in dejection.

"You couldn't talk her out of it?" There was still hopefulness in Fern's voice.

Althea shook her head. "There is no use in trying to evade the issue. You're going to have to come to terms with her."

"Suppose I go back there for a few days?"

"What good would that do?"

"Well, if I come and go for a while, perhaps she will get used to the idea — the novelty will wear off, so to speak." Althea looked away from her hopeful eyes. "Fern, you know that is nothing but procrastination. It won't fool Mrs. Henshaw."

"In the meantime I could say I have written to my mother about it and she doesn't mind."

"Fern! That's ridiculous. She'd say your mother doesn't know anything about it — that your mother doesn't realize that we're living together in my rooms and sleeping in one bed."

"Other women have done that in the past. My mother wouldn't think anything of it. When I was in boarding school I used to go to stay at some of my schoolmates' homes and we doubled up." Fern paused for a moment. "Oh, my mother would be upset if Mrs. Henshaw wrote and told her I was living with Adam Milner or some other man." Fern stopped, seeing the disgust on Althea's face. She got up and went to lean over her, saying in a conciliatory tone, "Of course you know I wouldn't think of doing that — never would have." She straightened up. "It's funny. You know, on the other hand, Mrs. Henshaw would think that was more forgivable than this.

"Than this? Then 'this' is something different — just as she says, something that can't be accepted." Althea spoke from the soreness she still felt from Mrs. Henshaw's attack.

Fern, uncertain how to respond, said, tentatively, "It isn't anybody's business but our own. If we accept it —" She stopped, as if realizing that something more lay behind Althea's mood. "What really did she say to you, Althy, about us?"

"That we must not go on living together, that we'll ruin

258

our lives, that it's unhealthy, that people will shun us."
Fern was sobered. "As plain as that? What are we going
to do, Althy?"

"What are *you* going to do?"

Fern took refuge in words. "I really wonder about her.
She's never shocked by anything anybody does. She'll
help anybody regardless of what they've done, if she thinks
they're alone and abandoned by everybody else. She accepts
what Elsie does — living with a man she is not married to —"

"Elsie is in a special place with her."

Fern glanced at her and went on, "and besides that was
something she did once herself. She was a friend of the
Fabians — Bernard Shaw, Beatrice Potter, Bertrand Russell.
They are far from conventional. Why does she act like this
now?"

"She's not shocked. She's upset — because we're doing
what she has always run away from. We're two women
living together."

Fern came to lean over her again. "What's so strange
about that? Girls live together all the time. London is full
of them. It's taken for granted that if a girl isn't married
she'll pair off with another girl — for protection, to share
expenses. Are you sure that she means what we think she
means — about us?"

Althea's eyes flashed as she looked up at her. "People
always recognize themselves in other people."

Fern stared at her in surprise. "What do you mean?"
Then a recollection came to her. "Oh. I see. Your aunt.
You think she knows about your aunt."

"She knows about aunt Marjorie because she knows
about herself."

"Oh," said Fern.

"Mrs. Henshaw knows perfectly well that we're not
just two girls living together to share expenses. For one
thing, I don't have to." Althea sat in thought for a few

moments and Fern did not speak. "There's always my aunt Marjorie. Marjorie means something very special to her — something that goes back to the time they were young girls together in school. She tries to suppress her feelings — has tried for years. She thinks it is wrong to have them. She is really very cruel to Marjorie, but she doesn't realize it. I've always known this but I've never said it even to myself. If I told her that, she would justify it. She would say it was a necessary pain — pain that cleanses from guilt — her guilt and Marjorie's."

"Whew!" Fern's whistle was incredulous. "That sort of guilt is terribly crippling."

"She doesn't see it that way."

They lapsed into silence, each of them struggling with her own thoughts. After a while Althea said suddenly, "Oh, I forgot something else! Victor is going back to the States."

"What!" Fern's face was at once alive with delight.

"Some people with political pull have got him a visa to enter the country for a concert tour. It's been decided he is not an anarchist nor a communist."

"Well, I'll be —! There's nothing she can't do if she sets her mind to it, is there? Mary must be very happy about this."

"They leave on the Aquitania in two weeks time. Their fares are paid and all their other expenses."

"America, the land of milk and honey!" The exulting tone in Fern's voice faded as she said, "I'll have to go there to see them and that means —" She did not finish her sentence.

She went out to St. John's Wood and was talked to by Mrs. Henshaw. That was as much as Althea learned, because when she came back she was uncommunicative about the interview and talked at length about the Karandys. There were farewell parties being planned and she and Althea were invited. They went together to these — cheerful, noisy, disorganized gatherings of young people crowded into small flats or the back rooms of inexpensive restaurants. Victor had to be restrained from spending the money now available to him for travel across the ocean. A week before the Kranadys were to sail Mrs. Henshaw announced an open house for any of their friends to come and say goodbye.

Althea and Fern went there in the afternoon of that day. The springlike weather had fitfully come and gone and come again. They walked up the street to Mrs. Henshaw's house in the mild, hazy sunlight, noticing the first signs of greening in the gardens they passed. As had been the case since Fern's encounter with Mrs. Henshaw, they were chiefly silent when alone together. They both felt the constraint of something that seemed impending. Yet that feeling, which each recognized that the other felt, seemed to bring them into a closer intimacy.

All at once Fern said, "She is bound to say something to us — to you or to me. What will you say?"

"It depends on what she says to me. As far as I am concerned, you stay with me. What will you say?"

"I'm wondering if she has written to my mother and if my mother has written back."

"Have you written to your mother?"

"No." Fern glanced sidelong at Althea. "Oh, Althy, I know. I'm always waiting to see if something will happen so I won't have to. I hate writing letters — and how would I say what I would have to say?"

Althea did not answer.

But in fact, all through the afternoon, Mrs. Henshaw said nothing to either of them, except remarks about the happy change in the Karandy's affairs. The big room was full of people when they arrived. Mrs. Henshaw was bustling about, helping the servant girl carry trays and little sandwiches and scones. Fern volunteered at once to help and Mrs. Henshaw sat down in her usual chair by the tea table, first guiding Althea through the throng to the chair beside her. There were several bottles on the table, brought no doubt by various of Victor's friends, surrounding the tea urn. Mrs. Henshaw did not look at them. Apparently she had decided that they did not exist.

Mary, pink-cheeked from the wine she had drunk and the conviviality, came to stand next to Althea.

Althea said, "You must be very happy to be going home."

"Oh, yes, I am! And Victor is so happy. He was so discouraged. He was talking about going to Paris. He did not want to go, because Paris is so full of refugee musicians. But he thought that he could get some professional engagements there. I dreaded going there."

"Why?"

"Well, it is bad enough here in London — all these strange people who insist on claiming him as one of themselves. I had no idea, when we first met in New York, that he was so involved with them. Paris would be worse, though that is where he feels most at home. Paris is so full of suspicious characters, from everywhere. Oh, I am very glad to be going back to New York."

"Victor has a whole season of concerts lined up, hasn't he?"

"Yes, and perhaps at the end of the year he will be ready to settle down in the States. So long as he has plenty of music I don't think he cares where he is."

"I think he will find more and more musicians going there from Europe — from Germany — friends of his."

Mary nodded. "It must be terrible to be driven from your home." She went on chattering cheerfully for a few more minutes and then wandered away, drawn by a group of young women Althea recognized as American students.

She noticed that Victor was crouched on one knee beside Mrs. Henshaw's chair.

"Dear lady," he was saying, "I am so unhappy that you will not be there in that unsympathetic place to help me."

Mrs. Henshaw clucked her tongue. "Now, Victor, that is nonsense. It is not an unsympathetic place at all. Why, look what they are providing you with — a year of concert engagements and your expenses taken care of. That is very generous and must mean that you are popular."

"Ah, yes. Those people. But there is the ambience. There are so many who don't know music. They don't feel it. They think a musician can be bought and paid for like everything else. They come to my concerts because it is fashionable."

Mrs. Henshaw said sharply, "Victor, this is nonsense. You will find just as many people there who know music and who appreciate you. And as many musical friends as you have here."

Victor put his blond head on one side and looked up at her with an artfully roguish smile. What was it Mrs. Owens called him? thought Althea. The faun. Yes, it was obvious that he made deliberate use of his looks, his charm, his artist's unworldliness, when dealing with women, especially women no longer young. His strictness, his hardness, his self-assurance, he kept for his music. Althea remembered that she had seen him use the same sort of appeal, laced with a certain arrogance, with men. She remembered seeing him once, with Adam Milner, and the odd gleam in Milner's eyes and the rigid smile on his face.

Mrs. Henshaw looked severely at Victor but there was a certain indulgence in her manner. "Victor, you've nothing to complain of. And you must consider how happy this makes Mary."

Victor glanced across the room towards his wife. "Ah, yes. But you must understand — there is not much love

between her people and me. They do not value me for what
I am. Oh, yes. They will be pleased when I am spoken of,
praised in the newspapers and when I make money. But for
myself —"

Althea did not hear the rest of the low-voiced conversation because Mrs. Owens came lurching across the room and
fumbled for a chair. As Althea watched apprehensively, she
found one and dragged it closer to her. As usual she was
dressed in a flowing garment that reached almost to her
ankles and was spotted down the front with stains from
food.

"Quite a shindig," she said in her hoarse voice close to
Althea's ear. She gazed around the room for a silent moment,
finally fixing her attention on Mary. "Y'know, it's been
twenty years since I was in the States. There was the War,
too, since then."

Her heavy face was downcast. Althea said, "Would you
like to go back?"

Mrs. Owens was slow to answer. "I don't know. I used
to think I never wanted to. Grown away from it, if you
know what I mean. Back then" — Althea understood that she
meant when Charles Russet was alive — "I wouldn't have
considered it. Everything was so much freer here then — I
mean, Paris, especially. Life was so much more enjoyable —
more interesting, you know, not so hemmed in by false ideas
about morality. Queen Victoria, you know lived on in the
States long after she was dead and buried here. Of course
there was Charles. He wouldn't have thought of crossing
the Atlantic except for a brief visit to be feted as a lion,
say, in New York and Boston."

"But now you think —?"

"Yes, now I wonder about it. Most people have forgotten all about Charles and me. Or if they remember, it's
become history — part of the biography of a great painter.
And they've forgotten me. I'm not a great actress any more,

just a lone old woman. Perhaps it would be nice to go back
where I came from." She gave a sudden, hoarse laugh. "But
how would I get there and what would I live on?"

"You haven't any money at all?"

"Not a penny. Come to that, what do I live on here?
Janet, of course." She gazed as Mrs. Henshaw, still absorbed
in conversation with Victor. "I'm a leech on Janet."

Althea protested. "I am sure she doesn't think of it that
way."

Mrs. Owens gave her a sly smile. "She never has time
to think about such things — to reflect. She is too busy
with the next problem after she has one under control."
Her attention wandered then and Althea saw her eyes straying towards the bottles on the tea table. She's waiting, she
thought, for Mrs. Henshaw to be looking the other way.

A week later Fern said that they must go to see the
Karandys off. They were to sail in the Aquitania from
Southampton.

"Fancy, a stateroom on the promenade deck! No, I don't
mean we are going to Southampton. Everybody is seeing
them off in Waterloo Station."

"Everybody?"

"There'll be a crowd. You know how many people
Victor knows — or who know him, especially now."

When they got to the station they saw the farewell
party clustered like a swarm of bees on a wide bare patch
of the train platform. Mist was hanging in the iron rafters
of the train shed and the whistles and shrieks of the trains
were muted by the damp air.

When they got closer they saw Mary surrounded by
several young men and women, Americans Althea recognized
from parties to which she had gone at the flat of a couple
who were attached to the London branch of an American
movie company. Another group nearby were chiefly
foreigners speaking French or other languages, of various

degrees of affluence or shabbiness. At first they did not
see Victor, until they realized that he was crouched down
in the center of a gabbling group of people, doing something with a suitcase spread open on the ground. A tall
English girl said in a high voice that carried over the confused uproar of sound, "Victor, you cannot possibly get
them all into that bag!"

Coming closer they saw that Victor, surrounded by
several new, luxurious pieces of luggage which he had
bought to transport all the possessions he had accumulated
in London, was trying to stow into the suitcase a heap of
studio photographs in expensive frames — all mementos,
no doubt, of the distinguished people he had met. A slender,
dark-haired young man was helping him. He said, looking
up at the English girl, "He must take them. They will be
very important to impress the people who are arranging
his visit. See, this is Toscanini, with his signature and an
inscription to Victor, and this is Galli-Curci. He must get
all these in."

Fern crouched down beside Victor and took a photograph out of his fumbling hands. "Watch out," she said,
"You'll tear it. Look, Victor, you can get these all in if
you take them out of the frames." She began quickly
stripping the photographs out of the frames and tucking
them expertly into the suitcase.

Victor sat back on his heels. He was nervous and took
his handkerchief out of his breast pocket and mopped his
brow. The din around them increased. An engine gave off
a great hissing cloud of white steam that rose up into the
rafters, something else clanged in the distance, and there
were several shouts — all the things, thought Althea, that
make a railway station sometimes so like a scene from
some imagined enternity beyond the bounds of earth.

Suddenly the disorganized crowd of waiting people
galvanized into an orderly throng, moving towards the

train that had slid quietly down the track alongside the platform. A porter came with a trolley and loaded the Karandys' luggage onto it and wheeled it away to the luggage van. Althea and Fern stood together watching the train glide quietly out of the station.

There was no sign of Mrs. Henshaw.

"Where do you suppose she is?" asked Fern.

"I suppose she said goodbye to them beforehand."

The question lying unspoken between them was, Should they go and seek her? In the two weeks while the Karandys were getting ready to sail there had been no private moments when either of them found herself face to face with Mrs. Henshaw. In the end neither of them brought out the question. They took the bus across the river and parted when Fern got off at Drury Lane.

Their uneasiness about Mrs. Henshaw underlay the delicious sweetness of their being together through the night and for much of the day. To Althea especially this passage of her life came to have a golden quality. This feeling was enhanced by the fact that there was a distance now between herself and all her ties of the past. She rarely saw the family acquaintances who up till now she had obediently visited in their hotel suites and rented flats. The people she saw by day, in lecture halls and study groups, had been not long ago complete strangers. She dealt with them now as intellectual equals who knew nothing of her before she came to London. Her senses had become open to the most transient nuance of thought and feeling, to the lightest touch of the impact of other minds and personalities. It was Fern, she knew, the daily, bodily presence of Fern, that brought about this transformation. She no longer lived an aseptic, sterile life remote from the effect of sexual stimulation. Fern made sure of that, Fern ready to kiss and caress her at every meeting after the briefest separation, Fern provoking gaiety and freshness of spirit at every meal, finally

Fern in bed, insistent, desirous, awakening her own eagerness to respond. She realized that this euphoria stretched
every nerve in her, heightened every response, till the most
commonplace event, scene, or person became lit with a
brilliance of responsive sensation in her, brought a quiver-
ing aliveness in herself of her feeling of life itself — as when,
going home from a chamber music concert in which the
music became almost unbearable in its piercing beauty,
she saw the Brompton Road not merely as a wide avenue
of pavement and stone but as splendid, broad and proud,
transfigured by the brilliant sunset.

And at night, lying sleepless beside the quietly breathing,
satisfied Fern, the other side of the coin was presented to
her. Looking back she knew now that before Fern she had
gradually come to believe that there was more to the difference between herself and the sort of girl her family
deemed normal than the fact of her crippling. Her mind
had been slow — she marvelled now at how slow — to fit
together the elements of that difference — her view of
Marjorie's female friends, her own repugnance at the love-
sickness of her friends at school, mooning over boys. In
her mind now there was very vivid — brought out of the
shadows where it had lain for so long — the remembrance
of the stress of Marjorie's farewell to Mrs. Henshaw on the
train platform in Washington. She had accepted until now
the idea that the barrier between herself and life as lived by
her relatives and friends was her iron brace. She knew now
that this was not so. And she smiled wryly to herself in the
darkness at the idea that poor foolish Miss Atwood had
formed part of that catalyst that had brought her to this
self-awareness.

But where were they — she and Fern? Ah, as Fern would
have mimicked — that was the rub. The English spoke of
Sapphism — the love of women for other women — naming
it for the great poet of ancient Lesbos. She had read — during

her sessions in the British Museum Reading Room — some
of the works of Havelock Ellis and of Freud — both men,
she noted to herself in passing — and she rejected these
strange ideas of theirs about what they called inversion,
thinking thereby to counter the strictures of religion and
traditional morality. Their supposed rationalization, she
thought, Radclyffe Hall had adopted in her novel and in
her own life, making out of something natural, joyous,
fruitful a sickness and a tragic fate. She could not identify
with the heroine of *The Well of Loneliness* because the
whole basis of this thought seemed false — that women
who preferred women were failed men. She knew she was
not a man nor an inverted woman, whatever that might
mean. She was as much a true woman as Fern. She had
never wanted to be a man nor to take the part of a man in
life's affairs. Her only idiosyncracy was that she disliked the
idea of physical intimacy with any man. She pitied the
women who might be persuaded by Radclyffe Hall's eloquent book that they were pariahs in society, somehow
morally and physically defective. That, she thought, was
the real perversion — the distortion of a natural preference
into something evil and unnatural. And yet how many
women had been convinced that what they were was a
mistake of God or nature — how many women would suffer
from the scorn and reviling that many people would heap
on them because they were now to be identified as sapphists?

And Mrs. Henshaw was one of those who had been
frightened and disoriented by these fearful anathemas of
religion and mistaken medical opinion. This had disrupted
her emotional life and still so dominated her that, with the
intent of friendship, she strove to disrupt the fulfillment
of the love between Fern and Althea herself. But there was
nothing sick in herself, Althea knew well, that did not
come from the consciousness of her crippled leg and warped

body. There was nothing sick nor shameful in what she meant to Fern or Fern to her.

Thinking all this, she realized that it was quite a long time since she had had a letter from Marjorie. The thought of this came again when Mrs. Tyndal came to fetch away the breakfast tray and brought two or three letters but none with Marjorie's handwriting on the envelope. The fact awakened a sense of uneasiness. Marjorie had never been careless in her letter-writing responsibility. Her letters had come with a regularity that seldom deviated except for the vagaries of the sea passage. When had she had a letter from Marjorie? It must be three weeks.

The question hung in the back of her mind through the morning. When she came back to her rooms in the afternoon she hunted through the accumulation of mail in the drawer of the desk that stood in the corner of the room. She found three of Marjorie's most recent letters and reread them, aware of the fact that she had merely scanned them when they arrived and had promptly forgotten what they said. There was so great a gap now between the reality of her life with Fern and these echoes of the past. The first thing that struck her now was that they were brief, much shorter than usual. Marjorie had a rambling style that filled several sheets reporting chiefly on family news. She had got into the habit of referring to Gwen, to something that Gwen was doing or that she had gone somewhere with Gwen. In these letters there was no mention of Gwen at all. And was there a certain stiffness, a certain incommunication in spite of all the words? If anything was the matter with Marjorie she would never hear of it from her other aunts unless there was very serious illness. She had had a letter from the aunt who had been in London at Christmas. It had said nothing except that Marjorie had not joined a family gathering to celebrate a wedding anniversary.

Otherwise it was a list of complaints about the trouble of traveling, the outrageous behavior of the customs officials, the tedium of settling down again at home.

As she pondered Althea heard the front door open and the sound of Fern's footsteps on the carpeted stairs. Fern opened the door and came in, tossing an armful of play-scripts onto a chair.

"Well, that's that," she said, and without waiting for Althea to speak explained, "I won't have a chance at that part. Oh, well — what's the matter, Althy? Why so gloomy?"

She had come across the room and seized Althea in her arms, kissing her on her neck. Althea, enjoying the firm hug, shook her head, "I'm not gloomy. I've just realized that I haven't had a letter from Marjorie for almost a month."

"You think she is sick? Wouldn't What's-her-name, that friend of hers, write and tell you if that was so?"

"Gwen?" Althea looked at her in astonishment. She would never have expected Gwen to write and now she thought, Why was that? "I don't think so. She probably doesn't know anything about me except that I'm Marjorie's niece who is living in London. Marjorie hasn't said anything about her for some time."

"Oh." Fern dismissed the subject. "I've seen Mrs. Henshaw. I was mooning along Bond Street looking in the shop windows and she came along behind me and took my arm and went walking along with me."

As Fern paused Althea prompted her. "What did she say?"

"At first she just talked about Victor. She'd had a letter from Mary, who is very happy to be home and her folks are trying their best to get along with Victor. The fact that he's having a triumphal tour must have something to do with it. I said that was nice and probably Victor was happy and easier to get along with. She agreed to that, and then

she said she had other news. Elsie is going to the States. I
remembered Elsie, didn't I? Well, Elsie is going to join
some sort of study group in New York as a representative
of the ILO. I said, how nice for Elsie, since she loves New
York. How soon was she leaving and would she be in London
in transit? And Mrs. Henshaw said Oh, no, no, she would
not come to London. She would leave from Cherbourg.
But there was a bit of a problem. The U.S. authorities take
a dim view of Elsie's political and social opinions. She be-
longs to some radical groups. She has been outspoken in
the newspapers abroad, about advocating radical changes
in the relations of labor organizations and governments.
They say she is a communist, hidden if not admitted. Also,
perhaps she may not be allowed to enter the country on a
charge of moral turpitude — she doesn't think people ought
to get married. 'You see,' said Mrs. Henshaw, 'Elsie is so
outspoken. It is not always wise to voice one's opinions
too freely.' I felt like saying, wouldn't that be hypocritical,
but I couldn't quite bring myself to say it to Mrs. Henshaw.
She is certainly no hypocrite herself. She went on talking,
saying she would so much like to join Elsie for a while
during her stay in the States, so I suppose she really expects
Elsie to get clearance to enter the country. By that time
we were almost to Oxford Street and she said she had to
take a bus. But just before she left me she stopped dead in
the middle of the sidewalk and said sternly, 'Fern, you
must come back to my house. I insist upon it. No, don't
give me excuses. There is no excuse I will accept.' And
there was I, standing on one foot and then the other and
everybody passing us looking annoyed because we were
taking up too much of the pavement. She gave my arm a
final squeeze and said, 'I shall expect you before the week
is out,' and took off down the street with that quick, short
step of hers. 'Now remember,' she said, turning around just
before she got too far for me to hear.''

Althea listened carefully, seeking to pick up what might truly be going on in Fern's mind. "What do you intend to do?"

Fern came and sat down opposite her and leaned her elbow on the table. "I'm not going to do anything right now. She can't come here and carry me off to St. John's Wood by force."

"No," Althea agreed and said nothing further.

Fern looked at her after a while. "You don't like that, do you?"

"Like what?"

"Anything hanging in the balance. You'd rather have a clearcut yes or no about it. But, Althea, a clearcut decision would mean that I would have to go back to her."

"Why?"

Fern sighed. "Otherwise I'd have to have a blazing row with her and I can't do that, Althy."

"No, you couldn't."

The edge to Althea's voice was not lost on Fern. Fern laughed in spite of herself. "Yes, that's right. I'm a coward about having a fight with anybody about anything. But, really, you know, if I just don't do anything, what can she do?"

Althea's gaze was full of half-contemptuous reproach but she said nothing.

The days passed and nothing happened beyond the routine of their lives. A letter finally came from Marjorie, full of apologies for the delay in writing.

"I've been so busy," she said. "We have been having a big fundraising drive and you know this isn't a very good time to ask people for money. Some of the older of us have been attending benefit dinners, the idea being that people with money will be reminded of all the achievements of the Red Cross in the past."

She went on with news of her sisters and other nieces

and nephews. As usual there was a blandness about her reports of her relatives. The reason, Althea had long since recognized, was that there was only the blood tie to link her to them. With her mother's death, Marjorie was more and more drifting away from the family circle. She wasn't able, thought Althea, to take the shortcut I have. There was no word of Gwen.

One day soon thereafter Althea woke to a fine spring morning. Instead of the fog that shrouded the sun and whitened the window, a pale band of sunlight lay across the rug. Its light brought Althea up through the last layer of sleep. She lay still, enjoying the feeling of Fern's back pressed against hers. Here they were, warm and snug, hidden from the world, of which for these precious moments she could be oblivious. The prying eyes of the curious, the pitying, the disgusted — how familiar to her were the expressions on the faces of people who saw for the first time her shriveled leg in its iron brace, her crablike walk with a cane. She could not remember that Fern, when they first met, had ever shown any of these feelings. Nor — her innate honesty made her remember this also — had Mrs. Henshaw, back on that faraway afternoon in Marjorie's house.

Marjorie. The stray thought brought back the uneasiness that the overdue letter had not dispelled. Marjorie, she knew, always tried to cover her own dismay, unhappiness, uncertainty, with a nervous flood of words, talking at great length about trivial things or at least things that were not at the center of her interest. The letter seemed to have this quality — a great flow of detail about her activities at the Red Cross, of which usually she never spoke except in passing.

Althea felt Fern move beside her and presently Fern took her hand and raising it to her lips kissed the palm.

"Look," said Fern, "the sun is shining." She raised her head and poked at her pillow. Althea buried her face in the curve of Fern's shoulder. Fern shifted her position to bring her body closer. Althea, aware that it was her wasted leg that lay next to Fern's, nevertheless pressed against her.

"Do you mind it, darling?"

"Mind what? That the sun is shining?"

"No, of course not. Do you mind, really, that I've got a bum leg?"

Fern made an impatient sound in her throat. "There you go again. Althea, NO. How many times do I have to tell you?"

"I've never asked you before."

"Well, then, why do you ask me now? Althy, I love you. I'm sorry about the old leg. But we can't do anything about it, so why think about it — unless it hurts you."

Althea squirmed closer to her. "I've always had to think about it. There isn't anything I can do without thinking about it — whether I can do something that I want to do or whether it will stop me. Don't you remember, when I first met you, how you had to help me on and off the bus and things like that? And how you had to consider, whether we could go somewhere you wanted to take me, because there might be too many steps?"

"You're a lot more independent now, Althy. You were too timid. You do a lot of things now you didn't used to think you could do."

"Because you've given me the confidence to try."

"Is that all?" Fern's voice held the familiar mischievous note. She shifted again in the bed to lie on her side, looking down at Althea. "Is that all?" she repeated, her hand travelling softly, gently over Althea's stomach and then to the soft hair at her crotch. She lowered her face over Althea's, seeking her lips.

Althea waited for her, luxuriating in the tantalizing anticipation. Suddenly, when Fern was closely on top of her, she reached up and seized Fern fiercely in her arms. Thin and sticklike though they were, they were strong arms. Fern, laughing, burrowed under her to clasp her close. They rocked together in the heat of love.

For an hour or more they played, until Mrs. Tyndal knocked on the door of the sittingroom. Fern, leaping out of bed, threw a dressingown around her and went to let her in with the breakfast tray.

"Such a lovely morning," said Mrs. Tyndal, putting the tray down on the table. "Such a pity to waste any of it."

"We wouldn't think of doing that," said Fern, looking beyond Mrs. Tyndal's shoulder to glance through the bedroom door to Althea.

When she had gone Fern brought a cup of tea to Althea, sitting up in bed. The gaiety of the last hour had left Althea. Fern tried to ignore the change in her, going back to the tray and lifting the metal covers to see what Mrs. Tyndal had brought.

"Ah, I've got a kipper," she said. Replacing the cover she went back to help Althea get up.

Sitting at the breakfast table, Althea said moodily. "I wonder if she suspects anything."

Eating, Fern said, "Of course not. Why should she?"

"For obvious reasons." Althea's voice was sharp. "Don't put your head in the sand."

But Fern refused to be cast down. "Why? Because we sleep in the same bed? She knew that would be the case when you asked her if I could come and stay with you. Besides, you forget. There are lots of places in the world — even in the States, I'm sure, though I'm not an authority on that — where females share beds. I'll bet there were not enough beds to go round in Mrs. Tyndal's family back in Wales. And let me tell you, there are girls in boarding schools who share beds. I know, because I've done it."

Althea was silent for a moment. A sudden memory came to her of an anecdote Marjorie had once told, about her schooldays in the Scottish school. Obviously Marjorie and Janet had slept together even when they went for their holiday in the Swiss pension.

"Mrs. Henshaw may have made her suspicious."

Fern looked over to her knowingly. "And why is Mrs. Henshaw suspicious? Guilty conscience? You know, if you've done something yourself, you're more likely to suspect someone else of doing it. Well, I don't think we should let them think we know about such things."

"Oh, Fern!" Althea exclaimed impatiently. "Why don't you just face Mrs. Henshaw and have it over with?"

Fern gazed at her thoughtfully. Yes, there was always this restless need in Althea to have things certain, uncompromised. Her own instinct was to acquiesce, to yield, to be fluid — after all, if you let someone else win a contest, you did not need to admit defeat yourself. You could go around if you couldn't go in a straight line. But there was no use quarreling with Althea.

Fern said in a reasonable voice, "What should I say to her? I can't come out in the open and say, No, I won't come because Althea and I are in love and we are living together. And if I don't say that, nothing else I said would convince her that I'm not eventually going to give up and do what she wants. She knows how to win by persistence. You've noticed that. She's like iron, you know, when she gets an idea in her head and she'll bend anyone to her will."

"You're afraid of her."

"Well, I suppose I am. But even if you're not afraid of her, she has a way of making you do what she wants. You've seen that. Don't you remember how she arranged things for Victor? People give in to her in the end. And even Mrs. Owens is putty in her hands. She has made her cut down on her drinking. Not that that will last, I suppose, when Mrs. Henshaw isn't right there with her."

They wrangled a little more, with no result, until Althea left to go to a lecture. Fern said she would not leave so early. She had an interview with a theater manager that afternoon.

So Althea was alone in their room, working on a paper in the middle of the afternoon. She did not notice the sound of the front doorbell and was only conscious of someone — she knew it was not Fern — climbing the stairs when she realized that Mrs. Tyndal's voice was mingled with Mrs. Henshaw's. She waited then, alert, till the voices reached her door and there was a knock, a sharp, brisk knock. When she said Come in and the door opened the two women stood there for a moment. Mrs. Tyndal, smiling nervously, leaned forward and said in a deprecating tone, "I know you do not like to be disturbed when you are studying, Miss Richards, but as it is Mrs. Henshaw —"

Mrs. Henshaw stepped into the room. Because the day was unseasonably warm, she wore no wrap over her grey flannel suit. She put her canvas carryall down on the nearest chair and came across to kiss Althea's cheek. Mrs. Tyndal quietly closed the door.

"How are you, Althea dear?" As Mrs. Henshaw sat down in a nearby chair, Althea could not see that there was any change in her manner from her usual kindly warmth.

"Oh, I'm fine. I'm pretty busy with this paper I am writing on economic struggle disguised as politics."

Mrs. Henshaw listened attentively as she went into detail and for a while they discussed the interrelation of economics and political history. But it was obvious to Althea that in spite of her amiability, Mrs. Henshaw's mind was set on something else. Finally, in a pause, she said, "Althea, I have come to speak about you and Fern. She cannot continue to stay with you. It is quite inappropriate."

Swallowing her rising anger, Althea said, "Why don't you talk to Fern, then? It is up to her to decide whether she wants to stay."

"I have spoken to her. Naturally she wants to stay. It is plain to me that Fern finds it difficult to make a harsh decision. She is a sweet girl but too maleable. It is you who will have to prevail upon her to come back to my house."

"I can't do that."

Her flat refusal silenced Mrs. Henshaw for a moment and Althea asked, "Why are you so concerned that she should be with me? I am not a dangerous person."

"Of course you are not — except to yourself — and to Fern."

"I cannot see why I am dangerous to Fern. I love her. I think she loves me. That is all there is to say."

There was another silence. Althea was surprised that there was no outburst of angry indignation from Mrs. Henshaw. Instead, Mrs. Henshaw said, in a surprisingly sympathetic voice, "My dear girl, I would not for any reason deny that this is what you feel. There are times when we feel this attraction to our own kind. But don't you realize — this cannot continue. It is not what society exacts from a woman. Women who ignore this fact cut themselves off from the current of normal life. You are young. You are governed by your emotions just now. Such things cannot last — they should not be allowed to. It is my duty to prevent you from destroying your life. If you don't stop this, both of you will regret it for the rest of your lives."

"Why should that be? I do not believe that it is necessarily so. If Fern and I are willing to take the risk, it concerns nobody but ourselves."

"Oh, no! You're very wrong there. Althea, I cannot let you do something that will bring the greatest distress to your aunt. She thinks everything of you. How can you be so callous —"

Althea's self-restraint snapped. "I'm not the one who is callous! I'm not the one who has made Marjorie unhappy all these years. Marjorie has loved you all her life. Do you think I don't know why she always has these women coming and going in her life? I know it is because of you. She loves you and she has always loved you and you ignore that — you pretend it is something that doesn't exist. *That* is callousness!"

Althea stopped abruptly, appalled by her own words. There were things after all that one knew but should not speak. She looked apprehensively at Mrs. Henshaw.

Mrs. Henshaw was looking at her aghast, and for a while she could not speak. Althea waited, frightened, as if she were a little girl who had accused an adult of some dreadful crime. She looked away but she was aware that Mrs. Henshaw was clasping and unclasping her hands, a pink flush in her face, her whole slender body rigid and trembling from the shock to her emotions. Presently she got up and walked toward the window. There was a profound silence in the room. It was filled, Althea felt, with the ghost of the last thirty years of Marjorie's and Mrs. Henshaw's lives.

Mrs. Henshaw came back to stand over her. She had regained control of herself but now her face was pale and set.

She spoke as if short of breath. "Never accuse me of slighting her. You don't know what you are talking about — nobody can know what there is — what there always has been — between us. Do you not realize that it is I who have had to fight this battle for both of us — that she is weak? Do you think that it has gone easily for me to be the one who must be strong and struggle against what would destroy us? Do you think I speak lightly when I say that you must not take this path? That I don't understand the price that must be paid?"

Gathering up the remnants of her courage, Althea looked

up at her. "Why should we have to do that? Why should we deny ourselves the real happiness of our lives? There is no reason for it — none that Fern and I recognize. Nothing will destroy us. We shall not let it."

"You don't know what you will meet —" But she did not complete her sentence. She stopped as if aware of a sound. It was Fern, Althea realized, running up the stairs. The door opened and Fern burst into the room. She stopped abruptly when she saw Mrs. Henshaw. She glanced quickly from her to Althea and back again.

Her presence seemed to bring Mrs. Henshaw back to normal. "Ah, Fern, I'm very glad to see you. This will simplify my errand. I find it very difficult to catch up with you these days."

Fern said hurriedly, alarmed by the tension she felt in the room. "I've been very busy chasing after film producers and theater managers. I'm sorry, Mrs. Henshaw. I have received your notes but things happen so fast I haven't had time —"

Mrs. Henshaw interrupted ironically. "Especially when one does not really want to answer. But I won't be put off, my dear. You have been here quite long enough with Althea. If it is really true that you find you are too far away from the theaters at my house, I'm sure we can find you a convenient place of your own."

Althea sat silent, waiting to see what Fern would do. Fern, obviously feeling the pressure from both of them, seemed to waver for a moment, as if ready to take the easier course. But all at once she shrugged and said, "Well, I don't want to leave Althea. She doesn't mind my staying here. Do you, Althy?"

The question was a desperate attempt to bring Althea to her rescue. But Mrs. Henshaw struck in, "I have just convinced Althea that it is most inappropriate for you to stay here. These quarters are far too cramped for two people."

She glanced towards the door of the bedroom which was open enough to give a glimpse of the bed.

Althea's suppressed anger burst out in a small spurt. "Oh, no! That is not true. You haven't convinced me of any such thing." Seeing the expression in both Mrs. Henshaw's face and Fern's — both of them were astonished at this flat contradiction — she hurried on, "I'm sorry to be so blunt, but you cannot really believe that I have accepted what you say."

This time it was Mrs. Henshaw who reacted in anger. A rosy flush came into her pale face. "Althea, this is outrageous! I have come here to save you from a very grievous error —" She suddenly stopped, as if the flood of words she was launched upon had all at once dried up or her will to say them had failed. She stood staring at Althea. From her there now seemed to emanate a tremendous surge of feeling — despair, confusion, anguish. Althea, overwhelmed, hung her head. Fern watched in surprise as Mrs. Henshaw automatically picked up her canvas carryall and began to walk to the door. Without another word she opened it and went out.

For a while the room was very quiet. Fern stood as still as she could, leaning on Althea's chair, listening to Althea's breathing, which gradually subsided from noisy to calm. Finally she thought it safe to say, "Why on earth did she act that way?"

Althea, still far away on the sea of emotion that Mrs. Henshaw had created, said tiredly, "Because I'm Marjorie's niece — because she and Marjorie have always been in love with each other — because she has spent so many years trying to deny this to herself — because nobody else has ever confronted her with this — has ever asked her if it made any sense."

Her words petered out. Fern said softly, "Whew! Did you really talk to her like that?"

Seeing that Fern was looking at her with a worried frown, Althea said, "I've upset her very much. I made her bring it all out. She's tried to live her life on the surface — as a protection against her own feelings — trying to deny the most important thing in it, the most important person, pouring her strength and all her soul into other people's troubles. She's upset because I spoke of her and Marjorie — she's tried to keep it buried. And I told her that she has been cruel to Marjorie."

"Oh, Althy! She wouldn't be able to stand that!"

"But it is true."

"And the truth often hurts. You don't dodge things, do you, Althy?"

Althea did not answer. After a moment she said, "What are you going to do if she does write to your mother and says that you've been seduced by a woman?"

"And I get cut off with a shilling? Well, I haven't an income yet — not what you'd call a regular wage. I'd have to sponge on you. But you know, that's not what would happen. My dad would come storming over here to have it out with me. And we'd have a blazing row. I'm of age, so he couldn't drag me off bodily to Berlin kicking and screaming."

Her purposely facetious tone did not dispel Althea's seriousness. "Would you let him scare you away from me?"

"Althy." Fern knelt down by the side of Althea's chair. "I know you know that I'm not brave — I'm an arrant coward, in fact. But nobody is going to scare me away from you. Althy, it is not just words when I say I love you. I do — I have — ever since we first met. I've never felt that my life had any real meaning before I met you."

She was gazing up at Althea with a half-apologetic, half-pleading look in her eyes. Althea made a sound in her throat, unable to articulate words. I cannot give her up, she thought. I would destroy myself if I did. But shall I destroy her if I don't?

Fern, made anxious by her failure to respond, said timidly, "Althy?"

Althea looked into her eyes, still dumb. She finally managed to croak, against the weight that oppressed her, "We'll sit tight. You'll stay here."

Fern's face cleared into a sunny smile. "Right you are!"

Althea, seeing the cheerful relief with which she got up and began to move about the room with her natural unconcern, felt thankfulness in her own heart.

But in the days that followed Althea had to struggle against the sense of tragedy that Mrs. Henshaw had created. In spite of this she felt certain that Mrs. Henshaw would not write to Marjorie to complain about her — or if she did, it would be in veiled terms, giving every reason for being concerned except the truth. For the emotional tie between them which Mrs. Henshaw had tried to bury for so long was now coming inexorably to the surface. How could she write and complain to Marjorie because her niece had found such a friend as they had once been to each other?

Thinking this way brought Althea the remembrance of Marjorie. How often had she, in her new way of living, forgotten Marjorie, discounted Marjorie, in her heart neglected Marjorie? What would her adolescence have been without Marjorie? Her iron brace — that was always the symbol of her bitterness. That was the barred gate that had closed her off from the freedom of a commonplace life, made her a prisoner within the confines of the prejudices of her family. But Marjorie had stepped in, Marjorie had accepted the burden she had seemed to be, Marjorie had opened the path of escape.

But then there was Mrs. Henshaw herself. She owed a

great deal to her kindness, her instinctive sympathy. There was a well of compassion in Mrs. Henshaw, a pure source of the good she did for those whose last resort she so often was, a source never sullied by even an unconscious self-interest. Even now, when she had put herself in opposition, she had not done so in any spirit of self-satisfaction. She had been caught, in fact, in a net of her own devising. It would be easy to rejoice that she had earned her present anguish for the lifelong pain she had inflicted on Marjorie — faithful, soft-hearted, yearning Marjorie. But this Althea could not feel. She could not triumph over Mrs. Henshaw.

She and Fern did not talk about it and Mrs. Henshaw did not come again to see them. When Althea asked Fern if she had heard from her mother, Fern said Yes, but it was just her usual letter, nothing about Mrs. Henshaw except that her mother sent her love, as she always did. Althea did not hear again from Marjorie.

Fern said finally that they should go and see Mrs. Henshaw. So on a day of drizzling rain they took a cab to St. John's Wood. Mrs. Henshaw's house seemed unusually quiet, as if empty of people. When they entered the sittingroom they saw Mrs. Henshaw sitting by her big desk, some papers in front of her. Mrs. Owens was slumped in a deep armchair close to the gas fire and Fern went over to talk to her.

Mrs. Henshaw said, "Ah, Althea, my dear. Do come and sit down here. The tea will be here presently." Automatically she picked up some knitting lying on top of a heap of papers.

Althea sat down in the chair she pointed to and waited.

Mrs. Henshaw said, "I have some news. I was about to come and tell you about it. I have heard from your aunt." She waited as if to see how this statement would affect Althea. Althea, who had not had a letter from Marjorie since the last brief message of two weeks before, felt a twinge of alarm.

Mrs. Henshaw went on. "Did you know that she has been ill?"

"What! She hasn't mentioned anything —"

Mrs. Henshaw interrupted smoothly, "But you haven't heard from her recently, have you? She says she has been unable to write. And I'm sorry to say that I find her sisters very self-centered women. It does not occur to them that Marjorie's friends — and you — might want to hear of her illness, when she herself is unable to write."

"But what is the matter with her? How is she now?"

"She must be over the worst, because she has written me a wee note. She says she hopes to be on her feet soon. She excuses her sisters. She says she did not really inform them of her condition until she had to."

There was a strange hardness in Mrs. Henshaw's voice. Why, thought Althea, she is really upset. "But what was she ill with?"

"She has not said in so many words. It began I believe, with the flu." She knitted rapidly, silently, for a few moments. "She seems very much depressed." She looked up suddenly at Althea with a piercing gaze. "I am afraid she was taken advantage of by that woman who was staying with her." She took off her glasses and rubbed the lenses with her thumb. "Poor Dawkins is very much at the mercy of those who realize how easily she can be victimized. I think I have asked you this before: Who is this person?"

"I don't know, except that she was someone Marjorie met in traveling for the Red Cross, before I came abroad."

"Did you have the impression that she was — unusually interested in her?"

Amazed at being asked this question, Althea stumbled. "Why, I don't know. Well, yes, maybe she did seem to be extra excited by having met her and the idea that she was coming to stay. She seemed to be looking forward to being alone with her."

Mrs. Henshaw raised her eyebrows. "She welcomed your coming to London, you mean. How like Dawkins! She was ashamed of herself."

There was a triumphant note in her voice. Althea said hotly, "There wasn't anything for her to be ashamed of!"

But Mrs. Henshaw smiled. "I know her very well, my dear. She is now disillusioned — and sorely hurt. She offers so much and gets so little in return. That is what made her ill — when the flu prostrated her she could not recover her spirits."

Althea wanted to scream at her, How can you sit there gloating over her unhappiness? But watching Mrs. Henshaw's face, she decided that it was not that. Mrs. Henshaw was actually reproaching herself and seeking to disguise the fact. Althea said, "I've known something must be wrong because I have been writing to her and she hasn't answered. I was getting worried enough to think of writing my other aunt — the one who was here in London at Christmas. But Marjorie would not have liked that."

"Oh, no! Don't do that! Indeed Dawkins would not like it." Mrs. Henshaw leaned over to select another ball of wool from her carryall. "No, I am going to see for myself — as soon as I can arrange it. She has asked me to come to her." She did not look at Althea as she said this and she was busy with the ball of wool as she went on. "I have taken very much to heart what you have said about — about —" Althea was astonished by the obvious emotional confusion that disrupted Mrs. Henshaw's usually calm face to the world. "My dear, you must believe me when I say that your aunt has always meant more to me than anyone else in life."

Althea could say nothing. Mrs. Henshaw, after a pause when she put aside her knitting for a moment and sought her handkerchief, said in a firmer voice, "Althea, my dear, I realize that you have a special burden in life. Your aunt has always been aware of it, too, of course. But you must not assume that you are cut off from the normal way of living. There are those who will always love you for yourself — you are indeed very lovable. I can only hope that disillusionment of any sort is not in store for you. You are courting social ostracism. That is very hard to bear, whatever you may think at this moment. It will be doubly so if you come to find that you have been deceived."

Althea rushed to protest, "But that is not what Fern is to me — a substitute for something else!" And trying to lighten the charged atmosphere, she added, in a less fervent voice, "You know, I don't really think that Mrs. Tyndal will ask me to leave because Fern has come to stay with me."

At the hint of laughter in Althea's voice Mrs. Henshaw became a little pink. She responded, "Mrs. Tyndal is a dear good little woman but fortunately she is not sophisticated."

There was silence for a while. Althea, listening to the sound of Fern's voice across the room talking to Mrs. Owens, wondered if she had really offended Mrs. Henshaw. But after a while Mrs. Henshaw said, obviously leaving behind what they had been talking about, "In the meantime, I have a great deal to do. I do not see my way at the moment to find the means to go to the States. But I must go to Dawkins. I must go there not only because she has asked me to come but because I must protect her."

Althea answered silently, Just be there, just your being there.

On the way home in the cab Fern said, "Did she tell you she is going to the States? Mrs. Owens says she is."

"She intends to go, yes. It's a question of money."

"But your aunt would be overjoyed to send it to her, wouldn't she?"

"Oh, yes, but she's too sick to think of it."

Fern looked at her out of the corner of her eye. "Are you going back there?"

Althea hesitated. "I want to go — I ought to go — to look after Marjorie. But I won't if Mrs. Henshaw goes. That's what Marjorie would want."

When they were back in Mrs. Tyndal's house, Althea said, out of a long, moody silence, "You see, I think poor old Marjorie has been confessing to her over the years all the details of her affairs with these other women. I am sure Mrs. Henshaw hasn't been pleased about them. But she's held off saying so. This last one — Gwen — has upset her, because it seemed to be going to be more permanent. It didn't turn out that way, but she's really stirred up now. You can see why I wouldn't want to be there if she is going to be."

"Althy, do you mean she is jealous?"

Althea shrugged. "It's more than that. I think she has always assumed that Marjorie is her property, even if she didn't claim her. But now it looked as if someone else might. She'll be stern with poor old Marjorie. But Marjorie will be delighted." Yes, thought Althea, Marjorie will be delighted — at last to be claimed by Janet — Marjorie over the years always striving for Janet's approval, or if approval was withheld, then at least welcoming chastisement as a proof of love — Marjorie, so forceful with other people and so weak and yearning for the Janet of her youth.

"But if she hasn't the money to get there —"

"Well, we'll wait and see for a bit. I must not interfere."

Several days went by during which Althea tried to concentrate on the reading she should be doing. Fern came and went, anxious not to interrupt her yet excited by the prospect of being in a film being made by the new Gaumont British studios. She compromised by telling Mrs. Tyndal every daily incident.

But one day she broke in on Althea's studying to say, "Mrs. Henshaw has found the money to go to the States."

"How?"

Fern grinned at her. "Guess! It's Elsie, of course."

"Elsie?"

"You remember that Elsie went to New York a little while ago. She has written to ask Mrs. Henshaw to come over and join her. It seems her assignment there will last several months. She has sent her money for the ship passage. You know, we've wondered what Elsie means to her — or what she means to Elsie. She always talks as if Elsie needs her love and sympathy. They act like mother and daughter. Perhaps she is the only mother Elsie has ever had."

Althea brooded. Elsie, the dazzling creature from paradise, brandishing that cruel bright sword of destruction. The old image of Elsie rose before her from the shadows into which she had thrust it, hidden now by the idea of Elsie as a hapless child rescued by Mrs. Henshaw.

Fern touched her gently. "Wake up, Althy. What are you thinking?"

Althea raised her head. "I've never thought of Elsie as a victim of any sort." But as she spoke there came back to her the memory of Elsie spurned by the man she adored — Elsie raging in the torment of rejection there in the lamplit hall of Marjorie's house — of Marjorie and Mrs. Henshaw trying vainly to soothe her rage — of Martha's neglected dinner waiting —

Fern was looking at her with her head on one side. "Perhaps she has a vulnerable side. Mrs. Henshaw often sees it in people. Anyway, it seems that Mrs. Henshaw is looking for a berth on a ship sailing from London soon."

"She's going on a freighter? Didn't Elsie send enough money for a passage on a liner?" There was indignation in Althea's voice.

"I don't know. Mrs. Owens didn't say."

It was Mrs. Henshaw herself who explained when they went to see her.

As they sat in the sittingroom talking in low voices as

the quietness around them seemed to require, Althea asked, "What is she going to do with this house?"

"Oh, she has found someone to take over the lease. You know how she is — always resourceful. Whoever it is will keep any of the lodgers who want to stay."

"What about Mrs. Owens?"

"Oh, I found out — she is taking Mrs. Owens with her. That's why she is going by freighter. She's stretching the money to pay for two passages instead of one. The freighter is much cheaper. Shh — she's coming."

Mrs. Henshaw came towards them with her usual brisk step. She was hatless and coatless and her canvas carryall was already lying on top of her desk, which meant that she had been in the house when they arrived.

She said, "Ah, there you are Althea," and sat down in her usual chair, saying to Fern, "My dear, will you go and fetch the tea?" As Fern went out of the room she said to Althea, "I expect that Fern has told you that I am indeed going to the States. Mrs. Owens and I sail in a few days. It is very short notice but this is the only sailing I can be sure of that will be suitable. I have heard from your aunt again. She seems much better and says she is eagerly awaiting me. She has also —"

She stopped as Fern came into the room with the tray of tea things. Mrs. Henshaw said to her, "You saw nothing of Mrs. Owens?"

"Not a sign," Fern answered, putting the tray down.

Mrs. Henshaw began to arrange the tea cups. "That is just as well. She is probably napping. Althea, your aunt has come up with an admirable suggestion. She says she can certainly find a purchaser — some museum or art gallery — which will want to acquire Charles Russet's portrait of Henrietta. The proceeds, if properly taken care of, will surely provide her with the means of living."

Fern, surprised, said, "But I thought she would never consent to part with it."

Mrs. Henshaw dropped a lump of sugar into a cup of tea. Althea watched her fine-chiseled profile. It was as usual in repose, urbane and untroubled. "She was hard to persuade. It means so much to her, of course. But after all, what can she do? I have pointed out to her that it is a treasure that should not be further endangered, that in entrusting it to a museum or art gallery she is really doing greater honor to Charles' memory than keeping it selfishly hidden in precarious circumstances. She feels the force of that argument. Marjorie has been in touch with the director of the Metropolitan Museum. He is wildly excited at the idea of acquiring such a masterpiece and one that has been given up for lost. Henrietta is not a fit guardian for it. She knows this and at last I have got her to agree. By the time we arrive at her house, Marjorie will have paved the way for us."

They sat and talked then in a casual way about Althea's course of studies, about Fern's prospects in the theater. She had a chance to get into films, said Fern. Of course, everyone she knew looked down their noses at the idea but she was excited by this new challenge.

After a while Mrs. Henshaw, who had picked up her knitting while they talked, wrapped it up into a roll and stuck the needles into it and thrust it into her canvas bag. There was a finality about her actions that seemed to go beyond this piece of work. She had, she announced, one more language lesson to give.

Fern said impulsively, "Can you tell us the day you're sailing and the name of the ship? We'll come and see you off"

"It is the *Cymric*," said Mrs. Henshaw, "sailing from the port of London. It is a freighter, of course, and therefore I shall not know the exact day until the agent calls me to tell me. I shall let you know as soon as I hear."

She was putting the tea cups back on the tray and when she finished, Fern picked it up and carried it back to the kitchen.

Mrs. Henshaw said to Althea, "Your aunt has sent me quite a large sum of money. She is always very thoughtful in that way. But I am not changing my plans. The money will be useful when I am there."

"Will you be with her for very long before you go to stay with Elsie in New York?" Althea asked the question with premeditated guile.

Mrs. Henshaw shot her a look of half-annoyed surprise. I suppose, thought Althea, she did not know I knew about Elsie. She said shortly, "I am not staying with Elsie in New York. Oh, I shall certainly visit her. No doubt we shall all be going to New York to deal about the portrait. "No" — she looked directly at Althea — "Elsie is happy and prosperous. She has no need of me. Your aunt does. I shall be staying with Dawkins."

She gave Althea no chance for a reply but came over to help her out of her chair.

When they got home Fern picked up the *Times* that Althea had read that morning and looked in the shipping news. The *Cymric* was indeed berthed in London and ready to sail. The date would be announced soon.

"Do you think she really will let us know?" Fern asked.

"Oh, yes," said Althea.

And in fact within a few days Mrs. Tyndal gave Althea a message when she returned from the British Museum in the afternoon. Mrs. Henshaw had called to say that the *Cymric* would sail the next day at three o'clock. She enclosed two boarding passes.

"We can take the train," Fern said. "That will bring us close to the docks."

They left in plenty of time. The rain was not more than a fine mist. When they walked out onto the big concrete dockside, looking for a gangway, Althea was a little dismayed at the small size of the vessel that was to cross the Atlantic. In the midst of gazing they found the sailor guarding the gangway and Fern showed him their cards. They walked up the gangway and began to search among the untidy clutter of a freighter's sailing day to find Mrs. Henshaw.

They found her at last wrapped in an enormous tweed overcoat, bundled against the chill breeze drifting up the river, sitting under an overhang to shelter from the wet, on a deck chair. Mrs. Owens, similarly wrapped up, lay in the deck chair beside her, asleep with her head on one side, her mouth open.

Fern said, "Hallo!" and Mrs. Henshaw looked up. For once her hands were still, gloved and tucked under the edge of the robe drawn around her legs. "Ah, you've come," she said. She was silent after that. Fern began to wander about within a few feet of them. Althea leaned against the rail, looking over the side of the ship to watch the oily water lapping quietly in the dock. The mist had cleared somewhat and a wind had come up to drive the clouds higher, though they still pressed close. Several noisy gulls came and whirled about, screaming overhead. Althea sniffed at the dark river smell, so pungent and so promising of the sea.

Fern came to stand beside her, leaning her back against the rail, her elbows supporting her weight. They stood watching the two women in the deck chairs. Obviously Mrs. Henshaw had not wanted any other people to come for this departure.

"She must have got rid of everybody else ahead of time," said Fern, "otherwise there would be a mob here."

Althea nodded.

Then Fern said, softly, "I hate to see her go. Don't you?"

Again Althea nodded, thinking about Marjorie.

Fern went on, "She's such a rock. She must have spent the best part of her life in the midst of catastrophe — personal or general. But she's unshakable and she's always there when you need her."

Once more Althea nodded and touched Fern's arm. Mrs. Henshaw seemed to be peering through misted lenses in their direction her nearsighted vision fumbling with various shapes on the deck. She said, as they came over to her, "Althea, my dear, do take care when I'm gone. Fern, you must look after her."

"Oh, right you are!" Fern exclaimed, smiling at Althea. "I hope you won't be seasick. It seems such a small ship."

Mrs. Henshaw gazed about her vaguely. "Oh, no. I am a very good sailor." She glanced at the woman asleep beside her. "I trust Henrietta will stand the voyage well. It is so tiresome to be ill at sea." Then she seemed to dismiss the thought.

They were interrupted by the appearance of a burly, redfaced man in a brass-buttoned blue jacket and peaked cap. Captain Bone, said Mrs. Henshaw, losing her vagueness when he came up to them. He had come, he explained, to tell them regretfully that the young ladies must go ashore. But he stayed for a polite few minutes of general talk about the prospects for good weather, the nature of his cargo — English china and French glassware and some less delicate things. Mrs. Henshaw and Mrs. Owens, he said, were his only passengers. He seldom carried women in his ship — "not because of the old sailor's superstition," he said, his bright blue eyes laughing at them, but because his accommodations were too rough really for ladies. He had done his best to make them suitable for this voyage. Mrs.

Henshaw must have talked him into it, thought Fern.

His stream of small talk began to slacken and Mrs. Henshaw, noting the fact, put out a hand to draw first Althea and then Fern to her for a kiss on the cheek, saying, "I am sure that Marjorie will let you know of our arrival."

Captain Bone interjected heartily, "Don't worry, young ladies. We'll take good care of both of them. And now you must go ashore."

He saw them down the gangway and waved as they walked out onto the dockside to look up. There was no bustle now, as if the ship was closed up and had already taken leave of the shore, held to it only by the slender ropes still attached to the bollards on the dock. The day, with its half-hearted attempt to blow clear, had become still and soundless with a smooth grey sky as evening drew near.

Fern wiped away a tear. Althea, used to Fern's easily expressed emotion, patted her arm. Fern tucked her hand under her arm as they began to walk the length of the dock.

"She never admits to any discouragement but she seemed a little sad."

"She's not discouraged," said Althea.

Fern, surprised by the positiveness of her tone, said, "What, then?"

"She's thinking of something else. She has left us behind. She is thinking about herself and Marjorie — what's gone by in the past and what's coming."

"Oh," said Fern.

They walked slowly out into the road, toward the dinginess of the railway station, past the silent griminess of closed warehouse doors. Althea imagined the ship's departure. Tonight, just after darkness had fallen, Mrs. Henshaw would be dropping down the river, through a night filled with thousands of little lights, the great city slipping by on

either side, till eventually the ship reached the open sea.
Althea broke the silence. "This is a hard thing for her —
to go back to mend the past. This is a brave undertaking."
"I see," said Fern. "But even that won't daunt her."

A few of the publications of
THE NAIAD PRESS, INC.
P.O. Box 10543 • Tallahassee, Florida 32302
Mail orders welcome. Please include 15% postage.

Lesbian Nuns: Breaking Silence edited by Rosemary Curb and
Nancy Manahan. Autobiographies. 432 pp.
ISBN 0-930044-62-2 $9.95
ISBN 0-930044-63-0 $16.95

The Swashbuckler by Lee Lynch. A novel. 288 pp.
ISBN 0-930044-66-5 $7.95

Misfortune's Friend by Sarah Aldridge. A novel. 320 pp.
ISBN 0-930044-67-3 $7.95

A Studio of One's Own by Ann Stokes. Edited by Dolores
Klaich. Autobiography. 128 pp. ISBN 0-930044-64-9 $7.95

Sex Variant Women in Literature by Jeannette Howard Foster.
Literary history. 448 pp. ISBN 0-930044-65-7 $8.95

A Hot-Eyed Moderate by Jane Rule. Essays. 252 pp.
ISBN 0-930044-57-6 $7.95
ISBN 0-930044-59-2 $13.95

Inland Passage and Other Stories by Jane Rule. 288 pp.
ISBN 0-930044-56-8 $7.95
ISBN 0-930044-58-4 $13.95

We Too Are Drifting by Gale Wilhelm. A novel. 128 pp.
ISBN 0-930044-61-4 $6.95

Amateur City by Katherine V. Forrest. A mystery novel. 224 pp.
ISBN 0-930044-55-X $7.95

The Sophie Horowitz Story by Sarah Schulman. A novel. 176 pp.
ISBN 0-930044-54-1 $7.95

The Young in One Another's Arms by Jane Rule. A novel.
224 pp. ISBN 0-930044-53-3 $7.95

The Burnton Widows by Vicki P. McConnell. A mystery novel.
272 pp. ISBN 0-930044-52-5 $7.95

Old Dyke Tales by Lee Lynch. Short stories. 224 pp.
ISBN 0-930044-51-7 $7.95

Daughters of a Coral Dawn by Katherine V. Forrest. Science
fiction. 240 pp. ISBN 0-930044-50-9 $7.95

The Price of Salt by Claire Morgan. A novel. 288 pp.
ISBN 0-930044-49-5 $7.95

Against the Season by Jane Rule. A novel. 224 pp.
ISBN 0-930044-48-7 $7.95

Lovers in the Present Afternoon by Kathleen Fleming. A novel.
288 pp. ISBN 0-930044-46-0 $8.50

Toothpick House by Lee Lynch. A novel. 264 pp.
ISBN 0-930044-45-2 $7.95

Madame Aurora by Sarah Aldridge. A novel. 256 pp.
ISBN 0-930044-44-4 $7.95

Curious Wine by Katherine V. Forrest. A novel. 176 pp.
ISBN 0-930044-43-6 $7.50

Black Lesbian in White America by Anita Cornwell. Short stories,
essays, autobiography. 144 pp. ISBN 0-930044-41-X $7.50

Contract with the World by Jane Rule. A novel. 340 pp.
ISBN 0-930044-28-2 $7.95

Yantras of Womanlove by Tee A. Corinne. Photographs.
64 pp. ISBN 0-930044-30-4 $6.95

Mrs. Porter's Letter by Vicki P. McConnell. A mystery novel.
224 pp. ISBN 0-930044-29-0 $6.95

To the Cleveland Station by Carol Anne Douglas. A novel.
192 pp. ISBN 0-930044-27-4 $6.95

The Nesting Place by Sarah Aldridge. A novel. 224 pp.
ISBN 0-930044-26-6 $6.95

This Is Not for You by Jane Rule. A novel. 284 pp.
ISBN 0-930044-25-8 $7.95

Faultline by Sheila Ortiz Taylor. A novel. 140 pp.
ISBN 0-930044-24-X $6.95

The Lesbian in Literature by Barbara Grier. 3d ed. Foreword by
Maida Tilchen. A comprehensive bibliography. 240 pp.
ISBN 0-930044-23-1 $7.95

Anna's Country by Elizabeth Lang. A novel. 208 pp.
ISBN 0-930044-19-3 $6.95

Prism by Valerie Taylor. A novel. 158 pp.
ISBN 0-930044-18-5 $6.95

Black Lesbians: An Annotated Bibliography compiled by
J. R. Roberts. Foreword by Barbara Smith. 112 pp.
ISBN 0-930044-21-5 $5.95

The Marquise and the Novice by Victoria Ramstetter. A novel.
108 pp. ISBN 0-930044-16-9 $4.95

Labiaflowers by Tee A. Corinne. 40 pp.
ISBN 0-930044-20-7 $3.95

Outlander by Jane Rule. Short stories, essays. 207 pp.
ISBN 0-930044-17-7 $6.95

Sapphistry: The Book of Lesbian Sexuality by Pat Califia. 2nd
edition, revised. 195 pp. ISBN 0-930044-47-9 $7.95

All True Lovers by Sarah Aldridge. A novel. 292 pp.
ISBN 0-930044-10-X $6.95

A Woman Appeared to Me by Renee Vivien. Translated by
Jeannette H. Foster. A novel. xxxi, 65 pp.
ISBN 0-930044-06-1 $5.00

Cytherea's Breath by Sarah Aldridge. A novel. 240 pp.
ISBN 0-930044-02-9 $6.95

Tottie by Sarah Aldridge. A novel. 181 pp.
ISBN 0-930044-01-0 $6.95

The Latecomer by Sarah Aldridge. A novel. 107 pp.
ISBN 0-930044-00-2 $5.00

VOLUTE BOOKS

Journey to Fulfillment	by Valerie Taylor	$3.95
A World without Men	by Valerie Taylor	$3.95
Return to Lesbos	by Valerie Taylor	$3.95
Desert of the Heart	by Jane Rule	$3.95
Odd Girl Out	by Ann Bannon	$3.95
I Am a Woman	by Ann Bannon	$3.95
Women in the Shadows	by Ann Bannon	$3.95
Journey to a Woman	by Ann Bannon	$3.95
Beebo Brinker	by Ann Bannon	$3.95

These are just a few of the many Naiad Press titles. Please request a
complete catalog! We encourage and welcome direct mail orders from
individuals who have limited access to bookstores carrying our publications.